The Hills and the Valley

THE HILLS AND THE VALLEY

Janet Tanner

CENTURY

LONDON MELBOURNE AUCKLAND JOHANNESBURG

To my daughters Terri and Suzanne with my love

First published in Great Britain in 1988 by
Century Hutchinson Ltd
Brookmount House, 62–65 Chandos Place
London WC2N 4NW

Century Hutchinson South Africa (Pty) Ltd
PO Box 337, Bergvlei, 2012 South Africa

Century Hutchinson Australia Pty Ltd
89–91 Albion Street, Surry Hills,
New South Wales 2010, Australia

Century Hutchinson New Zealand Ltd
PO Box 40–086, Glenfield, Auckland 10
New Zealand

ISBN 0 7126 1940 2

Printed and bound in Great Britain by
Anchor Brendon Ltd, Tiptree, Essex

1

As the train slowed to a grinding halt the girl in the crisp checked cotton dress swung open the carriage door and climbed down onto the platform. Passengers disembarking behind her jostled past and she stood hesitantly, clutching at the brim of her straw boater which she held in front of her like a breastplate. Her face was flushed from a mixture of excitement and nervousness – a pretty face, round and even-featured and surrounded by a mass of honey coloured curls which had bounced into their usual irrepressible halo the moment her hat had been removed.

She should not be here, of course, at Bristol Temple Meads railway station at twenty minutes past eleven on a Thursday morning. She should be at her desk in the big sunny room at her Convent School in Bath with the rest of her classmates in the Lower VI, listening to Sister Bridget droning Ovid – or perhaps Virgil. But Barbara Roberts had never been unduly influenced by what she should be doing. If there was something she wanted badly enough she usually managed to find a way of getting it. And she had wanted to come here this morning more than she had wanted anything for a very long time.

A small smile lifted the corners of her mouth as she remembered how innocent she had managed to appear when she had gone to Sister Claude, her headmistress, after Prayers this morning and pleaded an appointment with the dentist.

'I'm very sorry, Sister. Mum did write a note for me but I must have left it behind. It's such a rush at our house in the mornings . . .'

Behind her thick spectacles Sister Claude's pale eyes had been shrewd and Barbara's heart had lurched uncomfortably. But somehow she had maintained what Ralph Porter, her stepfather, always referred to as her butter-wouldn't-melt-in-the-mouth expression.

'You can ring Mum if you like,' she said boldly. 'You can reach her at her office number. But the trouble is she will be very busy.'

The hint had gone home. Sister Claude knew very well that Amy Porter, Barbara's mother, was indeed likely to be very busy. She headed not one but two businesses, Roberts Haulage and Roberts Transport, family concerns which had been started in the 'twenties by Barbara's father, Llew. After his death she had built them up almost from nothing until now they operated all over the country and incorporated a coal haulage business and a fleet of charabancs into the bargain. Sister Claude had never been certain how she regarded a woman in business, particularly if she happened also to be a wife and mother. But that did not alter facts. Amy Porter had chosen to send both Barbara and her younger sister Maureen to the Convent School and the not inconsiderable bills were paid each term without delay, something which could not be said for all the pupils. With costs mounting and daily talk of an approaching war threatening to throw everything into even greater uncertainty she could not afford to upset any one of her 'parents'.

'Where is your dentist, Barbara?' she had enquired, folding her finger tips together in the way that the girls said jokingly made her look as if she were at prayer.

'Mr Wenham Browne in the Circus, Sister.' It was the truth. Only – please don't let her ring *him* to check that I have an appointment today, Barbara prayed silently.

'Hmm. And what about your sister? Don't you usually have your dental appointments together?'

'Yes. But not this time. This is special. I have to have my crown checked.' Barbara's fingers were tightly crossed in the pocket of her blazer. Let Sister ask Maureen if she wanted to. Maureen was briefed – the girls had worked it out together on their way to school – and though Maureen, serious to the point of being a 'goody-goody' in Barbara's opinion, had not approved, Barbara knew she would not give her away. Let Sister ask Maureen – but not Mum or Mr Wenham Browne's receptionist . . .

Her prayer was answered.

'Very well, Barbara. You may tell Sister Bridget you have my permission to be absent for an hour. But straight there and straight back, if you please. No detours round the shops. And conduct yourself as a young lady should. I know you do not always find that easy, but we have a reputation to maintain. Whilst you are in uniform you are an ambassador of the school. Kindly remember that.'

'Yes, Sister. Thank you, Sister.'

She had almost run out of the office and down the stairs between the heavily wood panelled walls. She had done it! It had been easy! Now all that remained was for her to get to the railway station without being seen and onto a train for Bristol.

And she had managed it. There had been a nasty moment when she had thought there might not be a train, but it had arrived and now she was here in Bristol. All that remained was to discover which platform Huw's train would be arriving at in ten minutes' time and she would have achieved what she had set out to do – what she had been determined to do since Huw's letter had arrived yesterday with the morning mail.

'Huw is coming to Bristol tomorrow,' Amy had said, reading the letter as she spread marmalade on her toast. 'He has to pick up a plane and fly it back to his base.'

'Pick up a plane! What a funny thing to do!' Maureen had said, checking books into her satchel, but Barbara had almost dropped her coffee cup in excitement.

'Does that mean he'll be coming home?'

'I shouldn't think so. I imagine he will have to go straight to the airfield,' Amy replied, propping up the sheets of blue paper covered with Huw's unmistakably untidy hand behind the milk jug. 'I'm sure the RAF don't allow their pilots to wander around as the whim takes them.'

'But we haven't seen him for ages. His last leave was months ago,' Barbara protested.

'Has anybody seen my dictionary?' Maureen enquired.

Barbara ignored her.

'Well, if he can't come home to see us, why can't we go to Bristol to see him?' she demanded.

'Don't be silly, Barbara.' Amy popped the last piece of toast into her mouth and stood up, fixing the circle of checked gingham over the top of the marmalade jar with an elastic band. 'How can we do that?'

'If we went to the station we'd be sure to see him.'

'Maybe, but we can't, can we? I shall be at work and you and Maureen will be at school.'

'We could miss school just this once,' Barbara pleaded. 'I've only got Maths and Latin and . . .'

'Certainly not. I pay good money for you to learn Maths and Latin.' Amy checked her watch. 'Come on, the pair of you. If we waste any more time I shall be late at the office and you will miss your bus.'

'Babs, have you had my dictionary?' Maureen persisted, and the usual morning rush to get out had taken over once more.

But Barbara's mouth had set in a stubborn line. Let the others be off-handed about it if they liked. Let them do what they liked. If Huw was going to be in Bristol then somehow she was going to make sure she was in

Bristol too. If she could only see him for five minutes it would be worth it!

All day, whilst she was supposed to be concentrating on her lessons, she had thought about it and at last she had come up with her plan. Now she stood triumphantly on the crowded platform and knew that this far, at least, it had worked.

'Mind your backs please!' A porter was walking the length of the train slamming doors again in readiness for departure and Barbara touched his sleeve.

'Which platform does the Maidstone train come in at?' Her voice was almost lost in the roar as the engine let off steam.

'What's that?' He barely paused in what he was doing and she had to run a few steps after him to repeat her question.

'The train from Maidstone.'

He shook his head impatiently. 'There's no train here from Maidstone.'

'But . . .' Barbara was horrified. 'I have to meet someone coming from Maidstone.'

The porter was still walking, talking over his shoulder as he went. 'You want the Paddington train. Platform Two. T'other side of the line.'

'How do I get there?'

'Down them steps, along, and up t'other side.'

'Thanks.'

In her eagerness she almost started to run, then remembered Sister Claude's admonition and slowed to a walk. Maybe she was in Bristol when she should be in Bath but whilst she was wearing her convent dress she had better try to behave like a young lady.

It was rotten to have to wear a uniform, though. Barbara looked down at the print frock, the white socks and boringly sensible brown sandals with loathing. If only she could have worn her new green dress with its swirly skirt and decent stockings and shoes! If only she

5

could have looked really nice for Huw so that he could see she was growing up instead of having to come to see him looking like a schoolgirl.

I'm sixteen and I still look about twelve, Barbara thought in disgust.

The steps leading down to the underpass were almost as crowded as the platform had been and smelled of accumulated steam, smoke and grime. A bit like stale egg sandwiches, Barbara thought. A train rattled by overhead, and the station announcer's voice droned distantly and incomprehensibly. Up the steps on the other side she went into the dull grey light that filtered in through the smoke-blackened glass of the high vaulted roof and glanced off the dirty red-brick walls. Suspended from the steel girders was the sign, a large '2' in black on dirty white.

Barbara walked along behind the clustered passengers and stood between two wooden benches looking out of the station enclosure along the line for the first sign of the approaching train. Five minutes more and it should be here. What if it was late? She would already have some explaining to do back at school as to why her dental appointment had taken so long. But worry about that when the time came. For the moment just think about Huw . . .

The minutes dragged by and Barbara counted them off on the enormous clock which was suspended above the platform. Then, when she had begun to think it would never come, she saw it snaking along the line. She moved forward with the surge of humanity, aware of a moment's panic.

In all these people – would she see him? Supposing after going to all this trouble she missed him! Or supposing he wasn't there at all – had been forced to a change of plan perhaps?

And then she saw him, swinging down onto the platform, and wondered how she could ever have been afraid she might have missed him. Tall, broad-shouldered, his dark good looks enhanced by his air-force blue uniform. She began to run, not caring that her boater was being battered as she pushed through the mass of bodies.

'Huw! Oh Huw! Over here! Huw!'

He turned and saw her. She saw the surprise on his face swiftly followed by a delighted smile and her heart seemed to burst within her.

Huw. She'd have crossed an ocean for him, braved anything to see him – much more than just old Sister Claude. Huw, her adopted brother, whom she had adored for as long as she could remember.

She had been just three years old when he had come to live with them, a scruffy under-nourished boy of eight with a thick but musical Welsh accent and the look of the streets on his dark narrow face.

To the rest of Hillsbridge, the small mining town, centre of the Somerset coalfield, where she had been born, he had been something of a mystery. Why, they had asked with nodding heads and knowing glances, why should Amy Roberts decide to take in a lad like that just because his mother had died of pneumonia while staying in a Hillsbridge boarding house, leaving him orphaned? All very well for her to say simply that he was Welsh, as Llew, her husband, had been and she could not bear to see him sent to an Industrial School along with all the other waifs and strays and boys who were out of control or just plain wicked. All very well for Charlotte Hall, Amy's mother, to explain with a certain amount of bluster that Amy had been a little unhinged by the shock of Llew's death in an accident at the depot yard. It was a peculiar thing, very peculiar indeed, and there was more to it than met the eye – there had to be.

But Barbara had been too young to hear the speculation and she had neither known nor cared that

Huw was causing Amy problems and to spare. To her, right from the start, Huw had been a hero, the big brother she had longed for. As a child she had followed him everywhere, running after him like a puppy dog. She had been unaware of how much he had hated both her and Maureen at first, hating them because they were clean and tidy, with bows in their hair and neat white ankle socks, hating them because they had a mother and he did not. She had been deaf to Amy's entreaties to 'leave Huw alone', for Amy, even as she grew to love Huw, had been terrified he might lead her daughters into trouble. And gradually, as he had settled into his new life, he had begun to grow fond of her and make a fuss of her.

The change had come, though Barbara had been too young to realise it, when Amy had married Ralph Porter. At first, Huw had rebelled against the authority which Ralph had represented, but hard won respect had come, and the bond had been cemented when Ralph had done what Amy, because of her youth, had been unable to do, and formally adopted Huw. Life had settled into a good and easy pattern, the long sunny days of childhood – and they had been the sunnier because Huw was there.

It was Huw who had taught her to ride a two-wheeled fairy cycle, a thrilling Christmas present when Amy and Ralph had decided she was big enough to graduate from her tricycle – not an easy feat when the only flat lane near their home, Valley View, was full of pot-holes. He had run beside her tirelessly, hanging onto the saddle, and picked her up and dried her tears when she fell off, grazing her hands and knees and scratching the paint on her precious machine. It was Huw who found a way to mend Rosie, her doll, when she lost her head, twisting a piece of wire to hold it on again, albeit a little skewed. And it was Huw who warned off the boys from Batch Row when they wrecked the tree house that she and Maureen had built and furnished lovingly with remnants of Amy's net curtains and some old cracked pieces of china. Much later when one of them had followed Barbara home one night in the dusk and tried to steal a kiss he had caught up with him and knocked him down in the mud, bloodying his nose. The boy had gone home with his tail between his legs; he had not bothered Barbara again.

And all the while the bond between them had grown stronger. When Huw had his first girlfriend Barbara had suffered agonies of jealousy. To see him with that stupid simpering Judy Button whose Uncle Herbie was Amy's foreman and right-hand man, made her burn inside, and only her inner certainty that she, Barbara, was far more important to Huw than Judy could ever be, kept her from actually doing some of the drastic things she longed to do, like pulling Judy's long brown Alice in Wonderland ringlets, or puncturing her bicycle tyres. And eventually her restraint had been rewarded. Huw had come in one night scowling and kicking over the milk bottles which Mrs Milsom the housekeeper had put out rinsed and ready for the roundsman and there had been no more Judy.

The next trauma had been the greatest – when Huw had announced that he wanted to join the RAF. In her heart Barbara had known for a long while that one day it would happen. Huw had always been fascinated by flying, just as his Uncle Jack, Amy's brother, had been. Uncle Jack was now a schoolmaster in a seaside town in South Somerset, but during the Great War he had flown a de Havilland with the RNAS, and when the children went to spend holidays with him he sometimes took Huw gliding – a sport he had managed to take up in spite of losing a leg in the war. Barbara had only to see Huw's face after those trips to know where his heart lay and sometimes when they curled up with late night cups of cocoa, listening to the wireless and toasting their toes at the big open fire in the living room, he would talk to her about it.

But it had been a shock, all the same, when he had actually applied for a five-year Short Service Commission. She had cried bitterly after they had waved him off for the first time to the Civilian EFTS where he was to undergo his first instruction in the art of learning to fly and the house had seemed empty without him.

'For goodness sake, Barbara, buck your ideas up!' Amy had instructed her when she could no longer stand the sight of her long face and the way she was mooning about the house. 'Huw has only gone to Desford, not the moon.'

Barbara had said nothing. There was no way of making someone understand how desolate she felt, particularly when they were determined not to understand. Mum doesn't seem to need anyone, she thought. Not Maureen and me, not Huw, not even Ralph. I don't believe she knows what it feels like to really miss someone.

Of course, like most things in life, there were compensations and Barbara discovered them when Huw came home for a weekend kitted out as an Acting Pilot Officer RAF (On Probation). The uniform suited his dark good looks and he cut such a dashing figure that Barbara's heart swelled with pride. She had insisted on being allowed to accompany him to the railway station when he left to do the fortnight's square bashing and drill and discipline which would turn him into a real serviceman, and walking down the road, holding proudly onto his arm, she had been aware of all the admiring and envious glances he attracted. There were those, of course, who snorted and asked in loud whispers: 'Who does he think he is, anyway? I can mind the time when . . .' But there would always be people like that, especially in a small town, people who, having achieved nothing themselves, resented the fact that someone else might have done.

They did not bother Barbara any more than they had ever bothered Amy. But as the months slipped by and 1938 became 1939, Barbara realised that storm clouds were gathering on the horizon. At first, she took little notice of the talk of war, for war to her was not real, not something which actually happened in real life. It was a vague threat, no more, to be dismissed in favour of more interesting topics, like tennis and films and the latest music hits. Then one evening she had overheard Amy and Ralph discussing it – and how it could affect Huw.

'He's flying fighters now,' Amy was saying. 'That means he would be right in the thick of it, doesn't it?'

Barbara stood stock still in the doorway.

'Yes, I'm afraid it does,' Ralph replied.

There was a silence, then she heard Amy sigh.

'Oh well, let's hope it won't come to that.'

'I'm afraid that's a pretty vain hope,' Ralph said. 'If you want my opinion, Chamberlain did nothing but buy time when he went to see Herr Hitler and came back waving his piece of paper. It won't last, Amy. It can't. Hitler has his sights set on far wider fields than his own and sooner or later we're going to have to use force to stop his little game.'

Another silence.

'Let's hope it's later rather than sooner,' Amy said after a moment. 'The thought of another war makes me feel sick inside. I can still remember the last one too well. My brother Fred was killed in France and the boy Dolly was going to marry. And our Jack lost his leg when he was shot down and was lucky to get back alive. Oh no, I can't believe we'll go into all that again in a hurry.'

'We shan't have any choice,' Ralph said and the matter-of-factness of his tone chilled Barbara. She knew about Uncle Jack's leg, of course, and she had heard of an Uncle Fred and the others who had been killed, though it had meant nothing to her. Now, for the first time, she thought of them as young men, not so very different to Huw, and a sensation of prickly fear crept over her skin.

Throughout the months of spring and early summer her anxiety ebbed and flowed with each turn in the tide of news from Germany. Then familiarity began to breed contempt and by midsummer, when everyone said war was inevitable, Barbara was feeling quite bullish. If Adolf Hitler was the monster everyone made him out to be then he had to be put in his place – and who better to do it than Huw and the other young men like him? They would soon teach him a lesson he wouldn't forget! Barbara thought.

But as she ran towards him across the platform at Bristol Temple Meads railway station that June morning, laughing her welcome, all depressing thoughts of war were far from her mind.

Huw caught her by the arms, swinging her up and round, then holding her back to look at her. 'Barbara! What on earth are you doing here?'

She laughed. 'Surprised to see me?'

'You can say that again!' He hugged her. 'Shouldn't you be at school?'

'Yes. I'm playing truant.'

'Barbara! You don't change.'

'Nor do you,' she said proudly.

'I thought those nuns might knock some sense into you.'

'No chance. Surely you didn't think we'd let you come to Bristol and not make the effort to get in to see you?'

He glanced at his watch. 'I'm not going to be able to stay long, I'm afraid. But what do you say to grabbing a quick cup of coffee?'

'Lovely,' she said.

The station buffet was muggy, smoky and stale. Beneath a glass counter sandwiches curled sadly and at one end a tired looking woman was dispensing mud-coloured tea from an urn. Barbara followed Huw to an empty table and waited, wriggling her nose at the fumes from the overflowing ashtray, while he fetched two cups of coffee. The tired looking woman seemed to brighten considerably while serving Huw and Barbara, and smiled to herself. Trust Huw! But then, he did look so handsome, she would have defied any woman to keep a long face when he was around.

He came back carrying two cups of coffee and set them down on the table, pushing the overflowing ashtray aside.

'Sugar?'

'No thanks.'

'Of course, I forgot. You're watching your figure, I suppose.' He stirred two spoonfuls of slightly tea-stained granules into his own cup. 'So – what's been happening at home?'

'Not much. At least, nothing different. Mum is still busy with her businesses and Ralph is still busy with his. Maureen is an unbearable little swot and . . .'

'You shouldn't talk about your sister like that,' he admonished teasingly.

'Why not? That's what she is. Oh, I know she's clever and she'll probably do very well, but I mean . . . She's always got her nose in a book. And the nuns single her out as a model student. Yuk!'

He laughed. 'What about you?'

'What about me? I'm still at school because Mum and Ralph insist I get a good education. I don't know why they won't let me leave. They might just as well and then I can get on with what I want to do.'

'And what's that? The last I heard you were planning to seek the bright lights.'

13

'Oh, that's gone by the board.' Barbara sipped her coffee; it was bitter and half cold but with Huw sitting opposite she scarcely noticed. 'I think I'm going to join one of the women's services. If there's going to be a war I want to be in it.'

'Barbara.' Huw's face grew serious and he leaned towards her across the table. 'If there is a war – and I'm pretty certain there's going to be – it's not going to be any picnic.'

'You'll be in it.'

'That's different. I'm a man. Not that they'd let the women do anything dangerous, I suppose, but still . . . ' He felt in the pocket of his uniform jacket and got out a packet of Players and a cigarette lighter.

'That's new isn't it?' Barbara said curiously. 'I haven't seen that one before.'

He ignored her, lighting his cigarette and drawing on it deeply.

'Can I have one?' she asked, holding out her hand.

'No.'

'Why not?'

'Because you are not old enough. You're not old enough to join up, either.'

'I'm sixteen!' she protested. 'I'll be seventeen soon!' He only smiled and she flared suddenly: 'I wish you'd stop treating me like a child! It's because I'm wearing this stupid school dress, I suppose. I hate it. I absolutely hate it!'

He smiled at her, his eyes narrow behind the curling smoke.

'When you talk like that you not only look like a child, you sound like one. But you are growing up, Barbara, I grant you that.'

She returned his gaze, uncertain whether to be flattered or annoyed. Then she decided this stolen episode was too precious to spoil with petty squabbling.

'Tell me what you're doing,' she said. 'If you're allowed to, that is. It's much more interesting.'

They sat chatting over the bitter coffee, Huw regaling her with tales of life in the mess at his RAF station and she listened intently, laughing at their escapades. Then Huw glanced at his watch again.

'Barbara – I'm going to have to go.'

'Oh Huw . . .' There was a sudden catch in her throat. All this and over so soon . . .

'You know I'd stay longer if I could. Though I'm not sure you shouldn't be going yourself. How are you going to explain to the nuns?'

'Oh, they won't suspect a thing. They live in another world.'

'That is more than can be said for Squadron Leaders,' Huw said ruefully. He stood up. 'Come on, Barbara. I'll see you to your train.'

'No, it's all right. My platform is miles away. If you've got to go – go!'

'I think perhaps I'd better.' He chucked her under the chin. 'Be good.'

'And you.' Tears were springing in her eyes; angrily she blinked them away.

'When have I ever been anything else?'

'Plenty of times if the stories Mum and Ralph tell are true.'

'All right!' He raised a hand in surrender. 'No need to go into all that now. Bye-bye, love.'

'Buy Huw. Come home soon.'

With a smile and a wave he was gone. She stood watching while his airforce blue uniform was swallowed up in the crowds, swallowing at the lump in her throat. Then, with a characteristic lift of her chin, she turned and went back down the steps looking for a porter who could tell her how long she would have to wait for a train back to Bath and which platform it would go from.

Barbara had been back at school for only ten minutes when the summons came.

'Sister Claude wants to see you in her office.'

Her heart sank. It could only mean one thing. She had been too long and suspicions had been aroused. On her way up the staircase between the wood panelled walls her imagination worked overtime on what excuses she could offer. She had seen someone taken ill, perhaps, and stopped to do what she could. Or rescued a kitten from a tree and become ledged herself. A bit unlikely, one had to admit, but it would also account for the bent brim of her boater – another sin that was going to need explaining.

And if I have to make up a story it might as well be one that shows me in a good light, Barbara reasoned.

She tapped at the headmistress's door.

'Come!'

A nun shouldn't have a harsh voice like that, Barbara thought. It should be soft from praying and singing Aves, not sounding like a sergeant major. She opened the door and went in.

Sister Claude looked up and her expression told Barbara her worst fears had been realised. There was something very unholy about the tight set of her narrow lips and the way her eyes glared from behind her spectacles.

'Well, Barbara,' she said.

'Sister.'

'You know why you are here, I'm sure.'

Barbara opened her eyes very wide and attempted an innocent expression.

'I'm sorry if I was a long time at the dentist's, Sister, but on the way back I saw the most terrible accident. A poor woman stepped off the kerb and . . .'

'Barbara!' Sister Claude thundered.

'Yes, Sister?' She said it with less conviction.

16

'Save yourself the trouble of lying. It only adds to your wickedness.'

'But Sister . . .'

Sister Claude closed an exercise book she had been marking with a snap and laid it on a pile with the rest.

'I happen to know, Barbara, that you have not been to the dentist at all. You have been to Bristol.'

Barbara's jaw dropped. This she had not expected.

'How . . .?' It was out before she could stop it.

'You may well ask that, Barbara. Suffice to say that very few movements of a girl in the uniform of our convent go unnoticed – and *all* are known to God.'

'Oh.'

'Yes, I hear you were in Bristol, Barbara. Bad enough, but that is not all, I fear. I understand you were on the station meeting some *boy*.' She spoke the word with distaste, as if boys belonged to some strange alien race, Barbara thought.

'Not some boy, Sister,' she protested. 'Huw.'

'Huw?'

'My . . . my brother.'

'Don't lie, Barbara. You do not have a brother.'

'Well, he's not my brother exactly . . .' Barbara broke off. She had not realised Sister Claude did not know about Huw, though she supposed there was no reason why she should. Now she wondered just how she could explain him. My stepfather's adopted son, sounded so far-fetched, even though it was the truth. In her present mood Sister Claude would never believe her. 'He lives with us,' she said lamely.

Sister Claude's tight lips told her exactly how truthful she was being.

'I had thought, Barbara, that a school such as ours would have set your feet on the right path for life. I don't know where you met this boy, I don't know what possessed you to lie to me and to miss your lessons to go

17

cavorting with him. But one thing I do know. I shall not stand for it. This school has a reputation to maintain . . .'

Oh God, she's going to expel me! Barbara thought in horror.

'. . . and I shall do all that is necessary to maintain it. What will your mother have to say about this, Barbara?'

'She . . . I . . .' Useless to protest that Amy would have no objection to her being with Huw. She certainly *would* object to her missing lessons and telling lies to do it.

'You realise she will have to know about this?'

Barbara swallowed. 'Yes, Sister.'

Outside the door Barbara let out her breath in a long, sustained 'Phew!' So she hadn't been expelled – more was the pity. In the end Sister Claude had cared more about her fees than the school's much vaunted reputation. But she would certainly tell Amy – and Amy was going to be furious . . .

Barbara straightened her shoulders and tucked an irrepressible curl behind her ear.

Oh well – trouble in store.

But she knew it had been worth it and that given the same circumstances she would do the same thing again.

In her office at the yard which served as headquarters for both Roberts Haulage and Roberts Transport, Amy Porter signed the last of the day's mail, replaced the cap of her Parker fountain pen and tucked it away in her bag.

As usual the depot had been a hive of activity and it seemed to Amy she had scarcely had time to draw breath since she had unlocked the office at 8 o'clock that morning. Never mind, she liked it that way, liked to see the lorries busy and the diary full. She would willingly have worked out estimates and costings until the figures sang in her head and written dockets till her fingers blistered if the need arose. She could remember all too clearly the days when things had been very different – the days when she had first inherited the tiny struggling business from her first husband, Llew Roberts, who had been killed in this very yard when he was crushed by a lorry he had been working on. Roberts Haulage had been a two-vehicle concern then, employing only one driver and two mates, and she had fought long and hard, not only against the day-to-day problems but also against the prejudice she encountered as a woman, to turn the business into the thriving concern it was today – six lorries, two of them artics for working long hauls such as Llew could never have imagined when he brought his first small lorry home from Birmingham in 1922, a coal haulage company and a charabanc business which was run from a separate depot in Purldown, some three miles away.

There had been times, and plenty of them, when Amy had wondered just what she had taken on, times when she had fought the seemingly endless battles with more desperation than fervour, times when she had not been able to see how she could pull the business out of a downward spiral of cancelled contracts and mounting expenses, but there had never been a moment when she had admitted defeat. At first, it had all been for Llew's sake to make certain the dream for which he had lived – and died – did not die with him. But later she had to admit it had not only been for Llew but for herself too. They had thought she would fail, all of them. Charlotte, her mother, who disapproved of her stubborn stand whilst failing to realise Amy had inherited that very same stubbornness from her; Eddie Roberts, Llew's brother, who had thought the business would automatically become his on his brother's death; the whole town of Hillsbridge, standing by watching and waiting for her to fall flat on her pretty face because she was a woman dabbling in a man's world, a woman daring to step outside the bounds of convention.

Only Ralph had believed in her – Ralph Porter, who was now her husband. 'Oh I knew you could do it, Amy,' he had once told her casually. 'The day we first met, when you took that lorry for a drive and ran into my car, I told myself you were a woman to be reckoned with', and his eyes had twinkled wickedly as he said it. But at the time she had believed even Ralph was against her, deeply involved in his own expanding timber empire, joining with the other men of the business clique to keep her out.

Amy signed the last letter, blotted it and pushed the pile across the desk.

It was the same desk that Llew had bought second-hand when he had started the business, scratched and inkstained but also large and comfortably solid, but there was another set at right angles to it now, a light modern desk topped with a typewriter and a stack of efficient looking wire trays – the desk which accommodated Violet Denning, her secretary.

'There we are, Vi. You'll see these catch the post, won't you?' Amy said.

The girl looked up, keeping her place in the ledger she was marking up with her finger.

'Yes, I'll make sure they're there in good time, Mrs Porter.'

'And if Deacons ring tell them I've arranged things so that we can do the job for them tomorrow as they wanted.'

'Yes Mrs Porter.'

'If it's Mr Deacon himself you'd better make my excuses – you know he always likes to speak to me personally.' A small smile lifted one corner of her mouth – with some clients her femininity had been a positive advantage especially since she had become successful as well, but she had the way of dealing with them off to a fine art. 'I'm off now, Vi. You'll make sure everything is locked up properly when you leave, won't you?'

'Yes Mrs Porter. Don't worry. You get off home.'

Amy nodded, satisfied. Letting the reins go a little, even where mundane chores were concerned, had not come easily. After running the business single-handed she had felt herself responsible for everything that happened at the yard. But with expansion she had had to learn to delegate – there was no way she could possibly do everything herself. And Vi was a good girl, steady and responsible with a pleasant manner which the customers liked. She had been well trained at a secretarial college in Bath and her shorthand and typewriting speeds were good – essential as far as Amy was concerned, for patience had never been her strong point. But Amy fancied that Vi's telephone manner had been learned not in any college but at her mother's knee, for Vi was the daughter of Edna Denning, who had operated Hillsbridge telephone exchange from the front room of her cottage for many years until a purpose-built office had been erected.

I wonder what Llew would say if he knew I had a secretary? Amy wondered as she paused in the doorway looking back at the girl who was once again busy with her work.

It was a thought which occurred to her sometimes at odd moments and while she found his imagined surprise amusing it also struck a chord of sadness. Maybe she was married again, and very happily, but that did not mean she had forgotten Llew, who had been her first love, the father of her children – and the boy who had made the dream of starting a haulage company into reality. Sometimes it all seemed so long ago, like part of another life, sometimes it might have been just yesterday when they had sat side by side on

21

one of the grassy slopes that surrounded the Hillsbridge valley, where dust-blackened buildings clustered around railway sidings and pits, a young couple in love and with all their lives before them – or so they had thought. 'I don't want to work for anybody else,' Llew had said. 'I want to be my own boss. I'm going to get a lorry. Motor transport is the thing of the future.' She had almost laughed at him then. Back in 1922 there had been more horses and carts than motor vehicles on the roads in Hillsbridge. But he had been right and now it seemed to Amy very unjust that he should not have lived to see his vision realised.

Yet with the sadness there was also a pride and a joy which made Amy's heart swell when she thought of what she had done and she knew that if Llew had not died she would never have had this chance to discover herself. Whatever had happened to the business, whether it had been successful or not, she would have been simply Llew's wife, mother of his children, and a glorified unpaid housekeeper. Although at the time she had wanted nothing else, now she was honest enough to admit it would never have satisfied her.

She pulled the office door closed behind her and stood for a moment on the woodplank step looking around the yard that was her domain, a small, still-pretty woman in a smart blue linen dress with crisp white collar and cuffs. Hard work had helped to keep her figure trim where it might otherwise have run to plumpness, and her hair, well cut to help retain its natural curl, bounced irrepressibly around her face much as it had always done. One day, perhaps, it would turn snow white almost overnight as fair hair so often does, with barely a moment of greyness. But there was no sign of that yet. With the sunshine on it, Amy's hair was the same glorious honey gold it had always been.

Yes, she thought, looking around the yard with a

small surge of that ever present pride, I haven't done badly. What had once been an open area was now surrounded by garages and stores, a rest room with toilet facilities for the men and a workshop where the mechanic Amy now employed could attend to the maintenance of the vehicles. The workshop had an inspection pit; Amy had insisted on that. After what had happened to Llew she wanted to be quite certain that no-one should ever have to jack up a lorry again. Only the office was the old original – a wooden shed with a tarpaulined roof. Replacing it was the next thing Amy planned to do but at the moment, with a war threatening, it would just have to wait. She could have had a new office, of course, years ago if she had been prepared to allow Ralph to finance one for her. In the bitter cold of the first winter after they were married he had offered to do just that.

'It's like an icebox in here,' he had said when he called into the yard one day and found her hunched over her little paraffin heater wearing her coat and scarf, her fingers almost too numb to hold her pen. 'You need a properly constructed building, like the one you've had put up for the men. For heaven's sake ring round for a couple of estimates and get it done.'

'I can't afford it just now. I've reached my limits for capital expenditure.'

'You can't think properly if you're half frozen. If your company balance won't stand it at the moment I'll make you a loan, interest-free.'

She shook her head. 'My company pays its own way.'

'A loan, Amy. Come on now, don't be stubborn. I don't like to think of you working in conditions like these. Besides which it's doing nothing for your looks. Your nose is like a cherry.'

Under other circumstances Amy might have laughed. That day she had simply been too cold. But she had no intention of letting Ralph help her out. It would have

23

been all too easy to allow her companies to be amalgamated into his when they had married – had they ever got around to discussing it. But Amy's fierce pride had strengthened her then, and it strengthened her now.

'You can leave my nose out of it, Ralph Porter,' she had retorted. 'And kindly leave me to manage my business in my own way. When I want assistance I'll ask for it.'

Ralph had shaken his head and given up, irritation at her shortsightedness conflicting with admiration for her determination to stand on her own two feet. Amy had gone out and bought two new heaters which raised the temperature to an acceptable level on all but the most icy days and the old office still stood, a monument to her independence.

As she crossed the yard Herbie Button emerged from one of the garages, wiping his hands on a piece of waste. Herbie had been with Llew from the very beginning and he was loyal, trusted and true; some years ago Amy had made him foreman but it was a small enough tribute to a man whose help and loyalty had left Amy with a debt she knew she would never be able to repay. Now he ambled towards her, a tall spare man in a pair of much washed blue overalls.

'Going home then be 'ee, Missus?' he enquired mildly.

Amy smiled. Even after all this time it still amused her to be addressed as 'Missus', a title Herbie had adopted because he had found it difficult to call her 'Mrs Roberts' and well nigh impossible to adapt to 'Mrs Porter'. To him, as to so many of the older folk in Hillsbridge, she was Amy Hall and always would be, no matter how many husbands she may have. But it wasn't right to call her by her Christian name since she was his boss – and so to Herbie at any rate she had become 'Missus'.

24

'Yes, I'm going a bit early today, Herbie,' she told him. 'Ralph and I are going out this evening. I think everything is under control here.'

'I think so, Missus. I shan't be going for a bit, anyway, so I can keep an eye on it all.' He finished wiping his hands, stuffed the rag into his pocket and proceeded to wipe them again on the bib of his overalls. 'An' I'll make sure your young lady locks up safe while I'm at it.'

'She will, Herbie. You can leave the office to her,' Amy said hastily. Herbie's one fault was a slight officiousness born of an over enthusiastic sense of duty and she did not want him treading on Vi's toes. 'Goodnight. See you tomorrow.'

'Goodnight, Missus.'

He went off in the direction of the men's room and Amy crossed the yard and let herself out of the small gate into the lane. In the old days when she had lived in Hope Terrace she had driven to the yard in her little Ford motor car, but after marrying Ralph and moving into Valley View with him she almost invariably walked. It seemed lazy to use the car for such a short journey unless it was raining hard or she needed to go into Hillsbridge to see her accountant or Arthur Clarence, her solicitor, and she found the fresh air helped her to get into the mood to concentrate on work in the mornings and cleared her head after a long day spent on costings and rotas, wages and insurance matters.

Now she stepped briskly out along the lane which ran between the yard on the one side and a steeply sloping field on the other, enjoying the light fragrance of the cow parsley which grew shoulder high in the hedges and hearing the faint musical trickle of the underground streams that ran from the high sloping valley wall into the river which provided a natural boundary to the yard on its far side. Beyond the river was the railway line, beyond that again the batches rose, elongated ridges of colliery waste that had come from two or three of the Hillsbridge pits. There was no tipping on these batches now, a fleet of trucks carried the waste further along to a new incline, and fir trees had been planted on the dusty black slopes in an effort to beautify them. But in summer the trees themselves turned almost as black as the coal waste they grew on and sparks from passing trains set them alight with monotonous regularity. Sometimes the fires would burn for days in spite of the efforts of the local Fire Brigade, running along in the combustible ground to re-emerge in a new spot, and where the fires had burned nothing was left of Sir Richard Spindler's precious trees but an army of charred skeletons. When she had been a little girl Amy had liked to watch the fire engines tackling the blaze, sometimes from below, their hoses using the water from the river, sometimes from above. But after the terrible fire at Ralph's timber yard when Huw had almost lost his life she had come to dread seeing that first thin spiral of smoke that signified batch-on-fire and the wail of the fire hooter could turn her stomach to water.

This afternoon, warm June day though it was, there was no fire. Amy reached the triangular patch of grass where the moon daisies stood in tall white clusters and began to climb Porters Hill, where she had collided with Ralph's Morgan whilst driving the lorry and set in motion a chain of events which had changed all their lives. It was a steep hill, no more than a lane's width from burgeoning hedge to burgeoning hedge, and her feet crunched on the loose gravel which Ralph used to help keep the pot-holes at a manageable level. Amy was a little out of breath by the time she reached the gate and she smiled wryly to herself. She hadn't used to get out of breath on the hill no matter how she hurried. Maybe it was old age creeping on – or, more likely, since she was still only thirty-six years old, the cigarettes she indulged in when she was relaxing – and sometimes when she had a thorny problem to solve as well.

I'd better try and smoke less, she thought.

Valley View was a big rambling house with white-painted gables and shutters and so many chimneys it gave the appearance of an irate hedgehog. From the outside it had changed little since the days when Ralph had lived there as a bachelor – there remained a slightly wild feel about the garden where trees and bushes jostled for light and air, roses rioted and clumps of misty blue forget-me-nots encroached onto the daisy-studded lawns. Water lilies the size of meat platters obscured the greenish surface of the fishpond, and honeysuckle and morning glories filled the air early and late in the day with heavy sweetness. The small patches of garden where Barbara and Maureen had attempted to grow their own phlox and snapdragons had long since reverted to nature, for they had grown tired of their efforts and Amy never had the time nor inclination to supplement the efforts of old Freddie Burge, the gardener.

It was within Valley View that Amy had left her mark. When she had first set foot in the house she had thought how much a man's house it was, all dark paint and heavy furniture. Good, sensible – and so depressing! The only room which had shown any sign of a woman's touch had been the one occupied by Flora, Ralph's invalid sister. But Amy had soon changed that, introducing a touch here and there to lighten the sobriety and then gradually, as the big, high-ceilinged rooms came to need redecorating, lighter paintwork and modern wallpaper, chintzy curtains in summer and deep rich velvet ones in winter had followed. Sadly Flora had died three winters ago and her room was now a drawing-room which Amy had been able to furnish from scratch. Only the kitchen remained totally un-

27

changed. That was the domain of Mrs Milsom, who had been Ralph's housekeeper for more years than he cared to remember. When Ralph had announced his engagement to Amy she had gone to him, her plump chins quivering, and stated that she supposed her services would no longer be required. But Ralph had been able to assure her that was not the case. As Amy wished to continue running her businesses, they would be severely inconvenienced if Mrs Milsom was to leave.

Today was Mrs Milsom's afternoon off and she had gone to spend it as she often did with her sister who lived at Withywood. Amy unlocked the front door and let herself in. The hall was cool and dark, smelling of polish overlaid with the scent from a vase of roses from one of the enormous bushes that rioted in the garden. She went through into the kitchen and slid the kettle onto the old fashioned range which Mrs Milsom had refused to change for a modern cooker. Oh, for a good cup of tea! But even before the kettle boiled she heard the distinctive sound of Ralph's Morgan coming up the hill. So he had been able to get off early today too, she thought, and they would be able to have a leisurely meal before getting ready to go out. She crossed to the window and as the Morgan swung around the corner and into view she burst out laughing.

Not only Ralph, but Barbara and Maureen too. They were piled one on top of the other in the single bucket seat beside Ralph, holding onto one another and the dashboard of the open-topped three-wheeler sports car. She opened the door to greet them and issued her customary warning as they piled out.

'Mind your skirt, Babs! Maureen – be careful you don't burn your leg on the exhaust – it's red hot!'

'It's all right, Mum, we know!'

'Don't fuss! We've done it hundreds of times!'

'Yes, and you've burned your socks hundreds of times too,' she rejoined. 'There's not room for both of you in there. I'm surprised Sergeant Button hasn't seen you riding like it before now and given you a piece of his mind.'

'They're all right, Amy. They enjoy it, don't you girls?' Ralph swung himself over the side of the car on the driver's side with the ease of years of practice and and advantage afforded by being over six feet tall and, in spite of approaching middle age, athletically built.

Looking at him standing there beside the car Amy found herself remembering the first time she had seen him when she had run into this same precious car with the lorry. He had been wearing the flying jacket and boots then which were a necessity in an open car on a cold spring day instead of the open necked shirt and cavalry twills he was sporting today, and his hair had been thick and dark. Well, it was still thick, but the black was now etched at the temples with grey and his moustache, too, was pepper and salt. But this in no way detracted from his good looks. He was, Amy thought, as attractive as he had ever been, as if he had somehow been made for maturity. A small quiver tickled the pit of her stomach and she gave herself a little shake. Nine years married and he could still do this to her!

'I would have thought you wanted your brains testing, all of you!' she said. 'I can just imagine the ructions if I asked them to squeeze into one seat of my car!'

'Oh, your car! Your car's just a boring old Ford,' Maureen teased.

'I couldn't very well pass them by and not pick them up now could I?' Ralph demanded. 'There they were, plodding along the lane . . .'

'*I* just plodded along the lane!'

'And if I'd seen you I'd have picked up you as well.' Ralph came around and kissed her. 'Especially as you look as if you've had a hard day.'

She flipped at him with the back of her hand. 'I do not!'

'All right, let's go and have a cup of tea anyway. I hope you've got the kettle on.'

'Of course.'

A high-pitched droning, loud in the still air, made them all look up. A plane was passing over, quite low, the sun glinting on the silver tail, the red white and blue bullseye marking on the fuselage clearly visible. For a moment they were all silent watching it. Once an aeroplane had been a fairly rare sight, now the skies seemed to positively hum with activity – another portent of the war which everyone was coming to believe was inevitable.

'Training flight, probably,' Ralph said. It was a sensible assumption; there was a flying school in Filton and another at Hullavington, just over the border in Wiltshire.

'I bet it's not,' Maureen said. 'I bet it's Huw with the plane he picked up, coming round to have a look at us. Has anybody got a white hanky – Ralph?' She fished her own small square of lace edged cotton out of her pocket and began to wave madly.

'Don't be silly. He went hours ago.' Barbara's voice was impatient and Amy looked at her in surprise. That didn't sound in the least like Barbara. Normally she would be first to hop up and down and wave – particularly where Huw was involved. And Maureen, too, was looking a little shamefaced suddenly where usually she would have snapped back in that inimitable way sisters have . . .

'Never mind Huw – how about that cup of tea?' Ralph said and Amy came back to earth with a jolt.

'The kettle is probably boiling away like mad.'

They went into the kitchen. Whilst they had been outside the kettle *had* come to the boil and steam hung

30

in a heavy cloud around the chains of the gas lamp and drifted towards the corners of the room.

'Drat!' Amy pulled the kettle off the hob and went to open a window.

'What's for dinner? I'm starving!' Maureen dumped her satchel on a chair.

'Cold pie and salad,' Amy said pouring water into the teapot. 'It's Mrs Milsom's day off.'

'I don't like salad.'

'If this war comes and they start food rationing you'll think yourself lucky to eat what you can get,' Amy said tartly. 'And put your satchel away. I don't want it cluttering up the kitchen.'

Maureen picked her satchel up again. 'I only put it there for the minute. I'm taking it upstairs to do my homework now.' She tossed her head so that a thick braid of hair, a duller gold than Barbara's, fell across her slightly flushed face. 'And anyway, Babs doesn't like salad either, do you Barbara?'

There was no reply from Barbara and glancing at her Amy saw that she had not been listening. There was an anxious expression on her usually sunny, open face and Amy's earlier impression was reinforced. Something was worrying Barbara.

'What's wrong, Babs?' she asked.

Cornflower-blue eyes flipped up to meet hers and the guilt was clearly visible in them before they flipped away again.

'Nothing.'

'Are you sure?'

'Oh, leave me alone, Mum.'

Amy sighed. Sixteen was not an easy age to be, though Barbara seemed to weather it with less difficulty than some of her friends, if the stories she heard from their mothers was anything to go by. Oh well, let Barbara be for the moment. She'd find out later what it was. Just some confrontation with one of the nuns probably over a piece of skipped homework. Barbara was not a scholar and never would be, and Amy could feel some sympathy with her. She had never seen the sense of learning for learning's sake, either. Yet when she had met the real world head on she had knuckled down and made a success of it.

'Do you two want a cup of tea?' she asked.

'Not especially. I'd rather have Mrs Milsom's lemonade if there's any left,' Maureen said.

'There isn't.'

'Salad and *tea*. How boring. Well, I'm going to do my homework. Coming, Babs?'

The two girls left the room and Amy took two cups over to the table where Ralph had settled into one of the large old kitchen chairs. As she put them down he caught her wrist pulling her towards him.

'Good day?'

'Not bad.' She relaxed against his shoulder; it felt good and solid. 'How about you?'

'The usual. All the war talk is causing a bit of panic. I must say I'm particularly worried about the Swedish end if it comes.'

Ralph had interests in a Swedish timber company which had extended the Hillsbridge business through a depot in the port of Gloucester.

'Sweden won't get involved will it?' Amy asked.

With one arm still around her waist Ralph reached for his tea.

'Everybody is going to be involved this time whether they like it or not. Warfare has changed in the last twenty years, Amy. And leaving everything else aside, shipping is sure to be difficult, if not well nigh impossible. I'm stockpiling all I can, of course. The price is certain to go sky high. But I can't pretend that I think the future is anything but bleak for any of us.'

'Oh, it's so unfair!' Amy exploded. 'Just when the girls are getting to an age when the world should be their oyster, it looks as though everything is going to have to go into cold storage again. And Huw. I can't help worrying about him, Ralph. I keep thinking of what happened to Jack – and Jack was lucky.' She shivered, levered herself away from Ralph and reached for her own tea with an angry movement. 'Wouldn't you think the powers that be would have more sense than let it start all over again? Why can't we just mind our own business?'

'Bullies don't go away if you ignore them, Amy,' Ralph said. 'They just get more and more drunk on their own power and the time comes when you have to either make a stand or submit. I don't think I'm ready to submit, whatever it might cost me.'

'Not even if we lose the businesses that we've worked so hard for?'

'No.'

'Not even if our children get killed in the process?'

Ralph set down his cup. She had never seen him look so serious.

'No, Amy. Not even that.'

'Oh, my God,' she said.

They were silent for a moment each in their own world. Then Ralph went to pull her close once more but she broke away.

'I'm going up to see Barbara.'

'Why?'

'There's something wrong with her. I want to find out what it is.' Suddenly it seemed desperately important that her daughters should not waste a moment of what little of the halcyon days might be left to them on silly petty quarrels and anxieties.

She went upstairs. The girls had their own rooms, tiny twin rooms on the far corners of the house, barely larger than boxrooms, but it was better than sharing. There were less quarrels that way. She tapped on the door of Barbara's and pushed it open a fraction.

'Can I come in?'

'If you like.' Barbara was standing by the window, staring out. Her back presented a straight, uncompromising line.

Amy closed the door behind her.

'Babs – what is the matter? Did something happen at school today? Don't say nothing, because I know there is.'

'Nothing . . .' Then Barbara swung round defiantly. 'Oh, I suppose I might as well tell you. You'll have to hear sooner or later. I played truant from school and went to see Huw.'

'You . . . ? Oh, Babs!'

'I know. I shouldn't have done it. I told Sister Claude a story about having to go to the dentist and I got caught out. Someone saw me at the station and told her.'

'Oh, Babs!' Amy said again. 'That was very wrong of you.'

'I know. But I don't really care. Not even if I get expelled . . .'

'Expelled!'

'She threatened. But she won't do it. She's just a lot of hot air. And even if she did do it, oh Mum – don't look like that!' Barbara's lip wobbled suddenly. 'I'm sorry, but I did want to see Huw so much.'

'I see,' Amy said.

'You don't, Mum. Everybody keeps talking about a war coming and if it does, goodness knows when we shall see him again. He might . . .' her voice trembled, 'he might even be killed. Well, he might! Flying aeroplanes is all very well, but suppose he crashed. Oh Mum, I couldn't bear it!'

'Babs, Babs – don't talk like that!' Amy coaxed, but Barbara's wide worried eyes showed the depth of her fear. Amy pulled Barbara to her, holding her the way she had as a child, with the golden head against her

34

shoulder. 'Babs, darling, nothing is going to happen to Huw.'

'How can you be so sure?' Her voice was muffled.

Amy did not answer. She knew there was nothing she could say. Barbara was only voicing her own fears, fears she preferred not to acknowledge but which were there all the same, dark shadows in the quiet of the night. She pushed aside Barbara's blazer, dropped carelessly onto the bright cotton bedspread, and sat, pulling Barbara down beside her.

'Oh Mum!' Barbara whispered into her shoulder. 'Mum, I'm so scared!'

'Don't.' She fumbled in her pocket for a handkerchief and gave it to Barbara. 'What did Huw have to say anyway? How is he?'

'He's fine.' Barbara brightened. 'He bought me a coffee. We talked.'

Listening to her daughter's eager voice as she pushed the spectres back into the dark corners where they belonged, Amy felt a new disquiet. No, not new. Something which had bothered her now for a very long time. Barbara was too fond of Huw. She always had been. Just the natural bond between a boy and girl who had been brought up as brother and sister, perhaps. And perhaps something more . . .

Oh no, not that, thought Amy. Please God, not that. For if it should turn out to be more I don't know what I would do . . .

'Amy!' Ralph called from downstairs. 'Don't forget we're going out!'

Amy tucked one of Barbara's curls behind her ear and traced the line of her cheekbone with a tender finger.

'Don't worry any more, Babs. I'll settle Sister Claude.' She stood up and crossed to the door, looking back at her daughter. Bouncy, irrepressible Barbara – she looked so vulnerable now sitting there in her school dress with a single tear stain streaking between the dusting of freckles. She is just a child, she thought. You are a fool to credit her with more adult emotions. And if one day what she feels for Huw turns out to be more than that you will just have to deal with it. When the time comes.

'I have to go now, Babs,' she said. Then, as an afterthought, she popped her head back around the door. 'And though it was very naughty of you – I'm glad one of us got to see Huw.'

Barbara was smiling at her as she closed the door.

2

High above Hillsbridge on the south-facing side of the valley bowl, Greenslade Terrace – the Rank as everyone who lived there knew it – stretched a finger of grey stone cottages above a sloping patchwork of gardens which reached almost to the railway line far below. In the years since it had been built to accommodate some of the miners who earned their living in the Hillsbridge collieries it had scarcely changed. A little porch had been added here and there and some of the stone bakeovens on the opposite side of the cobbled lane which led past the back doors had been done away with or converted into garden stores. But, for the most part the houses were just as they had always been, walls blackened by coal dust and soot from the trains that constantly chugged up and down the two railway lines which served the town, yet with paintwork bright and clean, window panes sparkling in the sunlight and brass door knockers lovingly polished. There was running water at the stone sinks in the tiny sculleries but only one or two houses boasted a bathroom – toilet facilities were still shared privies in the same blocks which had housed the bakeovens, and baths were mostly still taken as they always had been in tin tubs in front of the open fires which burned all the year round for cooking as well as heat.

Some of the families had moved out, of course, and young couples had taken their place. The Brimbles had left number 9 to move in next door to their daughter Sarah, who had married the eldest of the Hall boys, Jim. And Jacob Cottle and his wife, whose hearts had been broken when their only son Bert had been killed at

Ypres, were both dead and buried now. But the Bryant familly still made the walls of number 4 echo with their noisy laughter; Colwyn Yelling, who had never married after coming home shell-shocked from the Great War, still carried on his bootmending business in what had once been the washhouse of number 19, while Peggy, his mother, still brought babies into the world and laid out the dead, and at number 12 Molly Clements still took in washing which she hung out to dry in billowing white sails over the long gardens. At number 10 henpecked Charlie Durrant, whose wife Martha had been the scourge of the Rank, had taken on a new lease of life since she had died three winters ago. He wore shiny leather shoes now instead of his boots and talk had it that he had a young lady friend.

'Who she is I don't know, but from the powder and paint on her face she's no better than she should be,' Peggy Yelling had told Charlotte Hall – who, of course, still lived at number 11.

'You've never thought of moving, I suppose, now that all the children have gone?' Peggy had asked her once and Charlotte had reacted violently.

'Move, Peg? I should think not! This is my home and has been ever since James and I were married. The only way they'll ever get me out of here is in a box, feet first!'

She had thought of it, of course, mostly when she was struggling back up the steep hill with a load of shopping. The Co-op delivered once a week, but she still liked to go to market for the weekend's provisions and after each winter it seemed the hill grew steeper and longer. 'I'm sixty-four now and not getting any younger,' she would say when James fussed about her breathlessness and the way her face grew flushed. He could no longer do the hill, of course, and hadn't been able to since a bad bout he had suffered in 1926 when the miners' chest disease, which now went by the fancy name of pneumokoniosis, had finally managed to incapacitate him. It was a miracle he was still alive, most folk said. By all the rules he should have been dead and buried years ago. But he was still hanging on, a tribute to Charlotte's loving care and good cooking, though sometimes his fight for breath was painful to hear. If they moved to a house somewhere on the level perhaps James would be able to get out a bit, even if it was in a wheelchair.

But convenient or not, Charlotte never gave a serious thought to moving. As she said to Peggy, this was her home and always had been. She had raised her family here – Jim and Jack, her pride and joy, Fred who had been killed in the Great War, scallywag Ted, in Australia now for the past ten years and doing well by all accounts, and Harry, who had forsaken managerial posts to become the Miners' Agent. And her daughters, too – placid, immovable Dolly, who had always been plump and now was downright cuddly, and Amy of whom she sometimes despaired and yet was always secretly proud. Amy, wilful and determined, who in spite of doing some things which might have shamed them all had still managed to marry Ralph Porter, one of the richest men in Hillsbridge, and send her two daughters to a private Convent school in Bath, a quite unheard-of status symbol.

It was their home too – a central core to their lives where they could gather together with all the grand-children at Christmas and know that whatever else might change, their home never would.

'I should think they'd have a fit if ever we moved', Charlotte would say.

This Saturday morning, however, any thoughts of moving or her own encroaching old age were far from Charlotte's mind.

It was a perfect September day, the kind of day when a clear blue sky above the still-green trees made a feeling of glad-to-be-alive spring in all but the most miserable breasts. Charlotte had been to market early, 'Before it gets too hot,' she had told James, and now she was very glad she had, because she had a visitor. Margaret, Harry's wife, was Charlotte's favourite daughter-in-law and when she came to call Charlotte always put aside the round of endless chores and made time to sit down and share a cup of tea with her whilst exchanging news.

Today, with the sun warming the cottages up and down the Rank, they had taken their cups and the biscuit tin and gone to sit on the low wooden bench outside the back door.

'Are you sure you don't mind, Dad?' Margaret had asked James, mindful of the hours he spent without much company in the cramped little kitchen, but he had smiled, a gentle smile that warmed his rheumy blue eyes.

'Mind m'dear? Of course I don't mind. You get on out and enjoy the sunshine while you can. You start back to school next week, don't you?'

Margaret was a teacher. After qualifying at college she had come home and taken a post at Sanderley, a village three miles north of Hillsbridge and the self-same school where Jack had once hoped to teach. She was a warm friendly girl with soft brown hair and a pleasant open face and her inborn sympathies had been nurtured by the home in which she had grown up. Her father, George Young, was a prime mover in the local Labour Party, a man genuinely committed to righting the inequalities of society and smoothing the path of those less fortunate than himself. From her childhood days Margaret had been encouraged to help with fund-raising and give a little of her pocket money to charity, and when the terrible General Strike had reduced half of Hillsbridge to poverty she had seen her home become a clearing house for gifts of clothing, blankets and food

40

for the needy. It had been her involvement with all this which had attracted Harry to her in the first place – that and the lovely way her face lit up when she smiled. In those days she had sometimes been afraid he wanted her not for herself but for all that her family stood for. Now she knew different. For Harry and for Margaret there had quite simply never been anyone else.

Now she settled beside Charlotte, raising her face to the warm September sun.

'I'm glad we're on our own, actually. Much as I love Dad I really wanted to see you alone. I've got something to tell you.' She turned, no longer able to keep the joy out of her voice. 'I'm going to have a baby. Harry and I . . . You're going to be a grandmother again.'

'Oh, am I?'

Margaret's face fell. 'You don't sound very pleased.'

'Oh, Margaret love, of course I'm pleased if that's what you and Harry want.' Charlotte hesitated. Joyous event or not she had never been able to summon up any great enthusiasm when told of an impending birth. Much as she loved every one of her children, in her day more babies had been inevitable and usually more of an occasion for commiseration than congratulation. Nine long weary months followed by another mouth to feed. Each time she had become a grandmother the same doubts had arisen, too deeply seated to be easily put aside. Would the mother be all right? Too often in her day the mother had not. Would the baby be fit and healthy? Again she had had her worries justified when Dolly's Noel had been born 'not quite all there', as Charlotte put it. And now . . . well, with the world in its present turmoil, was it a fit place to bring children into?

'If it's what you want,' she said again.

'Oh, it is!' Margaret's face was glowing again. 'You don't know how much!'

'That's the main thing. What does our Harry think about it?'

'He's as pleased as I am.'

'And when is the baby due? Not yet awhile I suppose.'

'Not until March. I've really only just found out about it but I couldn't wait to tell you. I feel like shouting it from the rooftops but you can't do that sort of thing, can you?'

'No.' Charlotte cast a shrewd glance at Margaret's slim, almost boyish figure. 'What will you do about work?'

'I think I can carry on until Christmas. Then I'll have nearly three months to rest and exercise and make all the preparations.'

Charlotte smiled wryly. Rest and exercise! That was the modern way for you! In the old days it had been work work and more work right up until your time.

'Well, good luck to you,' she said. 'Hey look – here comes Peg back from market. You'll be wanting to book her up for when your time comes I dare say.'

A plump fair-haired woman had turned the corner of the Rank carrying a laden shopping bag. Peggy Yelling was as old as Charlotte but somehow managed to look younger – because she had had fewer children, Charlotte thought. It always came back to the same thing . . .

'No, don't say anything to Mrs Yelling yet,' Margaret said swiftly. A faint rosy colour had come up in her cheeks.

'Oh, why's that then?' Charlotte asked.

'Because – well, I might not be having the baby at home,' Margaret said awkwardly.

'Oh! Not have it at home?' Charlotte was startled. 'Why ever not?'

'Because . . . well I just might not,' Margaret said defensively. 'Don't say anything to her about it, please.'

Peggy was almost within earshot now and Charlotte

was unable to question her further though she was determined to get to the bottom of it as soon as they were alone again.

'Morning, Peg,' she called. 'Nice morning.'

Peggy stopped, propping up her shopping bag against the leg of the wooden bench.

'Weather's nice, yes. I don't know that the news is so good.'

'Oh, what do you mean by that?'

Peggy took a handkerchief out of her pocket and wiped her perspiring forehead.

'Well – this war. It's going to come, isn't it?'

'Oh, I don't know. I think it's a lot of bluff. They'd never be that silly would they?' Years of living with James had endowed Charlotte with some of his simple optimism.

'The Territorials have been called up,' Peggy said. 'One of the doctors from South Compton is gone and that Conservative chap they say is going to be our next MP when Mrs Lincoln gives up. All his meetings have been cancelled. There's notices up all over the place. And now they're calling for men between forty-five and fifty-five to join the TA. When they start wanting the old 'uns you can bet it's serious.'

In the moment's silence that followed the chimes of the town clock striking eleven carried up across the valley in the clear morning air.

'Well, I'm going to look on the bright side,' Charlotte said stoically. 'Look, Peg, it was bad enough last time, wasn't it? And this would be ten times worse. They reckon there'll be bombing and gas attacks. Well, nobody could be fool enough to start something like that, surely?'

'They must think it's going to come though – to the cities anyway,' Margaret said. Her face had gone serious. 'That's why they're starting evacuations.'

'Yes, I heard about that.' Peggy finished mopping

her brow and tucked her handkerchief back into her pocket. 'There's some coming here, isn't there? I was reading about it in the paper yesterday.'

Margaret nodded. 'They are expecting five train-loads in Bath today and some of them will be sent out here to Hillsbridge. Mum's Womens' Committee is involved with looking after them when they arrive and I'm supposed to be helping out. It will be quite a job finding them all somewhere to stay, and it won't only be the children but mothers with young babies as well.'

'However will you manage?' Peggy asked.

'We shall just have to find people willing to take them,' Margaret said. 'We've been drawing up lists, but I don't think we've got enough. Actually, I thought of you for one, Mum. It's something else I wanted to ask you about. You've got a spare bedroom, haven't you?'

'Yes, but I like to keep that in case our Jack and Stella want to come up and stay – or one of the grandchildren.'

'It's not going to be easy, I know, but I'm afraid we're all going to have to make some sacrifices before it's over,' Margaret said.

Charlotte bristled. 'What about your mother? She's got room for a couple up there, hasn't she?'

'Yes, she's already promised to take at least one, perhaps two,' Margaret said and Charlotte felt a moment's irritation. Trust Gussie Young. She always had been a bit of a do-gooder. Charlotte herself, though more than willing to do whatever was necessary to help her own children, had always been inclined to feel that charity should not only start at home but also stop firmly at the back door.

'The authorities are sending some provisions with the evacuees,' Margaret went on. 'Enough tinned meat and milk and biscuits to last over the weekend so you need not worry about whether you'd have enough in your larder.'

This made Charlotte bristle afresh.

'It wouldn't be *that* that would worry me. I always keep a good table, you should know that. It's just that I don't fancy taking in strangers. Especially Londoners. Your house wouldn't be your own.'

Peggy retrieved her shopping bag.

'Oh well, no sense worrying about it. But if you're really stuck I might be able to take one. If our Colwyn clears all his junk out of the small room that is.'

'Thanks, Mrs Yelling. I'll remember that,' Margaret said gratefully.

Peggy set off along the Rank towards her own house and Charlotte stared after her feeling vaguely betrayed.

'I should have thought that was the last thing Colwyn would want,' she said tartly. 'A strange child in the house. You know what his nerves are like. Now then, Margaret, you were just telling me about the baby when Peggy came along. You might not be going to have it at home, you say? Why ever not? There's nothing like being at home, I say. You wouldn't get *me* into a hospital, I can tell you . . .'

Before she could go on Peggy, who had reached her own door and gone inside, re-emerged, gesticulating wildly.

'Lotty! Quick – go and put your wireless on!' she called. 'Mr Chamberlain is going to make a broadcast!'

Charlotte and Margaret looked at one another, dawning apprehension reflected in their eyes. Then they ran into the house.

'What be going on?' James asked, startled.

'The wireless – Mr Chamberlain is going to make a broadcast!' Charlotte bustled over to the set, turning the knobs and twiddling. 'Oh come on, come on! Why does it take so long for this thing to warm up!'

A few crackles of static seemed to answer her then the

voice of the Prime Minister filled the room, solemn and overlaid with tones of foreboding.

When he had finished they remained silent for a moment or two. They had expected it, even Charlotte in spite of her protestations to the contrary. But now it had happened they were stunned by the enormity of it.

'So, that's it then.' It was James who broke the silence, his wheezing voice almost as solemn as Neville Chamberlain's had been. 'We'm at war.'

'Yes,' Charlotte said. 'God help the boys who will have to fight it.'

'God help us all.'

Through the open window they heard voices. 'Have you heard the news? We're at war! We declared war on Germany at eleven o'clock. Mr Chamberlain just broadcast . . .' Up and down the Rank people called to one another and eyes searched the skies as if expecting to see the first German bombers with their cargoes of death. Margaret picked up her bag.

'I'd better be going. Maybe the evacuees will be here sooner than we think.'

'All right, Margaret. When shall we see you and Harry?'

'I don't know. Now . . . I don't know anything now . . .' She sounded as if she were in a state of shock and Charlotte for once was unable to argue.

'Take care then. Come when you can.'

It was only when she had gone that Charlotte realised she had never got to the bottom of why Margaret was not having her baby at home. Events had overtaken her. What had seemed so vitally important a few short minutes ago had ceased to have more than the slightest significance. Mr Chamberlain had broadcast and the world had turned upside down.

'Oh my Lord!' Charlotte said shaking her head. 'Where do we go from here?'

Her only reply was James muttering as he always had done in moments of crisis. 'Never mind, m'dear. Never mind. Worse things happen at sea . . .'

And Charlotte, still shocked, was unable to keep a sharp response from springing to her lips.

'Oh, for goodness' sake, don't you understand? We're *all* at sea this time!'

Although Hillsbridge, along with the rest of the country, had been rocked to its very foundations, very little seemed to happen that first weekend when England was at war.

In the bar at the Miners Arms and the George, the two public houses which faced one another across the main street, the talk was almost entirely of the terrible events which had overtaken them, and a few young hotheads marched into an army recruiting office in Bath only to be told that for the moment their services were not required and to go home and wait for their call-up papers. Margaret Hall, along with the rest of the band of willing volunteers, waited for the rest of the day and on Sunday, too, at the railway station, yet no trainloads of evacuees rolled in.

It was late on Monday afternoon before the first of them arrived, bussed in from Bath, and they managed to take the reception committee by surprise by their sheer numbers and the lateness of their arrival.

'Oh my goodness, whatever are we going to do with them at this time of night?' Captain Fish's daughter, Elinor, stalwart of both the WI and the St John's Ambulance, groaned as the pitiful procession filed off the hired charabanc and a fleet of private cars disgorged still more and even more into the Market Square.

'We'll sort them out, don't worry,' Margaret said, but she was almost as shocked by the sight of them as she had been by the declaration of war itself.

Dear Lord, but they were a pathetic sight! Pale, undernourished children, each clutching a bag of food and chocolate and the cardbox box containing their gas mask, each with a label pinned to their clothing, for all the world as if they were just another piece of baggage. Some of the little ones had been crying; their faces were tear streaked and ribbons of slime ran from their noses to their upper lips, while the older ones wore mulishly defiant expressions as they tried to be brave about finding themselves here in this alien place. Most looked as though their clothes were hand-me-downs or had come from a stall at a jumble sale, the girls with darned handknitted cardigans buttoned unevenly over the cheap cotton frocks, the boys mostly wearing shorts which were either too small or too long, so that their battle scarred knees were almost hidden by voluminous grey. Socks had long since rucked down around skinny ankles, hair had been cut with the pudding basin. Like a truckload of mute young animals they herded together looking at the willing workers who greeted them with eyes that were hostile yet frightened.

There were a few women with the party, haggard women who should have looked young, judging by the babies in their arms. Their clothes, too, were cheap and unfashionable, and one had a bristle of curlers escaping from the headscarf she wore turban-style.

They were from the East End of London and to them Hillsbridge might have been the moon. To the people who waited to greet them they were an astonishing sight, poorer looking even than the children from Batch Row and scruffier than the gypsies who used to come with the fun fair to winter each year in the Market Yard.

As soon as they were assembled the volunteers set to

work, attempting to match children to the people who had offered to take them in. But it was soon clear it would be no easy task and the Square soon came to resemble a cattle market.

'Mrs Parfitt – you agreed to take one.' Margaret led a small boy who looked as if he had been crying towards a sharp featured woman in a smart floral dress and marking off a name on her list as she went. 'This is Johnny Cooper, six years old, from Peckham. Can I leave him with you?'

'No thanks.' Winnie Parfitt shook her head vehemently. 'I don't want a boy. They do too much damage. I'd rather have a girl.'

'But . . .' Margaret looked around helplessly. Useless to try and persuade Winnie if she had already made up her mind. That would only make the child feel more unwanted than he already did.

'I'll have *her*.' Winnie nodded vigorously towards the most respectable of the girls.

'I was going to take that one,' another woman, whose name Margaret did not know, spoke up. 'At least she looks clean, which is more than you can say for most of them. I said I'd take one in when they came round and asked me but I shan't unless I can have some say which it is. I don't want one with fleas or anything like that.'

'I'm sure they haven't got fleas,' Margaret pleaded.

'And I'm sure they have – if not worse!' the woman argued. 'Look at that one over there – she hasn't stopped scratching since she got here.'

Margaret sighed and persisted and gradually the band of children grew smaller as they were matched with volunteer families and taken off home to be given a meal – and in some cases a good scrubbing.

Those who were left were the most difficult cases, however, and by the time the volunteers had been exhausted there was still a small cluster of them, mostly boys, rejected for the same reason Mrs Parfitt had given

– that they would be likely to be too much of a handful – and the siblings, brothers and sisters who were clinging tightly to one another in an effort to avoid being split up.

'This is a pretty state of affairs,' said Elinor Fish as she marched across the cobbled yard to Margaret, still waving her sheaf of papers on which the names had been mostly ticked off by now. 'What are we going to do with the rest of them, I'd like to know?'

Margaret passed a hand through her hair. She was so tired that every movement was an effort and she felt slightly sick – perhaps because the hands of the town clock were now showing a quarter past seven and she had had nothing to eat since midday. But she had no business feeling tired, she thought. She was a great deal younger than many of the volunteer helpers here today and the most important thing was finding beds for the night for these poor children.

'There's nobody left on the list is there?' she asked.

Elinor Fish shook her head. She was a tall straight woman who had inherited her military bearing from her father and the crisp navy blue uniform of the St John's Ambulance Brigade suited her. But she now wore the harrassed expression of a woman facing an impossible task.

'Nobody. In fact, one or two who were on it changed their minds when they saw the state of the children. If this goes on it's going to have to be made compulsory for people with the room to have them.'

'If only Harry was here we could bundle some of them into the car and take them round to anybody we can think of who has the room'.

'Good idea,' Elinor agreed. 'But since we haven't got a car we'll just have to make them walk. A bit of exercise won't do them any harm.'

Margaret looked at the children doubtfully. Of course exercise did nobody any harm and most people got plenty of it. But these children looked on the point of exhaustion and to drag them off on an endless trek from door to door seemed the height of cruelty – especially since it would probably involve a climb up one of the steep hills which were the only way out of Hillsbridge town centre.

'What about Holly Bush House?' she suggested. 'They've got plenty of room and it's not too far to walk.'

'Oh, I don't think so,' Elinor said swiftly. Holly Bush House was the home of the Dowlings, one of the most prominent families in Hillsbridge. 'They would feel most out of place there.'

Margaret felt a stab of irritation. In Elinor Fish's book it was one thing to push unwanted guests onto ordinary families, quite another when it came to imposing on people she knew socially.

'Well, what about the Rectory? Or Dr Carter's? If the children *do* have fleas at least he'd know what to do about it.'

'We could try the Rector, I suppose,' Elinor said doubtfully. 'Though it's a bit much to put something like this on a housekeeper. If he had a wife it would be different.'

'Well, we've got to find somewhere for them to go or we'll be here all night.' Margaret was beginning to feel irritable.

'Let's make a start in Market Cottages,' Elinor suggested. 'That's the closest and at least it's on the level.'

Not very hopefully Margaret agreed with her. The cottages in Market Row were small ones, two up, two down, and she couldn't see many of them having room for an extra child. But as she herself had said, something had to be done or the children would be sleeping under the stars.

Two of the other volunteers, looking equally harassed, joined them and the remaining children were split into three groups, one to tour the houses in Glebe Bottom, one to be despatched to the Rectory and one, with Margaret as leader, to try Market Row.

'Come along then, children,' she said, summoning up her best schoolroom manner.

'Where are we bleedin' going now?' The speaker was one of the bigger boys, a gawky lad with a narrow, aggressive face.

'To find you a bed for the night.'

'I don't want a bed here,' a small girl wailed. She was clutching tight to the hand of her older sister and her small face was streaked with dirt and tiredness. 'I want to go home!'

'That wouldn't be a very good idea,' Margaret said gently. 'It might not be very safe. There could be bombs.'

'We ain't afraid of bombs,' the big boy said. 'We ain't afraid of anything.'

'I'm sure you're not. But it's still best for you to be here for the time being,' Margaret said. 'Come on, let's go, shall we? The sooner we do, the sooner you can have something to eat and a nice cup of tea.'

With her small group she started along the road in the direction of Market Cottages. They followed her with a mixture of reluctance and defiance and her heart bled for them. How strange and terrifying this must seem to them!

At the first two houses she tried Margaret drew a blank, met by a shaking of heads and a door firmly closed in her face. At the third she managed to settle one of her charges, the small boy who had been turned down by Winnie Parfitt, and by the time they had reached the end of the road two houses further on 'Nosey' Parker's wife reluctantly agreed to take the older boy. But nobody, it seemed, had room for more than one child and Margaret was reluctant to split up the pair of sisters.

'We're stopping together,' they insisted when Margaret tried to suggest gently that it might be necessary and her ready sympathy went out to them.

They were an odd pair, as scruffy as any of the children, the older one tall and gangly with her cotton dress so short that Margaret caught an occasional glimpse of her knickers, the younger small and under-sized so that her frock, an obvious hand-me-down, reached almost to her ankles. Both had cropped hair, probably as a result of an edict of 'the flea lady', both looked pale and wan and disturbingly old before their time. Yet in contrast to this both were possessors of the most beautiful dark brown eyes Margaret had ever seen.

At the end of the row where the lane narrowed and began to curve steeply upwards towards the dairy and the Co-operative farm Margaret stopped. Pointless to go any further. The farm manager's wife was a sharp shrewish woman who would almost certainly turn them away though Margaret suspected that if compulsory billeting was brought in she would be found to have plenty of room. But in the end what good would that do? Forcing children into homes where they were not wanted would be a recipe for disaster in her opinion.

Sighing she turned back.

'Are you all right, girls?' Even as she spoke the words she knew it was a stupid thing to say and the older girl glowered back at her scornfully.

The younger one, however, was close to tears.

'I'm tired!' she wailed.

'Keep quite, our Marie,' the older girl warned.

'But I am! Oh 'Lainey, I'm tired!'

'Keep quiet, I said!' The older girl, Elaine, punished her sister with a vicious kick on the shin and the little girl's tears, held back for so long by sheer effort of will, overflowed.

'Don't start blubbering!' Elaine said in disgust.

The child puckered up her mouth in an effort to stop the tears but it was useless. They flowed down her dirt streaked cheeks and she scrubbed at them with a grubby hand.

'Oh don't!' Margaret dropped to her knees beside the child, searching in her pocket for a handkerchief. 'Don't cry, love.'

'I want to go home!' It was a soft pitiful mew like a lost kitten and suddenly Margaret made up her mind. She couldn't tramp these children round the streets any longer. She would take them home with her. It couldn't be a permanent arrangement, of course, for she was out at work all day and they needed to be properly looked after, with a good breakfast to go to school on and a square meal to come home to at night. But at least it would mean their ordeal didn't have to last any longer tonight.

'Come on, I'm going to take you back to my house,' she said.

There was no response of gratitude. The older girl still merely glowered at her, the younger began to trudge along, head bent, on feet that scuffed the ground with each exhausted step.

Seeing her weariness, Margaret dropped to her knees beside the child.

'I'll carry you, love.'

She picked her up. The roughly cut unwashed hair against her chin made her wrinkle her nose and the girl's shoes, reinforced with metal studs beneath the toes like a boy's to make them last longer banged against her hip but she felt a sense of satisfaction.

At least she was doing her bit towards the war effort. It might not be much, but it was something.

'They can't stay, you know,' Harry said. 'They'll have to go as soon as you can find someone willing to take them.'

After reluctantly allowing Margaret to give them a good scrub and ravenously wolfing down a supper of bread and cheese, the girls had at last gone to bed, sleeping side by side in the double bed in the spare bedroom. This in itself had caused a stir for at first they had insisted they wanted to sleep *under* the bed as they did at home.

'You can't sleep *under* the bed!' Margaret had protested.

'Why not? The bed's for our Mam. We're all right underneath.' Elaine, the older girl, had sounded resentful.

'But this is a nice bed,' Margaret had coaxed. 'You'll be much more comfortable in it. It's all made up – look!'

Still the girls had refused to get in and it had been Harry who put his foot down.

'I don't care what you do at home. Here we sleep in the bed, not under it,' he said decisively.

Now at last all was quiet and Margaret and Harry were relaxing in their comfortable kitchen, Harry stretched out in his shirt sleeves in his favourite chair, Margaret curled up on the arm, resting against him.

'They can't stay here,' he said again. 'We'll have to find somewhere else for them to go tomorrow.'

'But I have to go to school tomorrow,' Margaret said.

'Exactly. And what is going to happen to them?'

'I suppose I shall have to take them with me. They'll have to go to school eventually so they might as well start tomorrow.'

'But you can't drag them all the way to Sanderley every day. They'd be much better off in Hillsbridge with their friends. And anyway,' Harry said, 'it's going to be too much for you. Looking after two difficult girls and holding down a job – you just can't do it. Especially in your condition.'

'Oh, I'm all right,' Margaret said impatiently, but

she had to admit to herself that she didn't feel all right. In fact she felt extremely tired.

'No, we must sort something out tomorrow,' Harry said firmly.

'The trouble is they were all in such a state!' Margaret shifted her weight slightly. 'You can understand people not wanting to take them in. You can't believe it really, can you, that anyone could live like that.'

Harry did not reply.

'At least these two are clean now and have a good meal inside them,' Margaret said. 'But they looked so lost, Harry. I couldn't do anything but bring them home with me.'

He settled his arm comfortably around her waist.

'Knowing you, love, I don't suppose you could.'

'They're just children, after all,' she said defensively. 'I mean – think what Huw was like when Amy took him in. And look at him now. A credit to her.'

Harry's heart sank. Sorry as he felt for the children he did not want Margaret making herself ill by doing too much in her condition.

'I still say they've got to go,' he said decisively. 'There are others better able to look after them than you. Now – are you ready for bed?'

She nodded.

'I certainly am. It's been a long day. And it will probably be an even longer one tomorrow.'

Within a week Hillsbridge was beginning to feel other repercussions of the newly declared war than simply the arrival of a coachload of evacuees.

The TA left en masse, off to an 'unknown destination' as the *Mercury*, the local newspaper, phrased it and half the town was at the station to see them off. Lighting restrictions came into force so that vehicles were obliged to use sidelights only and every house was required to fix up some sort of black-out at the windows to ensure no crack of light showed once the lamps were lit at night. And petrol rationing was announced to come into operation the following week – 'Lord knows how we'll manage,' Amy said to Herbie. 'Let's just hope the Hauliers Association can sort something out.'

But in spite of Harry's resolution that it should be otherwise, the young evacuee sisters remained still installed in his spare bedroom at the end of the week.

To begin with, he supposed, the girls had remained simply because it was easier to let them stay rather than find alternative accommodation for them. By the time she had risen earlier than usual to cook them a breakfast and hurried home from school to prepare an evening meal, Margaret was too tired to go out knocking at doors to find someone willing to take them, and for all his good intentions Harry could not see that it was his place to do it. But as the days went by he sensed that Margaret did not intend to try very hard to rehouse the girls. They were both still reserved and resentful, but as a professional where children were concerned Margaret regarded this as a challenge and, ungrateful as they might be, they did seem to be settling in – more than could be said for some of the children, Margaret had told him – or in fact some of the women. Already two of them had returned home saying they preferred to face the threat of bombs to staying a moment longer in this alien place. And the big boy for whom they had managed to find accommodation in Market Row had been caught trying to stow away in a coal lorry which he thought might take him to Bath from where he could catch a train back to London.

The two girls installed in Harry's spare bedroom showed little sign of wanting to follow suit, however. The little one, Marie, still cried sometimes at night, it was true – through the bedroom wall he could hear her soft sobs and her older sister's sharp reprimands – and though he and Margaret tried to draw them out they positively refused to hold a conversation of more than a few words. Yet they ate heartily, wolfing down everything that was put in front of them, and they seemed to be treating the spare room as 'their' territory.

'They really are making themselves at home,' Margaret said and Harry knew what she meant, though he would have put it less kindly. He had had to go into the room to fix a lead for a table lamp for them – Margaret had insisted they needed to be able to put on at least a small night light if they woke in the night and became frightened by the strange surroundings – and he had felt almost like an intruder. They had pitifully few possessions yet somehow they had imprinted themselves on the room like an animal on a new lair. Stepping across the threshold was like entering alien territory, something which, in his own house, was an unnerving experience.

'I think we ought to let them stay for a bit,' Margaret went on. 'It's a shame for them to be pushed from pillar to post again just as they're settling in. And they're no trouble. We've managed this week very well.'

Harry sighed. 'What about all the extra washing they'll make?'

'I'm going to send it down to Molly Clements to do. And I can send our sheets as well, so I shall have less,' Margaret said. 'And there's another thing. They don't seem to have a change of clothes, Harry, apart from a spare pair of knickers – and they're in such a state I would be ashamed to put them on the line. I shall have to take them to shop and sort them out before I can let them go to somebody else.'

'Surely "somebody else" can take them to shop if they need clothes?'

'I wouldn't feel right about it,' she said determinedly. 'But can you imagine, coming all the way from London with only a pair of holey knickers and no clean vest – especially since they sleep in their underwear!'

'No, I can't,' Harry said truthfully. In his home, like Margaret's, he had always been exhorted to make sure his underwear was decent – in case he was run over and taken to hospital. 'I just don't see why it has to be your problem.'

'You've changed, Harry,' Margaret reprimanded him. 'There was a time when you wanted to help those less fortunate than yourself.'

Harry brought his hand down hard onto the table.

'Dammit, as Miners' Agent I spend my whole working life sorting out other people's problems and since I've been on the Council, most of my spare time too. But you have to keep a sense of proportion about these things, Margaret. I don't want you overdoing things, just when you should be taking life a little more easily.'

'I'm fine!' she assured him. 'I'm a perfectly healthy young woman! Just think, when your mother was expecting you she had a household to look after, not just two little girls.'

'Well, they'll have to go before the baby comes,' Harry said. 'We shall need to get the room ready for it.'

Margaret smiled, knowing she had won the first round of the battle.

'The war might be over by then, you never know.'

The first opportunity she had for taking the girls to buy the clothes they needed was on the Saturday morning and Margaret woke them at the usual time with a cup of tea.

'What's this for? Is bleedin' Hitler here?' Elaine said rudely, humping the bedclothes over and burying her head.

'No, but I want you to get up all the same. Come on now,' Margaret urged.

'But it's Saturday, ain't it? We don't go to bleedin' school on a bleedin' Saturday.'

'That's true. But I want to take you to shop.'

'What for?'

'To buy you some underclothes.'

'We've already got bleedin' underclothes.'

'And what are you going to do while they're being washed? Stay in bed? Come on now, drink your tea and get up like good girls.'

'Bleedin' stupid,' came the muffled voice from beneath the bedclothes and the enormous brown eyes of Marie, the younger child, seemed to echo the sentiment.

As she prepared breakfast Margaret heard the thud that announced that the girls were out of bed and a few minutes later they came into the kitchen, wrinkling their noses at the delicious aroma which had done far more than Margaret's words to persuade them to get up.

'Smells good, doesn't it?' She smiled over her shoulder and popped the plate piled high with bacon rashers and fried bread back into the oven to keep warm. 'I still have the eggs to do though so you have time to brush your hair and wash the sleepy-dust out of your eyes.'

The girls exchanged glances. Not a day went by but this stupid woman insisted on them washing themselves – why they simply could not imagine.

'Draw yourselves some water,' Margaret instructed. 'You know how to do it.'

The girls approached the kitchen sink with some trepidation. They had been shown how to use the contraption over the sink, but that didn't mean they liked it. As Elaine swung the long spout so that it suspended over the small tin bowl in the sink Marie hung back nervously, anticipating the spurting gas when the tap was turned on. As it came even Elaine jumped and two pairs of brown eyes stared wide and frightened as if hypnotised by the small blue flame.

'That will do! You've got enough there now,' Margaret said and reluctantly Elaine turned off the tap, saw the small blue flame die, and ran some cold water into the bowl.

While they washed and dried their faces on the kitchen towel Margaret cooked the eggs and dished them up onto the piping hot plates. Then she set them one each side of the kitchen table.

'There you are then. Come and get it.'

They dropped the towel on the rag rug by the sink and piled into their places, picking up the crisp bacon and bread whole in their fingers and dipping it into the egg yolk.

'Elaine – Marie – use your knife and fork!' she admonished. They eyed her resentfully. They didn't like using knives and forks. Food tasted better eaten with their fingers. But they had had this battle before and lost. Awkwardly they armed themselves with cutlery, holding their knives like daggers.

Margaret sighed and shook her head. She could only get so much into them at a time and if they were actually using the knives and forks, that was something.

When they had eaten Elaine retired to the lavatory and Margaret decided to take the opportunity to establish a little rapport with the younger girl. When her sister was there the child aped her sullenness, but once they were separated Margaret felt she had some hope of getting through to Marie.

Now she turned from washing dishes in the bowl at the sink and passed a wiping up cloth to the little girl.

'How would you like to dry some things for me? Be careful not to drop the plates – and the knives and forks go in this drawer here . . .'

Marie took a plate, her tongue creeping out of the corner of her mouth with intense concentration as she dried it and Margaret smiled to herself. Oh yes, Marie was quite sweet once away from her sister's influence. It wasn't her fault that she had been brought up in a deprived environment and Margaret thought how rewarding it would be to teach her to enjoy some of the good things of life.

The moment was short-lived, however. Elaine, returning from the lavatory, stopped in the doorway glaring at the domestic scene.

'What d'you fink you're doing, our Marie?' she demanded.

Marie immediately looked guilty. 'Helpin' wiv the dishes, Lainey.'

'Well don't – see!' Elaine's face had gone weaselly and her voice shrill. 'You're not her skivvy.'

Marie, still holding the cloth, looked from one to the other of them uncertainly.

'Nobody here is a skivvy, Elaine,' Margaret said briskly. 'Not Marie and not me either. I've just cooked your breakfast and Marie is helping me to clear it up again.'

'But you're paid to do it,' Elaine said defiantly. 'Our Mam said to watch out for people like you.'

Margaret began to feel angry, not so much because of what Elaine had said as because the hostile look was back on Marie's face once more.

'I assure you I am not making money out of you being here, Elaine,' she said forcefully. 'In fact I very much doubt if what I shall get will cover the bacon and eggs you have just enjoyed, and it certainly won't cover the cost of kitting you out with new clothes. So let's not fight about it, shall we?'

Eventually they were ready to leave for the shops and set out, the girls lagging behind so that Margaret found it impossible to carry on a conversation with them.

Saturday was market day, and though the market was not the great social occasion it had been when Margaret was a child, with all manner of fascinating tradesmen plying their wares until late into the evening and the band playing for the entertainment of shoppers, it was still a hive of activity during the daytime. Stalls spilled out of the great domed market hall into the yard outside and the big, brightly coloured van selling Gallipoli's homemade ice-cream was parked on the opposite side of the road, on the forecourt of the Miners Arms.

'We'll get an ice-cream when we've finished our shopping if you like,' Margaret offered and the girls' faces brightened. Ice-cream to them was a rare treat indeed – they could remember having it only once in their lives, when the Salvation Army had taken a group of them on a day trip to Brighton, but they knew they had enjoyed every last melting lick of it.

Margaret led them past the stalls and under the subway that passed beneath the first set of railway lines which bisected the main street. Then, they walked along the pleasant tree-lined road which followed the curve of both the lines and the river to the large square stone building which housed both the Co-operative confectionary shop and the drapers. As they passed the confectionary shop windows Margaret saw the girls' eyes go round again at the sight of the newly baked bread and jam tarts in the window and smiled to herself. Difficult they might be but there was one sure way to their hearts – through their somewhat deprived stomachs!

The drapery shop was busy. Margaret joined the queue and the girls wandered around the shop looking at the goods that were displayed and the card stands advertising Sylko and Cash's name tapes. Once again, they seemed totally awe-struck as if they had never been inside a shop like this one before. When it was her turn she called the girls over and noticed the look of distaste the assistant threw them.

'Evacuees, is it?' she asked in a loud whisper.

'Yes.' Margaret had no intention of discussing her charges with Mercy Marshall. 'I want some vests and knickers to fit them – and some liberty bodices too.'

Mercy pulled the appropriate drawers out of the fitting and spread the garments on the counter – cream interlock vests and knickers and neat fleecy-lined liberty bodices, complete with the buttons for the attachment of suspenders.

'There we are then – or did you want navy knickers?' she asked with a glance that suggested she thought navy might be more suitable for these two young customers.

'White,' Margaret said, then thought better of it. There was no knowing what these two would get up to – and no point making washing. 'On second thoughts perhaps navy would be better.'

Little Marie reached up to the counter, feeling the fleecy-lined liberty bodice with fingers that had some-how become grubby since Margaret had last insisted on her washing them.

'Don't touch!' Mercy Marshall snapped.

The child withdrew her hand sharply and cowered away as if half expecting to be struck, while her sister glowered and moved away impatiently to continue her examination of the wares at the rear of the shop.

Margaret sized the underwear with an expert eye.

'I'll take those – two pairs – and those. That will do nicely, Mercy, thank you. Now, what about ankle socks . . .'

At that moment she was interrupted by an angry shout at the rear of the shop. 'Hey you, what do you think you're doing? Just you leave my bag alone, you little turk!'

Margaret swung round to see a large red-faced woman rushing towards Elaine. The child moved quickly and a shopping bag full of groceries overturned, spilling its contents across the floor.

'Elaine!' Margaret called sharply.

The girl turned to run, dodging a customer who was just entering the shop and diving out onto the pavement.

'Look! Look what she's done!' The red-faced woman was beside herself. 'My shopping!'

'Oh, I'm so sorry,' Margaret apologised. 'I don't know how she managed to do that . . .'

'I do!' the woman said angrily, piling groceries back into the bag. 'There were cakes right on the top – I've just bought them. She was trying to take one!'

'Oh, surely not!'

'She was! I just happened to turn round and catch her nicely. Yours, is she?'

'Well, not really . . .'

'One of those evacuees, I suppose. They're going to be nothing but trouble. And that's another of them!' The woman stabbed an accusing finger at Marie, who was cowering behind Margaret. 'Little savages, all of them. My next-door-neighbour has one and he doesn't even know what the toilet is used for. Did it in the corner of the room, he did. Well, I don't know that I want my cakes after she's been fingering them.'

'Let me buy you some more.' Margaret was flushed with embarrassment. 'I'm so sorry, really I am.'

'It's not your fault, I suppose,' the woman said, slightly mollified. 'They should never have sent them here amongst decent people that's all.'

Margaret grabbed Marie's hand and led her to the counter. The child looked as if she expected to be punished for her sister's behaviour and her brown eyes were huge in her small pale face.

'You stay with me, Marie,' Margaret said sternly.

She paid for her purchases, stuffed them into her basket and still holding onto Marie in case she should try to run off after her sister, left the shop. There was no sign of Elaine in the street now.

'Where do you think your sister has gone?' she asked Marie. The child said nothing and in spite of her anger Margaret could not help feeling sorry for her. It wasn't her fault, and she could not think even now that Elaine had actually intended to steal a cake. With everyone being so hostile towards them it was no surprise that she turned and ran.

Back in the Market Square there was still no sign of Elaine and Margaret stood for a moment wondering what to do. It was possible she had gone home. Margaret decided she had better abandon her shopping trip and go home to see, though she had not yet bought any of the weekend essentials. That was going to mean another trip out whether Elaine was there or not. And as for the ice-cream she had promised the girls – well, they could certainly go without that!

Margaret and Harry lived in a large pleasant semi-detached house on the corner of Ridge Road where she had lived with her parents before her marriage. Climbing the hill she kept her eyes about her but there was still no sign of Elaine and it was without much hope that she pushed open the gate and walked up the drive. A stitch was starting in her side and she felt tired and breathless. She couldn't bear the thought of having to go back down to Hillsbridge for the shopping.

She rounded the corner of the house dragging Marie with her then stopped, relieved. There sitting on the back doorstep and idly chalking on the path with a sharp white pebble was Elaine. Instantly, Marie wrestled her hand free of Margaret's and ran to her sister. Margaret followed more slowly.

'So there you are.'

Elaine went on scratching with the stone without looking up.

'Well?' Margaret said briskly. 'Don't you think you should explain yourself?'

The thin shoulders merely shrugged.

'What were you doing touching that woman's shopping bag?'

Another shrug.

'Were you trying to help yourself to the jam tarts on the top?'

The thin faced upturned to look at her.

'Would you believe me if I said I wasn't?'

'Yes,' Margaret said. 'If you tell me you weren't, I would believe you.'

'I weren't.'

'All right,' Margaret said. 'In that case we'll go indoors and forget about it.'

A slow sly smile spread across the peaky features. The girl said nothing, getting up and turning around so that Margaret could see only the back of her cropped head, and something in her attitude disturbed Margaret.

A thief and a liar – or just a misunderstood child of the slums – which was she? For all her experience with children Margaret was not sure. But for the moment she thought there was little she could do but give her the benefit of the doubt.

3

The gold and blue days of September slipped by but no enemy planes were seen in the skies above Hillsbridge and after the first burst of activity life returned almost to normal – a normality which seemed somehow incongruous since England was at war and was punctuated more by petty annoyances than by fear or danger.

It was a nuisance to have to think about some sort of a blackout being in place before lighting a lamp when darkness fell, particularly since the shops had sold out of any sort of suitable dark materials since almost the first day; a nuisance not to know for sure what timetable the buses and trains were running to – if they were running at all, and a nuisance to have to register with a coal dealer to be sure of a supply of fuel through the winter months.

The quiet that reigned in the town was strange, too, for all the works' hooters and sirens were silenced by order; the fire hooter would be used only as an air raid warning siren and there could be no room for confusion; if a siren sounded people must be in no doubt what it meant. But since there were no air raids the silence was uncanny, reminding folk uncomfortably of the days of the General Strike. There had been no sirens then, either, and the unnatural quiet had ushered in a time of great hardship.

'Trouble is, my missus don't know when to expect me home for my dinner any more,' Ewart Brixey said to the group of regulars gathered in the Miners Arms. 'She always listened for the hooter and put the taters on.'

There was a general murmur of agreement. Whatever the reasoning behind it the people of Hillsbridge did not like a change of routine.

'Talking of sirens, have you seen th'ick evacuee girl who's stopping with Ethel Bennett down at Pit Cottages?' Tommy Clements enquired, taking a pull of his pint of beer. 'She's a bit of all right and no mistake!'

'And she's got a young'un, so you mind your p's and q's,' Ewart warned.

The evacuees – 'vackies' as they had come to be known – were still a talking point in Hillsbridge and yet another source of annoyance. The children, like the two Margaret and Harry Hall had taken in, were branded 'a lot of little savages' and the women for the most part were worse, walking the streets with their hair full of curlers, pushing to the front of the queue in the Co-op grocery shop and talking loudly in their Cockney accents which the locals described scathingly as 'th'ick awful twang'.

'What you going to do about that motor bike o' yourn, Ewart?' Walter Clements, Tommy's father, asked, changing the subject. 'You'll have to lay 'un up now that petrol's being rationed, won't 'ee?'

Ewart, the proud possessor of a handsome old Norton and sidecar, aimed a glob of phlegm at the spittoon.

'I shouldn't think so, Walt. Not yet anyway. I can get enough for what I want. It's them with motorcars that'll be having trouble.'

'That's one good thing about this war,' Stanley Bristow said and they all turned to look at him. Stanley had always been a taciturn man; these days he said even less than he had used to.

'Oh, what's that then, Stanley?'

'It'll bring back the horse,' Stanley prophesied. 'All them as got rid of their horses and carts in favour of motorised transport will be wishing they never had, that I do know.' He sipped his beer and added sagely: 'You don't need no petrol for a horse.'

The other men exchanged looks and smiles through the haze of smoke.

Stanley had once been the owner of the livery stables and he had never got over the fact that the government had requisitioned his horses in the First War. It had broken his heart, some folk reckoned, and was the cause of him being such a pessimist in his old age.

This time, however, there was something in what he said. You didn't need petrol to keep a horse going. Perhaps there would be those in Hillsbridge who would wish they had less fancy means of transport before much longer – and for the most part they were the people for whom the men in the bar at the Miners Arms had little time – the nobs.

'You'm right there, Stanley,' Walter said, voicing the feelings of the men round the table. 'The roads will be a lot better when there's less traffic on 'em.'

And on that sentiment they drained their glasses and set them up for another round before walking home through the clear dark night.

There was someone in Hillsbridge, however, who was less than pleased with the imposition of petrol rationing – to whom it could spell ruin if it bit really hard.

'As if I didn't have enough problems, now I've got to worry about keeping the lorries I've got left on the road!' Amy Porter said to her husband when the rationing was announced. 'I've lost three of my best men to the armed forces, the War Office want two of my lorries and now to cap it all I have to apply for coupons to get my petrol! Honestly, Ralph, I don't know how I'm going to keep going.'

'It'll sort itself out, Amy. As I understand it you can apply for a supplementary allowance as long as you can

70

show that it's for necessary haulage. You might even be able to do work for the Ministry. There's bound to be a lot of stores and equipment to be moved when things really get going.'

Amy experienced an uncomfortable jab of *déjà-vu*. She seemed to remember Llew saying something similar to her in the dark days of the General Strike. She had been horrified then at the prospect of profiteering and had quarrelled with him about it. But that had been in the days when Llew had been running the business and she had been sufficiently on the outside to be able to afford scruples. And of course the situation had been quite different. Then, it had been blacklegging to carry goods that trades unionists would not; now it would be in the national interest.

'What about you?' she asked. 'How is it going to affect you?'

They were talking, as they so often did, as they prepared for bed in the big pleasant room which overlooked the valley. Only tonight there was no view of the soft, dark, starry sky above the ridge of batches that Amy loved; the window was covered from corner to corner with a heavy old chenille tablecloth which Mrs Milsom had unearthed for the purpose.

As always Ralph had beaten her into bed. He would lie propped up against the pillows watching as she removed her make-up at the dressing table mirror and brushed her honey gold curls, never impatient because he enjoyed seeing the ritual and too often it was the only time in their busy lives when they were alone together.

Tonight, however, he seemed abstracted.

'Ralph?' Amy prompted, opening a pot of night cream and leaning forward to examine the tiny wrinkles that were forming in spite of her ministrations around her mouth and eyes. 'How are you going to manage?'

'Oh, timber is definitely going to be one of those very

71

necessary commodities. Though shipping is going to be hazardous – maybe impossible. And I've lost three of my men too, and there may be more once the call-up gets into its swing. More serious for me than for you, actually.'

'Why?'

'If the worst comes to the worst you can always try to acquire some smaller lorries, then you can take on younger drivers. As long as they're competent you could catch them between seventeen and eighteen now that the test has been abolished. But two-and-a-half tonners wouldn't be much good to me.'

'Thank heavens I've still got Herbie!' Amy said, slapping the last bit of cream onto her face and rubbing it in with more vigour than finesse. Then, as another thought occurred to her, she swung round on the stool. 'Ralph – *you* won't have to go, will you?'

'Not as things stand, no. The top age limit is forty-one. But that could change if things go on for long.'

Her eyes narrowed. 'You said that almost as if you hope they will!'

'Yes.' He folded his hands behind his head, staring into space.

'What do you mean – *yes*?'

'Well, I was in the last show. I don't much care for the feeling that I'm getting too old to be any use.'

'You – old!' She tipped her head to one side, teasing him. 'Since you have a business to run and a home and family, I'm jolly glad they don't know just how young and fit you are! Or how many things you are decidedly *not* too old for!'

She expected him to grab her then and pull her down onto the bed but he did not.

'I've been thinking, Amy. I want to do something,' he said. 'They want more ARP wardens. I think I'm going to volunteer for that.'

'Oh but surely you've got enough on your plate!'

'That's hardly the point. Unless we can win this war none of us are likely to have a plate to have anything on.'

She spun round. '*If* we can win? What do you mean by that? Of course we'll win – and teach that nasty little German a lesson!'

He smiled. 'Your patriotism does you credit, Amy. But that "nasty little German" as you call him has got to be reckoned with. He fancies the idea of ruling the whole of Europe, you know. And he's built himself a pretty efficient war machine. It's not going to be a pushover. It's going to be a hard struggle – especially if he invades.'

'Invades!'

'He'll try it. Mark my words. And we've all got to do our bit if we are to make sure he doesn't succeed.'

Amy was silent for a moment. Ralph sounded so serious and over the years she had learned to respect his opinions. Then her natural optimism reasserted itself.

'He's got a nasty shock coming to him, I'm sure of that. And I suppose if you've made up your mind to be an ARP warden there's nothing I can say that will make any difference.' She turned out the light and went to the window, unpinning the carefully secured make-shift blackout.

It was a clear fine night; by the light of the moon the valley looked peaceful and beautiful, the silhouette of the banked firs along the ridge of batches darker than the velvet sky, the river a slender silver thread winding its way between the trees which overhung its banks. Impossible, almost, to believe that a war was going on somewhere out there beyond the black guardian hills; even more impossible to envisage it touching their lives, encroaching on this serenity. And yet . . .

She looked up at that midnight-blue sky shimmering with a million stars and imagined that one of them might be the winking lights of a plane. Not that a plane would be flying with winking lights to advertise its position now, she supposed. It would move through the darkness with as much stealth as its throbbing engines would allow, unseen by the naked eye yet with this panorama in shades of black and silver spread out beneath it, the landscape marked out like a map by the hedgerows and trees and the shining thread of the river . . .

'I wonder where Huw is?' she said. 'Do you think he is flying tonight?'

Ralph did not reply. Anxiety stabbed at her suddenly, sharp and sickening.

'He will be all right, won't he?' she asked.

Still Ralph said nothing. He could see all too clearly the course this war would take, and the dangers for Huw and all the young men like him. Too many of them would die before it was finally won or lost. Too many would climb fearlessly into the cockpits of their Spitfires and Hurricanes and Lancasters and would never return. Pray God Huw would not be one of them.

'Ralph!' Amy said. There was real alarm in her voice and he stretched his hand out to her.

'Come to bed, love.'

Her heart sank like a stone. Ralph was not going to pander to her with false assurances. She knew him better than to expect that he would. But what comfort was there in that?

She crossed the moonlit room, turned back the covers and slipped into bed beside him. His arms went around her, holding her, and the strength of his body against hers felt good.

Whatever happens, whatever comes, I should not grumble, Amy thought. I have been very lucky, luckier than most people I know; perhaps luckier than I deserve.

But knowing it did nothing to ease the hollow, aching dread that had begun inside her and for all her

74

optimism Amy knew that this was going to be a long, hard war.

In the kitchen of a cottage in the lower reaches of Purldown, Alec Hall, the only son of Amy's eldest brother Jim, snapped the lid back onto a tin of cream gloss paint, wiped the worst of it from his brush on a sheet of newspaper and straightened up to survey his handiwork. Not bad, even if he did say it himself. By the soft light of the gaslamp the cupboard door and skirting boards gleamed fresh and wet and above all *clean*. Quite a change from the way it had looked when he and Joan, his fiancée, had seen it for the first time three months earlier. Then it had been, not to put to fine a point on it, filthy – a dirt which not even the dark brown paint had concealed. The huge stone sink had been grained with dirt, the cracked window panes so crusted that Alec doubted a blackout would have been necessary to keep the light from showing down the valley, and every corner festooned with cobwebs. The cottage had stood empty for the last year since the old widow who owned it had died – and judging by the state of it Alec had thought it could not have had a good spring clean for many years even in her lifetime.

At first Joan had balked at it.

'Surely we can find something better than this, Alec?' she had said, standing in the centre of this very kitchen as if to get too close to the walls or any of the fitments might contaminate her.

'Maybe. But this is in a nice position,' Alec had argued. 'It's going cheap, too. I don't know that we could afford more. And you'd like a place of your own, wouldn't you?'

'Well, yes, I would. You know that's what you

always said – we'd wait to get married until we could afford a place of our own. But this wasn't quite what I had in mind.'

'Just wait till I've finished with it,' Alec said. 'You won't know it and that's a promise.'

'How long is it going to take you?' Joan had asked doubtfully.

'Six months maybe, but . . .'

'Six months!'

'That's not so long, is it? Six months out of a lifetime?'

'No, I suppose not. But I just can't wait for us to get married Alec and it seems as far away as ever.'

'No it doesn't,' Alec had argued. To him it had seemed a frighteningly short time, but at least it provided a respite. If they had found a cottage in good condition which they could have afforded Joan would have wanted to get married right away – a prospect which made Alec go cold inside.

At twenty-six Alec was no more ready to get married than he had been at nineteen, perhaps less so, for now he saw those friends who had been so eager to fall into bed with the first pretty girl who came along caught in a tender trap of their own making. They were no longer free to stay drinking in the Miners Arms or the Working Men's Club until closing time – or if they did they had someone to answer to. They had to be sure their wage packets went home intact or face the wrath of someone with the power to make their lives a misery. And more often than not they had a couple of squalling kids to disturb their night's sleep. It was not a prospect that enthralled him and the more he thought about it the less he liked it.

'You take after your Uncle Ted,' Sarah, his mother, had said to him once. 'He was just like you; we thought he'd never settle down.'

The idea had pleased Alec. His Uncle Ted had

emigrated to Australia ten years earlier and to Alec he had the aura of a romantic figure. But even Uncle Ted had succumbed in the end and married Rosa Clements, who had lived next door to the Halls in Greenslade Terrace and adored Ted since she was a little girl. As far as he was concerned, Alec supposed, the same went for him and Joan.

They, too, had known one another from childhood days for Joan had lived two doors away from his home in Pit Cottages, and as she was the same age as his younger sister May and played with her along the Rank he had been delegated to escort the two girls to the Church school in Hillsbridge. Later, this escort duty had been extended to seeing them home from the dances which were held in the room under the Palace Cinema and when May had got herself a boyfriend he had been left alone with Joan. He could never remember actually asking her to go out with him, it had just happened somehow, and he had gone along with it. Joan had grown into quite a pretty girl, if a little plump, but his father had always advised him to pick a girl he could grab a hold of rather than one of the fashionable skinny-ribs and on that score Joan was always accommodating. She liked nothing better than a kiss and a cuddle though she always put her foot down over going further, a fact which intrigued Alec whilst frustrating him. He went through a few minor flings with other girls but when they came to an end Joan was always there waiting and almost without realising it she had become a habit.

It was when he woke up one day to the fact that most of his friends were married, or about to be, that Alec had finally succumbed to Joan's gentle pressure and agreed to become engaged. They had gone to Bath to buy a ring – a nice little diamond that had cost Alec the best part of two weeks' wages – and everyone had supposed that he would be the next at the altar. But somehow each time the subject of setting a date had arisen he had shied away.

First there had been his exams as an excuse – he had followed his Uncle Harry's example and qualified as an examiner at Starvault Pit where he worked, though he knew it was unlikely that he had either the ambition or the ability to rise further – certainly not to the dizzy heights of Uncle Harry, who was now Miners' Agent.

Then there was the excuse of saving up enough money to make a decent start and perhaps to buy a house of their own. For quite a long while that had satisfied Joan who had liked the idea of having a home which reflected Alec's status. But lately even that had worn a little thin. Joan had begun to be impatient and now the only thing which stood between Alec and final capitulation was the work which needed to be done on the cottage they had decided to buy.

Alec washed his paintbrushes in a jar of turps in the kitchen and wondered how much longer he could spin out the decorating and renovations without rousing Joan to what he privately called 'one of her paddies'. Though generally good-natured and amenable she occasionally lost her temper utterly and completely, something which Alec, a typically peaceful member of the Hall family, found profoundly disturbing.

But perhaps I ought not to spin it out for much longer, Alec thought. With this war who knew what would happen? The bill for conscription had been rushed through when the war was just a few hours old and just because no one from Hillsbridge except the reservists had actually been called up yet didn't mean they wouldn't be. The thought of leaving the job of renovating the cottage offended Alec's orderly mind even if leaving Joan a spinster did not. Finish the cottage and then worry about how to keep his freedom for a few more precious months, perhaps that was the best way . . .

Raised voices carrying through the wall from the adjoining cottage interrupted Alec's train of thought. A man shouting. A woman's shrill protest. Alec paused with the brush still suspended in the jar of turps listening. He could not make out the words but without doubt there was one hell of a row going on – the walls of the cottage were thick solid stone, not like the paper thin ones they were building nowadays.

Good grief they're going at it hammer and tongs! thought Alec. Even Joan, with her temper up, made less noise. There was a thud followed by another as if furniture was being overturned and Alec shook his head in disbelief, then went on packing up his brushes. It was nothing to do with him if his neighbours wanted to have a full scale row in their own home. He just hoped they wouldn't do it too often!

After a while Alec heard what sounded like the back door being slammed and then all was quiet. His neighbour must have gone out to cool off, Alec decided. He knew the man slightly – Eric Latcham, who worked at one of the pits in South Compton – but apart from passing the time of day if he saw him in the garden Alec had never really spoken to him. And if he's got a temper like that I don't know that I want to, Alec thought.

He finished cleaning his brushes before putting them away and packed up the sheets of paint-streaked newspaper from the floor. Time to be going home – after a hard day's work and an evening's decorating he was just about ready for bed, though he might stop off at the Miners Arms for a pint on the way, he thought. He put on his jacket and let himself out of the cottage. The moon was shining but it took a moment or two for his eyes to adjust after the brightness of the gas-lit kitchen and the outhouses where he had left his bicycle were in deep shadow. He locked the door, pocketed the key and turned around – then almost jumped as he saw a darker shadow cowering back against the door of the outhouses. Someone was there.

'Oh – goodnight,' Alec said.

For a moment there was no reply but a soft sobbing breath. Alec peered more closely, curious in spite of himself. The figure moved slightly as if uncertain whether to stay in the shadows or move away and Alec saw that it was a woman.

'Goodnight,' she said, but her voice was shaky.

'Hey – are you all right?' It came out before he could stop it though he was instantly embarrassed by his own boldness. This must be Eric Latcham's wife, he guessed, though in all the times he had been to the cottage he could never recall having seen her. And it was she, not Eric, who had gone out when the door had slammed.

'Yes, I'm fine,' she said in the same shaky voice. She moved awkwardly away from the outhouses and in the light of the moon he saw a tall but slightly built girl wearing a cardigan over a floral print dress. Her hair was short and dark but he could see little of her face as it was in shadow and half of it was obscured by her hand.

'That's all right then. I've – I've just been doing some decorating. I'm the new owner here . . .' Alec crossed towards his bicycle.

'Oh good.' She made to attempt to move and on impulse said:

'I'm Alec Hall, by the way. I don't think we've met.'

'No. I'm Bryda. Bryda Latcham.'

'Well, I expect we'll get to know one another better before long.' He bent to put on his cycle clips and still she stood uncertainly. Then she blurted out:

'I'm sorry if we disturbed you tonight.'

'No, no – you didn't . . .' He was embarrassed again.

'It's Eric,' she said all of a rush. 'He gets in a temper sometimes. But he doesn't mean any harm. You mustn't take any notice of him. He – well, you know what it's like when you have a drink.'

Alec looked up at her quickly, overbalanced and knocked into his bicycle. It rolled on its handlebar against the wall almost falling over and the girl made an instinctive grab to save it. As she did so she removed her hand from her face and in the light of the moon Alec clearly saw the angry weal and the swollen cheekbone which she had been trying to hide.

'Oh – your bike – I thought it was going to fall . . .' She half-laughed, quickly covering her face again.

'Thanks. It's all right.' He took it himself.

She shivered and pulled her cardigan around her with her free hand.

'It's going cold, isn't it?'

'Yes, nights and mornings . . .' Oh, the strain of conversing normally when he had seen – and she knew that he had seen . . .

'I'd best be going then,' Alec said. He picked up his bicycle and swung his leg over the crossbar. 'Goodnight then.'

'Goodnight.'

She was still standing there as he rode away. Afraid to go back in, he thought. It was hardly surprising if Eric had been hitting her about. The thought shocked and angered him – that a big bloke like Eric should take his ill temper out on his wife. But still it was none of his business.

The Miners Arms was blacked out but Alec guessed that some of his mates would still be there enjoying a pint. He propped his bicycle up against the wall and climbed the three broad stone steps to the door, which had also been blackout trapped.

As he had expected the usual group of regulars were gathered around the tables – Ewart Brixey, Tommy and Reg Clements and their father Walter, and Colwyn Yelling, though Stanley Bristow had already left. 'At my age I don't want to be out in this blackout!' he had explained. As Alec went in they greeted him cheerfully and when he had bought himself a half of bitter at the bar he took it over to their table and pulled an extra chair into the circle.

'Thee'm a bit late bain't 'ee, Alec?' Ewart was always the first to come out with what everyone else was thinking. 'You bin courtin' I s'pose.'

'Working, more like,' Alec said amiably.

'Oh ah – tell us another! Look, he's got white on his coat! You've been round the outhouses with Joan!'

'Fat chance. I've been painting.'

'Painting! That's a new name for it. Painting! I like that!'

'So does Joan,' Reg Clements said and there was a roar of ribald laughter.

Alec laughed with them and took a pull of his beer.

'Straight up, I've been decorating the cottage we're buying. Doing up the kitchen.'

'She didn't take long to get you in harness, Alec!' Tommy joked. 'If she's got you decorating now, what'll she be like when she's got a ring on her finger?'

'It had to be done,' Alec said mildly, wiping the foam off his mouth. 'We couldn't live in the place as it was.'

'Where's the place you'm buying, Alec?' Walter enquired.

'Down the bottom of Combers End. In Purldown really. Next door to Eric Latcham.'

'Oh ah.'

'Do you know the Latchams?' Alec asked.

'I d'know Eric,' Walter said. 'I knew his father. I can mind when he worked at Middle Pit.'

'What are they like?'

'You ought to know if you'm going to live next door to them.'

'I've hardly seen them,' Alec admitted. 'I do know Eric of course but . . .' He broke off, unwilling to relate his experience of the evening. 'What about his wife? Who did he marry?'

'Bryda Deacon,' Tommy said immediately. 'We were at school with her weren't we, Reg? You remember her don't you, Alec? Pretty girl, dark. She'd be older than you, but surely you remember her?'

Alec thought. Bryda Deacon. Yes, now he came to think of it he could remember her. As Tommy said she had been a pretty girl with a mass of brown wavy hair and a pair of legs that had made the boys whistle. Now, however, he found it difficult to equate that girl with the wraith who had cowered in the shadows of the outhouses.

'They had a little 'un, didn't they?' Reg said. 'About a year ago. Though she lost several before that, I heard.'

'I seen her not so long ago,' Ewart said. 'In the doctor's surgery it was, when I had that bit of an accident underground and did me ribs in. She were in there with the little 'un waiting her turn. She had changed though – I'm not surprised Alec didn't know her. She'd got very thin and she were as white as a sheet. I put it down to whatever it was she'd done to her eye.'

Alec shifted in his chair. 'Her eye? What had she done to it?'

'I heard her telling the woman next to her she'd walked into the door. A real shiner it was though. Nasty.'

Alec said nothing, unwilling to put into words what was going through his mind. Rough and tough these miners might be, ready enough to join in a brawl or take the strap to a son who needed to be taught a lesson, but wife beating was not their way and for the most part it would never enter their heads that someone they knew might indulge in it. Even with the evidence of the row he had overheard and Ewart's description of

83

Bryda's black eye, he could scarcely believe it himself. But one thing was for very sure. Healthy young women didn't make a habit of walking into doors.

'Have you heard about th'ick rook that brought down a power line?' Tommy asked, changing the subject. 'T'were in the paper – Newhaven, it were. The bird perched on the wire and brought the whole bloody lot down and the rook fell on a sheep in the field and set his wool on fire.'

'Dead, were it?' Ewart asked.

'Oh ah, the rook were, but the sheep were all right. The firemen had to put it out. But a lot of folk's Sunday dinners were spoiled when the electricity went.'

'They should have gone out to the field – they could have had roast rook if not roast lamb!' Ewart chortled and the conversation turned away from the Latcham family. But when they had finished their pints and left the Miners Arms, Alec was still thinking about Bryda and seeing her face both pretty and happy as he vaguely remembered her and thin and marked as it had been tonight.

He didn't like it. There was not a thing he could do about it – it was none of his business if she had married a man who took his temper out on her in that way. But as he pedalled home along what the locals still referred to as 'The New Road' it worried him all the same.

4

It was quite dark by the time Margaret left the school where she taught. There was no moon tonight and as the dark November air hit her she shivered, turned up the collar of her coat and pulled her woollen cap further down over her ears.

Not a night to be out and the prospect of having to walk the two miles home from Sanderley was far from inviting. But there was nothing for it. Since petrol rationing had been introduced Margaret had refused to allow Harry to come and fetch her as he sometimes used to do when she was late – the coupons were far too precious and their little supply might be needed for an emergency.

Not that she was late too often these days. Most out-of-school activities had ceased with the dark evenings and Margaret was usually able to leave soon after the children and get home in the greying dusk. Tonight, however, she had had no alternative but to stay late. There had been a staff meeting and with all the new wartime regulations there had been a great deal to discuss. Margaret had sat with the other two teachers huddled around the temperamental coke stove in the cramped little office which Tom Freke, the headmaster, rather grandly called his study, drinking mugs of tea and wondering how much longer it would take to get through the endless list of items Tom had drawn up on his agenda – a review of procedure in the event of a daytime air raid, how Christmas would be celebrated at the school this year, and a rundown on how the evacuee pupils were settling in.

This last item had made Margaret think again of her

own two 'vackies', Elaine and Marie. They were no longer at Sanderley school with her – the committee had deemed it unsuitable to expect two children, and 'townies' at that, to walk the two miles each way and they had been found places at Hillsbridge Board School. Fair enough in many respects, except that it meant they were usually home before she was, but Margaret had devised a hiding place for the back door key beneath a flower pot in the coal shed, and they were able to let themselves in and have the kettle on the boil by the time she too arrived home.

It was on evenings like these that it was inconvenient, though, and as Tom Freke's voice droned on, detailing dates and times for the Christmas parties, Margaret's mind had wandered to the two girls who would, she knew, be in the house on their own unless Harry had been able to get off early. They could go on and have their tea, of course. Knowing she would be late this evening she had cut bread and butter this morning before she left home, sandwiching it together with a thick layer of her mother's homemade blackberry and apple jelly to hide the fact that the butter was no more than a scrape and wrapping it up in greaseproof paper before putting it in the breadbin to keep fresh. And there was seed cake too, also homemade, and they were perfectly capable of boiling the kettle to make a cup of tea. The fire worried her a bit. It was well banked up to last through the day while they were all out and she hoped they would not try to poke it to life. A coal rolling out onto the hearth rug could easily cause a fire. She had told them not to touch it, of course, but they were not the most obedient of girls, particularly Elaine.

Left to her own devices Margaret was fairly sure that Marie could be quite a lovable child. She was sunny natured and did as she was told – when Elaine was not there to incite her to do differently. But Elaine was altogether another kettle of fish. She was cheeky and ill-mannered and it sometimes seemed to Margaret that to ask her to do something was to make quite certain she would refuse to do it, either by deliberate disobedience or by sly evasion. She was, Margaret thought, one of the least likeable children she had ever encountered.

And that was not all. For Margaret was beginning to suspect that she might also be dishonest.

At first, she had been unwilling to believe such a thing was possible. When she had mislaid the moiré band which Harry had given her the first Christmas she had known him and it had turned up amongst Elaine's few pathetic bits and pieces in the girls' room, she had thought that Elaine had merely borrowed it to try it on because it was pretty and then been afraid to admit it. Then, the first time she found herself with ten shillings less in her purse than she had thought she had, she told herself that she must have changed the note to buy some item or other which she had forgotten about. But when a couple of shillings she had left on the mantlepiece went missing she had seriously begun to wonder. They had been there when she went to school in the morning she knew; she had taken them out of her purse purposely not to spend them. But that evening when she went to get them to feed them to the gas meter they were no longer there.

'Did you take some change off the mantlepiece?' she had asked Harry.

'No. Why?'

'Oh nothing. I thought I left some there. I must have used it to pay the baker,' she said, but she knew she had not and the incident in the Co-op drapery shop when the woman had accused Elaine of trying to steal cakes from her bag had come back to Margaret. She had been willing to try and make excuses for the child then. Now she was not so sure.

It was a worrying thought that a girl living under her roof might be stealing from her and Margaret was not sure what to do about it. Should she set a trap for her so that at least she would know whether she was mistaken in her suspicions or not? She shrank from the idea. It seemed a thoroughly inhospitable thing to do on the basis of two missing shillings and a ten shilling note which she might or might not have spent herself. Besides, Margaret was not sure that she wanted to know if Elaine was a thief. With doubt removed she would have to do something about it and the flimsy relationship she was building with the girls would be damaged beyond repair. Not that there was much of a relationship with Elaine, if she was honest, but at confrontation time Marie would certainly take her sister's part and any hope of a bridge with the younger girl would be gone for good.

Perhaps if she is taking things it is just because she's unsettled and unhappy, Margaret thought. Their lives were in such a state of upheaval, finding themselves among strangers in a strange place with even the friendly cows in the fields looking like monsters from another planet and their home and their mother way out of reach. Perhaps when they settle down a bit she'll stop behaving in this way.

She dared not mention her suspicions to Harry. He would, without a doubt, believe the worst and be very angry. He was already against her having them and trouble of this sort would be just the ammunition he needed to insist they should be found a new billet. But Margaret did not want that. Though she knew that there was a great deal of sense in what he said and she should not be trying to hold down a job and look after two problem girls in her condition, she was reluctant to admit defeat. She was, after all, trained in teaching children if not actually bringing them up. She *should* be able to handle problems like this one.

Margaret turned out of the school yard and started along the road that led from Sanderley to Hillsbridge.

It was a straight road and mercifully in this direction mainly ran downhill. At first, it led through the outskirts of Sanderley and Margaret glanced longingly at the houses she passed. It was already dark and no chinks of light showed at the windows but she knew that behind the blackouts the families would be gathered around their fires, having their tea. Perhaps in some of them mothers would be feeding babies, as she would soon be doing. In spite of the cold wind which seemed to be blowing right through her coat, Margaret felt a glow of warmth and excitement and momentarily forgot the problems of her 'vackies'. For as long as she could remember she had loved babies – even as a little girl she had liked nothing better than to push out the neighbours' prams – and as soon as she and Harry were married she had begun to long for one of her own. At first it had not been practicable. She had needed to work both to justify her training and to add her income to Harry's to set up home. But soon she had been unable to bear the thought of putting it off any longer and the months of waiting and longing had begun. How endless they had seemed! Sometimes Margaret had despaired of ever encountering the first tell-tale signs. Suppose I can't have a baby, she worried and the thought had started a deep despair inside her. So often babies came when they were not wanted – what supreme irony it would be if she, wanting one so much, was never able to conceive. Never to feel new life moving within her. Never to hold her own child, and Harry's, in her arms. Never to bury her face in a small, sweet smelling bundle or examine tiny perfect hands and feet and know that they belonged to *her* child – hers!

But now these fears had receded to the world of shadows. The longed for baby was a reality. She remembered with a thrill the first time she had felt it move – nothing more than a faint tick that might

89

almost have been her own heart beating with excitement. But when it had come again she knew it was not and she had pressed her hands to her still flat stomach and caught the glow of happiness, holding it, cherishing it. Now, at least, her slim boyish figure was beginning to become rounder, her breasts fuller, her waist was thickening. And when the baby kicked as she lay in bed at night she would take Harry's hand and press it to the spot whispering: 'Did you feel that? Did you feel it?'

Now, walking along the dark pavement which reached to the point where a crossroads marked the perimeter of Sanderley, she was aware of a slight crampy discomfort and slowed her pace from brisk to moderate. Exercise wouldn't hurt her. Dr Carter had assured her on that point or she would not still be walking the two miles each way daily. But she had no intention of exerting herself. She would do nothing which might pose even the smallest risk to the baby. If she was cold she could always warm up over the fire when she got home. And an extra five minutes would be neither here or there to Elaine and Marie.

As she thought of them again the rosy glow of happiness which anticipating the arrival of the baby had brought faded again. In some ways she almost wished that Harry had had his way in the beginning and found a new billet for them. Having them there when the baby arrived would pose problems and nothing would be quite the way she had planned it. She had thought it would be just her and Harry and the baby, now unless the war ended unexpectedly or their mother came and took them back to London there would be Elaine and Marie too. But it was too late to worry about that. She'd cope. She had to.

Margaret reached the crossroads at the end of long straggling Sanderley, crossed and began walking along the straight road that would lead her out into the country before dropping over the hill into Hillsbridge.

The road ran between fields and on either side it was overhung with trees, trees which had now lost most of their leaves but which whispered and creaked in the biting wind. The leaves that had fallen lay like a carpet on the roadside and in places had drifted into sodden mounds. Margaret avoided them as best she could but in the pitch dark it was not easy and she cursed herself for having forgotten her torch. Not that it would be much good – the lighting restrictions extended to torches too. Harry had covered the bulb with tissue paper for her as the regulations insisted but even that tiny light must not be directed at the sky or the ground and carrying it at the right angle for two whole miles was tiresome.

Her thoughts having gone full circle, Margaret once more directed her mind to the problems Elaine was causing. This morning there had been a new development. Margaret had been unable to find a brooch she wanted to wear, a pretty little bar pin set with a tiny horseshoe. It was not in the jewellery box on her dressing table where she always kept it and a quick rummage through her clothes in the wardrobe had failed to turn it up still pinned to a dress or blouse. Instantly she had become suspicious whilst desperately trying not to be. When had she worn it last? Perhaps she had lost it then. Or put it somewhere silly when she had taken it off – the corner of a drawer or one of the odd cardboard jewellers' boxes which had come with presents and been stored in case she should one day need them. Or perhaps it had fallen down the back of her dressing table. All day, at odd moments, she had racked her brain trying to come up with an answer – any answer which would mean that she did not have to question Elaine and perhaps learn that the girl had been prying in her bedroom when she was not there.

Margaret sighed and managed to avoid a pile of leaves. Behind her she heard a car coming across the flat and edged closer into the side of the road. There had been a lot of accidents involving pedestrians since the lighting regulations had come into force – with half their headlights blacked out it was difficult for drivers to see people walking. Again Margaret wished she had her torch. If she had she could have turned to face the oncoming vehicle and he would have seen the pinprick of light, though it was also forbidden to shine torches in a way which might blind drivers.

The car was coming fast now – no, not a car, it sounded more like a motor cycle engine. Margaret relaxed slightly. A motor cycle wouldn't drive as close in to the side of the road. Another moment and it would be past her and gone. As it approached she half turned towards it.

And then it seemed everything happened at once.

Later, Ewart Brixey was to explain to Sergeant Button as clearly as his shocked mind would allow, 'I was coming across the flat on my motor bike and sidecar and suddenly I saw something in the side of the road. I slammed on my brakes and there must have been leaves on the road. I just lost it, Serg, I couldn't do a thing. The bloody bike went haywire. It weren't my fault – honest to God it weren't.'

But to Margaret in that moment the apportionment of blame was something which scarcely mattered. She was aware only of a flash of intense, paralysing fear and a sense of inevitability which was somehow suspended out of time. Then, there was the numbing shock of something striking her, a peculiar weightless sensation as she flew through the air and the sickening thud as her body hit the cold wet road.

The silence was broken by the angry hum of the engine still-running, impotent like a trapped bumble bee, and the descending whirr as the spinning wheels slowed and stopped. But Margaret was aware of nothing. Nothing but a blackness, darker than the night, which hovered for seemingly endless seconds and then descended, relentlessly, until she was lost within it.

Amy was at home, working on a pile of accounts at the dining room table, when the telephone rang. She had never lost the habit of bringing work home with her for she always felt guilty just sitting and listening to the radio, as if she was somehow wasting precious time and she had never been one to knit or sew. And with the efficient Mrs Milsom still in residence there was no need for her to bother her head about household chores.

Besides, what had once been a habit was now a boon. As Ralph had suggested she should, Amy had managed to get some Government contract work and that added to labour shortages meant there was never enough time to complete all her paperwork while she was at the yard.

When Ralph was not out on his ARP warden duties he sometimes worked in the evenings, too, and they would sit in companionable silence occasionally discussing a problem and always rounding off the evening with a glass of whisky.

'I hope the war doesn't mean we can't get a drink or I shall grind to a halt!' she said one evening.

Ralph had merely laughed. 'Do you good to do without. You're too fond of the bottle for your own good, my dear.'

Amy had been outraged.

'I don't drink much! Just a little to relax me and help me sleep. I'm no worse than you, anyway.'

'A man is allowed to like whisky – a lady shouldn't,' he had teased and Amy snorted her disgust. She had never stuck by the rules of what a lady should or should not do. If she had she would not be where she was today.

Tonight, however, it was still too early to have started on the whisky and Amy was fortified merely by a cup of coffee. Ralph was out at an ARP training session and when she heard the telephone begin to ring she cursed softly at the interruption and called out to Barbara to answer it. A moment later the door opened and Barbara popped her head in. She looked pink and anxious.

'Mum, it's Uncle Harry. He wants to speak to you.'

Amy was surprised. Harry rarely rang simply for a chat.

'What does he want I wonder?' she mused.

'I don't know. He sounded funny. I think there's something wrong . . .'

Amy went into the hall and picked up the telephone. 'Hello Harry.'

'Amy – something has happened. It's Margaret.'

'Margaret!' Her first thought was the obvious one. 'You mean the baby?'

'No. She's had an accident. Walking home from school. She's been knocked down.'

'Oh, my God!' Amy said. She was suddenly shaking all over, transported back through time to another accident. 'Is she all right?'

'I don't know. They've taken her to hospital. I'm going now.'

'You want me to come with you?'

'No – no need for that. I'm taking her mother with me. But we've got these two damned girls here. They haven't had anything to eat yet and I don't like to leave them. Do you think you could . . . ?'

'Yes, of course. I'll be right there.' Amy was trying to think as she spoke. 'I've got the car – and some petrol. I'll be with you in five minutes.'

'I won't wait if you don't mind, Amy. Just as long as I know you're coming.'

'Of course. You get off, Harry. And Harry . . .' she

paused, her voice breaking slightly, 'I hope everything will be all right.'

'Yes. Thanks. I don't know how long I'll be, Amy.'

'Don't worry about it. Don't worry about a thing – except Margaret.'

She replaced the receiver. Her mind seemed to have gone blank. No, not blank. A kaleidoscope of whirling thoughts none of which she could get hold of. Barbara was hovering in the doorway, her face anxious.

'It's Auntie Margaret. She's been knocked down,' Amy said. 'I've got to get over there and look after their evacuees while Uncle Harry is at the hospital.'

Barbara's response was immediate. 'I'll come with you, Mum.'

'Will you?' Amy felt a rush of gratitude followed by a swift stab of surprise. Barbara was displaying none of the panic she was feeling, just serious sympathy and a calm strength of purpose which only the young whose own lives have never been touched by tragedy can feel. For an instant, Amy felt that she wanted to lean on her, take advantage of that inviolable young strength and this too surprised her. Barbara was her daughter – she, Amy, had always been the one to do the protecting and provide the sure harbour for Barbara's life to ride at safe anchor. This must be a portent of what happened in old age when the strong became the weak, dependent suddenly on the very young they had protected. The sense of frailty it embodied lasted a moment only; Amy was herself still too young to depend on any strength but her own. But the thought of Barbara's support was even so a comforting one.

'I may be late,' Amy said. 'It depends on how long Uncle Harry has to stay at the hospital. In fact, I may have to stay all night. Thanks for the offer, Babs, but I think you had better stay here with Maureen. You can tell Ralph what has happened when he gets back. And you'll be able to get yourselves off to school in the morning.'

'If you're sure . . .'

'Yes, I'm sure,' Amy said. 'I'll let you know what's happening as soon as there is any news.'

She fetched her coat and scarf and put them on. Her papers were still spread out across the table and she took a moment to stack them together and ram them back into their folder. There would be no more work done tonight. Taking her car keys and bag she went out into the dark November night.

Margaret lay in the ugly functional hospital bed surrounded by dark green screens. Her face was as white as the freshly laundered pillow slip, her hair, mussed up, fanned out in a halo around it, her arm with the drip tube snaking into it lay still and lifeless-looking on the dark green bedspread.

On the hard ward chair drawn up beside her Harry eased his position slightly without once taking his eyes off that deathly pale face. Dear God but she looked terrible. The thought was a leaden weight in the pit of his stomach and he reached out and touched her hand, curling his fingers round it.

Why had he let her walk home in the dark? he asked himself for the umpteenth time since Sergeant Button had come to the Miners' Welfare Office where he was working late and broken the terrible news. Why had he not insisted on going to fetch her? But he was always so busy, tied up with the problems of the men he represented, and Margaret was so determined he should not waste precious petrol on unnecessary journeys, saying with a certainty that would not be brooked that she would be all right. And somehow it had never crossed his mind that she would not be. Margaret was such a capable person and he had been proud of her for it, glad she was not the sort of clinging vine some men had for wives.

So, perhaps he had not taken such good care of her as he should. But that did not mean he did not love her. He did and always had. There had never been anyone for him but Margaret and he thought there never would be.

She has to get through this! he thought fiercely. She has to! Nothing else matters. No, not even . . . Just as long as she gets through.

The prospect that she might not was too terrible to contemplate, too terrible to allow even a moment's fleeting thought.

That bloody idiot Ewart Brixey! he thought viciously. If I could get my hands on him God alone knows what I'd do to him! But Ewart Brixey was in hospital too, not here in Bath but at the Cottage Hospital just outside Hillsbridge where less serious cases could be dealt with. Ewart, who was known to ride his motor cycle and sidecar at reckless speed, had suffered only a broken leg while Margaret . . .

Harry's throat filled again as he looked down at her still white face, disfigured down one cheek by angry gravel rash. He leaned closer, as if his nearness could transfer some of his own strength into her broken body. He would stay here just as long as they would let him and when they decided it was time for him to go they would have to drag him away.

Into the long night Harry Hall kept his lonely vigil.

She came gradually back through the layers of consciousness, drifting, becoming aware of her aching body and the expanse of white ceiling above her, drifting again. Someone was holding her hand. Painfully she moved her eyes, shimmying across the dark green screens until a face blurred, then came into focus. Harry. Of course, who else? Warm contentment flooded her, her eyes heavy from the effort of moving closed

97

again. As if from a long way off she heard sounds of life going on, voices brisk and cheerful, the rattle of a trolley. She lay in her suspended world, not wanting to return to reality. But one voice was separating from the others, low, soft, yet close by. Harry's voice.

'Margaret? Are you awake? Can you hear me, love?'

The mists of that other world were falling away. Memory was returning, some images sharp and frighteningly clear against the thick curdled cream of the rest of her thoughts. The sounds of a motor cycle engine. Brakes applied fiercely. Tyres squealing. The shock as the corner of the sidecar caught her. The moment's weightlessness. The sickening thud. And the darkness closing in . . . A sob caught in her throat. Harry's fingers tightened on hers.

'Ssh! It's all right! You're all right . . .'

'I couldn't help it!' she said. It was an effort to speak – her jaw felt stiff. 'I didn't do anything. I only . . .'

'It wasn't your fault. We know that. Oh Margaret . . .'

And suddenly those other thick-cream thoughts were centralising like the aches and pains in her body and limbs to one terrible core.

'My baby!' She was almost screaming now, anxiety lending her strength. She tried to move her hand to place it on her stomach and could not. 'My baby! Is it all right?'

'Margaret, love . . . Don't worry about anything now. You're going to be OK. That's all that matters.'

She twisted her eyes up to his face again, saw the anguish there, and knew. There was no need for words. Nothing could erase the truth.

'Oh God, oh God!' she whispered. The pain was sharper now, a tight steel band pressing around her heart. And then the mists were closing in again, merciful mists now, clouding what could not be borne.

Margaret gave up trying to fight them and the darkness came once more.

Harry brought her home two weeks before Christmas, sitting in the front seat of his car with a rug wrapped around her.

It was raining, thick cold rain which overtaxed the wipers and flooded down the side windows and the greyness outside was an echo of the greyness in her heart.

She was still weak, still in pain from a collarbone and rib cracked when she had hit the ground, but she was on the mend.

'You should be fine by Christmas,' the doctor had told her and Margaret had thought, but not said, that she could not believe she would ever be fine again. Especially not at Christmas.

This should have been a joyful season, she thought. A season of hope. She and Harry should have been able to spend it knowing it would be the last one when it would be just the two of them, looking forward to next year when there would be a little stocking hanging by the fireplace into which she would be able to pop small cuddly toys, suitable for a baby's first Christmas. Instead, there would be the emptiness of knowing that the child she had carried within her, the child she had wanted so much, was dead.

Not that they would have been alone, of course. Elaine and Marie would have been there, and Margaret had been looking forward to making this a good Christmas for them, separated as they were from their mother. Now she did not even know if she would be fit to do that.

Her mother, Gussie Young, had had the two girls while Margaret was in hospital. Her own evacuee boy had been taken home by his mother a month earlier and rather than uproot Elaine and Marie completely again they had moved up the road to Gussie's house in Ridge Road. Margaret still intended to have them back when she was fit, but as yet there was no telling when that would be.

To reach home from Bath they had to drive along the very stretch of road where the accident had happened and Harry took one hand from the steering wheel and reached out to cover Margaret's for comfort. But she stared at the road impassively as if hypnotised by the same kind of fascination a stranger might feel when looking at the scene of some past disaster.

'Are you all right love?' he asked.

There was a hiatus, more as if she was adjusting to the fact that she was being spoken to than anything else. Then she said, 'Yes. I'm, all right,' and lapsed into silence once more.

Harry's heart sank. Margaret was usually such a chatterbox and her silence told more of the depth of her loss than any words could have done.

As the road began to drop away the Hillsbridge valley came into view, pit chimneys towering above the clustering lias stone buildings, grey, all grey, against the background of winter fields. Every other year as Christmas approached there had at least been brightness and gaiety in the shops to lighten the sombre hues of December, but not this year. Windows were blacked out and there were no displays to be seen, no dainty white lace-edged handkerchiefs and bright woollen gloves pinned artistically to trellises sprinkled with cotton wool to look like snow, no tempting hampers of groceries open to reveal a great heap of delicacies and at the County Stores, licenced to sell wines and spirits, a bottle of port or two. Even had the windows not been blacked out the people of Hillsbridge would not have enjoyed looking and anticipating Christmas this year, for with England at war feelings of patriotism and the need for austerity had been stirred in even the most self-indulgent breast.

Margaret neither noticed the absence of Christmas cheer nor cared.

Harry turned the car into Conygre Hill and as their house came into view she stared at it with the same impassivity. She had thought she would be pleased to see it after the impersonality of the hospital ward but now it made no impression on her emotions. Just a house. An empty house that would never echo to the sound of her baby's laughter.

Harry helped her out of the car and she walked, shivering slightly, to the door. Everything inside looked just as it had when she left it yet somehow slightly different, the rooms a different shape, the trapped smell of the breakfast Harry had cooked himself pungent and unfamiliar. For a moment it stirred her, then once more she relapsed into apathy.

Harry poked the fire to life.

'You sit down there, love. I'll put the kettle on.'

She did as he told her, too weighed down by self pity to argue.

A knock at the back door penetrated her daze. Then her mother's voice:

'Coo-ee! Can we come in?'

Margaret's heart sank. Her mother and the two girls. Harry had said they would be coming down to see her but she had not expected them so soon and she did not want to see them. It was all too much effort.

'Margaret love, so you're home.' Gussie was in the doorway, smiling her welcome.

'Hello, Mum.'

Elaine and Marie were behind her. Margaret registered that they were wearing new jumpers, identical fair isle. Gussie's handiwork, no doubt. She had always been a knitter, and since George, her husband, had died, the click of the needles had helped fill many a lonely evening. With an effort Margaret stirred herself.

'Hello, girls.'

Elaine was hanging back, scowling her familiar scowl. But as she spoke Marie darted forward, running across the room and throwing her arms around Margaret's neck. Momentarily, Margaret recoiled with shock but the little girl scarcely seemed aware of it. Her hair, grown longer now and smelling of sweet-scented soap, was soft against her chin, the thin arms pressed her tightly.

And somewhere within Margaret's tortured being something stirred sweet and sharp. She put her own arms round the thin frame, holding the child close. It wasn't her baby. Her baby was dead. But somehow she had come to be important to this child. She needed her and Margaret's heart reached out to her.

'It's all right,' she said softly. 'I'm all right. I'm home now.'

It was little enough. But it was a beginning.

5

The following Sunday just before ten in the morning a motor coach bearing the legend Roberts Transport left the forecourt of the Miners Arms bound for Bath. On board were twenty evacuee children, remnants of the army which had invaded the town in September, with their hosts and helpers, and as the coach rattled slowly up the steep hill from the town centre the chatter and laughter from the rear seats which they had vied for and squashed themselves into rose in a solid roar of excitement that almost drowned the tortured chuggings of the engine.

This was the moment they had been waiting for ever since the day they had arrived, more than three and a half months ago – the most wonderful Christmas present any of them could imagine. Treats had been arranged for them in plenty – every organisation, it seemed, wanted to give them a tea party or a social evening, every benefactor in the town was anxious to don the traditional red robes of Father Christmas and put in an appearance bearing a sack laden with more toys than most of the children had ever seen in their lives. But the tea parties and social evenings paled into insignificance before this very special treat. For today they were going to see their parents again. A special train had been laid on to bring them from London to Bath and the authorities had arranged for coaches and charabancs to take the children to meet them. The same coaches would then take them to their host areas for the day and back to Bath in time for the parents to catch the special train to return to London that evening.

In the corner of the back seat Elaine and Marie were as excited as the others although Elaine had still managed to assert her superiority and get the seat she wanted. They bobbed up and down, their faces pale with excitement beneath the bonnets which Gussie had knitted for them, chattering and laughing. This morning for once they had got up by themselves even before Gussie had woken them, washed without having to be cajoled into it, and dressed in their identical fair isle jumpers, but breakfast had been beyond them. They simply could not swallow, they were so excited.

'Never mind, we'll have a good dinner when we get back,' Gussie had said. She had a stew simmering on the stove and potatoes peeled and in the pot ready for boiling.

Now, sitting towards the front of the coach with the other adults, she turned to steal a look at them and smiled. Their anticipation was a joy to see and she wished that Margaret had been fit to come with them. Perhaps some of the spirit of the day would have infected her too – goodness only knows she could have done with it. The depths of depression into which she had sunk since losing the baby was worrying Gussie.

The coach arrived at the station with a quarter of an hour to spare before the train was due but already it resembled the square at South Compton on annual fair day. Children from all over the area had arrived and were being marshalled onto the platform to await the train's arrival.

'Stay close to me girls – I don't want to lose you!' Gussie instructed as they were borne along with the tide up the steps to the platform, but she might as well have been talking to herself. The girls, never inclined to take kindly to discipline at the best of times, were concerned only to find a vantage point and they were soon lost in the crush of excited children. Gussie shrugged resignedly and positioned herself near the top of the steps. At least they wouldn't be able to leave the platform without her seeing them go. She only hoped they would not get too close to the edge and fall onto the line!

Almost exactly on time the signals clanked and they saw the train come steaming around the bend. A long train – so many coaches – and half the windows down with mothers and fathers hanging out eagerly to catch the first glimpse of their offspring. The moment it drew to a stop the doors were open too and the children surged forward, clamouring excitedly. Their joyful whoops joined with the shouts of the parents and within moments the platform was a sea of happy humanity, embracing, kissing, tossing small children into the air and carrying them shoulder high towards the steps where Gussie stood.

Watching she felt tears prick her own eyes. The separation of families was one of the worst things about any war. And how quickly today would speed by so that it would seem like no time at all before they were back on the platform once more faced with the awful moment of parting.

The crowd was clearing a little now as parents and children departed to the waiting coaches determined not to waste one precious moment. Anxiously, Gussie scanned those remaining, a few too wrapped up in one another to be ready to leave yet, a couple of mothers running the length of the platform to small children who had remained with their hosts. And Elaine and Marie, standing alone, the anticipation on their faces turning to anxiety as they looked up and down the platform.

Gussie felt the first stab of alarm. There did not seem to be a single person not already paired with their children and the carriage doors were already being slammed as the porters and guard prepared for the train to leave once more. Gussie hurried across the platform to the children.

'What's the matter, girls? Can't you see your Mum?'

'No.' For once Elaine's composure was broken. She looked close to tears. 'She ain't here. She ain't come!'

'Oh, she must have!' She had had a letter herself from the girls' mother – the first she had received since they had been with her – promising that she would be on the train. The letter had been badly written in block capitals such as a child might write and the spelling was so haphazard it had not been easy to decipher the words, but the intention had been clear enough.

'Where is she then?' Elaine demanded.

A woman in a smart suit carrying an official looking briefcase was talking to one of the Hillsbridge organisers. Gussie took Marie by the hand and led the two girls over to her.

'My two can't find their mother,' she said.

The woman with the briefcase looked up and down the platform.

'Doesn't look as though she's come then, does it? Who are they?'

'Elaine and Marie Cooper.'

'Cooper.' The woman appeared to be thinking. 'Yes, I know Mrs Cooper. Can't say I've seen her today.' She looked around once more, then her lips tightened. 'She probably missed the train sleeping off a hangover,' she added quietly.

'A hangover?' Gussie could hardly believe her ears.

'Either that or she's spent the night with some man and couldn't tear herself away.'

'Oh my goodness!' Gussie whispered, shocked. 'Well, what am I going to do with them? What am I going to tell them?'

The woman with the briefcase turned to the children and her voice became softer as she spoke to them.

'Sorry, girls, it looks as if your mum isn't coming

after all. It's a disappointment for you I know, but there will be another time. The best thing is for you to go home now with Mrs . . .'

'Young,' Gussie supplied.

'. . . and try not to be too upset about it.'

They stared at her their faces pinched and bleak. Then Marie's mouth puckered.

'She's dead ain't she?' she wailed. 'The Germans have gone and got her!'

'No,' the woman promised. 'She is certainly not dead. Now try to be brave, there's a good girl.'

'Yeah, stop snivelling, our Marie,' Elaine admonished but for once she looked close to tears herself.

The last carriage door slammed, the guard blew his whistle and the train began to move slowly away from the platform.

'We'd better go,' the Hillsbridge organiser said to Gussie.

Without another word they each took hold of one of the children's hands and led them down the cold and echoing stone staircase to the waiting coach which overflowed now with happy and reunited families.

Instead of sitting in the back seat as they had done on the way to Bath, the two children squashed together in a seat with Gussie, fighting back the tears. And Gussie, soul of peace, had one of the most violent thoughts of her life as she looked at them.

Never mind Hitler, Gussie thought. If I could get hold of their mother right now I'd kill her myself. With my bare hands if necessary!

For the majority of the evacuee children Christmas began and ended with what was for most of them a memorable day with their parents, but one family in Hillsbridge had to wait until Christmas Eve for a longed for reunion.

107

Huw had been granted a few days' leave and the whole Porter household prepared enthusiastically for his homecoming.

Mrs Milsom put a couple of big old stone hot water bottles in his bed to make sure it was well aired, informed Smith the gardener that she would need another pound of sprouts for Christmas dinner and decided that an extra two dozen mince pies might just about satisfy the returning prodigal. 'A tray of a dozen never lasts two minutes when Master Huw is around,' she said to herself as she weighed up fat and flour and checked the stock of mincemeat in the pantry.

Ralph crossed the yard to the garage where Huw's car was laid up, checked it over and put the battery on charge. The car was a Riley Imp and very precious to Huw. He had bought himself a motor cycle for use at his base but Ralph felt sure Huw would want to drive the Riley while he was at home.

Amy went out to shop for the extra presents which she had thought would be too bulky to send to him by post – a book on the history of aviation and a pair of leather slippers lined with sheepskin, and Maureen insisted on keeping back a couple of paperchains when they had finished decorating the living room to festoon Huw's bedroom – a tribute Amy was not at all sure he would appreciate.

For Barbara, however, preparations took a slightly different direction. Everyone else seemed to be making arrangements for Huw's welfare; she concentrated on more personal things.

'I wish I could have a new dress,' she said to Amy.

'Whatever for? You have more than enough clothes,' Amy replied. The fact that she now had more money to spend than she had ever had in her life had not altered the slightly frugal approach that she had inherited from her upbringing – a good best dress and a couple of sweaters and skirts constituted a more than ample

108

wardrobe for a girl who still spent most of her life in school uniform.

'But it's nice to have something new to wear on Christmas day,' Barbara insisted. 'Couldn't I have one for part of my Christmas present?'

'I've already bought your Christmas present,' Amy told her. 'And with the price of things now a dress wouldn't be just *part*. It would be the main item.'

'Well, if I paid you back for it?' Barbara pleaded. 'I'm sure to get some money – Uncle Jack always sends a cheque and it would be such a shame not to be able to buy my dress *before* Christmas.'

Amy felt a slight pang. It seemed no time at all since the girls had thought clothes and even money the most boring of presents – all they had been interested in was toys.

'All right, Barbara, we'll see what we can do,' she promised. 'Just as long as you realise that if I *do* buy you a dress you owe me whatever we pay for it.'

So Barbara got her dress – a pretty cherry red wool with a Peter Pan collar. When they first saw it hanging on the rail Amy thought it would be too bright to suit Barbara's complexion, but she was wrong. The colour seemed to bring her to life, complimenting the honey gold of her curls and reflecting her vibrant personality. She looked young and fresh and sparkly yet at the same time more grown up than she had ever looked before and Amy felt a sudden unexpected lump in her throat as she looked at her.

'Well, Mum, what do you think?'

'It's very nice, Babs,' Amy said swiftly.

In addition to the dress Barbara insisted she needed something done to her hair. The salon in Bath Hill which they always patronised was heavily booked with clients wanting steam waves for Christmas, but as Barbara, like Amy, had never needed more than a trim for her naturally wavy hair they were able to fit her in.

'You're a very lucky girl, Barbara,' Mrs Baker, the proprietor, told her as she cut the hair so that it curled flatteringly around Barbara's pretty face. 'You'll never have to spend a fortune on perms like most people!'

And Barbara smiled at her reflection, accepting the compliment as a statement of fact but pleased all the same with the result.

Huw arrived late on Christmas Eve. They heard his motor cycle roar up the hill as they were putting the finishing touches to trimming the tree which Ralph, as usual, had obtained for them. It was a magnificent tree, over six feet in height and uniformly bushy, and Barbara was standing on a chair to attach the last of the glass baubles when she heard the motor cycle.

'It's Huw! He's here!' she cried, leaping down from the chair and setting all the baubles swinging and jangling. Then she stopped, overcome suddenly by a rush of uncharacteristic shyness. It didn't seem right somehow to go rushing out to meet him like a child. Instinctively, her hands went to her hair fingering the curls into place and instead of heading for the door with the others she ran upstairs to her room to touch her lips with the rose lipstick Amy allowed her to wear.

She did so want to look nice for Huw and it was very important to her that he should see that she was growing up at last. His remarks when she had met him at the station back in the summer about her not being old enough to smoke or to join the armed services had hurt her a little. The difference in their ages was not very great after all and in a few years' time would seem even less. But it was hardly surprising that he still thought of her as a child when she had been wearing school uniform. Barbara was determined that this Christmas he should realise that she was now a young woman.

Satisfied that she had done as much as she could

about her appearance without Amy and the annoyingly observant Maureen noticing that she was making an effort, Barbara went downstairs with all the composure she could muster. The sound of eager voices all chattering at once told her the family were in the kitchen and she pushed open the door.

The kitchen was full of the smell of yet another batch of mince pies baking and the pungent scorched smell of the taper with which Mrs Milsom had been singeing the last bits of fuzz and quills from the cockerel for tomorrow's dinner. Mingled with these was the scent of the pine needles that had got onto Barbara's hands as she trimmed the tree and the faint lingering aroma of fruit and nuts piled in a bowl on the table. Barbara drank in the warmth of the atmosphere without really noticing she did for she had eyes for no one but Huw, everything and everyone in the room existed only as a background to him.

He stood warming himself by the big old range, tall and handsome with his leather motor cycling jacket still done up to his chin and covering his air force blue uniform. For just a moment she stood looking at him, the love pure and simple welling up inside her. Then she could contain it no longer and she forgot all her self-imposed dignity and ran to him.

'Oh Huw – I'm so glad you could come!'

Was it her imagination or did he hesitate slightly before swinging her into his arms? Did some tiny spark take him by surprise and make for a moment's unexpected awareness? Then she was hugging him as she always did in greeting, her face buried in the stout leather of his jacket, her arms twined tightly around his solid muscular back.

Oh Huw – Huw – her heart echoed her voice and for a moment the others ceased to exist. Then she became aware of her mother's voice, gay, but with a slight edge to it.

'Barbara, for goodness sake let poor Huw take his coat off!'

She moved away, some of the awkwardness returning, but not enough to quench the fires of fierce joy. Huw was home if only for a couple of days. Huw was home, safe and well, the same Huw he had always been.

It was going to be a wonderful Christmas.

They spent a lovely, lazy Christmas day sleeping late because it had been the small hours before they had exhausted all they had to tell one another and finally gone to bed. After breakfast they opened their presents which Amy had stacked under the tree the last thing the previous night as tradition demanded. Considering it was a wartime Christmas there were plenty of them, some surprises, some not, all carefully wrapped and tied with coloured twine.

Ralph had bought Amy a pair of earrings set with sapphires – they sparkled darkly against the jewellers' floss in their small square box and Barbara could not help but notice the look they exchanged when she opened it. Every Christmas since they had been married Ralph had given her a piece of jewellery, usually with sapphires, so that it had become as much a tradition as the tree, but that had never detracted from Amy's pleasure in this expression of their love. Lucky Mum, thought Barbara, catching the shared glance through newly aware eyes.

In return, Amy gave Ralph a pair of gold cuff-links engraved with his initials and a bright woollen scarf, and for the girls there were twin bracelets of fine silver link, each set with a small star, and new night-dresses made of dainty flowered voile, too pretty and light-weight to wear in the cold winter weather, but as Amy explained, 'I thought that with the war on we might not be able to get things like that much longer.'

Huw, too, had managed to buy presents – another

scarf for Ralph: 'At least we're making sure you won't catch cold!' Amy laughed; perfume for Amy and a brooch each for the girls, dainty porcelain ovals hand-painted with a flower design. His packages were more clumsily wrapped than the others but Barbara melted inside at the thought of how long it must have taken him to tie the fiddly little bows.

There were all the usual stocking fillers too – the handkerchiefs and bath cubes and socks, all exclaimed over with delight.

With the present opening completed they toasted one another with sherry and tucked into the lunch of cold ham and pickles which Mrs Milsom had left for them, followed by the inevitable mince pies and chunks of delicious iced Christmas cake. Mrs Milsom had gone to have lunch with her sister but would be back during the afternoon in time to cook their Christmas dinner.

After lunch it was time to visit Charlotte and the rest of the family who had gathered at Greenslade Terrace. Warm, comfortable and full of sherry and lunch as they were they did not feel in the least like moving, but not to pay a visit 'home' would have been unthinkable on Christmas Day and Amy knew Charlotte would never forgive them if they failed to arrive. Ralph was to take the big saloon car which he used on the occasions when more room was needed than his Morgan could offer, but at the last moment Huw decided to drive his own Riley Imp.

'Who wants to come with me?' he asked and Barbara felt that his eyes were on her.

'I will,' she said, but Maureen answered just as quickly:

'Me!'

'You'll have to share it then,' Amy said. 'One there, the other back.'

'Maureen can go with Huw then and I'll come back,' Barbara said, preferring to save her ride and savour it rather than have it over and done with in the next few minutes.

She was glowing today, a picture that no one, not even Maureen, could fail to notice and appreciate, her face slightly rosy from the sherry, her eyes very blue, her hair shining fair in the light from the Christmas tree candles, and there was a dreamy quality about her mouth.

They piled into the cars and drove the mile or so to Greenslade Terrace. Half the Hall clan were there already, it seemed, replete and a little sleepy from having eaten their Christmas dinner at midday. Jim and Sarah were there, May and her husband and baby, and Alec and Joan, his fiancée. Dolly was in the kitchen brewing yet more tea, Bob and Fred, her sons, there under protest, sat in a corner discussing football, while Victor, her husband, his fog horn voice silent for once, was snoozing in a chair, and young Noel, whose birthday it was, played happily with a clown acrobat that had been meant for a child half his age. All their worst fears for Noel had been fulfilled; big and shambling he was a baby who would never grow up, but his moonlike face was good-natured and everyone adored him. Only the boys were missing – Jack and Stella had not come from Minehead this year and Harry and Margaret were spending the day with Gussie and the evacuee girls. And Ted and Rosa were half a world away in Australia . . .

'I had a card from our Ted,' Charlotte said when they had all found somewhere to sit. 'I expect you did too. I only wish he could be here, though. It doesn't seem right, Christmas and our Ted not here to give us a song.'

They were silent for a moment. It seemed so long since Ted had been there and they were remembering other Christmases when they had all gathered round the piano to sing carols, especially that memorable

114

Christmas at the beginning of the Great War when the boys had all lined up to do a comic drill with broomsticks for rifles. How lighthearted they had been then! Now they knew all too well that war was no joking matter. And there had been the Christmas when Noel was born too, another one to stand out in the memory. All that day they had tried to enjoy themselves while knowing Dolly was in labour and in the end Amy had rung Ralph to ask him to take her mother up to South Hill where Dolly lived to find out what was going on, something which had shocked the family who had then regarded Ralph as totally out of their class.

'You never know maybe one year Ted *will* be here,' James said stoically from his bed on the sofa. 'He's doing very well for himself by the sound of it.'

'Let's have a carol anyway,' Charlotte suggested. 'How about While Shepherds Watched? Who's going to start it off?'

Without waiting for them she started herself, her voice still good though she had trouble remembering the words, and they all joined in, even Victor waking up enough to add his loud voice to theirs. Victor was a little deaf as a result of gunfire in the trenches and he could scarcely hear his own rather tuneless voice.

'Can't somebody shut him up?' Amy, who had always found Victor irritating, whispered to Ralph.

After the carols Charlotte insisted on everyone having some tea although half of them were already full and others anxious to leave room for dinner. Much to Amy's concern she cut a plate of ham sandwiches and Christmas cake and they knew she would be offended if they did not eat at least a little. But the men at least seemed to have insatiable appetites.

'It's a pity the baby isn't big enough to have Father Christmas call,' Charlotte said to May. 'Do you remember when your Uncle Ted used to dress up for you? Never mind, maybe next year . . .'

Eventually, Amy said she thought they should be making a move.

'Mrs Milsom will be very upset if we let dinner spoil,' she explained.

Charlotte sniffed. She couldn't understand why Amy and Ralph did not have their dinner at dinner time like everyone else. It wasn't good for the digestion, eating so late at night. But she knew better than to say so.

They got their coats and while Charlotte stood talking to Amy, Ralph and Maureen for a few minutes longer, Barbara and Huw went outside to Huw's car.

It was a perfect December evening, the stars bright in a sky that was ink black and clear. Barbara shivered and knew it was partly from excitement. This was the moment she had been waiting for – when she would be alone with Huw. She sat beside him in the Imp and the sweet roar of the engine when he started it added to the feeling of excitement.

'It's been a lovely Christmas,' she said inadequately. 'I'm so glad you could come home.'

'If this war blows up big it could be a long time before I can come home again,' Huw said.

'Do you think it's going to?' Barbara asked anxiously. 'Nothing much seems to be happening at the moment.'

'Not here yet maybe,' Huw admitted, remembering how thoroughly frustrated by the lack of action he and his friends were. Four Hurricane squadrons had been sent to France to back up the British Expeditionary Force but his own, with its full contingent of Spitfires, was still based in Kent and had little to do but the sporadic patrol of the shipping lanes. What was more, reports filtering back suggested that even those 'in the thick of it' had little enough to do for the cold hard winter in Europe had put a stop to most activity in the air.

'You think it will blow up, though?' Barbara persisted.

Huw executed a neat gear change at the end of Greenslade Terrace and turned out into Conygre Hill.

'I don't think Hitler will give up in a hurry. But give us a chance to get at him and he'll change his tune – him and his precious Luftwaffe.'

Barbara shivered, the night air cold on her flushed face.

'Just as long as the Luftwaffe don't get at you.'

'Let 'em try! Our Spits are better than anything they've got.'

Brave talk. She cheered a little. Then another thought occurred to her.

'Are there any girls at your base?' she asked, shouting to make herself heard above the roar of the engine.

'Some WAAFs.' He accelerated over the first of the level crossings and turned left.

'What do they do?'

'Plotting. Typing. That sort of thing. And some are batwomen.'

'Batwomen?'

'Glorified domestics. You'd hate that, Barbara, if you're thinking what I think you're thinking.'

'Too right! I've no intention of spending my life clearing up after a lot of messy men.' But it had only been part of the reason why she had asked. She was thinking of pretty girls in flattering uniforms all too readily available . . . Still, he hadn't said, as he had the last time they had talked of her joining the services, that she was too young.

They were almost home now, rattling along the lane past Amy's yard where the lorries were parked up neatly for the holiday. Barbara did not want to go home. She wanted to go on riding for ever, just her and Huw . . .

He turned through the gates and steered the car into its garage. It was a big garage for a fairly small car with plenty of room on each side. She sat for a moment while he turned off the engine and the dimmed lights and suddenly they were in total darkness.

'Come on then,' he said.

'I can't see where I'm going.'

He got out and came around to the passenger side.

'Here – take my hand.'

She reached out blindly and her hand brushed his jacket. There in the dark she was very aware of his nearness. The garage seemed to be full of him – the smell of the leather jacket and the faint aroma of the smear of Brylcream he used to tame his thick dark hair mingling with the oil and petrol smell of the car. His hand found hers and held it firmly and the touch of his fingers, strong and safe, started a thrill of excitement deep inside her.

'OK?' he asked.

'Yes, OK.' Her voice was slightly breathless. She took a step, stumbled against him, and for a brief wonderful moment felt sure that he was feeling as she was. It was there between them, an electricity that sparked like the touch of bare wires, so potent, so primitive, that it almost took her breath away. She stood motionless wanting to catch the moment and hold it, never let it go. Then they heard Ralph's car on the drive and the fragile spell was shattered.

'Come on, this way.' There was a rough note in his voice and he turned, leading her by the hand towards the glimmer of moonlight. To all intents and purposes they were once more the boy and girl who had been brought up together, but Barbara knew with an instinct as old as time that for a moment back there in the darkness they had been more, much more.

'Here we are then!' Amy called gaily. 'Let's go and have our dinner. Christmas isn't over yet, you know!'

Laughing, still holding hands, they followed the others into the house.

*

I'll never forget, thought Barbara. 'Never, ever, as long as I live will I forget this Christmas Day.'

She was lying in bed in her room, the moonlight slanting in through the open curtains, making patterns on the wall and throwing deep shadows on the shiny linoleum beyond the patterned rug. It was late; the grandfather clock in the hall had long since chimed midnight, but Barbara had no thought of sleep. She wanted to savour and go on savouring every moment of this wonderful day – and especially the evening, imbued as it had been by the aura of those few stolen moments in the dark garage.

They had dined by candlelight, somehow finding room to do justice to Mrs Milsom's excellent meal in spite of all they had already eaten, and each time she had looked up from her plate she had found Huw's eyes on her. The first time she had blushed and looked away hastily, the second she had held his gaze, her lips curving slightly. Nothing had been said, beyond the usual family conversation, yet she had felt the pull of that electric attraction between them once more and thrilled to it. There had been crackers and Huw had pulled his with her, insisting on putting the paper hat it contained onto her honey coloured curls in spite of the fact that he had been the winner and she had a cracker of her own. There were indoor fireworks in the crackers too – little miniature cascades and glows which they lit on a saucer – but it was the tiny sparkler which Barbara liked best for Huw lit it from the candle and held it up to her chin so that its crackling incandescence was reflected in her eyes.

Afterwards, they sat around the roaring fire reading out the jokes and mottos, and playing that old favourite game Lexicon. There had been a magic moment then, too, for Huw had surreptitiously slipped her the cards she needed to make a word, though Ralph had noticed and accused them both of cheating. Then, at Maureen's insistence, a half-hearted attempt had been made at playing 'Man and his object'.

'We'll be *it*, Huw,' Maureen had insisted and though Huw had complied Barbara had felt that he really wished it was *her* who was going outside the door with him to decide what characters they should assume. In the event their charade had been easy to guess: 'Mr Chamberlain and his umbrella – I'm the umbrella!' Maureen had admitted amidst giggles, but they were all too tired to play another round for the warmth, the food and the drink were making them all sleepy.

They had sat for a while longer in the dying firelight unwilling to end what had been a lovely day, but eventually Ralph had said: 'Well, I don't know about the rest of you, but I'm going to bed!'

Now Barbara lay with the covers up to her chin, cuddling her stone hot water bottle in the crook of her arm and the warmth from it seemed to spread through to every corner of her body.

Oh Huw, Huw, today you noticed me – really noticed me! she thought happily. I wasn't just a little girl today. It was different – special. Oh, as long as I live, I'll never forget.

Barbara, thought Huw, and there was a new ring to her name as if over all the years he had spoken it he had never really listened to it before.

She had been a little girl to him for so long; at first a prissy little madam with clean ankle socks and bows in her hair whom he had despised and yet envied because she had what he did not – a home and a mother. Then, as he had settled down and come to accept her family as his own, she had endeared herself to him with her bold mischievous ways and her unstinted adoration and he had teased and spoiled her, watching her grow into an enchanting tomboy and then into a convent schoolgirl

120

who knew how to make people forgive her even when she was doing the unforgivable. Funny, determined and wilful, yet far more vulnerable than she would ever have admitted, Barbara was the person he supposed he cared for more than anyone in the world – except of course Amy, who had given him a home and love and taught him to love in return. Only now, since reaching manhood, could he fully appreciate just what she had done for him and what it had cost her. But Amy had filled the gap left in his heart when his mother had died. (Oh God, the horror of that night could make him break out in a cold sweat even now!) And Barbara – Barbara was just a child.

Until last night when he had come home for Christmas and seen her through new eyes.

Lying sleepless also Huw relived again the shock of the moments when he had realised it. Last night, when she had come into the kitchen to greet him had been the first. She had stood there framed in the doorway and though her face was as familiar to him as his own, seen every morning in the shaving mirror, he had been shaken by the change in it. Same fair hair, yet had it always curled so enticingly and he had never noticed it? Same blue eyes, yet with a tantalising sparkle. Same rosy cheeks he had seen on a little girl who rode behind him, squealing, on a toboggan in the snow, same mouth, yet somehow curving, sensual, appealing. And her figure. That of a young woman without doubt. Huw had felt the shock waves reverberate through his body as he looked at her. Barbara, yet not Barbara. Not a child. A lovely young woman.

Then there had been today in the garage. All day he had been watching her, trying to equate this strange young beauty with the Barbara he knew. Yet it had still come as yet another shock when they had stood close together in the darkness and he had felt the sudden desire to take her in his arms. He hadn't done it of

121

course. You didn't suddenly grab a girl you had grown up with. That was for pretty strangers who had made it obvious with their flirtatious behaviour that it was exactly what they wanted you to do. Yet never had he felt more inclined to recklessness. Maybe if the others hadn't chosen just that moment to arrive home he would have thrown caution to the winds and kissed her anyway. Maybe . . .

Perhaps it was just as well he was leaving tomorrow, thought Huw. Back to the familiar world of mess rooms and aeroplane hangars, back to the young men who talked in the RAF jargon that was now familiar to him. Back to the WAAF girls closer to his own age and the beauties of the nearby town who hung around young men in uniform, giggling and blushing and fluttering their eyelashes. To think about Barbara the way he was thinking about her seemed a betrayal of the trust she had in him and of the home that Amy had given him. Yet not even this creeping guilt could lessen the dark desire which had invaded his mind and senses.

Barbara, he thought again, and her name sounded like the haunting echo of some half-remembered melody. Little Barbara, grown overnight into a woman.

He was still thinking about her when he fell asleep.

'I'm worried, Ralph,' Amy said.

She could not sleep either, drowsy though she had been when they retired to bed. Then she had been lulled by wine and good food and the warmth, both physical and spiritual, which had been generated by the family gathering around the fire. Now, in the quiet of their bedroom, all the tiny pinpricks of anxiety which she had felt during the day yet been able to ignore gathered their forces to nag her into wakefulness.

'What's that?' Ralph grunted. He was half asleep already, partly buried under the blankets.

'Barbara and Huw. Haven't you seen the way they've been looking at one another all day?'

'No.'

'Well they have. I know Barbara has always adored Huw but this was different. And he was looking at her as if he had never seen her before.'

'You're imagining things,' Ralph muttered. He disliked Amy's habit of suddenly launching into full-scale discussions just when he was on the point of going to sleep; it was one of the few things about her that irritated him.

'I hope so,' Amy said. 'If there was anything between them I don't know what I'd do. Do you think perhaps we ought to have been more – well, open about things?'

Even now, though there were no secrets between them, there were certain subjects that were never mentioned. Too painful, perhaps, they had been consigned to the background of life, accepted and forgotten.

'You're worrying about nothing, Amy,' Ralph said, turning over and humping the blankets with him.

'I don't know. I really don't know.'

'Well, there is nothing you can do about it tonight. Worry about it if and when the time comes. Which I don't think for one moment it will,' Ralph advised, testily. 'And now, for heaven's sake, let's get some sleep.'

Two minutes later and he was snoring gently so Amy could say no more. But it was a long time, all the same, before she too fell asleep.

6

At the beginning of February Margaret decided she was fit enough to have Elaine and Marie under her roof again and nothing Harry could say would make her change her mind.

'They can't stay with Mum for ever,' she argued. 'It was never meant to be anything but a temporary arrangement and she's not a young woman to have all the extra work and worry. She's already wearing herself to a frazzle for the war effort.'

'She's not the only one,' Harry said pointedly, but Margaret refused to listen.

'They are my responsibility. It's not fair to push them onto her.'

'It's darned unfortunate they aren't among the ones who have gone home,' Harry said. As the weeks had passed and no threatened air raids had materialised one after another of the evacuees had returned to London. But Elaine and Marie had not been amongst them. Their mother seemed more than content for them to be off her hands and apart from the occasional letter which was so badly addressed that Margaret was amazed the Post Office was able to deliver it and a small parcel at Christmas they had heard nothing from her.

'I don't mind having them really,' Margaret had said stubbornly. 'It's not as if I'm at work now and it gives me something to keep me occupied.'

Harry sighed. It was true that being idle did not suit Margaret. The school board at Sanderley had already appointed a new teacher to take her place before she had had her accident and regretfully the Head had told her it was too late for her to withdraw her notice. But Harry could not imagine that Margaret would have any difficulty finding a new post if she were to look for one. She was an excellent teacher and highly thought of by all who knew her. But she was making no efforts in that direction.

It could be of course that she did not feel up to it, Harry thought. Although Dr Carter had said she had made a marvellous recovery physically, he knew she was still grieving for the baby she had lost. But he could not help feeling this was not the only reason for her preferring to stay at home.

Since the day when their mother had failed to arrive on the 'Parents Special' train to visit them, Margaret had become more and more protective towards Elaine and Marie and Harry suspected she was channelling some of her own loss and grief into becoming a surrogate mother.

The thought worried him. If she expended too much love on them she would end up by being hurt again for the day would inevitably come when they would return home to their own family, unsatisfactory as it might be. But try telling that to Margaret! She would only snap his nose off and say he was being ridiculous. Since the accident she seemed to snap all too readily.

The answer would be to start another baby of their own, of course, but it was much too early to think of that, Dr Carter had said.

So the children returned and Margaret devoted herself to looking after them and helping them to settle down – a mammoth task which meant she often looked tired and worried though she constantly denied that there was any problem.

One of the things she persuaded them to do was to join the GFS – the Girls Friendly Society – which met every Tuesday in the Church Hall. At first Elaine was prone to complain that the singing games they played were 'silly' and the first aid lessons 'boring', but they went along with surprisingly little argument and wore their badges pinned to their jumpers with something suspiciously like reluctant pride.

They were at GFS one evening in early March when Harry came home, later than usual, from a meeting of the Urban District Council. Harry had been a councillor now for more than three years and a member of the Labour Party for a great many more. In fact his dedication to politics had been the reason for the change of direction in his career. He had been all set to become the youngest colliery manager in the district when Sir Richard Spindler had called him to his office one day and issued what had been in effect an ultimatum – leave the Labour Party and take promotion, remain in it and see the chances pass him by. The interview had made Harry furious for he could not see that his politics had any bearing on his ability to do his job well, but Sir Richard had been adamant. The Labour Party was the enemy of management and if Harry persisted with what Sir Richard referred to as 'this political nonsense' he could not be considered to be serving the best interests of the colliery company. Harry had told him in no uncertain terms that he would not compromise his principles and left with the sick certainty that all the hard work he had put into passing his examinations had been in vain. Then, just when he was feeling at his lowest, Tom Heron, the Miners' Agent, had been forced by a heart attack into early retirement and Harry had applied successfully to succeed him. He enjoyed the new challenge for now he was able to use all his knowledge and expertise to the very end which had always most concerned him – getting a better deal for the men who worked the narrow Somerset seams – and it also left him free to work for the community in other ways. When he was elected to the council as one of the 'Labour Six', he

126

quickly proved his worth and it was not only the people he represented but also his fellow councillors who were privately convinced that Harry Hall would go far.

Since the war had started Council meetings had been held in the afternoons – to save having to buy blackout for the Council Chamber had been the official reason, but since the blackout had appeared anyway Harry had the sneaking feeling that the change had been pushed through by some of the members who preferred to miss half a day's work and be paid for it rather than having to give up an evening of their own time once a month.

Today, the meeting had gone on longer than it sometimes did thanks mainly to Eddie Roberts who had objected strenuously to one of the resolutions and Harry was still fuming as he sat at the table watching Margaret resurrect the plate of dinner which she had put back over a saucepan of water on the stove to keep warm for him.

'Eddie Roberts is a pain in the proverbial backside,' he said, making angry patterns on the tablecloth with the handle of his knife. 'He's a self-opinionated pompous blithering idiot. I can't stand him.'

Margaret stirred the skin off the gravy she had saved for Harry in the china gravy boat and looked around at him in surprise.

She knew Harry didn't like Eddie and knew too that the dislike was mutual. There had never been any love lost between Amy's brother-in-law and the Hall family since he had tried to cheat Amy out of the business when Llew, her first husband and Eddie's brother, had died. And though they were both members of the Labour party and so theoretically should have supported one another in council meetings there was often friction between the two men. But it was unlike Harry to wax so vehement about anyone, even Eddie.

'What has he done now?' she asked.

'To begin with he did his best to stop us suspending

the building of some of the new council houses at South Hill although we've been asked by central government to avoid any extra expense for the time being. Then, if you please, he tried to veto the wage rises for council employees which they desperately need to keep in line with the increase in the cost of living.'

'I hope this isn't too dried up,' Margaret said, putting the plate down in front of Harry. 'It was lovely when we had it.'

'It'll be fine. Quite honestly, I'm so hungry I wouldn't notice the difference anway,' Harry said, shaking salt onto the potatoes. 'What a meeting! Sometimes I wonder why I bother!'

'You bother because you care about getting things done.' Margaret sat down in the chair opposite him, resting her chin on her hand and regarding him seriously. 'You mustn't let Eddie upset you. He's just a lot of hot air.'

'Hmm. If only it was just that,' Harry said, tucking in. 'The trouble is I'm not so sure.'

'What do you mean?' Margaret asked.

'I don't trust him. I think he's doing his eye good.'

'Eddie? Oh surely not! I mean, I know he's out for his own good but surely he wouldn't do anything dishonest.'

'I'm not so sure.' Harry piled cabbage on his fork. 'I think he might be taking backhanders. Take his objections to holding back the building work to begin with. With the situation as it is he didn't really have a leg to stand on yet he argued black was white to try to get us to finish all ten of the houses. Then there have been several contracts handed out that have surprised me a bit. Unnecessary expense jobs pushed through, usually resulting in extra work for people Eddie has some connection with or benefitting them in some way. I noticed it first last year. There was that new building site at Riddicks Cross. Welsh's from South Compton were developing it and they applied to the council to have a new drainage system put in linking them to the main sewerage. Bloody cheek, really, but Eddie argued for them that they had thought that side of things had been taken care of by the council and hadn't catered for it. The whole development could have been jeopardised if they ran out of money because of the extra expense and he reckoned it was the council's responsibility anyway. So it went through.'

'Sounds fair enough to me,' Margaret said.

'But it's not. Their surveyors should have looked into it before they ever started the scheme. It's elementary,' Harry, himself a trained surveyor, argued. 'And when you look into it what do you find? Adam Welsh and Eddie Roberts are as thick as thieves. They do all their insurance through him and they often have a drink together in the George.'

'Oh,' Margaret said.

'And that's just one instance.' Harry paused. 'Have we got any bread?'

'Yes, of course.' Margaret fetched the loaf and cut a thick slice. 'What else then? What else has he been up to?'

'I think he's leaking information on tenders. In fact I'm damned sure of it. You know when there's a job to be done we invite tenders? Well, quite often just lately we've received one quotation late, right at the last minute after all the others are in. And it's always the lowest. Not by much, mind you, but just enough to win the contract. This time it was delivered a day too late. But Eddie argued that since it was the lowest and we would be saving the council money we should accept it anyway.'

'I'd agree with that,' Margaret said. 'After all, it's not the council's money. It's *our* money – the ratepayers. Of course you should economise wherever you can.'

'Stretching the limit by a day for a fiddling ten

shillings?' Harry shook his head. 'It's one thing if it's fair and above board. But I don't think this is. Of course we want a job done for the lowest possible price. But I don't like to see honest businessmen done out of work because Eddie Roberts happens to have a word in the ear of the opposition once they have submitted their prices. His cronies are undercutting, Marg, and they're doing it in collusion with him, I'm certain of it.'

Margaret pulled a face. 'I see what you mean. But what proof have you got?'

'None really. But I was given a wheeze today. Last meeting Thorne Sand and Gravel got the contract for supplying the necessaries to put up new outbuildings at the rear of the council offices. And who do you think was seen delivering building materials to Eddie's own home? None other than Thornes!'

'What does Eddie want with building materials?' Margaret asked, puzzled.

'I tackled him about it today. He says he is having an air raid shelter built in his back garden so that his mother will have somewhere to go if Hitler does start bombing.'

Eddie had never married – he still lived at home with his mother.

'You believe him?' Margaret asked.

'Oh yes, I dare say that part is true enough. Eddie is just the sort to want to go one better than anybody else.' Harry mopped up his gravy with the thick chunk of bread. 'What I'd like to know is whether he paid for it.'

'I see.' Margaret frowned. 'But it still comes back to whether you have any proof.'

'Not yet,' Harry said grimly. 'But I'll get it, Marg. If that's what he's doing, believe me, I'll get it.'

Margaret surveyed him anxiously for a moment. Harry was like her father had been, so straight. He couldn't abide anyone cheating the system. But going against someone like Eddie Roberts who held a lot of sway in the Labour Party could cause a great deal of unpleasantness and be dangerous. If her father had still been alive it would have been different. He would never have stood for it and he would have worked alongside Harry to winkle out the bad apple from the barrel. As it was Eddie could make a good deal of trouble . . .

'Be careful, Harry,' she warned.

'I'll be careful all right – just as long as I can get things straight and above board,' Harry said, laying down his knife and fork. 'Now – I'm feeling better than I was, but I've still got a corner left. What have we got for pudding?'

In the bedroom of the cottage in the lower reaches of Purldown Alec Hall humped the heavy old wardrobe back across the corner of the room and stood back, sweating.

'Well, what do you think of that?' he asked.

'Hmm, yes. It looks quite good there doesn't it? Unless the light might be better on the mirror if it was over there. . .' Joan Tiley, his fiancée, surveyed the position of the wardrobe, her plump and pretty face thoughtful.

'I'm not moving it again and that's final.'

Joan pouted. 'So why bother asking me if it's all right there?'

'To give you the chance to praise me up once in a while,' Alec said. 'It would make a nice change is all I can say. Nothing ever seems to be quite right for you.'

'Oh Alec, that's not true!' Joan objected. 'I told you what a lovely job you made of decorating the kitchen – and the living room too. You know I did. And if I do make any suggestions it's only because I want things to be just right. Goodness knows we've waited long enough to have a place of our own.'

'We're lucky to *have* a place of our own. Plenty of people never do.'

'Alec!' The pout became more pronounced as her pleasure in the arrangement of the bedroom furniture was overtaken by the feeling of anxiety which seemed to be there just below the surface almost all the time these days. 'Why do you have to be so bad tempered? Don't *you* want our home to be nice?'

'Of course I do.' But the undertones were still there. 'Why do you think I've put in so much time doing it up?'

'I don't know,' Joan said. 'Sometimes I wonder.'

'What do you mean by that?'

She hesitated. 'Sometimes I wonder if you're just putting things off. Six months, you said it would take to do this place up when we first got it. Well, it's getting on for a year and still you keep finding things to do.'

'You know what a state it was in.'

'But it's not in a state now. It's a little palace. Anybody would be proud to live here. But have we set a date? No. Every time I suggest it you come up with some excuse or other. I'm beginning to wonder if you really want to marry me at all!'

'Oh, don't be so stupid!' he retorted.

'I'm not being stupid. And you're so horrid to me . . .'

'Well, that's it!' he said crossly. 'I just spent a whole evening rearranging furniture to suit you and you accuse me of being horrid to you. I'm going home.' He crossed the bedroom and picked up his jacket from the bed. 'Are you coming?' he asked.

'You see? You're doing it again – snapping my nose off!' she wailed. 'I just can't seem to even *speak* to you these days. I don't know what's the matter with you.'

Alec did not reply. He was being snappy, he knew, but he couldn't help himself. He *felt* snappy. And she was right really though he would never have admitted

132

it. He was finding excuses to delay setting a date. He'd been doing it one way and another for as long as he'd known her. But it had got worse recently. Partly because he could feel the net closing in and partly because . . .

Alec, like all the Halls, was a master at shutting out thoughts he did not want to think and he stopped his mind now from forming the words to complete the sentence. But it was there all the same, a feeling he refused to acknowledge and yet could not eradicate. It wasn't just his fear of being tied down that made him delay his marriage to Joan. It also had something to do with the girl who would be their next-door-neighbour when they moved into the cottage.

Alec had only seen her a few times since that first night when they had talked across his bicycle in the back pathway. But he had found it impossible to forget her.

He had lain awake that night not thinking about her exactly but disturbed in a way he had been unable to understand and when he had finally slept, his dreams had been haunted by her once-pretty face disfigured by the marks inflicted by her husband's cruelty.

It wasn't right, he thought, for a man to hit a girl like that, particularly if she was his wife. Her home should be a place of safety with her man there to protect, not injure, her. Anger rose like bile in his throat. He'd like to get hold of that Eric Latcham and show him what a fist in the face felt like. Just wait till he saw him next time . . .

But of course he had said nothing. The next time he saw Eric Latcham in the garden they passed the time of day as usual though Alec was fuming inwardly. And of Bryda there was no sign. She was hiding her black eye from the world, no doubt.

It was several weeks before he had seen Bryda again. He was across the yard one Saturday afternoon clearing out the rubbish that was piled in the coal house when she came out of the back door with a child in a pushchair. She looked embarrassed to see him, trying to slip quickly by, but he spoke to her all the same.

'Nice afternoon.'

'Yes.'

'Cold though. I bet they're freezing watching the football up at the Town Ground.'

'Yes. Eric's gone.'

'To football?'

'Yes. He always goes to football.'

'Oh.'

'I must hurry to the shop and back before he gets home and have a cup of tea and his cockles ready for him. He always like a plate of cockles after football on a Saturday.'

She had hurried off along the path pushing the child in the pushchair, a slight figure in a jacket that looked as if it had seen better days and a scarf tied over her hair. But at least there had been no marks on her face. He hadn't hit her lately – or not where it showed.

Cockles! thought Alec and felt a strange twinge of something between nostalgia and regret. His father always had cockles for tea on a Saturday too, a big plateful swimming in vinegar. But they had been part of the warm scenario of a happy household, eaten in front of a roaring fire while the football results were discussed and the smell of home-baked cake wafted in from the kitchen. He couldn't imagine that sort of atmosphere in a house where a man knocked his wife about.

Sudden anger boiled in him and he had vented it on the rubbish. And when a box blew down over Eric Latcham's garden he had let it go. If Eric tackled him about it it would be a good chance to have a go at him; let him see what he thought of him.

But Eric did not tackle him about it. A man like that

134

only picks on someone too weak to hit back, Alec thought in disgust.

Each time he saw Bryda it was the same. A few brief exchanged words and she was gone. Yet he found himself thinking of her more and more, working outside as long as it was daylight in the hope of seeing her, glancing out of the window when he heard the door slam. Once he saw her scurrying by with her scarf pulled well across her face and wondered if she was again trying to hide the fact that Eric had been up to his old tricks. But if there were rows he did not hear them.

Now he shrugged into his jacket and turned to Joan.

'Are you coming? Or are you staying here all night?'

'Oh Alec!' She looked at him uncertainly then ran to him, burying her face in his chest. 'Don't let's quarrel, please.'

For a moment he remained stiff and unyielding, then he put his arms around her, overcome with guilt. It wasn't her fault that he felt so unsettled and edgy.

'I'm sorry,' he said. 'I didn't mean to upset you.'

Her hair tickled his chin, her body pressed close to his; nice hair, soft and springy, a nice body, plump and curvy, yet firm with youth. The irritation which continually needled at him these days began to fade, replaced by a warm glow of desire. She raised her face and he saw the tears welling in her eyes. Oh hell, he thought, he hadn't meant to make her cry. He kissed her, gently at first, then more deeply and as she responded his hands moved to caress the swell of her breast and her bottom, full and rounded beneath her flared serge skirt.

'Did I ever tell you you've got a smashing bottom?' he whispered.

For answer she pressed closer, her kisses becoming more frantic, and he pushed her back towards the bed. The mattress was bare, covered only by an old blanket Joan's mother had given them for although there was a

135

stack of new linen in her 'bottom drawer' Joan was afraid to make up the bed until the house was lived in for fear that it might get damp. As the iron frame of the bed touched the back of their knees he urged her down so they were sitting on it, still kissing, and slid his hand up under her skirt.

This was the point when Joan usually stopped him – so far, no further. 'Behave yourself!' she would say severely and refuse to kiss him any more until his hands were safely back where she wanted them. But tonight she made no protest. Above the tops of her stockings her thighs were plump and firm; as he explored all thoughts of Bryda, all anxieties about his future, all fears of the 'marriage trap' fled from his mind. He could think of nothing but Joan's body, her nearness and how he wanted her. Gently, he pushed her back on the mattress and she did not resist. Her skirt was rucked up to her waist now and those glorious plump thighs enveloped him. Carefully, he unbuttoned her blouse burying his face in her breasts and feeling her hands on his bare back; she had pulled his shirt out of his trousers and he had not even noticed it. He proceeded cautiously now for he was afraid that the next move on his part would be the one which would make her pull back, scolding him for his impertinence. Then desire lent him courage and he took her all of a rush and though he heard her moan softly she did not protest.

Too soon it was over, a brief snatched spasm of activity which had excited his body yet left him feeling strangely detached from her. Physically satisfied yet at the same time disappointed by the sense of something missing, he felt the first stab of guilt.

'Joan – I'm sorry . . .'

She moved beneath him. He rolled off her, propping himself up on one elbow, and saw the lazy smile curve her mouth.

'It's all right. After all, we're going to get married

aren't we? In fact I think we ought to set a date pretty quickly *now*.'

The moment she said the '*now*', the way she said it, he knew. He had thought he had been the aggressor and the instigator. Suddenly he knew different. He'd been caught well and truly, trapped by a nice pair of plump thighs just like many men before him.

No, be fair, he said to himself. She hasn't trapped you. You are supposed to be engaged to her after all. But all the same, now, knowing what he had done . . .

'Yes, I suppose we'd better,' he said. 'When do you want it – Easter?'

Her smile became broader.

'Oh yes, Easter would be lovely!'

She reached for him again pulling him back towards her and he held her. But there was no stirring of desire now, nothing but a heaviness inside. Over her shoulder Alec stared at the wardrobe that had started it all and wished that he could begin this evening over again.

'Well, girls, it looks as though we'll be going to a wedding!' Amy said.

'A wedding? Oh good! Whose?' Maureen, sitting up to the table ready for her evening meal, added the query almost as an afterthought.

'Your cousin Alec. He and Joan are getting married at Easter. Auntie Sarah rang me today to tell me.'

'Auntie Sarah *rang*?' Whilst some members of the family practically lived by the telephone, using it as a lifeline for business and all communication, others – Sarah and Jim included – had never thought of having one in the house and used what they regarded as a suspicious instrument only in the case of dire emergency.

'Yes. Time is short and she wanted to let us know as soon as possible,' Amy explained.

'I can't see that there's anything very urgent about

that,' Maureen said. 'They've been engaged for years. Why are they suddenly in such a hurry to get married?'

'I really couldn't say and it's none of our business anyway,' Amy said crisply.

Privately, her suspicions were always aroused when a wedding was arranged at such short notice just as most people's were. 'Of course our Jim had to get married in a hurry,' Charlotte had said when Amy had driven up that afternoon to discuss it with her and her meaningful look had almost shocked Amy. It was true Jim had gone to the altar a little sooner than he had intended and when Alec had been born there had been those who had done some counting on their fingers but this had never been mentioned in the family. To bring it into the open simply wasn't done.

'Perhaps he'll ask me to be a bridesmaid,' Maureen said hopefully.

'I shouldn't think so.'

'He might. I've never been a bridesmaid. Well – can I have a new dress anyway?' Maureen persisted.

Amy ignored her, glancing at Barbara. She was curled up on the leather topped coalbox beside the fire, completely oblivious to the conversation as she pored over a letter which had arrived for her in the morning post. It was from Huw, Amy knew, having recognised both the writing and the postmark and when Barbara had come home from school and she had given it to her the reaction had been just as it always was – an unconcealed delight which glowed on her face like the flickering reflected firelight coupled with an air of disconcerting secrecy.

'Barbara?' she said sharply. 'Did you hear what I said?'

'Hmm?' Barbara looked up, holding the letter close to her chest.

'Alec and Joan are getting married.'

'Oh, are they?' She might have been told the dustcart

was passing by outside for all the interest she took. Amy's anxiety expressed itself as irritation.

'I should have thought you'd be pleased. Most people like a wedding.'

'Will Huw be able to come home for it?'

'I don't know,' Amy said. 'I shouldn't think so.'

'Oh – well,' Barbara said and went back to her letter.

'I said, can I have a new dress Mum?' Maureen persisted.

'It all depends. I should think you've got more than enough dresses anyway,' Amy snapped, her mind still on Barbara and Huw.

It was all very well for Ralph to tell her not to worry – she *was* worried. All Barbara could think of these days was Huw – Huw – Huw. And with him writing to her so regularly she could no longer dismiss it as a one-sided crush on Barbara's part either.

'Mum – please . . .' Maureen begged.

'For goodness sake, Barbara, leave that letter and go and wash your hands. Mrs Milsom is ready to serve dinner,' Amy said crossly.

Margaret stood in the centre of the kitchen, a worried frown creasing her features. On the table beside her her handbag stood open; she rifled through it quickly, moving around letters, diary and comb to peer into the depths, then returning her attention to the purse which she was holding.

She had been sure there had been three pound notes in it yesterday. Now there were only two. For the umpteenth time she did a quick calculation of what she had spent since Harry had given her the housekeeping money. No, there was no way she could have spent all that. A pound was a lot of money. A few shillings unaccounted for she could have understood. But a *pound* . . .

Have I left my bag lying about when Elaine has been

in the room? Margaret wondered, and instantly hated herself for the thought. But it had to be faced. Too many things had gone missing and either turned up under suspicious circumstances or not turned up at all. The unpleasant possibility that the child was a compulsive thief seemed to be becoming more and more likely with each new incident.

I can't just let it go on unchecked, Margaret thought. If she is stealing I shall have to do something about it. But what? It was such a delicate situation and if she handled it badly she could completely upset the relationship she was establishing with the girls. Worse, she could push Elaine over the brink. At least she was behaving herself a little better now – nor had Gussie complained of anything going missing during the time they had been staying with her.

If she *is* taking things it's probably just because she's lonely and wretched, Margaret thought, recalling again the lack of contact the girls' mother had with them. I mustn't accuse. I must try to understand and then gently show her it's not very nice to help yourself to things that don't belong to you and particularly not nice to go to other people's purses . . .

The sound of a car on the drive outside made her look up and to her surprise she recognised Harry's Morris. Strange. What was he doing home at this time of day – and using up precious petrol too! She closed her purse quickly and put it back in her bag. She had still not told Harry of her suspicions and she did not want to. Not until she had sorted things out in her own mind and was sure. Harry would only huff and puff and make things much worse.

The door opened and he came into the kitchen unbuttoning his overcoat.

'Hello. It's nice and warm in here.'

'What are you doing home?' she asked.

He did not answer her directly. 'Have you got the

140

kettle on? I could do with a cup of tea. It's blooming cold out.'

'I haven't, but it won't take a minute to boil.' She reached for the kettle and filled it. 'But you can't tell me you came home just for a cup of tea. Your Miss Vranch always makes sure there's plenty of that at your office.'

'I wanted to talk to you. On our own, without those blessed girls listening to every word.'

She crossed and gave him a quick hug, sliding her hands under his overcoat.

'Well, it's nice to see you, whatever the reason. I get quite lonely here on my own all day. I shall be jolly glad to get another job – unless of course we manage to start another baby . . .' She looked up at him meaningfully and got quite a different reaction to the one she expected.

'You're not, are you?' he asked, looking at her seriously.

She shook her head.

'No, I'm not – more's the pity. Why do you say it like that?'

'Oh, just that – well, our circumstances might be about to change.'

'What on earth do you mean?'

'That's what I've come home to talk to you about.' He glanced towards the kettle, already singing on the gas. 'Make the tea and I'll tell you. It will go down better over a cuppa.'

'I want to know now! What is it Harry?'

'Wait . . . Oh, all right. It's just that I don't want to give you too much of a shock.' He held her at arms' length, his hands resting on her trim waist. 'How would you feel about being the wife of a Member of Parliament?'

'A . . . *what*? Harry – is this some kind of joke?'

'Not a joke, no. Look, the kettle's boiling, Make that tea.'

141

She did so, thinking she must have fallen asleep and be dreaming.

'It's like this,' Harry said, sitting down at the table as she set the pot and cups on the scrubbed wood surface. 'You know David Reece was the prospective Labour candidate for this constituency? Well, he's been called up to active service. He was a reservist and he received his papers a few days ago. That means the party has to find another candidate.'

'And they want you? Oh Harry!'

'I know. I could hardly believe it myself. I mean, I know I'm a loyal party member and a councillor and all that, but all the same . . . Of course, I may not be selected even if I agree to let my name go forward. There will be others on the shortlist. But Roly Everard thinks I stand a good chance with my background. "You're used to sorting out problems," was how he put it. And I suppose he's right. I sort out the men's problems every day. An MP simply sorts out problems over a wider spectrum.'

'I'm sure nobody could do it better than you,' Margaret said loyally.

'I don't know about that.' Harry grinned, looking pleased with himself in spite of his assumed modesty. 'Obviously, coming out of the blue like this we have to give it some thought. But quickly. Reece is definitely out of it and they can't be without a candidate for too long at a time like this. There has to be somebody to oppose Mrs Lincoln and her reactionary ideas.'

Mrs Lincoln was the sitting MP – a true blue Tory and a remarkable woman. But, as Harry said, the seat was there for the taking and with the mining industry making up a good part of the constituency there was plenty of support locally for the Labour Party.

'Well?' Harry said. 'What do you think?' Margaret got up, crossed to the pantry and fetched the jug of milk. A little flame of excitement was flickering inside

142

her but she calmly milked the cups and poured the tea before she spoke. Then she passed Harry his, looking at him steadily.

'I think you should let your name go forward,' she said. 'Be honest, Harry, it's what you have always wanted. Even before you knew me I think you wanted it and for years you have been working towards it. Perhaps you haven't even realised it, but I have. I knew you wouldn't be content to stay in local government or even to be the best Miners' Agent Hillsbridge has ever had. You're cut out for more than that. Let your name go forward and see what happens.'

'And if it came to it and I was selected, you wouldn't mind? It would mean a lot of separations I shouldn't wonder, nights away from home, that sort of thing. And a lot of work for you. You wouldn't mind?'

'Harry, I was born and raised to politics. Of course I wouldn't mind. Especially when I know it's what you want.'

'Even if I should get elected?'

'If you get elected I should be the proudest woman alive.'

He reached for her hands and they sat in silence for a few moments, each with their own thoughts. Then Harry laughed lightly.

'Of course we may be putting the cart before the horse. I might not even get selected.'

Margaret smiled back at him, her eyes glowing with loyalty and love.

'They'd be fools not to have you. Oh Harry, of course you'll be selected!'

On a Wednesday evening at the beginning of March Alec Hall was once again alone at the cottage, pottering from room to room and looking for any odd jobs which still needed doing.

There was very little need for him to be there. The house was in apple pie order, gleaming with new paint and with every conceivable defect attended to, but to Alec it had become a place of refuge. His home seemed to have been taken over by the arrangements for the forthcoming wedding. Sarah, his mother, and Joan were in a constant state of excitement, rushing here and there, fussing, fretting and planning, and when he was around they were given to pouncing on him to draw him into a discussion about one of the innumerable details which in his opinion at least were at best unnecessary and at worst a wicked waste of money. Marriage was, after all, basically a private business between two people; surely it should be enough to enter into it quietly along with the immediate family to wish them well and the minimum of fuss. Yet there seemed to be no end to the frills Joan was intent on adding now that she had finally persuaded him to walk down the aisle – and all had to be attended to in record time. The dresses were being made by a dressmaker who lived in South Hill Gardens, not just Joan's, which Alec assumed would be white, but also creations in pink organdie to be worn by the four girls Joan had asked to be bridesmaids. There were frantic fittings for these dresses and Joan said the dressmaker would have to burn the midnight oil to get them done. Invitations had been sent out to forty guests for a reception to be held in the Victoria Hall and a three-tier cake had been ordered from the Co-op. Add to this a photographer and cars to be booked, flowers ordered, and the details of the wedding service itself to be arranged and the whole thing had become a massive undertaking.

It was what women liked, Alec supposed, and since it was Joan's day he'd have to go along with it. But it was his firm intention to involve himself as little as possible and finding that any suggestion of taking himself off for a drink at the Miners Arms produced screams of

144

protest from both Joan and his mother that he should even think of such a thing when there was so much to be done, he had discovered his best course was to get out his bicycle and go down to the cottage on the pretext of having some necessary job or other in hand there. At least that way he got a little peace and quiet and he could always stop off for a pint on the way home with no one the wiser.

I don't know what I've let myself in for I'm sure, Alec thought, scrubbing a stubborn streak of paint off the kitchen window with a cloth dipped in turps. Sometimes I think I've been a bit of a damn fool.

It was a thought which had occurred to him frequently over the last weeks and it was worrying him more and more. In a vague sort of way he had expected that once the decision was made and plans were under-way he would accept the whole thing as inevitable. Well, that had happened, he supposed. But the inevitability did not make it any better. If anything it had made it a good deal worse, for try as he might to be philosophical about it, Alec could not rid himself of the kind of feeling that might be experienced by a prisoner about to be given a life sentence – and with the whole daunting court procedure still to be gone through into the bargain.

Perhaps when the deed was actually done he would feel better about it, Joan would be a good wife, not a doubt of it. She would make him a comfortable home, cook him the sort of wholesome food he was used to and, if the other evening was anything to go by, do a little more than simply keeping him warm in bed. They would have children, three or four probably since Joan had always said she favoured a big family, and he would settle down to being the head of the household. Not a bad prospect for any man of twenty-five. Alec only wished he could feel a little more enthusiastic about it.

145

He went into the little living room and switched on the wireless. He'd been lucky to get hold of it, he thought, as it warmed up and Donald Peers' voice came crackling through. It wasn't a new set – he had bought it from a man he worked with – but he had got a different battery for it and besides being a source of entertainment the wooden cabinet was attractive enough to make it a very acceptable piece of furniture. The same man had said he might be able to get hold of a gramophone, too – if he did it would be worth splashing out a few shillings on. If Joan could spend all his money on frills and furbelows for the wedding, darned if he didn't see why he shouldn't have a gramophone!

It was when the Donald Peers song came to an end that he heard the knocking at the back door and went back through the kitchen to answer it, wondering vaguely who would come calling. One of his mates, perhaps, suggesting he should slope off a bit earlier to the Miners Arms tonight? Alec did not think that in his present state of mind he would take much persuading.

He opened the door and the light spilling out showed him the slight figure of Bryda Latcham standing on the doorstep.

'Oh, hello!' he said, surprised and awkward suddenly.

'I'm sorry to bother you.' Her voice was hesitant.

'That's all right. You'd better come in. If a warden sees this light showing we shall be for the high jump.'

'Oh . . .' She hesitated. 'No warden is likely to be coming round the back here, is he?'

'No, s'pose not.' Perhaps she was afraid of being in a house alone with a man, he thought. Not surprising, considering the way her husband treated her. A moment later this idea was negated when she said:

'I was wondering if you could do something for me. The light has gone in my kitchen and I can't see to get the bulb out. Eric's out – he won't be back until gone ten – and I can't see to do a thing.'

146

'Oh, right you are. I'll come round.'

'You don't mind me asking?'

'Course not.' He closed the door behind him and followed her next door. As she had said her kitchen was in almost complete darkness, lit only by a faint glow which crept in from the hall, and he almost fell over a chair which she had placed beneath the light fitting.

'Sorry . . .' she said.

'It's all right.' He climbed onto the chair, removed the spent bulb and replaced it with one she handed to him. There was a click and the light came on.

'Oh, that's better!' she said. 'I hate being in the dark. Stupid really I suppose, but . . .'

'No, it's nothing but a nuisance. I hate it myself.'

In the glow of light which came from beneath the faded shade he could see the kitchen now as well as feeling it – a nice kitchen, homely and sparklingly clean in spite of the comfortable clutter, a heap of laundry waiting to be ironed on the oil-cloth topped table, two flat irons piled on the gas ring, a stewpan soaking in the sink.

He got down from the chair, turning to look at Bryda. And saw the livid mark at the side of her mouth, darkening to a deep purple bruise just above the line of her jaw. His stomach turned. As she realised he had noticed her hand flew up defensively covering the mark. But before he could stop himself he heard himself say: 'Has he been hitting you about again?'

The moment it was out he knew he should not have said it. Her eyes went dark and she seemed to draw back into herself.

'What do you mean?'

Leave it! the voice of caution urged him. But he could not.

'You know very well what I mean! He beats you up, doesn't he?'

'Well, he . . .' She looked even smaller and more

147

vulnerable now, on the defensive again. 'He doesn't mean it.'

'How the hell can he not mean it?' Alec said. 'How can you possibly hit a woman and not mean it?'

'He – he's got a temper. He gets drunk. He's always sorry afterwards.'

'I should bloody well think he is!' Alec exploded. 'I wish I could get my hands on the bastard!'

'No!' she protested violently. 'You mustn't say anything, please!'

Her eyes were huge in her thin face and she laid a trembling hand on his arm. Alec felt the pit of his stomach fall away.

'For Christ's sake . . .' he muttered.

And somehow she was in his arms.

For long moments suspended in time he held her. Then it was over. She drew away and he let her go, standing awkwardly, still stunned by the strength of his emotions. Her head was bent, eyes downcast behind a curtain of hair that almost hid her face. She could not look at him.

'I'd better be going,' he said roughly.

She moved then, looking up quickly.

'Don't go! Stay and have a drink – we always keep a bottle of beer in the house. Unless of course you're busy . . .'

He did not need asking twice.

'No, I'm not busy. There's nothing left to do in the cottage really.'

'You'll be moving in soon, I suppose. You're getting married at Easter, aren't you?'

'Yes. Supposed to be.'

She was bustling about now, trying to behave normally, fetching the beer, a bottle opener and a glass. Alec watched her, feeling a little as though he had already drunk more than was good for him and wondering why Joan never had this effect on him.

148

Bryda spread a freshly laundered shirt out on the table and took a flat iron off the gas ring, handling it carefully with a thick crocheted holder.

'It's funny really. I don't know a lot about you seeing we're going to be neighbours,' she said.

'No. We went to the same school though, didn't we?'

The awkwardness was still there but as they chatted it lessened. Bryda worked steadily at her ironing. Alec broke into a second bottle of beer.

When the clock in the living room chimed ten she became anxious again.

'P'raps you'd better go. If Eric were to come home and find you here . . .'

Let him! Alec thought recklessly, emboldened by the two pints. Then I could tell him what I think of him and perhaps give him a taste of his own medicine into the bargain! But he knew that he would not be the one to suffer. It would be Bryda who would taste Eric's revenge when he was not there to see fair play. He got up.

'I'll see you again then.'

'Yeah. See you again.'

'Thanks for the beer.'

'Thanks for doing the light.'

He hesitated in the doorway wishing he could take her in his arms again. From the other side of the table she smiled at him and it seemed the smile lit her face, blotting out the marks beside her mouth and the dark shadows under her eyes. He felt as if the pit had dropped out of his stomach.

'Night,' he said.

'Night.' He went out into the clammy darkness and closed the door behind him.

7

Harry was in his office at the Miners' Welfare Building. On the desk in front of him lay a file of legal papers relating to an appeal against dismissal by one of his members, to his left a pile of correspondence awaited his attention, at his right elbow a cup of coffee cooled and congealed.

There was a tap at the door, and Elinor Vranch, his highly efficient secretary, popped her head in.

'Mr Eddie Roberts to see you, Mr Hall.'

'Oh yes.' Busy as he was, Harry put the cap on his fountain pen and laid it down on the blotter. 'Show him in please, Miss Vranch.'

Not a flicker of surprise showed on the carefully made-up features.

'Very well, Mr Hall.' She went out and Harry heard her say: 'Mr Hall will see you now, Mr Roberts, if you would care to . . .'

'It's all right. I know the way.' The door opened and Eddie Roberts came into the office. 'Afternoon, Harry. What did you want to see me about?'

Eddie Roberts, Amy's brother-in-law, was a big man. Physically, he closely resembled his dead brother Llew – he had the same brown hair springing from a deep 'widows peak', the same clear blue eyes and good strong features which looked boyish in spite of the scattering of lines and paunches which had come from approaching middle age – and a liking for a little more whisky than was good for him. Here the resemblance ended. Llew's face had been characterised by openness while Eddie had a slightly shifty look; Llew's eyes had been frank and friendly, Eddie's were narrow and calculating. He had put on weight around his middle so that he was now solid rather than whippy but curiously it gave him no substance. Harry did not like him.

'Come in, Eddie,' he said easily, concealing his feelings. 'Have a seat.'

Eddie glanced at the watch which he wore on a chain across his waistcoat.

'I can't be too long. I have some calls to make. Business, you know.'

Once upon a time Eddie had set up as an estate agent in the town but it had not been a success. Now he made his living selling insurance door-to-door.

'I won't keep you long, but I thought it was best to ask you to call in when you were passing. It's a bit more private here than most places.'

Eddie's eyes narrowed. 'Why should we want privacy?'

'Because I'd rather no one overheard what I have to say to you.' Again Harry indicated the chair. 'For goodness sake sit down man. I can't talk while you're bobbing about there.'

Eddie sat. 'Go on then. It's about this business of you being put forward as a candidate for prospective Labour member, I suppose.'

'Well no, actually, it's not,' Harry said. 'It's about you, Eddie, and since you're in a rush I'll come straight to the point. I have reason to believe that you have been taking backhanders in exchange for contracts we arrange on the council.'

Eddie's jaw dropped. If Harry had had any doubts that his suspicions were correct they were dispelled in that moment; Eddie's guilt was written all over his face. Then he quickly recovered himself.

'What a bloody awful thing to say!'

'It's true though, isn't it?'

His directness disconcerted Eddie once more. A dark flush rose in his cheeks. 'And what proof have you got, I'd like to know?' he demanded.

Harry sat back in his chair, the leather patched elbows of his sports coat resting on the rounded wooden arms. 'At the moment, none.'

'Well then, I ought to have you up for libel!' Eddie blustered.

'I dare say if I did a little investigation I could come up with the proof without too much trouble,' Harry continued smoothly. 'Take that load of stuff you've had delivered to build yourself an air raid shelter for one thing. It shouldn't be too difficult to discover whether that was paid for, and if it wasn't the fact that it was you who swayed the council to give a contract to Thorne Sand and Gravel would look decidedly fishy. Then there's the business about Welsh's drainage system up at Riddicks Cross. And they are just two instances. I could name others, but I won't. I'm sure you get the gist of what I'm saying.'

'I can have an air raid shelter if I like! Nothing wrong in that!'

'Not if you pay for it like everyone else, no. But I don't think you did. Notice I say "think". The point is, Eddie, if I *knew* I'd have to do something about it and that would be very embarrassing for all concerned. Which is why I'm having a quiet word with you about it rather than going out for the proof I'm sure I'd find if I did.'

Eddie's face turned an even deeper shade of red.

'What are you going to do about it then, Harry?' he asked.

'At the moment, nothing. I don't want to cause a scandal. It wouldn't be good for the council or for the party. But if ever I have cause to suspect again that you're doing your eye good I shall have no alternative but to ask for an investigation.'

'I see.' Eddie blundered to his feet. 'You Halls are all the same, aren't you? Too damned big for your boots.'

'There's no need to be offensive,' Harry said steadily.

'And I hope you're not about to bring my sister into this because if you do I shall feel a good deal less charitable.'

Eddie snorted, on the point of saying more, then thought better of it.

'I won't detain you any longer,' Harry went on. 'I've said what I had to say and I hope that will be the end of it.'

'It won't be the end because I shan't forget this in a hurry!'

'Well, that's up to you, Eddie.' Harry stood up. 'I'll see you at council. Close the door on your way out, will you?'

For a moment Eddie glared, then turned and stormed out of the office. As the door slammed after him Harry sat down again, sighing. He rather thought that when Eddie Roberts had had time to cool down and think things through he would see sense. There would be no more suspect contracts and payments in kind through the back door. But Harry was in no doubt as to one thing. Like Amy before him he had managed to make a dangerous enemy.

At eight o'clock on Good Friday evening the bar at the Miners Arms was already crowded. All the regulars were there but tonight it was Alec Hall, usually one of the quieter of the customers, who was the centre of attention. Tomorrow he was due to be married and everyone was anxious to buy him a drink, make a joke at his expense, or hand out a piece of advice.

'Drink up, lad, and I'll get thee another,' Ewart Brixey said, draining his own glass. 'This be your last night of freedom. You might as well make the most of it!'

'I'm all right, Ewart, thanks all the same. I've still got half left.'

'Drink up!' Ewart insisted. 'We don't want you

riding home on that bike o' yourn tonight. We be going to carry you!'

'Leave the poor bugger alone,' Stanley Bristow interjected. 'Don't you take no notice of 'im, Alec. You'll want a clear head when you walk down that aisle tomorrow morning.'

'And all your strength tomorrow night!' Tommy Clements joked. There was a roar of appreciative laughter but Alec found it impossible to join in.

He had never felt so trapped since he was four years old and starting school, he thought. He'd hated it, hated the teacher, sour sarcastic Miss Williams, hated the smell of the coke-burning stove that gave out a great deal of smoke but very little heat, hated being made to lie down on a mat for three quarters of an hour every afternoon to have a sleep. He had run away several times but whenever he did his mother had taken him back; his mother, whom he had thought he could rely on to make things come right, dragging him along the street and saying firmly: 'I'm sorry, Alec, you've got to go. They'll put the attendance man on to me if you don't.' Trapped. Trapped. The glory of Friday afternoons, leaving the playground and knowing that for the whole weekend he would be free; the sick weight inside him on a Sunday night because tomorrow it would start all over again – at least until the holidays.

But there weren't any holidays in marriage. You were stuck with it for life. It was worse than going to prison when you came to think about it – there was no remission for good conduct. Alec took a swig of his beer, wishing he could drink himself into oblivion but it wouldn't do any good. He'd just have a thick head tomorrow to add to his troubles.

'You've got a good girl there,' Stanley ruminated. 'I always liked Joan.'

'Nothing worse than being married to a shrew,' Walter Clements said.

154

The men were silent for a moment. They all knew Walter was thinking of Ada, his first wife. She had been a shrew and no mistake. And a slut into the bargain. But she was Tommy's mother for all that and with Tommy sitting across the table it was not something you could mention.

'Trouble is you'm stuck with 'em,' Stanley Bristow said. 'That's why I never married. Give me horses every time. You know where you are with a horse.'

'You'd have a job getting a horse to keep you warm in bed at nights though!' Ewart joked.

'True enough. And there's plenty of blokes landed with a woman they don't want through looking for a warm bed *afore* they got married,' Tommy put in.

'More fools them,' said Stanley.

Alec pushed back his chair. Suddenly he couldn't stand the ribaldry and innuendo any longer. It was choking him up, just as the thought of getting married tomorrow was choking him up.

'Where be you going, Alec?' Ewart asked. 'You sit down. The drinks tonight are on us!'

Alec drained his glass. The bar was swimming round him, the warmth and the noise and the smoke all part of the nightmare.

'I'm going out for a breath of fresh air,' he said. 'I'll see you later.'

He went out. His bicycle was parked at the foot of the stone steps and he wheeled it across the road trying to make some sense of his chaotic emotions.

I can't do it! he thought. I can't marry her. Stanley is right, she *is* a good girl, but I can't spend the rest of my life with her. Not now. Once upon a time I thought it was just me, not wanting to be tied down. I thought perhaps everybody felt this way and got over it. Or if they didn't then I was just peculiar, couldn't have natural feelings for a woman.

But that was before Bryda.

You're mad – bloody mad! he told himself but it made no difference. The feelings which had been missing where Joan was concerned were all there for Bryda. Yet the funny thing was that scarcely a thing had happened between them which was not strictly proper.

Since the night when he had changed the light bulb for her he had spent many hours in her kitchen but for the most part they had only talked of everyday happenings, Alec drinking a bottle of beer (which he now took with him in case Eric should notice his store being depleted), Bryda doing some of the interminable chores that came with running a home and looking after a family. Sometimes she ironed, sometimes she darned, once she had been baking – an apple pie and a treacle tart which filled the kitchen with a smell of mouthwatering sweetness. But apart from the occasional touch of hands which set Alec trembling with desire they remained behind the barriers of propriety. The unwritten rule was there between them – she had a husband, he had a fiancée. Whatever they felt for one another they were going to have to live as neighbours.

Perhaps in his heart Alec had been nursing a dream that one day he would take her away from that brute of a husband of hers to a world where they could be together openly and he could banish the shadows from her eyes forever. But if so it had been just that – a dream, and one that was all the more impossible as the remorseless machine that controlled his life rolled along, sweeping him with it. He had agreed to marry Joan and that was all there was to it. He accepted it as a fact of life.

Until the night before his wedding when he suddenly knew that he simply could not go through with it.

The knowledge came to him like a bolt from the blue, frightening him into immobility. He stood in the centre of the road, his bicycle propped against him. He couldn't go through with it. He couldn't promise to love, honour and keep Joan as long as they both should live when the only person he wanted in the whole world was going to be living on the other side of a brick wall. But what the hell was he going to do about it? How could he pull out at this late stage? Everything was ready, even the bridesmaids' dresses which the dressmaker had sweated over late into the night. Some of the guests had already arrived, Uncle Jack and Aunt Stella had driven up from Minehead and were staying with his grandmother in Greenslade Terrace, and Joan's cousin Betty had arrived from Yorkshire. Everything would have to be cancelled. He went cold at the thought. Yet the insistent demon was darting inside him now.

You can't marry her. It wouldn't be fair to either of you. What sort of a life would you have, starting off like this, when all you want is to be with Bryda . . .

A car hooted and he looked up, startled out of his reverie, to see a set of partially hooded lights approaching fast. Quickly, he skipped to the side of the road thinking that if he was to get knocked down and killed it would settle things once and for all – and with no disgrace to Joan.

If only there was someone he could talk to! Uncle Harry, for instance. He was a sensible type and used to sorting out men's problems. But there was no time to go looking for him. And besides, without meaning to the men in the Miners Arms had told him all he needed to know.

'There's nothing worse than being married to a shrew,' Walter Clements had said. Well, that was what Joan would certainly become when she realised he did not love her. He could see it now, the bitterness and the recriminations, the constant urging to change not his ways but his feelings, something which would not be dictated to even by the strongest of wills.

'There's plenty got themselves landed with a woman they don't want through looking for a warm bed afore they got married,' had been Tommy's comment. True, very true, for him as for all the others. But mostly they had been trapped because there was a baby on the way. This was not so in his case. In the beginning he had thought there might be. But Joan had told him it was all right, she hadn't fallen.

Good Joan. Honest Joan. She could have made him believe otherwise and he would never have left her, unwed, to bring up his nipper. But she had told him the truth and now he was going to penalise her for it.

No, not penalise. She deserves more than I can give her, Alec thought. And the sooner I tell her so the better. Filled with dread though he was at the thought of the scene ahead of him, for the first time for weeks Alec also felt elated – and in control of his own fate.

He mounted his bicycle and pedalled along the New Road, the only flat road out of the centre of Hillsbridge, towards Joan's home.

'I don't believe it, Alec. I don't believe what you're saying!'

Joan stood in the little front room surrounded by the trappings of her forthcoming marriage. Her dress covered with an old white sheet to keep it clean and hide it from the gaze of visitors hung from the curtain rail. On the table the presents were arranged, each topped with a gift card, while a sheet of wrapping paper, eagerly torn from one present and still forming the rough shape of the box it had covered, lay discarded in a corner.

'I'm sorry, Joan,' Alec said wretchedly.

'Buy *why*?' Joan cried. 'You can't do this to me, Alec! Everything is arranged. Everything! All these presents – look!' She swept a distracted hand in the direction of the table. 'You can't call it off now! You can't!'

'I've got to,' Alec said. 'It wouldn't be fair to you.'

'Fair!' She was almost hysterical. 'You think it's *fair* to come here the night before our wedding and tell me you're not going to marry me? It's crazy. That's what it is. You've gone crazy!'

'No, I'm seeing sense. It's a bit late, I know, but . . .'

'Late? I should damn well think it is! Well I'm telling you *I* shall be there in the morning and . . .'

'Well I won't,' Alec said.

'Oh my God!' Joan ran to the door. 'Mum! Dad! Come here, please! Alec says he's not going to marry me!'

Her parents, alerted by the commotion, were in the hall outside. They came rushing in, their faces pictures of disbelief and distress.

'What's going on? What's all the shouting about?'

'Alec's calling it off. He's calling the wedding off!'

'He can't be!' Joan's mother cried. 'Alec, you can't be!'

'He is – ask him!'

'I'm sorry,' Alec said woodenly. 'Yes, it's true. I can't go through with it.'

'Oh my Lord!' Joan's mother looked on the verge of collapse.

'Now steady on – wait a minute.' Her father was struggling to remain calm. 'This is just wedding nerves. Everybody has them, lad.'

'No, it's not that,' Alec said. 'I should never have said I'd marry her. I know that now and . . .'

'You mean you've been leading my girl on? All this time?'

'Not leading her on, no . . .'

'What else do you call it? Well you can't pull out now. It's too late for that.'

'It's not too late till the ring's on her finger,' Alec said.

159

'And what are we supposed to do?' Joan's mother cried. 'Alec, for goodness sake, you'll break her heart. Look at her. How can you do this to her?'

Alec looked at Joan and almost weakened. Her plump pretty face was ravaged, her hair tumbled from running her fingers through it. She was not crying yet, the shock was too deep for tears. They would come later and he hated to think of her crying. But, however upset she was it was better than sentencing her to a life without love.

'I can't go through with it,' he persisted.

'And what about all the expense?' Joan's father thundered. 'This has cost us a packet, you know. The cake – trifles – sherry for the toasts . . .'

'Her dress and the bridesmaids',' her mother wailed. 'And the Minister. What will the Minister say?' Another thought occurred to her. 'Why don't you go and see him now?' she urged. 'He'll talk to you, Alec. You'll feel different if you both go and talk to the Minister.'

'No, I won't,' Alec said. 'Look, I'll see you right about the expense. I'll pay you back bit by bit I promise. But I can't go through with it.'

'What about your mother? Does she know?'

'Not yet. I thought I ought to tell Joan first.'

'What's she going to say?'

'I don't know.'

'No, I'll bet you don't! Go and get her in, Arthur. For goodness sake go and get his mother!'

'She won't change my mind either,' Alec said. He was shaking yet he had never been more certain that he was doing the right thing than he was at this moment. 'Nobody is going to change my mind.'

'Oh my Lord! My Lord!'

'I'm sorry,' he said again. He turned and walked out of the room. Joan's father made to go after him, then thought better of it.

'God rot you!' he shouted. The words echoed in the hall and filled Alec's ears. 'God rot you for doing this to my daughter!'

Alec did not turn around. He just kept walking out into the night.

He should have gone home, he supposed. He should have gone home and broken the news to his own mother and father. But he simply could not face another row now. They would hear soon enough – if they hadn't heard through the wall already. Joan's mother and father would be ready enough to rush around and paint it large and scarlet with him the villain of the piece.

Which was what he deserved to be, he supposed. The villain leaving the girl at the altar. But it wasn't all his fault, dammit. Joan had pursued him relentlessly for as long as he could remember. He had been too weak to resist. Well, just in time he had realised he had to stop being weak and make a stand for all their sakes.

But facing his mother and father was not a pleasant prospect. They wouldn't rant and rave as Joan's parents had – it was not their way. But they would be upset to think he was letting Joan down and there would be discussions long into the night as to what to do about the cancellation, the guests, the presents. Well, he'd said his piece. He had offered to pay any expense. And as far as he was concerned the guests could take their presents back with them when they left tomorrow. He could feel no emotion about it. All that had been spent, leaving a sort of flatness. And relief.

That still left the house, of course. God knew what they would do with that. Unless he was to live in it himself. He could keep an eye on Bryda then. Or more. If he could persuade her to leave her husband perhaps she would move in with him . . .

161

He was pedalling back along the New Road without any clear idea where he was going. Not the Miners Arms, certainly. He rode past the door quickly hoping no one would come out and see him. If he couldn't face the thought of his family just now, how much less could he take the crude jokes of the mates who still thought he was going to be a bridegroom tomorrow. Automatically he turned left, free wheeling down into Combers End. Past the drapers shop, past the fish and chip café, past the Palace Cinema where his grandmother had once worked as a cleaner. The road flattened out and he started pedalling with urgency, heading for the cottages at the lower reaches of Purldown.

No lights were showing at the windows – the blackout held. He fished his keys out of his pocket, fumbled to get them in the lock, dropped them. He was on his hands and knees scrabbling around in the dark to retrieve them when her door opened and a crack of light streaked the black path.

'Alec! Is that you?'

'Yes.'

'What are you doing here? I thought you'd be busy with the wedding tomorrow.'

He straightened up. He could see her slight form silhouetted in the doorway.

'No . . .' he hesitated. 'Can I come in, Bryda?'

'If you like. Eric is out playing cribbage.'

She opened the door and he followed her into the kitchen. She had been knitting; a ball of wool, needles and a length of half-finished garment lay on the chair. She removed it to the table.

'I'm really surprised to see you tonight, Alec. I never thought . . .'

'It's all off,' he said.

'What's off?' she asked, uncomprehending.

'The wedding. I called it off.' Because of you, he wanted to add. But he did not.

'Off?' she repeated. 'You mean you're not getting married?'

'No. I couldn't do it.'

'Oh poor Joan!'

'Never mind Joan,' he said. 'I don't feel so hot about it myself.'

And suddenly all the emotion that had turned to flatness was emotion again.

'Oh Christ,' he said. 'What have I done?'

She came to him putting her arms around him, asking no more questions, and this time it was she who was the comforter.

'Oh Alec, Alec . . .'

He buried his face in her shoulder and without realising it he was crying, silent tears forming in his eyes and running down his face.

'Don't,' she whispered. 'If you really didn't want to then you did the right thing. It may seem awful now but not nearly as awful as being married to the wrong person.'

'I know. I know.'

As the torment subsided a little he began to be aware of her nearness, not just as a comforter but as a woman and small barbs of fire ran through his veins.

'Oh Bryda,' he moaned.

In all these weeks they had barely touched. Now the contact unleashed the volcano within and they were kissing, clinging, exploring, their desperation for one another blinding them to everything else.

'Bryda, I love you. I couldn't marry her. I love you.'

'And I love you. Oh Alec . . .'

The oilcloth floor was covered only by a couple of bright rag rugs but it might have been a bed of silk and down. With a passion wilder than Alec would have believed possible they sought one another and it was even better than he had know it would be. Their mutual longing for one another swept them to heights neither had dreamed of, then let them slowly back into a valley of contentment. For a long while they lay without speaking as if they knew that to speak would be to break the spell. Then, as sanity returned she pulled away, getting up and straightening her clothing.

'You'd better go,' she said.

He looked at her in disbelief. 'What do you mean?'

'It's getting late. Eric will be home.'

'But . . .' He got up, buttoning his trousers. This was all backwards. When he and Joan had made love it had been she who had asked for the commitment afterwards. Now . . . 'What are we going to do?' he asked. 'Us – you and me.'

'What can we do?'

'But we – I love you, Bryda. And you feel the same – you know you do.'

'I'm a married woman.'

'But he's a pig. No, worse than a pig. A pig wouldn't do what he does to you.'

'He is my husband.'

'You could leave him. Come away with me.'

'Where?'

'I don't know. Anywhere.'

'But – what would you do?'

'I don't know that either. But it doesn't matter, does it? At least we'd be together.'

'Oh Alec, if only we could!'

'We can. We can do anything! God knows my name will be mud in Hillsbridge now I've jilted Joan. We could go . . .' He thought of Uncle Ted doing well in Australia. 'We could emigrate. Make a fresh start the other side of the world.'

'Oh Alec!' She looked undecided. For a glorious moment it all seemed possible. 'What about little Beryl?'

'She'd come with us. I'd look after her like my own.'

'Oh Alec!'

The back door opened.

In all the crazy elation of the last minutes they had both forgotten Eric, due home from his cribbage match. Now he stood in the doorway, a big rough-looking man, raincoat buttoned around his burly chest, cap pulled well down over his coarse-featured face.

'Eric – you're home!' Bryda said, her voice breathy and nervous.

He ignored her. 'What are you doing here?' he asked Alec.

'He just popped in. He is going to be our neighbour you know.'

'Then he'd better learn to stay in his own bloody house hadn't he?'

'Eric – you're ever so wet. It's raining out, is it? Take your coat off . . .' She ran to him as if to help him out of his coat.

Eric looked at Alec, bone dry without a coat, and his eyes narrowed.

'It's been raining an hour or more. How long has he been here that you didn't know?'

'Look here, Eric . . .' Alec began, but Eric's attention was now centred on Bryda. Beneath his gaze her hands flew to tidy her hair and fasten a button on her dress. Her face was flushed, the guilt written all over her.

A spasm of fury distorted Eric's face. His hand shot out and the flattened back of it caught Bryda full in the mouth. She staggered back, collided with the arm of the chair and sat down hard.

'Bloody bitch!' he spat at her. 'You're bloody cuckolding me, aren't you?'

Alec stepped between them. 'Leave her alone! If you want to hit someone, hit me! Go on!'

Bryda jumped up, blood trickling from the corner of her mouth, and grabbed Eric's right arm with both hands. 'Stop it! Stop it, do you hear? Go, Alec! You'd better go!'

'And leave you to him? Not bloody likely!'

'You little bastard!' Eric shook himself free of Bryda like a bull disentangling himself from a bramble. She staggered again, still groggy, and Eric came at Alec with raised fists. Alec sidestepped and Eric cannoned into the table so that the sugar basin bounced off and shattered on the floor in a welter of sugar and shards of china.

'Please go, Alec!' Bryda screamed. 'He'll kill you!'

As Eric rushed at him again Alec grabbed the first thing that came to hand to defend himself – an ornamental brass toasting fork. Holding it by the prongs he swung it at the charging Eric. The carved emblem on the handle caught Eric on the cheek and he checked, then came on, roaring with fury. Alec sidestepped and swung again. The handle of the fork connected with Eric's temple, the man's own momentum giving the blow extra force. To Alec's amazement he went down like a skittle, crashing against the corner of the range.

Christ I've killed him! Alec thought in panic.

Eric tried to rise and fell back again. Bryda flew across the kitchen dropping to her knees beside her husband. Blood was seeping from his cheek; an angry weal showed on his temple where the fork had caught him.

'Eric!' she screamed.

'Bastard!' Eric muttered, stunned as much by his fall as by Alec's blows.

Alec advanced, holding the toasting fork threateningly. 'Try again and you'll get some more! Bryda – get Beryl and come with me.'

'No!' She pulled a handkerchief out of her sleeve, dabbing at Eric's bleeding face. 'For goodness sake, Alec, go! Haven't you done enough?'

'I'm not leaving without you.'

'Don't be so foolish. What are you thinking of?' She

166

was crying now from pain and fright. 'I never thought it would come to this. Oh, get out! Get out!'

Alec took a step back, bewildered by the venom in her tone. 'But . . .'

'Get out! I'm not going anywhere with you. Can't you understand that? Oh, just leave us alone!'

'But he . . .'

'I'm used to him. We were all right before you came. You've just made things a hundred times worse.' She was still dabbing obsessively at the blood on Eric's cheek. 'Don't you understand? He's my husband!'

'Get out, Hall!' Eric said. He was beginning to recover himself a little. 'And if I see you around here again I swear you'll wish you'd never been born.'

'Go, Alec, for pity's sake – go!' Bryda moaned.

For a moment Alec stood there looking at them, then he flung the toasting fork down on the table and went to the door.

'Bryda . . .' he said helplessly.

But she was still on her knees beside Eric, ignoring him. Long after he had stumbled out into the dark wet night the picture remained imprinted on his mind.

'Oh my Lord, whatever next!' Charlotte said. 'Whatever can our Alec be thinking of?'

'Well, there you are, Gran. I thought you'd like to know right away.'

In an effort to maintain normality Charlotte crossed to the hob that jutted out over the open fire, turning the saucepan of potatoes which sat there simmering gently.

The last few days seemed to have comprised nothing but a series of shocks. First Jim arriving at the door on what should have been Alec's wedding day. Charlotte had been up early and was already dressed in the smart black silk dress which came out for special occasions; her black straw hat and a flower which she intended to

167

pin to the matching silk coat lay in readiness on the table. When Jim had told her the wedding was off she could hardly believe it and later, when she heard the story of what had happened between Alec and Eric Latcham, she had trembled again for the story resurrected too many memories she would have preferred to forget.

'Thank the Lord he didn't kill him!' she said with feeling and James knew she was remembering the terrible business when Ted had 'gone after' Rupert Thorne who had seduced his beloved Becky. Ted had done no more than Alec had done but by a stroke of ill fortune Rupert had died and Ted had stood trial for his murder.

'Thank the Lord it ended there!' Charlotte had said. 'They'll get over it in time, I suppose. But I wish it hadn't happened, all the same.'

And now this. Here was May, Alec's sister, standing in the kitchen and telling Charlotte that Alec had gone off to a Bath recruiting office and signed on for the army. Again, Charlotte had experienced a sense of *déjà-vu*. Fred had done the same, and Ted. Ted had ended up wasting years of his life in a prison camp and Fred had never come back at all. The war to end all wars it was supposed to have been. That was the reason her boy, along with thousands of others, had laid down his life. And what had happened? Less than twenty years later and it was all happening again. Only this time it was Alec, her grandson, who would be marching off to God knew where.

And all because of love. It was just like Ted all over again. Charlotte stared down at the bright coals in the grate and let the patterns dance before her eyes. Suddenly she felt very old. Life was like a switchback ride at the funfair, round and round, up and down, only the trouble was you couldn't get off. Not until the very end. And even then who knew what would happen?

I'll still be up there worrying about them as I twang my harp, Charlotte thought with a touch of wry humour.

Aloud she said: 'Where is he going, and when?'

'We don't know yet, Gran. He'll have to train first, of course. We'll let you know the moment we hear anything.'

Charlotte nodded. 'I wish you would.'

After May had gone she sat down in her easy chair resting her legs for a moment. Her ankles swelled badly these days, sometimes forming rolls over the top of her shoes.

'Oh, the silly boy!' she said softly. 'Let's just hope he won't be mixed up in the worst of it. This is going to break our Sarah's heart, especially coming on top of the rest of it. I know she's in a terrible state now about all the goings on.'

James wheezed and covered his mouth with a thin hand in which the veins, dark with coal dust, stood out in cords and knots. His blue eyes were rheumy and distant.

'Never mind, m'dear,' he said, resorting to his usual calm acceptance. 'Worse things happen at sea, you know. Worse things happen at sea!'

8

By the end of May when the horse chestnut trees at the Hillsbridge end of the New Road were heavy with fragrant mauve and white cones and the flowers in the dusty beds beneath them were beginning to bloom into a carpet of red, white and blue, the towns folk had forgotten the stir which had been caused by Alec Hall jilting Joan Tiley and getting into a fight with Bryda Latcham's husband, Eric. They had even forgotten the excitement of hearing that Harry Hall might be selected as prospective Labour Candidate for the constituency. For the war which throughout the winter had seemed so distant and unreal had suddenly erupted.

Hitler's troops had rampaged through France, driving the Allied force back until they were trapped on the beaches of Dunkirk, and the people of Hillsbridge along with the rest of the country had followed the news of their evacuation by a flotilla of small boats with a mixture of dismay and stubborn pride.

Unbelievably, Hitler was on the doorstep now, kept at bay only by the narrow moat of the English Channel. Hearts beat faster but faces remained set with stoic calm and even optimism. 'Let him try to take us the way he's taken France! Just let him try . . .'

More young local men were conscripted; every day it seemed there was news of someone else receiving their call-up papers and all those between the ages of twenty and twenty-eight who had not yet registered were required to do so by the twenty-fifth of the month. The Home Guard were busy drilling and arranging defensive fall-back positions should Hitler penetrate the coastal defences – in one practice at South Compton the entire unit had to be removed from one side of the barrier they had erected to the other when it was realised that any Germans marching inland from the coast would come upon their undefended rear. The auxiliary services, too, were all busy and though recruitment was still voluntary, rumour had it that before long service would be 'frozen' and none of the present number of air raid wardens, amateur policemen, firemen or first aiders would be able to resign.

The issue of gas masks was now complete – every man, woman and child had theirs in a cardboard box under the stairs – and they were advised to practise with them regularly. Everyone had to carry a registration card with them at all times. All signposts and station signs had disappeared and even the directions on AA boxes had been removed as the Government tried to ensure that should the Germans arrive as they were threatening to do there would be not a single tell-tale sign to let them know their whereabouts.

But most noteworthy of all was the news which broke towards the end of the month. At last the town had a real live hero of its own – Marcus Spindler, younger son of Sir Richard, owner of Hillsbridge Collieries and half the town besides.

Marcus Spindler had always been very much Hillsbridge's 'golden boy'. Whilst Henry, the elder son, was a serious young man who had been raised and educated as heir apparent to the Spindler estates which stretched far beyond the Colliery Company, Marcus had been allowed to shine in his own way. At his public school he had discovered more of an aptitude for sport than academic excellence – and since the school was famous and not more than five miles from Hillsbridge, his exploits were frequently reported in the *Mercury*. From school he had somehow managed to secure a place at Oxford and there he had gained the honour of two

171

'blues' – one in cricket, the other in rugby football. The *Mercury* had emblazoned his picture on the front page, and once again the people of Hillsbridge had murmured proudly: 'He's done well. You've got to hand it to him – he's done well!'

When the Spindler's chauffeur-driven car passed through Hillsbridge many people were still old-fashioned enough to tip their caps. And Marcus, charmer that he was, would nod and smile so that the same people would compare him with his rather shy elder brother and say 'He's not stuck up, either. He could be, but he's not!'

When war had come, Marcus Spindler had been one of the first to be called upon to serve his country. As a Captain in the TA he had been offered a commission in the regular army and Hillsbridge had seen him leave resplendent in his smart new uniform – the Welsh Guards. They would have liked him to be in the Somersets, but no matter. Wherever he was, Marcus Spindler would do them proud.

Now they knew he had not disappointed them. He and his company had been ambushed by a German patrol in Normandy during Hitler's push to the Channel coast, so the story went, and in the short bloody skirmish that had ensued they had all been killed. All but Marcus, who had been wounded in the leg and left for dead. But Marcus was not dead, far from it. With the same dauntless spirit which had helped him to carry his team to victory on the sports field he had somehow managed to drag himself over miles of rough country to find the rest of his battalion and warn them of Germans in the vicinity. Only then had he collapsed from exhaustion and loss of blood.

The rumour going round Hillsbridge was that he was going to be decorated, though all reports of the incident in the *Mercury* were necessarily muted for security purposes. Well, a decoration meant anything from the

Victoria Cross down. Hillsbridge, with loyalty and pride for its 'golden boy' in full bloom, was certain it must be the Victoria Cross.

That summer, when there was so little to be cheery about, it was a bright spot in a darkening sky. And as the storm clouds gathered the story was passed from mouth to mouth, everyone adding a little embellishment of their own, yet certain of the core of truth, nonetheless.

Marcus Spindler had showed the world that Hillsbridge was a place to be reckoned with. Where he had led the rest of them could follow.

Harry's interview for selection as prospective Labour candidate was set for a Saturday afternoon in June – to allow good time for the other three hopefuls to travel to the Party headquarters in the small market town some seven miles from Hillsbridge, Harry supposed.

The family had an early lunch, Elaine and Marie were sent off to spend the afternoon with Gussie, and Harry and Margaret set off in the car, Harry smartly dressed in his best grey suit with an appropriate red tie, Margaret wearing the dress she had considered most suitable – a pretty but modest floral print in shades of green with a matching jacket since she had nothing red in her wardrobe.

'It's funny really, I feel I have to impress though I've known most of the committee all my life,' Margaret said as they drove through the rolling green countryside. She was feeling ridiculously nervous and from Harry's silence she could tell he was, too, though on the surface he appeared calm.

The Party headquarters was in a square and rather dilapidated building in the oldest part of the town. Harry parked the car and they went up the flight of crumbling stone steps and into the small anteroom. Two of the other hopefuls were already there with their wives, sitting on the hard rickety sit-up-and-beg chairs and eyeing one another suspiciously. As Harry and Margaret went in they transferred their attention to him – perhaps because Roly Everard the agent immediately approached them in friendly manner, slapping Harry on the back and greeting Margaret with a kiss on the cheek.

'Good to see you both. You managed to find enough petrol to get here then? The first candidate is in with the Committee now so it will be another hour or so before they get to you. They're seeing you last,' he explained.

His wife, Gladys, another faithful party worker, emerged from the minute kitchen.

'How about a cup of tea?' she offered.

'Sounds just the job!' Harry said heartily but Margaret declined, trying to hide her nerves. It was going to be a long afternoon and the last thing she wanted was to be desperate to spend a penny during Harry's interview.

As they waited they made small talk but Margaret could see that Harry was becoming preoccupied and she guessed he was worried about the speech he was going to have to make. Harry worried about making speeches just as her father had done, she knew. Harry was no natural orator, either, and all his speeches were carefully prepared and practised endlessly in front of the bathroom mirror, though he was far better at the quick off-the-cuff rejoinder than her father had been. His job had prepared him for that, she supposed.

Slowly the minutes ticked by. The first candidate came out of the interview room looking rather pleased with himself and Harry's heart sank. The man looked a natural, big and bluff with an Honest Joe face and a flatteringly receding hairline, but when Harry heard him make a sotto voce remark to his wife about 'country folk' in a London accent he allowed himself to

174

hope that perhaps the man had overreached himself. It was all too easy for city folk, especially those from the capital, to underestimate the know how and ability of those they might regard as bumpkins and such an attitude would not go down well with the Committee who would brand it as 'cocksure'. The second candidate emerged looking less happy, the third decidedly disgruntled. And then it was Harry's turn. He and Margaret were ushered into the Committee Room where the eight-man executive sat ranged along the big old polished table. All familiar, friendly faces – except one. Harry was aware of Eddie Roberts' baleful gaze and felt his heart sink. If Eddie could make things difficult for him he would do it. Eddie was a man looking for revenge.

'Afternoon Hall, Mrs Hall. Thank you for coming.' Like Margaret, William Terry, the Chairman, was a teacher, an ex-headmaster and a highly respected union man. But despite knowing both Margaret and Harry well he managed to inject his voice with a modicum of formality. 'Perhaps you would like to tell us why you believe we should select you as our prospective Labour member.'

'Thank you.' Harry launched into his prepared speech and as she listened Margaret watched the faces of the Committee. Mostly interested, though old Fred Hobday, a County Councillor for more years than anyone could remember, looked as though he might be on the point of nodding off, and Eddie Roberts hand resting on his chin, eyes narrowed, was obviously watching for any weakness he could home in on.

Harry finished his speech. He had done well, Margaret thought proudly.

'Right. Now has anyone got a question they would like to ask?' William Terry enquired. 'I know we're all familiar with Harry's views and the work he has done for the Party over the years, but there may be some specific points we would like clarified.'

'Yes. We're all aware of your interest in industrial matters, but this is also a rural community.' The speaker was one of the country dwellers. 'Where do you stand on the issue of farm subsidies, Mr Hall?'

Harry had been prepared for this. 'I'm in favour. Particularly at the moment when we need to grow as much of our own food as possible.'

A few more questions were asked but Eddie had remained silent. Then just as it seemed the interview was at an end he straightened in his chair.

'I'd like to know how you are able to be a committed socialist, Harry, when so many of the closest members of your family have directly opposing interests,' he said.

Heads turned to look at him.

'Would you, for instance, feel able to vote for changes which might spell ruin for your own sister?' he asked smoothly.

Margaret felt her cheeks flush with anger. How dare Eddie bring Amy into this?

'I don't quite understand the question,' Harry said. 'I don't believe it is any part of our policy to ruin good business ventures which employ a number of people simply because they are successful. But let me say here and now that I am fully committed to furthering the cause of the working man and his family. Any legislation which assists that would have my full support, just so long as it's not a case of cutting off one's nose to spite one's face.' He knew he had used a cliché and instantly regretted it. 'My loyalty is totally for the people I would represent. No personal considerations would ever be allowed to interfere with that. On that I give you my word,' he added.

'Quite. I don't think your dedication to the cause is in any doubt, Hall, or we wouldn't have called you here today,' William Terry assured him. 'Now, if there are no more questions . . .'

176

'What a nerve!' Margaret whispered to Harry as they took their place once more in the outer office to await deliberations. 'Eddie knows very well you would never betray your principles for anyone!'

'He was just trying to get at me,' Harry said philosophically. 'I shall have to put up with a good deal worse than that if I'm selected.'

'Well, I very nearly told them what I thought about it!' Margaret continued angrily. 'I know you and Eddie have never seen eye to eye, but all the same . . .'

'How did you think it went?' he asked, changing the subject.

'Oh fine. You were wonderful.' She smiled up at him. 'I'm sure they'll choose you, Harry. It's a foregone conclusion.'

'You weren't that sure on the way here.'

'I was nervous then. That was before I heard you speak.'

'And you're not nervous now?'

'Well, I suppose just a little,' she admitted. 'But I'm sure they'll choose you all the same.'

They had to wait another nerve-racking half hour before the agent popped his head round the Committee Room door and asked Harry and Margaret to step back in. They exchanged glances, aware of the eyes of the other candidates upon them.

'Well, Hall,' William Terry began when they were once again installed in front of the large polished table. 'I expect you know what I'm going to say. We've discussed all the pros and cons and on behalf of the Committee I would like to ask you formally if you would be prepared to stand as prospective Labour candidate for this constituency. The Committee are unanimous in selecting you as their first choice,' he added.

Margaret felt the swell of pride begin within her. She had known it! She had known it all the time! Harry –

prospective Labour candidate. Perhaps Harry – MP!

Harry waited for the bubble of triumph and felt nothing. Flat. Numb. The interview and the tension had taken more out of him than he could have gussed.

But unanimous . . . he glanced at Eddie, sitting and staring impassively at the sheet of paper in front of him on which he had been making notes.. Eddie had voted for him. But why? Because he had seen how the land lay perhaps and had gone along with the majority view to save his own skin? He wouldn't come right out and oppose – Eddie was too devious for that. But it didn't mean he agreed with the Committee's choice and it didn't mean he would make things easy for Harry either. Oh well, the first rule of battle was 'Know your enemy'. Harry knew Eddie right enough, knew every little facet of his twisted nature – or so he thought.

He thrust Eddie and the battles ahead to the back of his mind.

'Thank you very much,' he said, smiling at the Committee. 'I am very honoured that you should put your trust in me. I shall be delighted to do everything in my power to repay that trust. And if we do not return a Labour member at the next General Election I assure you it will not be from lack of effort on my part.'

Margaret beamed thinking how proud and pleased her father would be if he were here now. And once again the thought flipped across her mind like a portent for the future.

Harry Hall MP.

Barbara Roberts was worried. As the war hotted up, coming closer and closer to home she could think of one thing and one thing only – Huw.

News of what he and his squadron were doing was necessarily sketchy for the letters he sent home were heavily censored, but reading between the lines they knew he had flown operational sorties over France and Belgium and been in the skies during the evacuation of Dunkirk. When the squadron was sent north for a week at the beginning of June Ralph had said that would be for recuperation purposes and Barbara had known he must have had a tough time to be in need of recuperation.

Now it was the middle of July, the squadron was at Hornchurch and in the thick of an action that was being dubbed the Battle of Britain. The Germans, still intent on laying siege to the island which alone in Europe was continuing to defy their might, were bombing convoys in the Channel and even attempting a strike at the fighter bases in the south east, and the RAF planes flown by young men like Huw were attempting to hold them back. There were reports of dogfights over the sea, with aircraft, both English and German, spiralling down trailing smoke to explode in a ball of fire or vanish forever.

Just thinking about it made Barbara go cold but she thought about it often all the same, as if to forget for a single moment of a single day would somehow mean disaster for Huw. As long as she was willing him to be all right then he *would* be all right, she told herself, but it was a strain all the same and even more of a strain to keep her anxiety hidden from her mother, from Ralph and especially from Maureen, who only mocked and told her: 'For goodness sake, Babs, there's nothing you can do about it. You might as well put it out of your mind.'

She could not. She did not even want to. It overshadowed everything, even her efforts to plan her own future. It was almost the end of her last term at school now, another week and she would hang up her straw boater for the last time, but she had still not reached any definite decision as to what she would do – enlist for a secretarial course so as to be able to help out with her mother's business as Ralph wanted her to, or try to join one of the women's services as she herself had wanted. It would be good to feel she was doing something towards the war effort, she thought, but if she did she would be sent heavens knew where and that might mean she would not see Huw for years. At least if she was here in Hillsbridge she was on the spot if he was able to get some leave and come home.

Yet if women were made liable for call-up as some said they soon would be the decision would be taken out of her hands. She would have to go. As she and Maureen rattled home on a service bus from Bath one afternoon in late July she stared thoughtfully out of the window, whilst beside her Maureen read a paper novelette which had almost been confiscated by one of the Sisters at school.

It was a hot day, the sky clear and blue above the thick green hedges, the sort of day when it was almost impossible to realise that a war was going on, but it lent no respite to Barbara's anxiety. Was Huw flying now? Was he even at this moment engaging his fire with a German fighter? She pictured him in the cockpit of his Spitfire, face drawn with concentration, and her heart contracted. She was unaware of the warm dusty air blowing in at the half-open door of the bus, unaware of its rattling progress. This daily journey had become such a part of her life that it no longer warranted the slightest attention, except that during the early months of the war services had been badly disrupted so that you never knew how long you would have to wait, or indeed how long the journey would take, for if the bus broke down as it often did there was no 'relief' to come to the rescue. But things were better again now. The bus company seemed to have adjusted to the fact that England was at war and the journey had reverted to being part of the daily pattern.

The bus gathered speed along the straight where

Margaret had met with her accident and began the long descent into Hillsbridge. As it rattled downwards the town came into view gradually above the curve of the hillside, first the broad spread of farmland and rich green fields climing up, up, on the other side of the valley till they reached the distant smudge of trees on the horizon with only the sky, azure blue, above; then the first tiers of cottages which spread like grey fingers across the steepening valley bowl; and lastly the town itself, the tangle of soot-blackened buildings, the railway lines, the yard and the tall brick chimney of Middle Pit where most of the Hall family served out their working lives. 'The Emerald Valley' Amy had once called it in a romantic mood just after her wedding to Ralph, but such a notion had never occurred to Barbara. She neither eulogised it nor blamed it, as some did, for being a blot on the rolling Somerset countryside. It was the place where she had been born and raised, and as much taken for granted as the air she breathed.

Towards the foot of the hill the bus slowed and Maureen raised her eyes from her novelette to see what was causing the delay. Just the train probably. It arrived from Bath at almost the same time as the bus and the girls might have used it had it not been for the fact that the branch line station it ran from was twice as far from their school as was the bus station.

Today the gates were not yet closed. It was not for that that the bus was stopping. But something was going on . . .

'Babs – look! Look, they've got the flags out!'

For one glorious moment as she emerged from her reverie Barbara thought that the war must be over. Why else would anyone fly flags? Then Maureen went on: 'It must be for Marcus Spindler, mustn't it? Gosh, how exciting!'

Barbara wrinkled her nose. 'Why should it be for Marcus Spindler?'

181

'Because he's a hero!' Maureen said impatiently. 'And he's coming home today. They've patched his leg up enough for him to be allowed out of hospital and instead of going on somewhere for convalescence he said he preferred to come home. Mum was talking about it at breakfast.' She gave her elder sister a critical glance. 'You don't listen to a word anyone says to you these days, do you? You're in a dream all the time.'

Because a number of people were milling about in the road near the level crossing the bus had come to a complete stop and Maureen jumped up, jamming her novelette into the pocket of her blazer and climbing over her sister's legs to grab her satchel from the rack.

'Come on, let's get off here while the bus is stopped and see him arrive!'

Reluctantly, Barbara followed suit. She had no special desire to see Marcus Spindler or anyone else arrive – unless of course it happened to be Huw. But Maureen was already halfway down the aisle, cajoling the conductor to let them off.

'This isn't the stop, you know!' he said, with mock severity, but he was a regular on this route and he liked the two girls. 'All right, go on then, just this once,' he said, shaking his head and grinning.

Once in the street the extent of the welcome which had been prepared was more obvious and Barbara and Maureen stopped for a moment, taking it in.

The town silver band, once able to win prizes at competitions from the Albert Hall down but now with its numbers depleted by conscription, was formed up on the platform. At the foot of the station approach a shining Rolls Royce was drawn up and waiting, the chauffeur, peaked cap set squarely on his head, tie knotted firm and tight against his Adam's apple in spite of the warmth of the afternoon, brushed an imaginary speck of dust from the immaculate bonnet whilst keeping one eye on the signal which would announce

182

the imminent arrival of the train. Overhead the bunting fluttered bravely and a large Union Jack had been hung across the parapet of the footbridge which spanned the lines between the two platforms.

Part of one of the platforms had been roped off – to allow Marcus and any other travellers to disembark in comfort, Barbara supposed – a very necessary precaution in view of the size of the crowds. Only the stationmaster, resplendent in his best uniform, and Police Sergeant Button were strutting importantly about in the roped-off section.

'Where do you think is the best place to watch from?' Maureen asked. 'There aren't as many people this side of the line, are there? And we'd have a really good view of him getting into his car.'

'But we'd be quite the wrong side when the train arrives,' Barbara pointed out. 'We wouldn't be able to see the band or anything.'

She opened the small wicket gate beside the large crossing gates and they crossed the lines where the sleepers made a flat path and onto the bit of the platform that was not roped off. Then they slipped along at the back of the waiting crowd and climbed up onto the long bench seat outside the waiting room window.

This caused a few murmurs amongst those who had been waiting longer and whose view was more restricted. There were some remarks about 'people having to sit where your dirty feet are!', but Barbara and Maureen pretended not to hear and before long several children had been hoisted up onto the seat beside them.

'It's like South Compton Fair Day, isn't it?' Maureen said, referring to the sideshows and rides which took over the High Street and Square of the neighbouring town every year on the last Friday in April.

Along the line a signal clanked, closer in it was echoed by another. In his signalbox high above the platform Desie Duery hauled on the wheel and the level crossing gates swung laboriously across the road, meeting in the middle with a small satisfying thud. All eyes turned to look along the line, watching for the first sign of the train rounding the bend alongside the sheds, and in the moment's silence before the band began to play again every ear strained for the unmistakeable sound of wheels on rails and the rhythmic expulsions of steam.

'Just think if we had come home today on the train instead of the bus we could have pretended all this was for us!' Maureen giggled.

The engine came into view and the carriages snaking behind it. The conductor raised his baton and the band struck up once more – 'There'll Always Be An England'.

As the train eased into the platform people began to cheer and wave Union Jacks so that the girls had to crane to see. A small group of dignitaries made their way out of the waiting room and into the roped-off-section of platform.

'Oh look – it's Uncle Eddie Roberts!' Maureen cried.

'Pompous ass,' said Barbara who knew that bad feeling existed between her mother and her uncle. 'Look at him fancying himself. It ought to be Uncle Harry doing the honours.'

As the train stopped old Reuben Tapper hurried forward as fast as his rheumaticky legs would carry him to open the door. Reuben had worked for the S and D for as long as anyone could remember. If it had not been for the war he would have retired last Christmas or so he told anyone who would listen. As it was with strong young men needed for jobs more vital than railway portering Reuben had managed to put off the day when he would hang up his cap for the last time.

Now he flung the carriage door wide stepping smartly back and raising his rather claw-like hand into the parody of a salute. The girls nudged one another and giggled, then the laughter died as a young man in the uniform of an army officer emerged.

'Wow!' Maureen said softly; it might have been an echo of the thoughts of everyone on the platform.

Tall, fair, he looked a little like a modern day Greek god as he stood framed in the open doorway. His face was slightly shaded by the peak of his cap yet this did not detract in any way from the clarity of his features – the clear strong lines of his jaw, the patrician nose and well-shaped mouth. His shoulders were broad beneath the tailored khaki, his hips athletically slim, and he stood so straight that at first glance the ivory topped cane with which he supported himself was hardly noticeable.

The people on the platform cheered so loudly that they almost drowned the band and he smiled, raising his free hand in a wave. Then as the dignitaries approached he started down the steps to meet them, shifting his wounded leg with a deliberation that brought a lump to the throat. It was almost possible to feel his pain and share in his determination that it should not show. The sun lent an aura to the khaki uniform and turned the fringing of fair hair beneath the cap to molten gold as he took that last deep step to the platform and steadied himself once more to proud erectness.

'Gosh, isn't he super?' Maureen gasped.

Barbara said nothing but in her heart she was forced to agree. Not as super as Huw, of course. But there was something about him which could not be denied, something which made the heart skip a beat and started a wave of emotion – pride and admiration, patriotism and pity.

Hillsbridge's own golden boy had come home from the war a hero and they had been here to see it.

Through the dark years that lay ahead it was a moment that neither girl would forget.

9

On a Saturday afternoon in August Harry Hall was cutting his front lawn, sweating a little as he pushed the mower over the uneven ground. He had allowed the grass to get much too long – there never seemed to be time for dealing with it and now the dandelions were sprouting up in the carpet of daisies so he had had to make time. Daisies he did not mind, dandelions really did make the lawn look like a wilderness.

Margaret would have done it if he had let her, but he would not. She had still not fully regained her strength and once when she had dragged the mower out and made a start on the lawn she had been so 'done up' that she had had to leave it and go and sit down and he had expressly forbidden her to do it again.

'It's my job. I don't want you struggling with it,' he had said. 'You can do the weeding and those girls can help you. It's about time they did something about the place. You wait on them as though this was a hotel.'

This afternoon, however, both girls were out. In an effort to give the 'vackies' something to interest them through the long summer holiday, the schools had set an essay project in conjunction with the Royal Society for the Protection of Birds known as the 'Bird and Tree Scheme'. This gave the city bred children an incentive to explore the countryside and lent a purpose to walks, rambles and nature study. Margaret had encouraged both Elaine and Marie to enter into it and today they had gone out immediately after lunch, armed with notebooks and baskets for collecting specimens of leaves and wild flowers. Harry and Margaret were alone for once with nothing to do but tidy the garden and they had set to work with a will. But Margaret seemed to have something on her mind. As he pushed the mower back and forth Harry noticed her sitting back on her heels deep in thought. And she certainly wouldn't be wondering which spike of green was going to turn into a flower and which should be pulled up as a weed, he thought – Margaret was a natural where gardening was concerned.

He stopped mowing, pulling out a handkerchief to mop his forehead.

'Penny for 'em.'

'What?' She looked up, startled.

'Your thoughts. From the look on your face they're worth a good deal more than that, though.'

Margaret straightened her back. Her expression was indeed serious.

'I'm not sure I'm going to tell you. I haven't really thought it through yet.'

'Thought what through?'

She rolled over into a sitting position, looping the skirt of her cotton dress over her knees.

'All right, I will tell you. It's nice to be able to talk without Elaine and Marie listening to every word. I've been offered a job.'

'Oh, have you!' He abandoned the lawn mower and dropped down onto the grass beside her. 'What sort of job?'

'Teaching, of course. They're going to need someone at the Church School from September on. It sounds like the job is mine if I want it.'

'Do you?'

'Well yes, I do. I miss the classroom and the Church School would be so convenient – just down the hill.'

'So what's the problem?'

She smiled. 'I knew you'd say that. You are, for one thing. You're so busy you're never here. And now that you're prospective Labour candidate – well, if a

187

campaign got under way you'd need a full-time wife to support you, not a harrassed working woman.'

'I think it's highly unlikely there will be a campaign just yet,' Harry said. 'Mrs Lincoln is not going to resign until there's a General Election.'

'But her health is a bit suspect isn't it?' Margaret said. 'Maybe she will have to go before then.'

Harry stretched his legs.

'Even if she did it's doubtful there would be a contest. There's a party truce on, remember. In the event of a vacancy the nominee of the sitting party would be returned unopposed. Unless the local committee decided to go against the Party Executive and contest anway, as they did in Kettering. I wouldn't like that. "Unofficial Labour" doesn't have quite the same ring to it. Though I can imagine Eddie Roberts pressing for it for just that reason,' he added thoughtfully.

'So you wouldn't mind if I went for the job,' Margaret asked.

'Not if you think you can cope with it. Not a bit. Though I can think of a job or two I'd rather you were doing. Like being the mother of our child, for instance.'

He saw her face cloud slightly. It still hurt, remembering the baby she had lost, and as yet there was no sign of another on the way. Margaret had tried resolutely to put it from her mind – the more she wanted it the less likely it was to happen, she thought. Perhaps even considering this job was an effort to tempt fate.

The sadness in her eyes and the sweetness of her sunwarmed face stirred him and he reached for her, pushing her back on the newly mown grass.

'Let's start again – like now.'

'Harry!' She rolled away. 'The neighbours could see!'

'Only if they were watching out of their bedroom windows.'

'Well they might be for all you know! Stop it this minute! Just imagine the newspaper headlines if anyone saw you! "Prospective Labour MP behaves indecently." I'd die of shame!'

'How can a man making love to his wife be behaving indecently?' he teased.

'It's where you do it that counts,' she said severely. 'In any case we have a great deal more gardening to do. This lawn is a disgrace!'

'All right, I give in,' he laughed. 'You're a hard woman, Margaret.'

She laughed, then cocked her head to one side, looking up at the sky. 'What's that?'

Harry followed her gaze. The sky which a few minutes ago had been clear blue and empty was suddenly full of planes. German fighters zooming in like angry gnats, Spitfires closing in from the opposite direction to head them off, the rays of the sun catching their fuselages and wings and sending off sparkling shards.

'Oh my God!' Margaret gasped.

Harry grabbed Margaret's wrist, dragging her towards the cover of the hedge. If the fighters were coming, the bombers would not be far behind. As they rolled beneath the leafy laurel he heard them – the drone of their engines making the earth and the air tremble.

'What are they doing *here*?' Margaret squealed. It was the first time that a raid had penetrated this far – they had mostly been confined to the south-east and many of the battles had been fought over the sea.

The guns were firing now; with hands pressed over her ears to shut out the noise she bobbed her head out to see what was happening, then bobbed quickly in again as the spurts of red and orange flashed across the sky like some erratic blow-torch.

Harry was watching over her shoulder.

'The bombers are turning round. They know they

won't get past those Spits. Pray they don't start dumping their bombs for a quick getaway. Christ! – that one's hit!'

Margaret risked another peep and saw the plane angling down with black smoke pouring from it. There was a muffled explosion as it hit the ground somewhere over the crest of the hill and out of sight. Against the blue she saw the billowing white of a parachute. And still the fighters darted and climbed, still the gunfire raked the sky.

'The children!' In the midst of the dogfight she remembered Elaine and Marie, somewhere out in the countryside collecting their nature study specimens, and began scrambling to her feet. 'What about the children?'

Harry grabbed her arm pulling her down again.

'They'll be all right. They'll take cover.'

'But they'll be so frightened!'

'There's nothing you can do, Marg. You don't know where they've gone. They'll be all right.'

For seemingly endless minutes the skirmish continued but the Germans were in retreat now and the battle was moving further away. She saw another plane on fire, losing height with smoke streaming from its wing in a black ribbon, but it was too distant to be sure what it was.

'Is that one of ours or one of theirs?' she asked. Her voice like the rest of her was trembling.

'One of ours, I think,' Harry said. He too sounded shaken. It was the suddenness of the incident which had been so unnerving. One minute a peaceful summer afternoon, the next . . . 'It's all right, they're beating them back. It's over now.'

'But where were they going?' she asked. 'What were they after?'

Harry brushed bits of twig from his shirt. 'Your guess is as good as mine. One of the Wiltshire aerodromes, perhaps. Or the army training camps on Salisbury plain. I don't know. Whichever it was, they won't get them – this time.'

'No,' Margaret agreed. Then the full force of his words hit her. 'This time' he had said, but there would be other times. The war had taken hold in earnest and this was just the beginning. Before it was over there would be many more dogfights in the sky, many bombers seeking to drop their loads of death, many men dying.

'Let's pray we can finish it quickly!' she said.

Margaret and Harry were not the only members of the family to witness the dogfight. Amy, Barbara and Maureen watched it from a bedroom window at Valley View and their faces, white with tension, reflected their thoughts.

It could be Huw up there in one of those Spitfires. It could be Huw, blazing fire and receiving it, bobbing, weaving, ducking. When they saw the plane spiralling down Amy stretched out her hands and the girls took them so that they stood close together in a chain, straining their eyes at the distant darting specks.

Please God, not Huw! Amy prayed silently.

Oh, those poor men! thought Maureen.

And Barbara, holding on to the panic inside her with a supreme effort felt as if all her worst nightmares were taking shape in the daylight. She had known what was going on, of course, but until now had only been able to guess at what it was really like. Now there was no more uncertainty. She was seeing it with her own eyes.

Even when it was over she seemed to see it still and knew it would haunt her dreams throughout the weeks and months to come.

*

Elaine and Marie were down by the river when the planes came. It was a pleasant spot. On both sides the meadows sloped bumpily down, scarred only by cow pats left by the herd of heifers that inhabited the valley and the river meandered cool and clear beneath the overhanging trees. At one point it broadened into a natural pool which Sir Richard Spindler, who owned the land, had leased to the council for a swimming bath and the girls had lingered there for a while, dangling their feet in the water before pressing on upstream, picking their way between the bushes and keeping a sharp eye out for the cows who sometimes lumbered down to the river to drink or take advantage of the shade.

Elaine and Marie did not like cows. Until they had come to Hillsbridge they had never seen one in their lives and although Margaret had told them they were quite harmless they treated the cows with suspicion bordering on terror. They were so *big* and Elaine and Marie disliked their baleful expressions and the way they had of suddenly charging across a field like a herd of wild buffalo.

Today there had been no cows to be seen, however, and the girls had been able to wander about in peace. Marie had picked a few celandines and some wild garlic to go into the basket Margaret had given her; she sniffed her fingers and wrinkled her nose at the strong smell of onions which clung to her skin. But Elaine had not bothered to collect any specimens. She had no intention of bothering to write an essay about birds and flowers or anything else – essays or 'composition' as she called it were strictly for school, not something with which to pass the holidays.

At first, when the planes came the two girls could not understand what was going on. They grabbed hold of one another, dropped their specimen baskets in the thick marshy undergrowth and turned frightened eyes

192

to the sky. They could see nothing; the heavy trees in full leaf hid all but the smallest trace of blue. But when they inched nervously out into the field they were able to see at least some of what was going on and they watched round-eyed with terror.

When it was over Marie began to cry very softly, little mewing sobs.

'I don't like it, Lainey! I want to go home!'

'Don't be soft,' Elaine admonished.

'I do. I want to go home. I want our Mam!' She rubbed at her cheeks with her onion-smelling hands.

'You'd get worse than that in London,' Elaine said. 'Every day, I 'spect. That's why they sent us here.' Her eyes were shining with a peculiar light. She had been a little frightened by the dogfight, though she would never admit it, but now she was excited. The adrenalin, pumping through her veins, was a new experience. 'I'd like it,' she said boldly. 'I'd like to be back in London. But you wouldn't. You're just a baby.'

'I'm not!' Marie protested, wriggling uncomfortably. When the gunfire had started she had wet her knickers; now they felt cold and clammy.

Elaine noticed her gyrations. 'What's the matter wiv you?'

Marie told her, still sniffling.

'There you are! You are a baby! Take them off. We'll hang them out to dry.'

Marie did as she was told and Elaine hung the offending knickers over a branch.

'Yer,' she said, suddenly making up her mind. 'I'm going back to London. I've had enough of this place.'

'You can't. They won't let you,' Marie gulped.

'Just let them try to stop me! I'll find a way!' The adrenalin was making Elaine believe anything was possible.

Suddenly Marie's expression became one of horror. She stood transfixed, her eyes huge, her mouth fallen open.

'Lainey – look!'

'What now?' Elaine began, then as she turned her own voice became a scream.

Just a few inches from her a cow's head was poking through the branches. All bravado forgotten she turned and ran, Marie following her, out into the alien green field where monsters lurked, leaving their specimen baskets and Marie's knickers still dangling from the branch. They went on running and they did not stop until they reached the road.

'I want to go home!' Marie wailed again and this time she did not mean London, but the safety of the house in Tower View.

For once Elaine did not argue with her.

'Do you want to go and see the German plane?' Ralph asked.

He had come home late in the afternoon and brought with him the news that one of the planes that had been hit in the skirmish had come down in a field just over the hill.

'A bit ghoulish, isn't it? Amy said.

'I thought the girls might be interested. It's probably the best chance they'll get of seeing a Jerry aircraft at close quarters.'

'Oh yes, please! Please take us Ralph!' Maureen begged eagerly.

'Barbara?'

Barbara nodded. She was still a little shaken by the afternoon's events but there was a creeping fascination all the same about the German plane.

'Are you coming, Mum?' she asked.

'I suppose so,' said Amy.

They all piled into the family car and Ralph drove up the hill and along the lanes. It was a perfect August evening. In the hedgerows the cow parsley grew taller than a man; out across the fields, thick and green, a hawk hovered in the still blue air. Once again it was hard to realise that this was a world at war and the glimpse of harsh reality which had been revealed to them that afternoon now seemed more like a dream.

Until they saw the plane.

Ralph parked at the field gate and they climbed over and walked along beneath the hedge until it came into view, lying there in the open like a great wounded bird. Surprisingly, it was still almost intact, the black cross on the fuselage clearly visible though a piece of the tail, marked with its swastika, lay some distance away at the edge of the field. Nearby the aircraft lay the unexploded bombs, guarded, as was the wreckage, by stern-faced uniformed men.

'There it is,' Ralph said. 'An ME110.'

They all stared in awe.

'What happened to the men?' Maureen asked.

'One bailed out. The rear gunner we think – they haven't found him yet. They took the others away.'

'Dead?'

'I'm afraid so.'

A Home Guard man recognised Ralph and strolled over.

'One less for the Luftwaffe,' he said cheerfully.

'Yes. Any news about the one who bailed out?'

'Not yet. He's hiding out somewhere. We'll find him, don't you worry.'

Amy shivered. 'I don't much care for the idea of a Gerry roaming around, especially after dark.'

'I expect he's far more scared of you than you are of him,' Ralph told her. 'He's probably been told he'll be shot, or worse, if he's caught.'

'So he will be if he comes anywhere near me. Not shot – but I'd certainly take my umbrella to him!'

Ralph laughed. 'See what I mean? Come on then. Let's go home.'

They turned back towards the lane, but Barbara was still standing looking at the plane as if mesmerised.

'Come on, Babs!' Amy called.

Barbara turned and there was a strange light in her eyes.

'Mum – I've made up my mind,' she said. 'I don't want to go to college. I want to join the WAAF.'

Over the next few days the arguments raged.

'You can't join the WAAF, Barbara. You're not old enough,' Amy said.

'I shall be next year.'

'So why not go to college until then.'

'Because I want to join up as soon as I'm eighteen. That would mean leaving college in the middle of term. It would be just silly.'

'The silly thing is to waste a whole year for no good reason. You were very keen to get your qualifications and take a position with one of the companies until just recently. I don't know what's got into you.'

'I want to join the WAAF.'

'Well, I don't want you to. I might as well tell you that straight.'

'Why not?'

'Why not?' Amy raised her eyes heavenward. 'Hundreds of reasons.'

'Give me one.'

'It could be dangerous. Most of the airfields are in the south-east and that's where the Germans are bombing.'

'Huw's in the south-east. I'd be in no danger at all compared to Huw.'

'That's different. Huw is a young man.'

'Why should it be different?' Barbara argued. 'The only difference I can see is that I am your daughter, and Huw is not your son.'

'I've always treated him as my own!' Amy flared. 'I brought you up as brother and sister and it wouldn't do you any harm to remember that.'

Barbara opened her mouth as if to say something, then thought better of it.

'Anyway, I'm not prepared to argue with you about this,' Amy went on. 'If you're still set on the idea this time next year then I suppose we shall have to think again. For the moment, my lady, you are going to college whether you like it or not. And that is my final word on the subject.'

Barbara hesitated outside the door of the Recruiting Office swallowing at the sudden lump of nervousness which seemed to be constricting her throat. Then she lifted her chin, pushed open the door and went inside.

A stern-faced woman in uniform was sitting at a bare table. Barbara looked at the iron grey hair, mannishly cut, and the tight uncompromising line of the lips and once again her courage almost failed her. Had there been a queue she did not think she could have stood the suspense. As it was there was no time for second thoughts for the woman glanced up at her, grey eyes snapping coldly, and indicated the chair opposite her with a quick jab of her pencil.

'Morning.'

'Good morning,' Barbara said, surprised.

The woman sat back in her upright chair. Behind her recruitment posters pinned to a screen made a colourful backdrop.

'So you want to join the WAAF.'

'Yes,' Barbara said.

'Good. That's the spirit. The more young people who are prepared to volunteer the sooner this war will be over.'

Barbara nodded vigorously. Her sentiments exactly.

What a pity her mother could not see it like that.

At the thought of Amy Barbara felt another qualm of nervousness. What on earth was Amy going to say when she found out what she had done? Barbara pushed the thought to the back of her mind. By the time Amy knew anything about it it would be too late. She would be signed on as a WAAF.

'Name?' The woman was uncapping a pen, all brisk efficiency. Barbara supplied the details.

'Age?' This was the one that had been worrying her. Barbara crossed her fingers tightly in the pocket of her jacket.

'Eighteen.'

'Birth certificate?'

'Oh – yes . . .' Barbara opened her bag and fumbled inside. She had rather hoped they might not ask for her birth certificate. She was not certain it would stand up to inspection, though she had worked on it for half an hour last night with lemon juice and some of Ralph's thick black ink. She handed it over nervously and watched the woman straighten it out on the desk. Not a flicker passed across the woman's face and Barbara breathed a little more easily.

A few more questions then the woman nodded briskly.

'Right. In a moment I'll ask you to sign this. Before you do so I should point out to you that it is a very serious offence to give false information – the penalty for doing so could very well be a jail sentence.'

Her eyes, hard as flint, met Barbara's then glanced obliquely for a moment at the birth certificate lying on the table. Barbara felt her stomach turn to water. She knew. Oh Lord, what had she done? A jail sentence! Oh jeepers!

The woman pushed back her chair and stood up.

'Excuse me. I have something to attend to in the back office. I'll be back in just a moment.'

She disappeared around the screen without a backward glance. For a second Barbara sat as if rooted to the chair then realised – this was her chance. She leaped up, almost knocking over the chair in her haste, grabbed her birth certificate and the completed forms and ran to the door. As she opened it she was terrified she would hear the woman's voice ordering her to stop but she did not and she ran out into the street, not daring to look over her shoulder or stop until she reached the corner and lost herself in the scurry of shoppers.

What a narrow escape! If they'd checked her birth certificate and found it falsified, if they had realised she had lied about her age . . . But they hadn't. Luck had been on her side. The woman had had to leave the room and she'd been able to get away . . .

Her step slowed as a thought struck her. *Had* it been luck – or something else? Had the woman known all the time that she was lying and made the chance for her to escape rather than having her arrested, or whatever it was she would have done? Barbara couldn't be sure. She simply thanked her lucky stars that she was not at this moment being whisked off by a military policeman to answer charges. Next spring she would try again. For the moment she had had quite enough excitement.

Oh Lord, I've got to alter my birth certificate back to the correct date before I can go and see them again, Barbara thought. Why do things never happen this way in romantic novels? Then, girls could even dress as boys to follow their loves to war and get away with it. Whilst she had done something as uninteresting as adding a few months to her age and risked a jail sentence. Life simply wasn't fair.

Feeling very much a failed adventuress Barbara walked to the bus station to catch her bus back to Hillsbridge.

10

Throughout the month of August the Battle of Britain raged on, squadrons of the Auxiliary Air Force and fighter pilots of the Fleet Air Arm now fighting alongside the RAF.

Losses were heavy, though not so heavy as the toll they inflicted on the marauding Germans, and Barbara lived in a constant state of anxiety. There was little evidence in the western corner of England of the battle that was raging over the south-east, but they knew about it all the same and Barbara's supreme moment of pride came when she heard what Mr Churchill had said in the House of Commons: 'Never in the field of human conflict was so much owed by so many to so few.'

Huw was one of 'the few'. But for how much longer could he fly day after day without getting caught? The bombers came now in smaller formations with much heavier fighter escort – the Germans had learned that their famed Luftwaffe were not going to wipe out the aerodromes of Kent and Essex as easily as they had first thought, but they were as determined as ever, sending in wave after wave of planes to try to achieve by sheer weight of numbers what they had earlier been unable to succeed in doing.

Barbara no longer thought about it every moment of every day, for to do so was more than could be humanly endured, but it was there in her heart all the same, a constant weight, an agony of waiting.

Letters arrived for her and for all the family more frequently now but they were shorter and much less detailed as if Huw, too exhausted by a day's flying from the first dawn 'scramble' to the last fading moments of dusk to push his pen across the paper for more than a few lines, yet somehow felt compelled to make contact with those he loved. As if he is afraid in his heart that each day might be his last – though he would never admit it, thought Barbara.

One such letter arrived during the first week of September – the very day that Barbara was due to begin her course of business studies at a commercial college in Bath. She was in her bedroom making sure her bag contained everything she would need when she saw the postman pushing his bicycle up the slope to the gate and she swiftly thrust the last items inside and ran down the stairs.

Amy was in the hall picking up the envelopes from the mat.

'Anything from Huw?' she called eagerly.

'Looks like it.' Amy began ripping open the envelope. 'It's addressed to all of us,' she added, seeing Barbara's face.

'What does it say?'

'Give me a chance!' said Amy. She was as anxious as Barbara though she would never admit it. Then her face whitened. 'Oh Lord, he got shot down!'

Barbara began to tremble. 'Is he all right?'

'All right enough to write,' Amy said shortly.

'What happened? What does he say?'

'I'll read it to you.' Amy took the letter into the dining-room and sat down at the table because her own legs were trembling too much to support her a moment longer. 'It's pretty brief – you know Huw – but here goes. "We were alerted late and didn't have the chance to get high enough before we met the Nasties. That's a pretty fatal situation – you need height and speed to control a fight and we didn't have it. We were sitting ducks. One of my mates was killed and I got a cockpit full of bullets. I think I managed to put a round into the

201

nose of a Heinkel but I couldn't hang around to see. Two 109s got onto me and shot me up. I had to bale out. Landed in a hop field with nothing more than a few cuts and bruises to show for it. But my Spit is a goner and I'm sick about that. Seven notches on her wing and she has to end up as scrap. Suppose I'm lucky not to be scrap, too, but all the same it hurts to lose a kite – especially when they are so damned precious!" There you are, he's unharmed, thank God. But how like Huw to be simply concerned about losing his plane instead of thanking God he escaped with his life! He could have been . . .' She broke off, swallowing hard.

'He's right, of course,' Ralph, who had been listening quietly, said. 'We're losing too many planes every day.'

'How can you talk about planes as if they were more important than men's lives?' Barbara asked passionately.

'I didn't say they were more important. But if we don't keep the numbers up we have no chance of defending this island of ours – and then none of our lives will be worth living,' Ralph said. 'As a matter of fact, I've been wondering if we couldn't do something about it.'

Barbara, re-reading the letter over Amy's shoulder, said nothing but Amy asked: 'Do something? What do you mean?'

'I thought maybe we could raise the money to buy a Spitfire.'

'*We* could?'

'Well – Hillsbridge and the surrounding areas. We could get a committee together and organise fund-raising events.'

'What would it cost?'

'I haven't gone into that yet. Several thousand I should think. But I thought I could start the fund off with a good donation and I'm sure people would be willing to do all they could. The rate we've been losing

202

Spits we'll be shot out of the air soon if we don't do something.'

'That's a marvellous idea!' Amy enthused. 'Hillsbridge's own Spitfire! Our little bit towards the war effort.'

'I'm glad you think so. I'll get on the telephone today and have a word with a few of those who might be interested in helping us. And now,' said Ralph, 'we'd better be going. Do you want a lift, Barbara, or are you going to miss the bus on your first day?'

'I'm ready,' said Barbara. She was still trembling from thinking how close Huw had come to death.

'We really should contribute something to the war effort,' Ralph said again from the doorway, obviously preoccupied as he waited for her to gather her things. 'If we don't the Luftwaffe is going to overrun England.'

That night when Barbara returned from her first day in the new business college they heard the news.

For the first time, London had been bombed.

And so it continued while the blue and silver of September became the russet reds and golds of October and into the dark and dreary days of November.

By the middle of September the Battle of Britain had been virtually won. The RAF had the Luftwaffe on the run and Hitler was obliged to disperse the barges he had waiting in the ports of Northern France and Belgium and postpone his invasion plan, Sealion, for the winter at least. But new tactics had been adopted. If the bombers could not get past the Hurricanes and Spitfires during the hours of daylight then they would come when they could hide in the darkness.

Every night, the air over London was heavy with the sound of the Me10s and the Dorniers droning in with their loads of death and destruction. Soon, the subway stations on the underground were being used as shelters where Londoners could gather nightly in comparative safety, but people were being killed in their homes and in the streets nonetheless and Margaret wondered sometimes about Elaine and Marie's mother. Whilst the other evacuees were in constant communication with parents who loved and missed them but who wanted them to remain out of harm's way, the two girls heard from their mother only rarely, a brief card or badly written note, and Margaret thought angrily that it really did seem a case of 'out of sight, out of mind'.

'I believe she's glad to be rid of them,' she said to Harry one night when the girls were in bed. 'It seems to me she's glad of the war as an excuse to let someone else look after them.'

That was before the air raid siren began sounding at night in Hillsbridge, too, as the German bombers extended their range and began aiming for the aircraft factories in Bristol and Yeovil along with their other city targets – Birmingham and Coventry, Southampton and Liverpool. When that happened Margaret shepherded the girls into the cupboard under the stairs where they all three sat cramped together playing 'Snap' and 'Strip Jack Naked' by the fading beam of a torch that Margaret kept handy on the shelf just inside the door.

It was the same in houses all over Hillsbridge when the siren wailed its stomach-churning warning. A few people, like Eddie Roberts, had their own shelter built in the back garden and they would troop out with their flasks of tea and hot water bottles to the comparative comfort of their specially equipped bolt-holes.

Most, like Margaret and her evacuees, took cover as best they could inside their own homes, using kitchen tables and heavy old sofas as makeshift shelters if there was no room in that universal favourite – the cupboard under the stairs.

Some, Charlotte and James included, preferred to ignore the sirens and carry on with their usual routine.

James had suffered another bad chest bout when the first chill of October had turned the air cold and damp; if it had not been for the new wonder drug 'M & B' prescribed by the doctor, Charlotte was convinced it would have turned to pneumonia and been the death of him. As it was he had rallied once again but there was no way she could move him from his bed in the front room every time the siren sounded and she sat beside him, stoic as ever, while the planes droned overhead, remarking, 'Well, at least if we go, we'll go together,' and 'If they drop a bomb on our house we shall be in good company'. Buckingham Palace had been hit by a bomb in September though mercifully none of the Royal Family had been injured and Charlotte, always an ardent monarchist, took comfort from the fact that she was able to share in the ordeal of 'our dear King and Queen'.

There were those, of course, who were out in the streets during those dangerous hours of darkness carrying out their duties. Ralph, as Air Raid Warden for Midlington, was out every night when he was not at committee meetings raising money for the Spitfire project and Barbara, thwarted in her desire to join the WAAF, had persuaded her mother to allow her to volunteer as a Fire Watcher.

Since bombing raids had switched to the hours of darkness the Germans had discovered the advantage of well lit targets – and the best way of illuminating town and countryside alike was by the dropping of incendiary devices. Some landed harmlessly in fields and gardens – one struck the garden that ran down steeply from the Durrants' house in Greenslade Terrace, sinking a deep crater in the patch where the Clements' pig had once uprooted the parsnips – but some landed on the roofs of houses, setting them ablaze, and the engines of the Auxiliary Fire Service were kept busy dashing here and there, bells jangling, to put out the fires.

Amy was not altogether happy about Barbara being a Fire Watcher but since Ralph had promised that the moment the siren sounded the girls would be sent under cover and as she still felt a trifle guilty about insisting that Barbara should do a full year at college before even considering volunteering for the WAAF, she had eventually allowed herself to be persuaded.

One evening in early November Barbara was out as usual with her team – three men and another girl, Jessie Bendall – when the siren sounded.

'OK girls – in you go!' Ron Hodges instructed them.

'What about you?' Barbara asked as she always did.

'Never mind about us. We'll be all right. You girls go under the Chapel. That's the safest place.'

They were in the main Westbury Hill where the Methodist Chapel stood tall and stately on a bank of high ground below a rising rank of privately owned houses. A flight of stone steps led up to the main doors at first floor level and beneath it a passageway linked the main road to a little used steep lane. It was to this passageway that Ron Hodges ushered the girls. Jessie went willingly enough but Barbara hung back a little, resentful of being bundled off the moment danger threatened.

When the air began to tremble with the throb of the bombers' engines, however, she was glad enough of the cover. The Chapel was a good solid structure – then she remembered photographs she had seen of the destruction in cities where buildings every bit as solid as the Chapel disintegrated like a pack of cards when a bomb scored a direct hit.

I wouldn't like that lot coming down on top of me, she thought.

The throbbing engines were coming ever closer. When they were almost overhead she heard the first piercing whine of an incendiary. As the roar rose to a crescendo, making heaven and earth tremble around her, she pressed her hands over her ears. Another incendiary whistled down, and another.

A dark silhouette appeared suddenly in the entrance to the passageway and Ron Hodges threw himself in breathing heavily.

'That was a close one! They're bloody peppering us!'

'Have they got anything yet?' Barbara asked. She had to shout to make herself heard above the throbbing of the engines.

'Not yet but if they go on like this they will and it will be like daylight for the bombers when they come. The buggers know what they're doing all right. Oh, sorry . . .' He broke off, embarrassed at having sworn in front of Amy Porter's daughter.

'I didn't even hear you!' Barbara shouted back and wanted to laugh. Fancy anyone worrying about their language in the middle of an air raid!

As she spoke the whistling sound came again, so close it sounded as if the incendiary was going to land on top of them. Barbara automatically ducked and they heard the thud as it landed close by.

Ron Hodges poked his head out of the passageway and swore.

'Right on the roof of one of them houses!'

Barbara straightened and risked popping out to look too. As Ron had said the incendiary had landed just below one of the chimney pots on the rank immediately above the Chapel. Already it was a mass of flames.

'We'll have to get the brigade,' Ron said.

The nearest telephone was three hundred yards away up the steep hill. Ron was a big man and not as fit as he might have been. Barbara had often heard the breath wheezing in his chest when he hurried. She made up her mind.

'I'll go.'

'You bloody won't!'

'Oh yes I will.'

Before he could stop her she ducked out of the alleyway and was running up the road beneath the garden walls of the houses. She could get to the telephone box three times as quickly as he could, she knew. She ran without stopping, though after the first fifty yards the steepness of the incline made her legs ache and her heart pump painfully, only ducking her head slightly as the incendiaries whistled down through the clean cold air. One landed in an allotment on the opposite side of the road, one had caught something alight on the other side of the valley – she could see the whole area bathed in the rosy flickering fire glow. But that was someone else's area. Not her responsibility. Gasping for breath, Barbara ran on.

The telephone box was on a lane which branched away at right angles from the main road and it sloped less steeply. Barbara turned into it thankfully, keeping close to the hedge that defined the garden of the end house. She reached the telephone box and yanked the door open, leaning against the glass panels and trying to catch her breath as she jiggled the receiver to try to get a dialling tone.

The wait seemed endless, the lines were busy. Barbara hopped up and down with impatience. Phones! She could have made it to the fire station in person by now if she had run the other way.

At last her call was answered and she blurted out her message.

'One of the houses in Westbury Hill has been hit. The roof is well alight. Can you send an engine?'

'You'll be lucky,' came the reply.

'But it's on fire! It's like a beacon for the bombers.'

'So is half Hillsbridge. OK love, thanks. We'll do what we can. Keep your head down now.'

The line went dead and Barbara was overwhelmed by a feeling of helplessness. How the hell could they cope with an attack on this scale? They simply weren't geared to it. And the whole sky seemed to be aglow . . . Well, if there was no engine to be spared, they'd simply have to do the best they could with buckets and hoses when the planes went away.

The heavy bombers were coming now. She could hear them thundering in. Better not risk running back down the road – better to stay where she was in the telephone box. Or was it? If a bomb landed anywhere in the vicinity all the glass could shatter. She crept out, ran as far as the corner and dived under the garden hedge. Then she lay in the cold wet grass with the twigs scratching her neck and hands listening to the horrid sound and wondering why in the world the Germans should be raiding Hillsbridge. It was a mistake. It had to be. They had probably set out to bomb Bristol and missed their target.

When the bomb fell it took her by surprise although she had been half expecting it. Even in her wildest dreams she had never imagined it could be half so awful. The fearful whine as it fell, the bang as it hit something solid, the ear-splitting reverberations of the blast that made it seem as though the whole world was caving in, the roar of cascading bricks and plaster that seemed to go on forever.

'My God, something has been hit!' she thought and only realised as she heard her own voice that she had spoken aloud.

She lay shocked into immobility for a moment then suddenly the sky was alive again, this time with a scurrying flight of British fighters. Gunfire traced the sky with bright streaks and the bombers turned tail. One loosed his bombs somewhere out over the open countryside as he tried to lighten his load for a quick getaway; she heard the dull thuds but no more explosions. They were going. The fight was further away now. Mesmerised, she watched it disappear over the top of the ridge on the Hillsbridge skyline.

Better get back now. There was work to be done. She was amazed by the coherence of her own thoughts. She picked herself up and started for the corner, running again. Then her heart seemed to stop beating.

The Chapel. The bomb had hit the Chapel. For a moment she could scarcely believe it, yet the scene, like something from Dante's *Inferno*, was all too real.

There was a fire tender in the road – the one she had phoned for and they had said they could not send? – but its hoses were trained not onto the burning roof of the house but into a pile of bricks and rubble which burned fiercely in the gap where the Chapel had stood. Mrs Miles, the shrill and none-too-bright elderly houseowner was standing in the road shouting at the firemen to 'Come quick – my roof's afire!', and Cliff Button, Herbie's brother, who was now Sub-Officer Button of Hillsbridge Voluntary Fire Service was shouting over his shoulder as he worked: 'Never mind your house, Missus! There's people in here!'

People. Ron Hodges and Jessie Bendall. Dear God, if she had not gone to the telephone *she* would have been in there, under the heap of collapsed masonry! She remembered the thought which had occurred to her when Ron had first told her to shelter in the passageway and knew it had been a premonition.

She ran to Cliff Button. He made to brush her aside as he had done poor panic stricken little Mrs Miles, then recognised her and swore.

'Barbara! Thank God! Jack Bull thought you were in there too.' Jack was another of the fire watching team.

'No. I'm all right. What can I do?'

'Nothing. Just keep out of the bloody way,' Cliff said grimly. She stood helplessly watching. The fire was out now, the firemen moved on to deal with Mrs Miles' blazing roof and the heavy rescue squad moved in. It was their first genuine emergency but their nights of training stood them in good stead and some of them were experienced in Mines Rescue work too. In the muted light by which they were working Barbara saw an arm exposed and clapped her hand over her mouth. Another minute and they had uncovered the body of Ron Hodges. Half his clothes had been torn off by the blast yet he looked remarkably untouched. For a moment Barbara thought he was all right. Then, as they laid him gently on the road, she could see he was dead.

She stood looking down at him, sick to her stomach, then a shout from one of the men caught her attention. Someone had heard a faint cry from beneath the mass of rubble. It could be that Jessie was still alive. The men worked more frantically now, clawing at the rubble with their bare hands in their haste. Barbara joined them, heaving at chunks of masonry with a strength she had never known she possessed and after a few minutes someone gave a cry.

'Steady now – steady! We're almost there!'

Barbara craned forward, hands pressed to her mouth, to watch the last careful excavation and found herself whispering a prayer of gratitude for the miracle which had saved Jessie. When the Chapel had collapsed one enormous block of coping stone had fallen from the arch above to form a cave and it had protected the girl from the shower of masonry and rubble. But to get her out would be a long and painstaking operation. One false move and the coping stone could slip and crush her.

Barbara crouched down beside the cave while the men worked, murmuring words of encouragement to Jessie. The girl seemed remarkably cheerful and Barbara was filled with admiration for her courage.

'Well, Barbara Roberts, you were the lucky one, weren't you?' she joked, only the strain in her voice betraying the trauma she was enduring. 'The whole lot came down, didn't it?'

211

'Uh-huh. Just like the big bad wolf and the little pigs in the fairy story. "I'll huff and I'll puff and I'll blow your house down." And I must say he's made a pretty thorough job of it.'

'What about the others? Are they all right?' Jessie asked.

Barbara bit her lip. This was hardly the moment to tell her about Ron.

'Never mind the others. It's you we're worried about.' With a smoothness born of desperation she turned the conversation to seemingly irrelevant topics – boyfriends and dances, fashion and the latest popular music.

At last the team leader gave the signal that he thought it was safe to lift her out and with great care they did so. Blood was streaming from a cut on her face and her feet and legs were bare. Otherwise she seemed almost unhurt. As she was placed on a stretcher and carried gently to the waiting ambulance Barbara followed.

'I'll go with her.'

'There's no need, Barb, honestly. I'm all right . . .' Jessie protested, but her teeth had begun chattering with delayed shock and Barbara reached for one of the rough grey blankets to cover her.

'For once in your life just try to keep quiet, Jessie Bendall,' she said sternly.

It was only when the ambulance pulled away that she realised that she too was trembling.

Dawn was breaking when Barbara walked up the drive of Valley View and tried to unlock the back door. She was so tired she scarcely knew what she was doing and could not understand why her key would not turn until the door was thrown open by Amy and Barbara realised it had been unlocked all the time.

212

'So there you are!' Amy said. She sounded almost cross.

'I'm sorry, Mum, I couldn't help it. There was a bomb. . .'

'I know. Oh darling, I've been so worried! I've been waiting up for you. Ralph found out you were all right but I couldn't go to bed until I'd seen with my own eyes.'

'Oh Mum!'

'And just look at the state of you!'

Barbara looked down noticing for the first time her coat was still covered in dust and brambles, her stockings torn, her shoes caked with rubble. She glanced in the mirror and her face gave her another shock for it was pale and dirt streaked and her eyes were puffy and red from tiredness.

'Never mind,' Amy said. 'Just as long as you're all right. That's all that matters.'

Barbara grinned wryly.

'You never know, Mum, I might have been better off in the WAAF after all!'

Two weeks later Ralph's Spitfire Committee held its first major fund raising event – a Grand Dance at the Victoria Hall.

The Fund had started well. A series of whist drives had provided a small but steady income and a Grand Christmas Draw was being planned with almost every local businessman being talked into donating a prize. But the dance, which she hoped would be the first of many, had been Amy's idea. 'We might as well give people some fun while parting them from their money. Heaven knows we could all do with something to take us out of ourselves,' she had said, and before she knew it she had been volunteered to lead the Dance Organising Committee.

'As if I didn't have enough on my plate!' she groaned to Ralph when they got home after the meeting, but he only smiled. Amy was never happier than when she was doing a dozen things at once.

In the event the dance took a great deal less organizing than Amy had feared. After sweet-talking some of Harry's colleagues on the council she was able to book the Hall for merely a nominal fee to cover the cost of heating and lighting, a local trio – piano, drums and piano accordian – agreed to give their services free of charge, and Stanley Bristow, who had run concert parties in Hillsbridge for as long as Amy could remember, volunteered to act as MC.

'It's a pity your Ted isn't still about,' he said to Amy. 'He could have done a turn for you. I've never knowed anybody with such a good voice as he had.'

'I know. But we can hardly get him back from Australia to sing at my dance,' Amy said with a smile.

She placed an advertisement in the *Mercury*, footing the bill out of her own pocket, for now that she had taken it on she was determined her dance should raise more money for the Spitfire Fund than any other event, and when tickets went on sale at the local newsagents they seemed to sell themselves.

'You'll be having to turn people away I reckon,' the girl in the newsagents said when Amy looked in to check progress.

Amy delegated the catering arrangements to a small band of women helpers, with the promise that she would loan Mrs Milsom to assist with any baking that needed doing, and Ralph put in hand the arrangements for a licensed bar.

By the night of the dance she was in a great state of nerves, terrified that for all her careful organisation there might be something she had overlooked.

'Stop worrying and enjoy it!' Ralph advised. 'What can go wrong?'

'Anything! The band could forget to turn up.'

'Of course they won't. Have you ever known them to miss an opportunity to deafen us all?'

'There's always a first time. Or something could go wrong with the heating in the Hall. You know they're always having trouble with the boiler. We could end up either roasting or freezing.'

'If we're roasting we open a window. If we're freezing they'll just have to keep playing "The Gay Gordons" or "The Lancers" to get everybody warmed up.'

'We could have an air raid in the middle of it!'

'That,' said Ralph, 'is one thing you can do nothing about. We shall just have to pray the Germans leave us alone. It's been very quiet the last couple of weeks and it would be just bad luck if they chose the night of the dance to pay us some attention again.'

Amy nodded. It was true, since the night the Chapel had been bombed everything had reverted to normal. No planes had come and apart from one false alarm the siren had been silent.

'Let's get down to the Hall,' she said. 'I want to make quite sure they've strung up the net of balloons properly. There's nothing worse than announcing a balloon dance, pulling the string, and finding nothing happens.'

'Come on then,' Ralph said with a smile. 'If the girls aren't ready they can walk down. They've had quite long enough to tog themselves up.'

The girls were ready, Barbara looking a picture in the red dress she had had last Christmas, Maureen in blue ('Marina blue, after our dear Duchess of Kent,' Charlotte insisted on calling it). They piled into the car and reached the Victoria Hall to find the band already there and setting up.

Amy took first turn on the door and found herself rushed off her feet as both ticket holders and those who had come hoping to pay on the door arrived. The landlord of The George had set up a bar and was soon busy, the refreshments, in spite of the strictures of rationing, looked delicious, and for once the heating boiler seemed to be behaving itself perfectly.

By ten o'clock Amy had relaxed in the knowledge that all was well.

'It looks as if Mum is enjoying herself,' Barbara said to Maureen as Amy was twirled past them by Frank Cottle the schoolmaster. 'She hasn't stopped dancing since Ralph took over from her on the door.'

It was true. Every one of the Spitfire Committee was determined to claim a dance from Amy while Ralph was otherwise occupied for in spite of being the mother of two almost grown up daughters she was as pretty and popular as she had always been.

'She's doing better than we are,' Maureen grumbled. 'There don't seem to be any nice boys here who are unattached.'

'Most of them are in the forces, I suppose,' said Barbara. 'Come on, it's a "Valeta". We can dance that together without looking silly.'

A few moments later the music stopped and Stanley Bristow came to the front of the stage.

'We're making this a prize dance,' he announced. 'I've got a surprise parcel for the first gentleman who can bring me a pair of ladies' knickers.'

There was a moment's silence, broken only by shocked giggles, then a big brawny man in shirt sleeves rushed between the dancers carrying his partner in his arms.

'Here you are, Stan!' he shouted.

'Well done, Walt!' Stan laughed. 'You see, folks, I didn't say *how* you had to bring 'em to me. You are wearing some, my dear, I trust?' he asked the flushed lady who had been lifted onto the stage.

The hall erupted with laughter.

'That's a bit rude, isn't it?' Maureen said.

216

But Barbara was not listening. She was staring at the main door, eyes round, face suddenly alight. Leaving Maureen standing, she pushed her way between the dancers towards the young man in air force blue who had just come in. Then, as she reached him she stopped, shy suddenly.

'Huw!' was all she could say. 'Oh Huw!'

'Well done, Amy. It's been a wonderful success.'

'It certainly has. You must organise another one.'

The dance was almost over now, people were leaving and stopping to congratulate Amy as they did so. She replied automatically, nodding and smiling, but her thoughts were no longer on the success or otherwise of the dance and across their shoulders she was watching one couple on the dance floor who seemed oblivious of all others.

Barbara and Huw.

It had been a wonderful surprise to see him, of course. He had got a three-day leave pass and hitched a lift straight home, he had told her, and she had been delighted that he should arrive tonight of all nights.

'Oh Huw, it's so good to see you!' she had said, hugging him, then holding him at arm's length and thinking how handsome, how *dashing* he looked in his uniform.

But her pleasure had been shortlived for it was soon obvious that Huw, though pleased to see all of them, really had no eyes for anyone but Barbara.

It was so long now since he had been home that she had almost forgotten her anxieties of the previous Christmas. Stupid imagination, she had told herself, and half expected that when Huw next turned up he would have a girl on his arm. Why, he could even be getting married before she knew it. He was twenty-two

217

years old now after all, quite old enough, and with a war on couples seemed to be heading for the altar when they had only known each other for a few weeks.

But tonight she had seen Barbara with Huw and all her old fears had been resurrected.

They had been dancing together from the moment he had arrived. Now, it was the last waltz and there they were in the centre of the floor, Barbara's cheek resting against Huw's chin. As the soft overhead light fell on them Amy saw that her eyes were closed, a dreamy smile playing about her mouth. And the way Huw was holding her was decidedly not brotherly.

Amy's heart came into her mouth. It was happening, just as she had feared. Barbara and Huw. Oh dear God, what was she going to do?

The music was haunting.

Who's taking you home tonight after the dance is thru'?
Who's the lucky fella going your way
Who'll kiss you goodnight at your doorway . . .

It was over. Couples were leaving the floor. But Barbara and Huw still stood there, looking at one another, just looking . . .

Amy hurried over to them

'We shan't bother too much with clearing up tonight – the caretaker will be in in the morning. Ralph has got the car . . .'

'There won't be room for all of us, will there?' Barbara said. Her face was aglow, flushed and smiling. She looked like a young woman in love.

'Oh, I expect we can all squeeze in,' Amy said.

'No, don't worry about us,' Huw said and Barbara added, 'We'll be all right, Mum. Huw and I will walk.'

Amy floundered helplessly, faced with unexpected suddenness by the very situation she had always feared.

'All right,' she agreed reluctantly.

At this moment there was nothing else she could do.

*

The moon was shining, clear and cold, as they left the Hall. The square outside was still busy with people stopping for a last word or calling goodnight to one another and a couple ahead of them had stopped to embrace in the subway that ran beneath the railway line. When they reached the road Huw put his arm around Barbara to see her across and left it there. She let her head rest against his shoulder.

'When I saw you come in tonight I thought I was dreaming,' she said.

'I thought I'd surprise you.'

'You certainly did that. Oh Huw, it's so lovely to see you. I've been so worried . . .'

'No need to worry about me,' he said. He used the breezy tone of all fliers, the boys who looked death in the face day by day, who 'scrambled' with their friends and tried not to notice the faces that were missing when they gathered again in the mess at night to drink a little too much and sing a little too raucously to the jangling accompaniment of the mess room piano, but the underlying tension was there all the same. She caught it and shivered.

'Cold?' he asked.

'No. Not really.'

But he pulled her closer all the same.

'It sounds as though I'm not the only one to have a narrow escape,' he said. 'You were lucky, Barbara. They shouldn't have allowed you to be out in the open when there was a raid on, you know.'

'Oh fiddlesticks,' she said. The horror of the bomb seemed a long way off now. 'Don't let's talk about the war. Let's pretend it's never happened.'

But what else was there to talk about?

'Wouldn't it be funny if when we have raised enough money to buy a Hillsbridge Spitfire you were to be the one to fly it?' she said.

'Highly unlikely.'

219

'You could, though. Stranger things have happened.'

They turned off the main road into the winding, sloping lane which would lead them past Amy's yard. The hedges on their right, taller by several feet than they were, were stiff and shining with frost; away on their left they could hear the soft gush of the brook as it flowed over the small weir and into the mill pond where once poor Grace Scott, sister of Uncle Jack's wife Stella, had tried to drown herself. Their footsteps echoed on the dry road. They might have been the only two people left in the world. They walked more slowly now. It wasn't so far to Valley View and they didn't want to get there. They wanted to go on being alone with the stars and the bright three-quarters full moon and the silence.

Because of the silence they must have heard the engine of the car almost at the moment it started up in the Victoria Hall Square. They heard it fade slightly as it drove around the horseshoe towards the main road – cars could not shortcut under the railway line as they had done – then grow louder as it came up the hill. Another moment and the lights, dimmed for the blackout, would be in view.

Barbara felt a moment's foolish panic as if a dream was about to be shattered.

'It's Ralph and Mum. Don't let them see us!'

She caught his hand and darted towards the Mill. It stood beside the lane, a gaunt building with a tower and high wooden loft doors where they hoisted the sacks of grain up and down on a pulley contraption. A path ran along the side of it, Barbara dived into it, pulling Huw after her. The deep shadow closed around them, she collapsed against the cold stone wall, laughing, and he leaned against her, blotting out her vision so that she heard, but did not see, the car as it passed by in the lane.

When it had gone he levered himself away, looking

220

down at her. In the half light his familiar face looked different, the face of a handsome stranger. Breath caught in her throat and suddenly the whole of her body was alive and tingling as a series of tiny shocks, sharp as the frost on the branches, ran through her. For a long moment they stood there looking at one another and there was a magic feel to the world as if suddenly it had all become one with the wonder inside her.

'I've missed you, Barbara,' he said.

And he kissed her.

She stood motionless, her hands spread out on the rough fabric of his greatcoat and the feel of his lips on hers and the nearness of him was dizzying. She parted her lips to his, wanting to drink him in, to make the moment last forever and ever and the glory of it swept her up on a dizzying tide. It was wonderful, just as she had always known it would be – no, more wonderful. Better than the wildest dream. Higher than the highest mountain. Deeper and stronger and oh . . .

For many minutes they stood there in each other's arms. Then his lips touched her nose, cold after the warmth of her mouth, and he rested his cheek briefly against hers before moving away.

'We'd better go.' His voice was low and regretful. 'They'll wonder what has become of us.'

'I don't care,' she said. 'Let them wonder.'

'No, I have to get you safely home.' He kissed her again and she clung to him kissing him even more passionately than before in an effort to keep him there. Anything . . . anything . . . only make tonight last forever . . .

Gently, he disengaged himself.

'You may not care, but I do,' he said. 'If I want your mother to let me take you out again I'd better get you home at a decent time.'

She giggled. What a funny thing to say – 'your mother' – as if she was a stranger not the woman who had brought him up. But he wanted to take her out again, not as a child to be indulged but as a girl. Of course he did! The world wouldn't be full of this wonderful enchantment unless he wanted her as much as she wanted him . . .

'I suppose we'd better,' she said reluctantly.

They walked the rest of the way with their arms around each other. Only when they came within sight of the house they let caution be the better part of valour and simply held hands. Huw opened the kitchen door and the warmth came out to meet them making their faces glow. Amy and Ralph were sitting at the table drinking cocoa but there was no sign of Maureen. Late as it was she had probably gone straight to bed.

'Hello Mum. Ralph,' Barbara said a little breathlessly.

'Where have you been?' Amy asked. Her eyes were sharp. 'We didn't pass you walking along the lane.'

'We stopped to look at the Mill,' Barbara said.

'Whatever for? At this time of night!' Amy got up abruptly passing a hand through her bubbly fair hair. She suddenly looked very tired. 'Do you two want cocoa? I put enough milk on for you. Though I expect Huw is about ready for bed if you're not, Barbara. What with his long journey and after all he's been through . . .'

'It's all right. I'm used to late nights,' Huw said.

'You go on to bed Mum. Don't wait up for us,' Barbara said.

'It's all right. I'm not *that* tired that I can't sit and have a cup of cocoa with you,' Amy said.

And if her voice was a trifle shrewish Barbara was too happy to notice it.

11

The lovely glow was still with her when she woke next morning. She lay for a moment with the sheets pulled up to her chin revelling in it as she remembered every detail of the previous evening from the moment she had looked across the dance floor and seen Huw standing there in the doorway to their last whispered goodnight.

Amy and Ralph had seen them upstairs, staying down themselves, so they said, to lock up, and Barbara had felt a stab of bitter frustration that she and Huw could not be alone again together if only for a few short minutes. But in the shadows on the landing he had kissed her lightly and his fingers had momentarily touched hers before he went off along to his room. She had stood in her own doorway watching him go and he had turned and smiled at her once before going in and closing the door.

Well, there was always tomorrow.

'If you think I'm going to college tomorrow when Huw is only going to be here for a couple of days you've got another think coming!' she had said.

Amy had opened her mouth as if to say something, then closed it again. Barbara had not noticed.

Now it was tomorrow and the previous night seemed a little like a dream. But her red dress lying across the chair where she had dropped it and her dancing shoes with dried mud still clinging to their heels kicked off beneath the dressing table told her it had not been a dream. It had really happened. Huw was here under their own roof again if only for a little while and the two days until he had to go again stretched away enticingly yet seeming already ominously short.

Barbara pushed aside the blankets and got up not wanting to waste a moment of it. Some time during the night the frost had given way to rain; when she pulled the thick curtains and looked out the valley was drab and grey in the heavy sunless light of day. She found a jersey and skirt and got dressed, hanging the red dress carefully in the wardrobe.

Oh, you lovely dress! she thought. Every time I wear you something wonderful happens. And it's all to do with Huw . . .

She hummed as she went downstairs. The kitchen was empty. Three cups, plates and cereal bowls were on the draining board, washed but not dried. Mum and Ralph must have gone to work and Maureen to school. And it was Mrs Milsom's day off. Barbara dried up one of the cereal bowls, filled it with cornflakes and helped herself to milk from the jug on the cold slab. She was halfway through eating it when the door opened and Huw came in.

'Hi there.'

'Oh hello!' She felt awkward suddenly, as if her feelings must be written all over her, and she was shy now at the thought of him seeing them.

'Everyone else gone, have they?'

'I suppose so. Do you want breakfast?'

'It's all right, I'll get my own.'

'There's probably bacon and eggs if you want it,' she said.

'No, this will do fine.' He filled another of the bowls with cornflakes.

They chatted for a while as they ate, not mentioning the previous evening, and Barbara made a pot of tea. While they were drinking it they heard the post come. Barbara smiled.

'No need to rush for it this morning. There's usually a mad scramble to see if there's a letter from you. And when there is of course Mum always opens it,' she said meaningfully.

'I'd write just to you if I could but it's had to be a family thing until now,' Huw said.

Barbara felt her cheeks flood with pleased colour.

'I was determined to stay home for you today,' she said.

'I'm glad you did.' He caught at her hand as she set down the cup of tea, pulled her down and kissed her. 'Morning, darling.'

'Morning!' She skipped away, thrilled by the kiss and by the 'darling' but now, with the dawning of confidence, feeling the desire to play hard to get just a little.

'Come here!' he ordered.

'Why?'

'Never mind why. Just come here and I'll show you.'

'What's it worth.'

Flirtatiously she moved just within his reach, pretending surprise when he reached out and caught her. He pulled her down again, this time onto his knee, holding her there and kissing her. She leaned against him, delirious with happiness.

'Huw! All these years and I never knew you were like this,' she teased.

'Barbara! All these years and I never knew *you* were!'

She traced the line of his nose with her finger. When she reached his upper lip he made a playful snap at it with his teeth.

'Hey, come on,' she said, jumping up again. 'Let's get these dishes washed up.'

'Spoilsport!'

The washing up took quite a long time since there was a great deal of tomfoolery with soapsuds and tea towels and quite a lot of kissing.

'What are we going to do today?'

'Don't much mind. We could go out for a walk. Or

we could just stay here and play some records on the gramophone.'

'It's up to you. Your choice.'

'I think,' said Barbara, 'we'll stay and play records for now and then go out for a walk when Mum and co. are due home.'

'That's not very nice,' he chided. 'I came home to see them too.'

'No you didn't. You came to see me.'

'All right, madam, I came to see you. But I can't leave them out altogether, especially not Amy. She's a very special person, you know. You take her for granted. I suppose it's only natural. But I have never forgotten that if it had not been for her I would have been raised in an Industrial School, as they were called in those days, where they used to send bad lads to have the devil knocked out of them.'

'Pity you didn't go there then!' she teased.

'If I had, I would not have met you. Or if I had met you, you wouldn't have looked at me twice, not a nicely brought up, convent educated girl like you!'

'Shame!'

'Yes, isn't it?' he said lightly. 'Never mind, that's *not* how things worked out, thanks to Amy. I've never known really why she did what she did and at the time I can't say I was very grateful to her. I was a little heller – took it out on her, ran away, did anything I could to get my own back on life. Not now though. Now I'm old enough to know better and I *am* grateful. And if you think I'm going to hurt her by avoiding her these few days I'm here you've got another think coming. We've got all our lives . . .'

He broke off and suddenly the shadow of the war was there again between them. But only for a moment. She was too happy to let it spoil things for long. 'All our lives' he had said. Oh Huw, Huw . . .

'I love you,' she said.

'And I love you.' He said it a trifle awkwardly and kissed her again.

'I think I've always loved you. Ever since I was a little girl. I knew. I just *knew*.'

He grinned. 'You were a good kid. I liked doing things for you. And then suddenly – you weren't a kid any more.'

'I should hope not!'

'Last Christmas when I came home I looked at you and I thought – Christ, she's grown up!'

'Kids have a habit of doing that.'

'Not always as nicely as you have. Barbara, you are the prettiest girl I have ever seen.'

'Do you see many?' she asked, experiencing a moment's jealousy.

'A few. But they just don't interest me. Not the way you do.'

'Are we going to play those records then – or are we going to stay in the kitchen all day.'

'I don't much care,' he said. 'As long as we can be together.'

'I know,' she said. 'Neither do I. Isn't it wonderful?'

It was a glorious stolen day, a day of laughter and kisses, some tender, some passionate. They played the gramophone but never got around to taking the walk – the weather was not really nice enough, they kidded themselves. The rain had closed in, hanging in a thick cloud over the valley and dripping constantly from the trees.

Amy came home early. She was in even before Maureen was back from school, looking, Barbara thought, a trifle strained and weary.

'I want to get a nice meal for you, Huw. It *would* be Mrs Milsom's day off, wouldn't it, just this one special day? What time do you have to leave tomorrow?'

Barbara looked up sharply. 'What do you mean – tomorrow? Haven't you got a three-day pass, Huw?'

'A three-day pass doesn't mean three days with us. It took him one of them to get here, didn't it? And I expect it will take him the best part of another to get back.'

'Oh no! I never thought! You never said . . .' Barbara felt cheated and shocked as if someone had thrown a bath of cold water over her.

'I suppose I ought to go fairly early in the morning,' Huw said. 'I have to be back by midnight and I'm not quite sure how easy it will be to get there.'

His motor cycle was off the road now, since he had loaned it to a friend who had drunk a little too much and wrapped it around a lamp post.

'Go by train,' Barbara said.

'Yes, but even trains are a bit uncertain these days.'

'And I don't think you can miss another day's college, Barbara,' Amy said severely.

'Oh Mum!'

'You've had all day today.' Amy glanced at her watch. 'Maureen's bus should be in now soon. You can take my car and go and meet her. It's pouring with rain.'

Barbara brightened. She loved driving Amy's car.

'All right. Are you coming with me, Huw?'

'Don't hog him, Barbara. I want to talk to Huw myself. You go for Maureen and Huw can chat to me while I'm peeling the potatoes.'

About to protest Barbara remembered what Huw had said about not leaving Amy out. Perhaps she was being selfish.

'All right.' She fetched her gabardine raincoat and a scarf. When she had put it on her face peeped rosily out of the hood. 'I won't be long.'

'Take care,' said Amy.

Huw and Barbara exchanged a secret smile and she went out humming.

228

The moment the car had left the drive Amy turned to Huw.

'I'm sorry, Huw, but I wanted to get Barbara out of the way. I have to talk to you alone.' Her voice was serious, her face drawn into tight lines. He looked at her in surprise.

'You worry too much. Things aren't as bad as you might think.'

Her mouth quirked but without humour.

'I'm afraid they are. But that's not what I want to talk to you about. Nothing to do with the war. It's about you and Barbara.'

'Oh!'

'I'm sorry, Huw. I'm really sorry to have to do this at such a time when you're trying to snatch a couple of days relaxation. But I can't see any alternative.' She pulled out a chair. 'Let's sit down, shall we?'

She sat and he perched on the table opposite her, waiting.

'You see, I can't help noticing the way things are going between you and Barbara,' Amy said. There was a little tremble in her voice. 'I am right, aren't I?'

Huw shifted slightly, feeling uncomfortable.

'Well yes, if you put it like that.'

'You are becoming fond of one another.'

'Yes.'

'More than fond.'

'Yes,' he admitted. 'Look, Amy, I know it may seem strange to you after all these years, but Barbara and I – well, I suppose you could say we have discovered one another. Since you've brought the subject up – I want to marry her.'

Amy blanched. 'You can't.'

He got up, crossed to the sink and leaned against it.

'I know it's a bit sudden, but I suppose at a time like this when you don't know from one day to the next what is going to happen to you things *do* happen more suddenly.'

'What does Barbara say about this?' Amy asked.

'She doesn't know yet. I haven't asked her. But it's been on my mind all day. I can't stand the thought of leaving her. I love her, Amy.'

Amy sunk her head in her hands and saw nothing but bright flaring patterns on a background of darkness. It was just as she had feared. Worse. The only blessing was that he hadn't said anything to Barbara yet. At least she could spare her daughter that. But there was no easy way out for Huw. No way at all . . .

'You can't,' she said.

'But I do. And she loves me. I'm sorry if it's a shock to you, Amy. I hoped you might be pleased.'

'No, I mean you can't. Really can't. It's wrong for you to love her and you certainly cannot marry her.'

The seriousness of her tone got through to him.

'What do you mean?' he asked.

'I need a drink,' Amy said. She hurried into the drawing room, poured two glasses of whisky, neat, from Ralph's bottle of Glenlivet and gave one to Huw. 'By the time I've finished I think you'll need one too,' she said wryly.

He took the glass and set it down on the draining board.

'What is all this, Amy?'

'Huw, you know that I took you in when your mother died.'

'Yes, and I am very grateful.'

'But you don't know why. Very few people do. I can think of only three. My mother. My solicitor. And . . . someone else. I never saw the need to tell you and perhaps change the parameters of your world. Now I see I was wrong. I should have told you long ago what I am going to tell you now. Did you ever know why you

230

and your mother had come to Hillsbridge just before
she died?'

'Not really. It was something to do with money.' He
was casting his mind back to the small boy he had been,
remembering how he had trailed miserably behind his
mother up a long hill to visit – yes, Amy. It was
something he had pushed aside with the passage of
years. The memory of 'the woman' as he had called
Amy then shouting at his poor sick mother and turning
them out of her house did not square with the Amy he
knew now. Somehow in the period of adjustment he
had blotted it out.

'Yes, it was to do with money,' Amy said. 'After your
mother's husband died she was more or less destitute.
She came to Hillsbridge to beg assistance from *my*
husband not knowing that he had been killed in an
accident at his transport yard.'

Huw's eyes narrowed.

'Why should she do that?'

Amy took a gulp of the whisky. It burned her throat.
'Because,' she said slowly, 'my husband Llew was your
father.'

The silence seemed to go on forever.

'I didn't believe it at first,' Amy went on, her voice
low yet perfectly audible in the quiet kitchen. 'I sent her
packing. Then, when she got pneumonia and died and
you were left all alone I thought I had better investigate
what she had told me. I questioned Mrs Roberts –
Llew's mother – and I discovered to my horror that it
was true. Llew had had an affair with your mother back
home in the Valleys. Her husband had accepted you as
his own, but after he died and she was desperate for
money, she turned to Llew for help. He had been
sending enough to support you but when he was killed
the money stopped. That was why she had come to
Hillsbridge – to find out the reason for her letters
remaining unanswered. And to beg for help. Times

231

were different then, you see, Huw. The depression and all that . . .'

'So you took me in because you felt guilty,' he said. It was taking shape now, all of it, and he could not understand why he had never questioned it before and come up with an answer that was somewhere near the truth.

'I took you in in the beginning because you were Llew's son. I loved Llew very much.' Her voice trembled. 'Then I kept you because I came to love you too. But you see now, Huw, why there can never be anything between you and Barbara. You and she have the same father. She is your half sister.'

'Oh my God.' For a moment he sat stunned, then reached for the glass of whisky and swallowed it all in one gulp.

'I'm so sorry, Huw,' Amy said. 'Under any other circumstances I'd have been so pleased, but . . .'

'You should have told me,' he said. 'God, Amy, I had a right to know.'

'Yes. I'm sorry. I'm really sorry . . .'

The door opened. The girls burst in.

'Hi, Mum, we're home!'

In the tension neither Amy nor Huw had heard the approach of the car. Now the girls stared, puzzled by the atmosphere in the kitchen.

'You weren't long,' Amy said. Huw sat, not speaking.

'Hang your coats up,' Amy said.

They looked at one another and Barbara looked at Huw. He avoided her eyes. They went out to the hall.

'Huw – please – don't tell Barbara,' Amy begged softly. 'I don't want her to know that her father . . .'

'I don't know,' he said. He looked like a boxer reeling from a low punch.

'Please!'

He got up. 'I'm going for a walk.'

'I'll come with you!' Barbara said eagerly, coming back into the kitchen.

'No,' he said abruptly. 'No, Barbara, I want to go alone.'

Barbara sat on the bus shrouded in wretchedness.

'What's the matter, Babs?' Maureen asked.

'Nothing. Leave me alone.'

'Sorry, I'm sure. I don't know what's wrong with everybody. You are all as snappy as snapdragons. I don't understand it.'

Barbara said nothing. She did not understand either – could not fathom the change which had occurred in the short time it had taken her to collect Maureen from the bus yesterday. She had left bubbling with love and happiness and returned to an atmosphere of tension. And Huw had hardly spoken to her since, seemed to be avoiding her. Why had he gone rushing off for a walk on his own like that? After the lovely day they had shared it did not make sense. And the whole evening had been the same, awkward and subdued. The meal had been rotten – hardly surprising as Amy had never been a good cook and since marrying Ralph had had little need to practise what skills she had possessed, but even taking that into account it had been worse than usual. And afterwards, though they had played their favourite games of Lexicon and Rummy at Ralph's suggestion, that curious tension had remained.

No more kisses, no chance to exchange a word even. And when she had left this morning and gone to kiss Huw goodbye she had sensed his withdrawal.

But why – why – what had gone wrong?

It must be something Mum said to him, Barbara thought. That she didn't want us to be together, that I'm too young or he's too likely to be killed, or something. But why should he take it like this?

233

Tears choked at the back of her throat and she stared out of the window of the bus swallowing at them angrily. She would not cry. She would not. And really there was nothing to cry about. Huw's feelings could not have changed in half an hour. It was something else that was making him different.

She would write to him tonight. She would tell him that whatever her mother had said she didn't care. She loved him and wanted to be with him.

Oh, please God let it be all right! Barbara prayed.

And please, above all, keep him safe!

Their letters must have crossed in the post.

Barbara received hers from Huw two days later. She took it up to her room to read filled with a sense of dread as if she already knew what it said.

'Dear Barbara. I'm sorry but what happened when I came home was all a mistake. Please try and forget it and go back to the way things used to be between us. Go out with other boys. You'll soon find someone who will make you forget me. I'm sorry if I hurt you. I didn't mean to. Love, Huw.'

She sat staring at it and the tears washed down her cheeks.

Forget him? As if she ever could!

The rain beat on the window, but not even the bleakness of the winter weather could match the bleakness in Barbara's heart.

12

Christmas came and went, a miserable Christmas by most people's standards. The shop windows which were usually a blaze of light at this time of year were covered with blackout paper and every conceivable extra which made Christmas festivities special was in short supply or not available at all. Sugar and butter were rationed, making it difficult to cook rich festive fare, and nuts, grapes, bananas and tangerines were nowhere to be found. As if even nature herself was tightening her belt against the war the holly bushes were bare of berries, so that when Amy sent the girls out to look for sprigs to tuck behind the pictures as she did each year they returned with an armful of sad looking branches, and Ralph rather felt that his regular contribution of a Christmas tree was something of an extravagance.

The new year augured no better. In the first week of January the meat allowance was reduced for the second time in as many weeks and the children were unable to buy sweets or chocolates – all available supplies were being sent to the forces, it was said.

In the third week of January Ralph's Spitfire Fund achieved its target. The idea had caught the imagination of everyone and many of the villages surrounding Hillsbridge had joined in with their own schemes to raise money, from collecting boxes left on the counters of shops and general stores to 'penny bun sales', from whist drives and dances to slide shows. A final handsome donation from Sir Richard Spindler made up the required £5,000 with £1.2s.3d. to spare! Everyone was full of congratulations for Ralph and his team but in the midst of the euphoria Amy could only be secretly glad it was over – coming on top of her long hard days at the office the raising of the money had meant a lot of extra work.

She was worried, too, about Barbara. At first she had been only grateful that Huw had behaved as he had and told herself that Barbara would soon get over the ending of her first love affair, but it had not been that easy. As she watched Barbara's misery day after day she began blaming herself. Huw had been right, she should have spoken out long ago, and she found herself remembering her mother's old dictum: Oh what a tangled web we weave, When first we practise to deceive!

Yet even now she did not see what she could have done about it. She had wanted only to preserve family harmony and the moment for telling Huw had never seemed the right one. She had gone on in the mistaken belief that it was something which need never come to light and by the time she had begun to realise what was happening between Barbara and Huw it was much too late.

God forgive me, Amy thought. I only did what I believed to be for the best and look how it has turned out!

On the Monday evening after the Spitfire Fund target had been reached a final meeting was arranged and Amy, anxious to find anything to take Barbara's mind off her broken heart, suggested she should come along with her and Ralph.

'Oh, I don't want to go to a boring meeting,' Barbara said.

'This one won't be boring – it might be fun!' Amy coaxed. 'The organisers from the villages will be there and we've planned a celebration to thank them for all their hard work. You're not fire watching this evening, are you?'

236

'No.'

'Well, there you are. You've no excuse.'

'Maureen isn't going, is she?'

'I don't think Maureen is old enough to be going into pubs even if it is the functions room. And she has her homework to do, anyway. Please, Barbara,' Amy said, making one last effort, 'I really would like you to come.'

'Oh all right, I suppose so,' Barbara said ungraciously.

She, Ralph and Amy were among the first to arrive at The George but soon the others were milling in, smiling and looking pleased with themselves. When the time came for the meeting to begin Ralph and Amy were required to take their places at a long trestle table which had been set out at the front of the room for the committee and Barbara sat at the back, prepared to be bored. Then, just before the meeting was called to order, there was a small stir when voices could be heard on the stairway leading to the functions room. Barbara turned towards the door and saw a stout middle aged man in an expensively-cut overcoat with a dark moleskin collar and an Anthony Eden style hat. His face, heavy-jowled, had the look of a man who might be a little too fond of his port, and she recognised him at once as Sir Richard Spindler. Following him into the room was a younger man, tall, fair and handsome, and although he was now wearing a dark suit instead of his uniform he, too, was instantly recognisable as Marcus, who had been given a hero's welcome home the previous summer.

The stir became more pronounced. Someone rushed forward to put out two extra chairs in the front row and the Spindlers were escorted to them, smiling and nodding like visiting royalty.

Typical! thought Barbara bad temperedly. Typical of them to swan in at the last moment expecting everyone to fall over backwards just because they had deigned to grace the meeting with their presence.

But as she listened – or rather did *not* listen – to the first of the rather self-congratulatory speeches, she found her eyes straying to the back of Marcus' head. The hair that had looked golden in the sunshine the day he came home looked no less dull tonight as the light from the overhead chandelier fell on it and tiny bristles gleamed like gold dust on the nape of his neck above the white shirt collar and dark grey of his suit. He really was a very good looking young man.

He had been invalided out of the army, Barbara had heard, and intended to help his elder brother run the estate side of the Spindler empire – whatever that might entail.

The speeches were over at last, everyone who had contributed to the success of the fund had been thanked and Ralph was on his feet holding the all important cheque.

'On behalf of the Spitfire Committee I have great pleasure in formally presenting this cheque for £5,000 to Sir Richard who has kindly agreed to pass it to Lord Beaverbrook on our behalf.'

Sir Richard rose and accepted the cheque amid a burst of clapping.

'Now I hope you will all join me in enjoying the remainder of the evening,' he concluded. 'A great deal of hard work has gone into this project. When we each have a glass in our hands I suggest we raise it to drink to the Spitfire – *our* Spitfire – and hope it plays its part in bringing a speedy end to the rascally exploits of Adolf Hitler!'

Waitresses, specially employed for the occasion, were moving between the rows of chairs with trays of sherries; Barbara took one and raised it with everyone else.

'The Hillsbridge Spitfire!'

The thick sweet sherry cloyed in Barbara's mouth as she thought of Huw, perhaps flying tonight in a fighter just like the one they were toasting.

238

They were making it sound like a game, she thought, endowing it as if it were a new cricket pavilion for the greater glory of the first eleven. But the war was not a game. It was life and death for young men like Huw.

The rows of chairs were being cleared away to turn the functions room floor into an open space where people could mingle and chat whilst they drank their sherry. Barbara was cornered by one of the village representatives who swore he could remember her as a little girl, though Barbara could not recall ever having seen him in her life before.

'Oh my, where does time go?' he asked ponderously, and when he reached the point of tweaking her curls and attempting to pat her bottom Barbara decided it was time to escape.

The trays of sherry were standing on a table near the door. Barbara exchanged her empty glass for a full one, sidled closer to the door, checked that no one was watching her and slipped out. The staircase was carpeted, leading downwards to the Lounge Bar and upwards to the rooms which The George let to paying guests. Barbara was just trying to decide whether to go up or down when a voice behind her said:

'Not leaving already, are you?'

She swung round to face Marcus Spindler. Colour rushed to her cheeks, then she thought – why try to deny the truth?

'Escaping,' she said and laughed.

'I thought as much.' He came down the two steps to the landing where she was standing. 'What do you say we escape together?'

'*You?*' she exlaimed quickly, then her flush deepened. 'I would have thought you were used to this sort of thing', she explained.

'That doesn't mean I have to like it.' He smiled. It was a nice smile, bringing deep dimples on either side of his mouth into play. 'The old man railroaded me into coming along.'

'That is exactly what my mother did to me.'

'So they have nobody to blame but themselves if we creep off,' he said. 'What do you say we get a proper drink?' He glanced in disgust at the sherry he was holding.

'I – well, yes, why not?'

They went down the stairs to the Lounge. It was half empty since most of its regulars were upstairs at the meeting.

'What can I get you?' he asked.

Barbara hesitated, wondering what sounded the most suitable.

'Gin,' she decided.

'And tonic?'

Taste vied with a desire for sophistication. Taste won.

'Orange.'

'Grab a seat,' he said. 'I'll join you in a minute.'

She crossed to a table in an alcove. He carried the drinks from the bar one at a time as if he could not use one of his hands and she noticed that his limp was still evident. Then he pulled up a stool to sit facing her.

'Here's to escape.' He raised his glass, half full of amber liquid, and drank. Barbara sipped hers and tasted the tart 'bite' of the gin beneath the sticky sweetness of the orange squash.

'I'm Marcus Spindler, by the way,' he introduced himself. 'Who are you?'

'Barbara Roberts. Ralph Porter is my stepfather.'

'Oh yes, the timber man.' There was something dismissive about the way he said it.

Had he not been so handsome Barbara might have been annoyed. As it was she said, 'I expect you know my uncle, too – Harry Hall. He's the Miners' Agent at the moment, though he might end up by being our MP.'

'Yes.' He smiled briefly. 'He just cost my father rather a lot of money. He talked through an annual paid holiday of six days per annum for his men, and time and a half payment for Good Friday and Easter Monday last year as well. It went to arbitration just after Christmas and my father was notified of the arbitrator's findings last week. He nearly had apoplexy.'

'Sorry about that,' Barbara said.

'Not your fault.'

'It doesn't sound as if you care much for my family,' Barbara said.

'Oh, I wouldn't say that. Hall is a good sound man, if a little misguided. Naturally, he does the best he can for his men while my father is mainly interested in making a profit. And politically speaking anyone in the Labour Party is to my father like red rag to a bull.' He laughed at his own joke.

'Ralph is a Tory,' Barbara offered.

'Most business people are. Anyway,' he said, 'we don't want to talk politics do we? Let's talk about you. What do you do?'

Barbara sipped her drink, gaining confidence as the gin warmed her throat. 'I'm learning business studies so I can be of help with Mum's companies. But if I had my way I'd be in the forces – as you were.'

She saw the shadow come into his eyes.

'Not any more.'

'No, but . . . I saw you arrive home at the station. We just happened to be passing,' she added quickly, afraid he might think she had gone there specially – a very unsophisticated thing to have done. 'And we felt so proud. To think someone from Hillsbridge should have been so brave!'

'It was nothing,' he said. He was looking at his drink now, not at her. 'I'm sure there are a great many Hillsbridge men who are braver than I.'

'You don't want to talk about it, do you?' she said. 'I

can understand that. It must have been awful for you. I just wanted you to know that we were very proud.'

He finished his drink. 'Would you like another one?'

'Oh no, thank you. Well . . .' she giggled. 'All right then – why not.'

He refilled the glasses. Again, she noticed the large amount of amber liquid in his tumbler. Not surprising really, when you knew what he had been through. Huw also drank more than he used to. Perhaps they all did, the young men who had to live with a knowledge of imminent death. She pushed the thought away. Thinking of Huw in danger or not was painful. Just for tonight she would not think of him at all.

They sat for a while chatting and Marcus had refilled their glasses once again when Amy put her head round the door.

'There you are! We wondered what had become of you!'

Marcus rose to his feet. 'I'm afraid I kidnapped her, Mrs Porter. Can I get you a drink?'

'Oh no, thank you all the same. We're just leaving. Are you ready, Barbara?' Amy asked.

'Yes.' Barbara got up reluctantly. She had been enjoying herself. 'Thank you for the drinks,' she said to Marcus.

'My pleasure.' As she slipped past him he touched her arm. 'May I telephone you?'

Barbara felt the flush beginning again. She glanced at Amy, waiting in the doorway, and looked back at Marcus, so tall, so handsome.

'If you like,' she said.

'You seemed to be getting on very well with Marcus Spindler,' Amy said in the car on the way home.

'He's very nice.'

'Yes he is. So good looking and a hero as well.'

'Not to mention his father's title,' Ralph said drily.

'Did I hear him ask if he could phone you?' Amy asked.

'Yes.'

'Well, you might sound a little more enthusiastic! Most girls would be thrilled to bits to have Marcus Spindler chasing after them.'

'He wasn't chasing.'

'Well, if he does phone and ask you out I hope you'll go,' Amy said. 'It would do you the world of good, Barbara. It's just what you need to cheer you up.'

'Mum, did you know Marcus Spindler was going to be there when you persuaded me to go to the meeting?' Barbara asked suspiciously.

'I thought he might be, yes.'

'Please don't start matchmaking for me,' Barbara said with asperity. 'I don't care for it.'

'I'm not matchmaking! I'm only saying he is a very eligible young man and I hope you realise how lucky you are.'

'Amy!' Ralph said warningly. 'Leave Barbara to make up her own mind. The last thing any girl wants is an interfering mother.'

'Well, I'm sure I'm not that!' Amy said huffily.

They completed the journey home in silence.

Marcus phoned the following evening.

'It's Marcus for you!' Amy called upstairs to Barbara when the telephone rang. In spite of the rebuff she had received from both Barbara and Ralph she was unable to keep the delight out of her voice.

'Hello, Barbara,' Marcus said when she had come to the telephone. 'I thought I ought to get in touch with you fairly quickly before you forget who I am.'

Barbara almost giggled. It would not be easy to

forget Marcus Spindler, she thought, but she had no intention of saying so.

'I wondered if perhaps you would allow me to take you out to dinner. Would you be free one evening this week?'

'I'll be fire watching tomorrow and Friday,' Barbara said. 'I don't believe I am doing anything on Saturday.'

'Do I take it that's an acceptance of my invitation?'

Barbara hesitated. She was not sure she wanted to go out to dinner with Marcus Spindler or anyone else, grand and grown up as it sounded, unless that someone else should happen to be Huw. But Huw had rejected her.

'Well?'

Oh, why not? thought Barbara. Mum is right, I can't moon about for ever.

'Yes, I should think that will be all right.'

'I'll look forward to it.'

Barbara put down the receiver and turned to see a pleased looking Amy hovering in the doorway.

'You're going out with him then?' she asked.

'Yes. Oh, for heaven's sake, Mum, stop looking like the cat that got the cream!' Barbara snapped.

'I'm sorry,' Amy said. But she wasn't. She was very, very relieved.

Marcus collected her promptly at seven o'clock.

When he knocked at the door Barbara hurried to answer it, anxious to escape not only her mother's proud scrutiny but also Maureen's envy. 'You lucky thing!' she had said when she heard who was taking Barbara out. 'He's an absolute dish and stinking rich, too. What a pity he hasn't got a younger brother for me!'

Barbara was wearing her red dress. She had put it on

reluctantly because it reminded her of special times with Huw. But it was the most suitable garment in her wardrobe and she could not go out with Marcus Spindler looking badly dressed.

'I know a nice little restaurant out in the country' he said when he had installed her in the front seat of his car – a handsome two-seater Bentley. 'Some of the restaurants in town are having problems with their menus since the advent of rationing but this one seems to be coping admirably.'

'How are they managing that?'

'It's as well not to ask questions like that. But a good chef can work miracles with plenty of fresh produce.'

He drove fast – though not as well as Huw she thought loyally. Whatever problems he had with his leg when walking did not seem to have affected his ability to put his foot on the throttle and keep it there. Barbara held tight to her seat and began to enjoy herself.

The restaurant turned out to be a large old country house. They were shown to a large pleasant room where a huge log fire burned in an open fireplace. Barbara studied the menu, leather bound and tasselled, and chose stuffed mushrooms to be followed by pheasant. Marcus ordered French onion soup and steak. Barbara gasped when she saw the size of it – one person's ration for a whole week, she wouldn't be surprised. She began to understand why Marcus had said it was best not to question where it came from.

He was an easy person to be with, she soon discovered, charming and amusing, with a seemingly inexhaustible supply of stories about his school and army days. But the stories stopped short of what had happened when his unit had found themselves on the run from Hitler's rampaging armies in France. On the subject of the tragic incident which had won him acclaim Marcus refused to be drawn and Barbara respected his reluctance to talk about it and admired his obvious modesty. Many men would have been eager to boast – Marcus preferred to draw a veil over the whole episode.

By the time coffee was served accompanied by a dish of assorted petits fours Barbara was relaxed and enjoying his company.

'Would you like a liqueur?' he asked.

'Oh, I don't know . . .' She had, she thought, drunk rather a lot.

'I'm having a brandy. Why don't you have the same – or perhaps something sweeter – cointreau or crême de menthe?'

'All right, I'll have a crême de menthe,' Barbara agreed. She liked the peppermint flavour.

He drew out a silver cigarette case and flipped it open to reveal a row of Black Russians.

'Have one?'

'Oh yes, why not?' Barbara said recklessly. Amy smoked – why shouldn't she? But when he lit it for her with his chunky silver lighter she drew on it very carefully. It would hardly be the right image to choke on the smoke.

'So!' He smiled at her lazily. 'Are you going to come out with me again?'

In the candlelight he looked very handsome, his fair hair falling in a soft lick over his high forehead, his perfect features highlighted by the shadows all around. She felt a tiny finger of excitement dart within her. Was it the wine and the liqueur – or was it something more? Whichever, she knew she had enjoyed herself more this evening than she had done for a very long time.

'Is that an invitation?' she asked playfully.

'You know very well it is. I hope, Miss Barbara Roberts, that you are not about to give me a hard time?'

'Now would I do a thing like that?'

'So – will you come out with me again?'

'Since you put it like that – yes.'

He smiled and drew on his cigarette. Behind the screen of smoke his eyes crinkled.

'Good. Now we've got that over we can enjoy the rest of the evening, can't we?'

Next morning over a leisurely Sunday breakfast the family questioned her thoroughly.

'How did you get on?' Amy asked.

'Fine. I'm seeing him again on Wednesday.'

'What did you do? You were very late,' Maureen said. 'I tried to stay awake but I'd already been to sleep for ages when I heard the car.'

'You shouldn't be so nosey,' Barbara said, hoping Maureen had not been peeping out of the window and seen Marcus kiss her goodnight. She was feeling a little fragile this morning from the effects of the wine she had drunk and also oddly guilty. A whole evening and she had hardly thought of Huw once. Now he was there again, a shadow over her pleasure.

She sipped her coffee remembering the way it had felt when Marcus had kissed her. Not as exciting as the kisses she had shared with Huw. That lovely dreamlike quality had been missing. But it had been pleasant, all the same. An experience she would not mind repeating.

Ralph turned on the wireless and when it had warmed up they listened to the news. More German air raid attacks. More vessels lost in the Atlantic. Allied forces crossing the border from Kenya to Somaliland. Discussions with the new Greek Prime Minister, Alexander Korizis. War – war – nothing but the war. When and where would it all end?

Glad of the diversion from her affairs to more important matters, Barbara helped herself to another piece of toast.

Three days later they received news of Huw's promotion

247

to Flight Lieutenant with the rider that he was now a flight commander on his squadron.

'Goodness knows he's earned it,' Ralph said. He felt inordinately proud of the lad whom he had first seen as a scruffy coal-black youngster who had slept the night in his coal house after running away from Amy's one long ago night in 1926. It had seemed then he had no destiny beyond being a troublemaker – how wrong that had proved to be! But in his more self-indulgent moments Ralph felt that he could take a little of the credit for the way the boy had turned out. Amy had given him love and kindness and a home, but he had taught him discipline and given him the firm hand he had undoubtedly needed.

'Flight Lieutenant!' Amy said, every bit as proud, and Maureen practically bounced with excitement.

'Are you going to put it in the paper? Oh you must! I bet he is the only flight commander in Hillsbridge!'

Barbara said nothing. The letter containing the news had been addressed to all the family – there was no special page for her, no mention of her even, and it hurt.

'Aren't you pleased, Barbara?' Maureen prodded her and added with a touch of malice, 'I suppose you're not interested in Huw any more now you have a hero of your own.'

'Oh shut up, Maureen!' Barbara said.

It was far from the truth. But at least it was a mast to which she could nail her pride.

I'll show you, Huw James, she thought. I'll show you you're not the only fish in the sea. And one of these days you'll be sorry for building up my hopes and then brushing me aside. You'll come running back, I know you will.

But even then the prospect of victory tasted bitter in her mouth and Barbara knew it would be a long, long time before she got over Huw – if ever she did.

13

On a Wednesday morning in March Harry Hall was at home nursing a bout of influenza.

It was very unusual for Harry to be ill – or to give into it if he was – but on this occasion, shivering and sweating alternately, with every bone in his body aching and his head feeling like a pumpkin he had bowed to pressure from Elinor Vranch and gone home to bed.

'You are no good to anyone in that state,' she had told him firmly. 'And what is more you are only spreading your germs around for the rest of us to catch.'

'She's quite right,' Margaret had said when she came home from school and found him there. 'The best thing for you is to keep warm and have a good rest. It's overwork that has brought this on if you ask me.'

'Rubbish,' Harry said and sneezed. 'Hard work never hurt anybody.'

'Maybe not. But when you overdo things you lay yourself open to the first infection that comes along. And goodness knows, Harry, you've worked yourself to a frazzle. It's no wonder you're ill.'

Her tone was unusually severe just as Elinor Vranch's had been and Harry wondered why it was that women became so bossy when a man was ill. But he felt too wretched to argue and in any case he knew deep down that Margaret was right. Since his appointment as prospective Labour candidate life had become one hectic whirl and he could scarcely remember the last time he had spent an evening relaxing at home.

Although there was no prospect of a General Election until after the war and, under the electoral truce, it was unlikely the Labour Party would contest the seat even if it did fall vacant, there was always a great deal of work to be done and many meetings to be attended. Added to this Harry remained a councillor at a time when council meetings seemed to run on longer and deal with more business than he could ever remember, and was still employed as Miners' Agent, a job which had become more demanding than ever for the war had thrown up many personal problems for the miners and their families and Harry was expected to deal with them.

'Harry Hall is a good bloke,' was a remark often heard in the Miners Arms and the Working Men's Club, the chapel schoolroom where the families went once a month to pay over their 'Club Money' to the representative of the Friendly Society, and the pit cage as it descended to the bowels of the earth. 'Harry Hall is a good bloke – he'll sort it out for you.'

As far as this went it was fine. Harry Hall *was* a good bloke – but as a result of his popularity and the success of his endeavours on behalf of everyone who sought his help it meant he never had a moment to call his own. From the time he got up in the morning, plotting and planning strategies with his image in the shaving mirror until he fell exhausted into bed at night, his mind was full of all the things he had to do, the causes he had to further, the people depending on him for help.

Margaret, who had started teaching at the Church School at the beginning of the Autumn term, complained that she scarcely ever saw him and when she did he was too tired to notice she was there.

'We'll never get around to starting a family at this rate,' she had said one evening when he had collapsed into bed almost two hours after she had retired herself.

'I don't think it would be a very good idea anyway with this war on. Who wants to bring a child into a

250

world like this?' he had mumbled in reply, heaving the blankets over his chin.

'That's no answer,' Margaret said. She had been dozing and was now feeling sleepy and loving. 'By the time the war is over we might be getting too old. Couldn't we just . . .'

But it was useless. Harry was already asleep.

When the 'flu hit him he had fretted and fought it, then given in thinking: 'I can't help it. They'll all just have to go hang for a day or two.' But as he began to recover he became restless again, working at a pile of papers at the dining-room table contrary to doctor's orders and in spite of feeling so weak that even turning a page was an effort.

He was busy this morning ploughing through the notes he had made for a man who wanted to appeal against conscription when there was a knock at the back door.

Harry swore to himself, propped the papers in such a way that he would be able to find his place easily again on his return, and went to answer it. Probably the baker he thought, pleased to find someone at home and wanting to be paid. The regular baker's boy had been called up and was now in the desert with the Eighth Army and the new one, a useless lad who could not even handle his delivery horse properly, was nothing but a nuisance. Harry decided he would give him a piece of his mind.

But it was not the baker. It was Mrs Franklin from next door.

Since moving into the house Harry had had little to do with the Franklins. Doug Franklin worked at the Co-op Dairy, so he was not one of Harry's flock and he and his wife Betty were strict chapel-goers who 'kept themselves to themselves'. Margaret was on fairly friendly terms with Betty, Harry knew, but his own contact with them had been limited to calling out

251

'Good day!' when he saw them over the garden fence and he was surprised now to see her standing on the doorstep with a coat pulled on over her pinafore.

'Morning, Betty,' he greeted her.

'Oh.' Betty peered past him into the kitchen. 'Margaret not at home, is she?'

'I'm afraid not. She's at school. And she'll be late this evening, too. She has a staff meeting,' Harry said, thinking it was odd that Betty should have expected to catch Margaret in the middle of a working day.

'Oh,' Betty said again. She was a sharp-featured woman with a bustling manner but today she appeared vaguely at a loss.

'She should be home by six o'clock or so,' Harry said, preparing to shut the door. The wind was whistling in, making him feel cold though he had been sure he was well on the way to being better. But Betty showed no signs of being ready to leave.

'Perhaps I could have a word with you then, Harry,' she said.

Harry began to feel annoyed. He had enough problems on his plate without taking on the ones that Betty Franklin wanted to discuss with Margaret.

'Can't it wait?' he asked. 'I'm off work sick. I'd ask you in but I don't want to pass on my 'flu to you.'

Betty showed no signs of being put off.

'It's all right, I *never* get 'flu,' she sad in the self-satisfied tones of one who is certain of her superiority over a whole army of germs. 'I'm sorry to bother you, Harry, but I feel I must talk to you right away.'

'You'd better come in then,' Harry said, admitting defeat.

She followed him into the kitchen.

'Well?' he said determined to retain some control of the situation.

'I hardly know where to begin. It's very embarrassing . . .' She hesitated, then went on all of a rush: 'It's those

252

two vackie girls of yours. Now I've seen a lot and said nothing. It's not my place to interfere, though personally I feel they need a lot more supervision than you and Margaret are able to give them. I've tried to make allowances, of course. They are a handful, I know. But this time . . .'

'Where is all this leading?' Harry asked, getting more annoyed.

'They came round to my place last night. Wanted to know if I could give them anything for a Sale they're having at their school – some sort of Bazaar in aid of the Comforts Fund. I told them I'd see what I could find. They came again this morning. I left them in the kitchen while I went upstairs to get the few knick-knacks I'd looked out for them. A couple of ornaments that belonged to my mother, it was. Rubbish, really, but they seemed pleased enough and went off with them.'

'Yes?' Harry prompted. He could see the pile of papers waiting for his attention and his head was beginning to ache again.

'Well, it's like this,' Betty said, becoming visibly more agitated. 'Since then I can't find my purse. It was in the fruit bowl on the sideboard before they came, where I always keep it. And now it's gone. I can't find it anywhere.'

'I see.' Harry's headache was forgotten now. 'Are you trying to say you think they have something to do with its disappearance?'

'I can't think anything else,' Betty said. 'I'm a Christian woman. I don't like accusing anybody of anything. But I can't find my purse anywhere. I've turned the house upside down looking for it in case I picked it up myself and put it down somewhere stupid, though I'm sure I wouldn't do that. And all I can think is – well, they were down there by themselves while I went upstairs. And now it's gone.'

'I see.' Harry's face was grim. 'Well, all I can say is you'd better leave it with me, Betty. I'll have a word with them this evening and see what they have to say for themselves.'

'They'll deny it, no doubt. I wouldn't trust them any further than I could throw them. Oh, the trouble those vackies have caused! Everybody falling over backwards trying to help them settle in and this is all the thanks you get. They're a poor lot. Never seen the inside of a church, most of them. I don't know — it makes you wonder what we're fighting for.'

'I promise I'll look into it for you,' Harry said hastily. 'Did you have much in your purse?'

'Not a lot, being as this is Wednesday. A ten-shilling note, I think, and 3s.6d. in silver and coppers. Oh – and the money I had put back ready for the insurance man. Half a crown, that was. I can't afford to lose it, Harry.' She was beginning to look flustered again and Harry felt sorry for her. Nearly a pound was a lot of money to someone like Betty. She would be ill able to afford to lose it. 'Oh, and there's some milk tokens too!' she went on, distressed as she made a mental inventory of her purse. 'And the raffle tickets I had off the WVS. I was in hopes of winning a dozen fresh eggs with one of those . . .'

'What is your purse like?' Harry asked.

'Black leather. A good strong purse. Our Ethel bought it for me the Christmas before last . . .'

'If you do happen to find it let me know at once will you?' Harry said.

When she had gone he began pacing the kitchen deep in thought. He was sorry for her but he simply could not believe Elaine and Marie could be responsible for the disappearance of the purse. Why should they be? In all the time they had been there, problems though there had been, there had never been any suggestion that they might be thieves. It seemed a ridiculous assumption to make and quite unfair. The silly woman had probably put the purse down in some unlikely place and forgotten all about it. Then, unable to put her hand on it she had panicked. That had to be the answer.

Because he was feeling chilly again he fetched an extra pullover and put it on then sat down to begin work once more. But now he found himself quite unable to concentrate.

He remembered the girls going next door this morning and hearing them come back again while he was in 'the back place' – the downstairs toilet that was little more than a cupboard, festooned with two garden chairs hanging on nails on the wall, Margaret's peg bag on the hook behind the door and two old tennis rackets stacked in a corner. For some reason Harry preferred 'the back place' to the upstairs bathroom, perhaps because it had the same tightly enclosed feel about it that his pigeon house had once had – the pigeon house that had been his haven in the old days when he had lived at home in Greenslade Terrace. Now 'the back place' provided him with that same sense of peace. He had taken the newspaper there with him this morning and he had still been there reading it when he heard the girls go out again on their way to school.

That, he supposed, was the reason he had not seen them with Betty's knick-knacks. Had they come back into the house to take them up to their room? And if so, why? Why hadn't they taken them directly to school if they were to be priced and put on sale there? Surely they would have been anxious for their teacher to see the treasures they had solicited. So why *had* they come back into the house and gone upstairs?

Any one of a dozen reasons, Harry told himself, but he was beginning to feel uneasy all the same. Perhaps he would take a look around and set his mind at rest. He marked his place in his papers once more and went upstairs.

The girls occupied the small room that had been going to be the nursery. He opened the door and took a step backwards at the muddle facing him. The bed had been 'covered up' rather than made, clothes and comics lay about everywhere. I didn't know they had so much stuff! Harry thought. Margaret must have bought them quite a lot without telling me. He looked around, shifting this and that, then opened drawers and rifled through. Plenty of rubbish but no sign of the purse. He moved the pillows, picking them up and dropping them back into place. Nothing. He turned back to the door relieved, then noticed the boxes containing their gas masks in a corner. Once they had carried the gas masks everywhere with them, nowadays they had ceased to bother. Harry flipped open the top of one box. And there, nestling beside the gas mask, he saw it.

'Oh no!' he said to himself.

He picked it up – a black leather purse, slightly worn – and opened it. Inside were the milk tokens Betty had mentioned and a little wad of raffle tickets. But no money. He stood for a moment holding it in his hand and wondering what to do. He should go straight round and tell Betty, he supposed, but he would like a chance to recover the money first – and ask the girls what they had been thinking of.

He glanced at his watch. Almost a quarter to twelve. The girls would be having their dinner hour soon. Although their school was so close they did not come home for dinner – with Margaret working it was not practicable. But today whether they knew it nor they *were* coming home.

He put on his overcoat and walked down the hill to the Board School. As he approached he heard the bell clang to signify the end of morning lessons and the almost instant chatter of childrens' voices as they escaped from their classrooms. He went in at the gate and marched straight through the cloakrooms, ignoring the children milling there.

In the first classroom a young woman teacher was cleaning the blackboard with a duster. She looked round, hair falling down from a velvet band which she wore Alice in Wonderland style around her head.

'Mr Hall! What can I do for you?'

'I'd like to take Elaine and Marie home with me,' he said.

'Oh dear – some trouble is there?

'A family matter,' Harry said grimly. 'Where can I find them?'

'I expect they've gone in to dinner.'

'Please fetch them,' he ordered.

'I think perhaps I ought to tell the headmaster,' she said, looking harrassed. 'While they are in school they are our responsibility you see.'

'I'll take responsibility,' Harry said firmly. 'I want them now.'

'Even if they're having their dinner?'

'Even if they're having their dinner.'

She went out, looking worried, and within a few minutes was back, following in the wake of the tall spare figure of the headmaster.

'I understand you want to take your evacuees out of school,' he began. 'May I enquire why?'

'A personal matter. I'd rather not say any more until I've spoken to them.' Harry, in spite of his 'flu, was at his most magesterial.

The headmaster nodded. 'Fetch them please, Miss Lane.'

The moment they came into the room Harry knew they were aware of his reason for being here. The guilt was written all over them. Elaine glaring at him defiantly, Marie hanging her head and looking as if she was about to burst into tears. They were already wearing their coats.

'Come along you two,' Harry said. His head had begun to ache again and the throb made him speak even more severely than he intended. They followed him unwillingly. He marched them back up the hill in silence. Then, in the kitchen, he took the purse out of the pocket of his overcoat and held it out accusingly. 'I would like an explanation of this.'

Marie looked as if she wished she could curl into a small ball like a hedgehog. Elaine stared at the ground and scuffed her toe against the leg of the table.

'Stop that!' Harry ordered.

She stopped. She was afraid of Harry.

'Well?' Harry demanded. No answer. 'I found this purse in your room', he went on. 'You stole it this morning from Mrs Franklin next door, didn't you?'

Still no answer. Harry opened the purse.

'There was money in it this morning. Nearly a pound. Where is it?'

They looked at one another furtively.

'If you don't tell me I shall send for Sergeant Button.'

Marie began to sniffle.

'I mean it!' he threatened.

'We spent it!' Elaine muttered. Her weaselly face was defiant.

'You're a liar as well as a thief,' Harry accused. 'You have had no opportunity to spend the money. I want it back this instant or I shall certainly call Sergeant Button.'

'Lainey – get it, please!' Marie whimpered.

Elaine shot her a disgusted look but she crept out of the room and upstairs. A few moments later she was back, flinging the money down onto the table. A threepenny bit rolled off onto the floor.

'Pick that up!' Harry ordered. Marie scuttled to obey. Harry counted the money. It seemed to be all there.

'Now we are going next door to see Mrs Franklin,' he

258

said. 'You are going to apologise for what you did. And you had better do it properly and I hope you can convince *her* not to call a policeman.'

Elaine's eyes went dark with terror.

'But you said if we gave you back the money . . .'

'I said *I* wouldn't call the police if you returned it. I can't answer for what Mrs Franklin will do. It was her purse you stole, not mine. But this I promise you. If ever I have cause to suspect you have done something like this again, I shall have no hesitation. There won't be a second chance for you then. I shall take you straight to the police station and let them deal with it.' He opened the back door. 'Are you ready? Come along then!'

White-faced they went with him. But when Harry knocked on Betty Franklin's door there was no reply. He saw the relief on the sisters' faces and was determined not to let them off so lightly. This had to be a lesson they would not forget.

'Perhaps she is at the police station now,' he said. 'There's nothing more we can do until she comes home. You two had better go back to school for the afternoon and we'll discuss this again later. I'll take care of the purse until we can return it. Come along, I'll see you back to the school gates.'

Elaine went morosely, obviously still shaken by the threat of the police, but with the immediate danger passed Marie had other things on her mind.

'We've missed our dinner now.'

'It won't hurt you to go hungry for once,' Harry said sternly. Knowing Margaret there would be a good meal on the table for them the minute she got in this evening; he had seen the pan of soup simmering on the stove and a cottage pie on the slab in the larder all ready for warming. But perhaps if the girls' bellies rumbled a few times this afternoon it would help to teach them a lesson. Harry was quite determined to prevent a repeat performance of today's scenario.

259

He left the girls at the school gates and watched them scuff miserably across the playground. Then he went back up the hill. His head was throbbing wretchedly and his legs felt so heavy it was an effort to move them. As he unlocked the back door he sneezed and the sneeze started a shiver.

I think I'll have a couple of aspirin and go back to bed for a couple of hours, Harry decided.

He was awakened by Margaret's voice.

'Hello! Hello! Isn't anyone at home?'

He fought through the muzzy layers and opened heavy lidded eyes to see her peeping around the bedroom door. She was wearing a woollen cap; beneath it her face was rosy from the cold.

'Oh, there you are! You went back to bed did you? Where are the girls?'

He fought the thickness in his head and turned to look at the clock which stood on the bedside table. Six o'clock. He'd slept for five hours!

'I'm sorry I'm late,' she said. 'The meeting just went on and on. I thought you'd all deserted me!'

He sat up. 'Aren't the girls home?'

'No. They haven't had their tea either. It doesn't look as though they've been in at all.'

'Where the devil are they then?'

'I don't know. That's what I'm asking you.'

A sense of impending doom penetrated his muzziness. 'We had a bit of an upset today. I had to get them out of school at dinner time.' He went on to tell her what had happened and saw her face change.

'Oh no! I thought they had stopped all that.'

'You mean something like this has happened before?' he demanded.

'Well – yes. Several times I've missed money and I've suspected Elaine.'

'Why didn't you say anything about it?'

'I wasn't sure. I didn't want to cause trouble so I was biding my time.'

'You mean they've been thieving and you've let them get away with it?'

'Not Marie. I'm pretty sure it's Elaine. But nothing has gone missing for ages now and I thought she'd got out of it.'

'What rubbish!' he exploded. 'If that's not encouraging her I don't know what is. I'd have thought you'd have had more sense, Margaret.'

'Well, all *you* seem to have done is succeeded in frightening them so much that they haven't come home!' Margaret said defensively. 'Where are they, Harry? That's what I'd like to know!'

'Yes, so would I,' Harry said crossly, getting up. 'And when we do find them they deserve a jolly good hiding.'

Margaret's lips tightened. She was firmly against corporal punishment which she did not believe achieved anything.

'I don't know what we're going to do,' she said. 'It's dark and cold and they've had no tea. We'd better go out and look for them.'

'They'll come home when they're hungry,' Harry said stubbornly but privately he was worried. The girls had had no dinner and no tea. They must be hungry already. But they were not here.

'We'll give them another hour,' he said. 'If they're not home by seven I suppose we shall have to tell the police. In the meantime, I'd better do what the girls were supposed to do and take Betty back her purse.'

'Well, I'm going out to look for them now,' Margaret said.

She walked the streets looking everywhere she could

261

think of but there was no sign of the girls. At seven she returned home. Harry was in the kitchen looking annoyed.

'Are they back?' she asked hopefully, though it was clear they were not.

'No. And since you obviously haven't found them either I suppose we had better phone Sergeant Button. The little idiots! The whole story will have to come out now and there would have been no need for it to if they hadn't behaved so stupidly. Betty was prepared to let the matter rest now she has her purse back provided we do our best to make sure such a thing never happens again – though personally I think it probably will. They are bad girls and that's all there is to it.'

'They're not bad, they're just deprived,' said Margaret, springing to the girls' defence. 'I should have thought you of all people would understand that. You are supposed to be committed to fighting for better conditions so that people wouldn't need to steal.'

'Elaine and Marie don't need to steal. They have all they could wish for here – and more. You're soft with them, Margaret.' He got up. 'But there's no point sitting here arguing about it. I'll phone Sergeant Button now. He'll have them back in no time. Wherever they are they can't have got far.'

Eddie Roberts was working late this evening. Whatever adverse effects the war might have had on other businesses it had certainly done the insurance trade no harm. People were more anxious than ever to insure life and property and Eddie saw no reason to point out the exclusion clauses to them unless they specifically asked. Even then he usually had a platitude to offer. 'Well – strictly speaking, of course . . . but this is a very good company, very fair. I know of a case . . .' By the time Eddie had finished his client was usually ready to sign

262

on the dotted line. Eddie Roberts was such a *nice* man, so cheerful, so helpful, it was a pleasure to have him calling.

It was just after eight o'clock when Eddie came out of a house on the main Bath road in Sanderley and walked down the path to where he had left his bicycle on the path by the front gate. With eyes not yet accustomed to the dark he felt for it and realised it was not there. At the same moment a car came along the road and by its shaded lights Eddie saw a bicycle wobbling off along the road in the direction of Bath.

'Hoi!' he shouted and began to run after it without much hope. Then there was a crash. Eddie got his second wind and ran harder to find the bicycle – *his* precious bicycle – lying in the road and two girls picking themselves up out of the gutter.

'What the devil do you think you are doing?' he demanded angrily.

They got up, rubbing their grazed knees and looking up at him fearfully. There was a moon and now his eyes had grown used to the dark he recognised them.

'You're the two vackies staying with Harry Hall, aren't you?' he asked. 'What are you doing in Sanderley – and where the blazes did you think you were going on my bike?'

The older of the two girls straightened up defiantly.

'We're going back to London.'

'On my bike?'

'No, stupid. We're going to Bath. Then we're going to get a train.'

Eddie almost laughed. 'You can't do that! Not without telling anybody. You can't go back to London anyway. It's being bombed nearly every night.'

'We don't care,' Elaine said. 'It would be better than staying here. Anything would be better than that.'

'What do you mean?'

'They're awful to us,' Elaine said plaintively. 'Really

263

awful, aren't they, our Marie? Well, *she's* not too bad, I suppose, but him . . . He says we've done things we never have and then he . . .' She paused dramatically. 'He hits us. He does! So we want to go home. Oh, please help us, Mister!'

'I'm hungry!' Marie wailed suddenly. 'Really hungry!'

'We haven't had anything to eat all day,' Elaine went on, prompted by her sister's outburst. 'Not a thing. We often don't.'

'You mean they don't *feed* you?' Eddie asked. He was beginning to feel strangely excited. He'd never heard anyone say a word against Harry Hall before, usually it was all sickening praise. This was a revelation!

'Well, we usually have our dinner at school,' Elaine said. 'But we didn't today. He wouldn't let us. He came and took us home to go on at us again. It was awful. That's why we're going, isn't it, our Marie?'

Marie nodded.

'Please help us, Mister!' Elaine said plaintively. 'You've got a kind face . . .'

Eddie was thinking furiously. What on earth was he to do with two vackie children in the blackout and him with only his bike? But he was determined not to let this golden opportunity slip through his fingers. For years now he had nursed a jealousy of Harry Hall and he had been looking for a way to put him down, Clever Dick that he was. When Harry had put a stop to his little sidelines on the council Eddie had made up his mind that one day he would get his own back, but instead he had been forced to sit quietly back and endorse him as prospective Labour candidate. Eddie had practically sweated with rancour and impotence. No matter how he dug about looking for something to pin on Harry he had always been unsuccessful. In all his dealings Harry seemed above reproach. And now suddenly this had been presented to him.

In secret Harry Hall was cruel to children. Helpless

264

evacuee children placed in his care. Hitting them. Starving them. Treating them so badly they were prepared to face the bombs in London rather than spend another night under his roof . . .

'You can't go to London, tonight,' he said. 'You'd better come home with me. You can have a meal and I'll look after you until we get something sorted out.'

'What about *him*?' Elaine asked. 'He'll make us go back with him!'

'No he won't. When the authorities hear what you have to say about his treatment of you I'm sure no one will make you go back there.'

'They might not believe us!' Elaine said. For the first time she sounded frightened. 'He'll call us liars – he will!'

'I don't think so,' Eddie said grandly.

'He will. He always calls us liars.'

'We did something bad today,' Marie said in a small voice.

'Oh, what was that?' Eddie asked, bending lower to hear her.

'We took some money from the house next door.'

'But only because we was hungry!' Elaine put in swiftly. 'We wanted to buy some food.'

'Are you hungry now?' Eddie asked. 'I expect you are. Well, I'm taking you home with me. I'll see you all right.' He picked up his bicycle and sat Marie on the crossbar. 'We shall have to walk, I'm afraid,' he said to Elaine. 'I can't ride with both of you.'

As they set out along the road there were expressions of triumph on both his face and Elaine's. Only Marie looked unhappy. She did not like the things Elaine had said. Of course, Elaine was her big sister and she was usually right. Marie always stuck by her through thick and thin. But this time she did not think Elaine was right.

Marie clung to the crossbar of the bicycle feeling confused, hungry and frightened.

*

265

'It's ridiculous!' said Margaret. 'The most ridiculous thing I ever heard!'

'Not only ridiculous but a pack of lies!' said Harry.

'Nevertheless, accusations have been made.' Sergeant Button shifted uncomfortably, taking refuge under his voluminous cape. He did not like this one little bit. He had enormous respect for both Harry and Margaret Hall, but he still had a job to do. 'You don't deny taking the children out of school today, Mr Hall, and making them miss their dinner.'

'No, I don't deny that. But I took them out for a very good reason. A purse had been stolen, Sergeant, and I found it in their room. I wanted to get to the bottom of it all.'

'The girls say they took the money because they were hungry. They wanted to buy something to eat.'

'Do you honestly believe that?' Margaret demanded.

The sergeant shifted again. 'There are people who take in vackies for the money they get for their keep and don't spend what they should on them.'

'And you're saying we are like that?'

'Not necessarily. But it does happen . . .'

'Not in this house, it doesn't!' Margaret marched to the larder, took out the pie and banged it down on the table in front of the policeman. 'Here is their tea, uneaten. The fact that they didn't have it is entirely their own fault. But I assure you that until today they have never gone hungry in their lives. Well – not since they have been with us at any rate.'

Sergeant Button's majesty wilted beneath her furious attack.

'They are a cartload of little monkeys, it's true,' he admitted. 'I've had more trouble with the vackies and the things they get up to than all the local youngsters put together. Being away from home I suppose they think they can get away with anything.' He paused, remembering it was not just the children who had caused him trouble. There had been one of the young women, soliciting openly outside the Miners Arms, and several cases of theft and shoplifting. 'Well, at least you won't be troubled with them any more,' he said.

'What do you mean?' Margaret asked sharply.

'They're with Mr Eddie Roberts. He has offered for them to stay with him for the time being and I reckon that would be best all round.'

'But they live here!' Margaret was distressed. 'All their things are here!'

'As far as I'm concerned I'm quite happy to bundle the lot of it in the car and drive it up to Eddie Roberts' house,' Harry said. 'He's got them, he can keep them, and good luck to him.'

'No!' Margaret protested. 'I'm not happy about that Sergeant. I'm sure I could get through to them if I had the chance and find out why they said those terrible things.'

'You've had plenty of chance to get through to them – and it hasn't worked,' Harry said bluntly. 'Let them stay where they are, I say. Well, what about the accusations against us, Sergeant? Will you be preferring charges?'

'I doubt it, Mr Hall. I shall have to make a few enquiries, of course, but I feel sure it will end there.'

'I wish you would take us to court,' Harry said.

Margaret's eyes went round with horror. 'Harry!'

'I do. At least then we could refute the allegations. As it is mud will stick. And Eddie Roberts will do his best to see that it does, no doubt. Can't you just imagine how he'll love to go round muttering "There's no smoke without fire"? I can!'

'It's unfortunate. Very unfortunate,' Sergeant Button said uncomfortably. 'But I still think it's best to leave them where they are for tonight. Perhaps you'll be able to sort something out tomorrow, Mrs Hall.'

'They are not coming back here if I can help it!' Harry stated.

Elaine and Marie arrived on the doorstep two days later.

'What are you two doing here?' Margaret asked coldly.

They looked at her sheepishly.

'Can we come back and stay with you?'

'I don't know about that,' Margaret said. 'I thought we ill treated you.'

'It's better than at Mr Roberts' house. You can't move there. His mother keeps telling us not to touch things,' Elaine said in disgust.

Margaret hid a smile. She had heard Amy talk of her former mother-in-law's fetish for tidiness.

'Well, I don't know,' she said. 'Mr Hall is very upset about the things you have said and done.'

'Oh, please!' Marie cried. She hurled herself at Margaret, clutching her skirts. Margaret was lost.

'All right, you had better come in,' she said.

'Things are going to be different from now on,' Harry said sternly. 'I'm telling you straight that if I had my way you would certainly not have come back. And if I ever have another moment's trouble from either of you, you won't get another chance.'

They returned his gaze submissively. What was it about these urchins, he wondered. They could do the unforgiveable and still worm their way back into your heart.

Of course, if he was honest, his motives were not entirely altruistic. Already, Eddie Roberts had begun to spread the rumours, a word here, a word there. 'Of course, nothing could be proved but . . .', always with

268

the look that said maybe Harry Hall was not all that he seemed. With the children back under his roof his case looked a little stronger. If he had really ill-treated them they would never have been so eager to return.

As prospective Labour candidate Harry felt he could not afford even a whisper about his character – and given the opportunity Eddie Roberts would do plenty of whispering.

'Very well, for the moment we will forget about it,' he said to the children.

But he knew there were plenty of political opponents now and in the future who would not be so ready to forget.

14

Throughout the spring of 1941 while the war gained in ferocity and momentum Marcus Spindler continued to court Barbara Roberts.

Britain was on the offensive now. Huw was night-flying as part of the fighter force which escorted the bombers to their targets in France – small groups of Lancasters and Halifaxes which flew down from their bases in Lincolnshire and Yorkshire and made their rendezvous with a close-support wing of thirty-six Hurricanes or Spitfires over the fighter base to create the formation known as the 'beehive'. Sometimes, Huw was a part of this, more often he flew with the target-support wings, timed to arrive in the target area at precisely the same time as the 'beehive'. As he watched the dark waters of the Channel pass beneath the wings of his Spitfire and the coast of France loom ahead Marcus was wining and dining Barbara; by the time the bombers had off-loaded their cargoes of destruction onto some French factory which was working for the Germans and turned for home, Marcus was kissing her goodnight in the deep shadows under the trees where he parked his two-seater Bentley.

She thought of him sometimes as Marcus held her, whispering in her ear the sort of sweet nothings which Huw never had. They rolled easily off his tongue and started a strange dark excitement inside her. It was pleasant to be told she was the most beautiful girl he had ever met, possible to believe it almost when good food and wine and the tantalising touch of his lips had filled her with excitement. It made her feel desirable and feeling that she responded accordingly, learning to kiss as he kissed, with tongue and teeth as well as lips, murmuring those intoxicating words of love against her skin. In spite of this she sometimes thought of Huw and it was like a sweet sad yearning which somehow only heightened the response she offered Marcus.

Forget Huw. Forget him. He doesn't want you. Marcus does. He holds you and whispers nice things to you. He spends a great deal of money on you and wants to be with you often. Forget Huw. Forget him!

Gradually the self-hypnosis began to work and she began to believe that Marcus could replace Huw in her heart.

At the beginning of April news reached Hillsbridge that Alec was with the British Invasion Force in Greece but it was one subject Barbara did not raise with Marcus, being slightly ashamed of her cousin's lowly status as Private when Marcus had been a Captain.

Then, on 18th April, the very same day that the *Mercury* reported seventy people dead from a bomb which had demolished a block of flats in Berlin, Marcus had news of his own.

'We're having a few changes in family business,' he told her as they drove around the lanes to their favourite restaurant. 'My brother has decided to volunteer for army service.'

'Really?' Barbara was surprised. Henry Spindler was his father's right arm. While Sir Richard ruled the colliery companies, Henry was responsible for administering the estates, the farms, cottages and other holdings which went to make up the Spindler empire. It was for this reason, she imagined, that he had so far escaped being called upon to serve his country, for the successful administration of Britain's assets could be considered in many ways essential war work, though when other young men from Hillsbridge had failed to put a case to satisfy the Exemption Board there had been occasional murmurings of unfair treatment. 'It's one thing if your name is Spindler, quite another if you're plain Smith or Jones' was one comment that had been made in the Working Men's Club on more than one occasion.

Marcus manipulated the Bentley around a bend with a burst of acceleration which made Barbara wonder just how much petrol he was burning – and where he managed to get it.

'The point is there should be a Spindler doing his bit,' he said. 'Unfortunately it can't be me now – this leg has put paid to that. So Henry is going to join my old regiment and I am going to take over his job.'

'But you don't know anything about it,' Barbara objected.

He laughed. 'Not as much as Henry does, maybe, but I'm learning. What do you think I've been doing all these months – sitting around and twiddling my thumbs? Of course not! I've been working with Henry, learning to do what he does. Which compared to being an army officer, with men's lives in your hands, is child's play.'

'Is it?' Barbara said doubtfully. The course she was engaged on was teaching her that there was a great deal more to business than she had at first suspected and she had already decided that although she would be having her eighteenth birthday the following week, she would see the course through to the end of the year at least before volunteering herself for one of the women's services.

'Do you wish you could be the one to go back into action?' she asked. 'Or are you glad your war is over now?'

He glanced at her, his well-shaped mouth curving.

'With a lovely lady like you by my side is there any doubt about where I'd prefer to be?'

She experienced the familiar flush of pleasure but refused to allow it to show. 'Seriously.'

'Seriously, it is not very nice to feel one is no longer of any use.'

'Oh, but that's rubbish!' she said hotly.

'Unfortunately, it is *not* rubbish.' He paused, seemingly on the point of saying something.

'At least you have the satisfaction of knowing you were invalided out a hero,' Barbara said into the small silence.

Marcus pressed his foot down hard on the throttle. The car shot forward.

'Yes,' he said and there was an undertone in his voice she did not understand. 'Yes. I suppose at least I have that.'

Henry Spindler left to begin his training as an Army Officer the following week in almost as much of a blaze of glory as Marcus had come home to.

The night before he left the Spindlers held their own private farewell party and for the first time Barbara was invited to their home.

The prospect of meeting his family did not intimidate her, but as they passed between the lodge gates and into the tree lined drive leading to Hillsbridge House she felt the first twinge of nervousness.

The house was so enormous! Even now, shrouded in blackout, she could imagine the way it must have looked when dinner parties or balls were held in peacetime with lights shining out of every one of the dozens of windows and illuminating the broad forecourt and the willows which overhung the lawns.

Marcus parked with an unceremonious screech of brakes, helped her out of the car and led the way up the flight of steps, guarded by magnificent stone lions, to the main door. Once inside, the brilliance encompassed her. The hall, larger than their own drawing-room, was illuminated by a crystal waterfall chandelier; a broad stairway swept upwards beneath a cupola, now hung with blackout. Barbara glanced furtively around, glad she had saved enough clothing coupons for the blue shantung which Amy's dressmaker had been able to turn into something more suitable for such an occasion than the 'utility clothes' which were all that could be purchased in the shops these days.

A door to the right of the hall was ajar, and voices were floating out, genteel voices with no hint of Somerset accents. As Marcus led her in she glimpsed pale gold velvet and brocade, fresh flowers and valuable antiques. His arm was around her shoulders as he made the introductions.

'My dear, how lovely to meet you at last. We've heard so much about you!' Lady Spindler was tall and slim, dressed in silver-grey silk. Her hair, too, was silver-grey, a shining cap; her features slightly faded yet still pretty, her long neck showed to perfect effect a double choker of pearls caught at the base of the throat by a small and perfect cameo. She reminded Barbara of a swan. Over her shoulder Sir Richard beamed at Barbara.

'Capital. I must say you know how to choose 'em, Marcus my boy!' He stopped short of actually clapping Marcus on the back but Barbara felt that he would have liked to do so. 'Now, my dear, what would you like to drink? Sherry? Or don't you indulge?' He laughed a little too heartily.

'Oh yes, she indulges, don't you, Barbara?' Marcus said, smiling at her. 'And so will I.'

'I knew *you* would,' Sir Richard said jovially. 'Drinks too much since his wartime experiences, you know. But I dare say it won't do him any harm.'

'As long as it doesn't make me garrulous, Father,' Marcus said and Barbara cringed. But Sir Richard, seemingly unaware of the sarcasm in his tone, rumbled on.

'They say the army marches on its stomach. Myself, I'm not so sure. Marches on the bottle if you ask me. Where would we have been in the Great War in the trenches without a rum ration?'

'Don't forget Barbara's sherry, dear,' Erica Spindler said gently.

'No, of course not. Marcus, introduce Barbara to your brother, will you? He's been talking to that blasted Clara Oldthorpe for the last half hour. And if he's off to war he may as well take the image of a pretty face with him as a plain one, don't you agree?' He winked at Barbara and she felt that as far as Marcus's father was concerned at least she had passed the test.

By the time they went in to dinner Barbara was enjoying herself. Henry Spindler, quieter and altogether more serious than Marcus, had been very sweet to her and if his companion Clara Oldthorpe, a doctor's daughter from Bath, had shot her the occasional less-than-friendly look Barbara counted that as yet another mark of triumph. When a girl was as plain as Clara Oldthorpe it must be very difficult to refrain from jealousy, Barbara thought, trying to be kind but unable to avoid the conclusion that the obviously expensive gown she was wearing did nothing whatever for her flat chest, thick waist and decidedly bandy legs.

Dinner was served by a maid in a black dress, cap and apron. Barbara recognised her as a Hillsbridge girl, one of a family who lived in the same rank as her Aunt Dolly, and fervently hoped she would not show any sign of recognition herself. She did not. She was far too well trained for that.

They were in the middle of dessert – wafer-thin crêpes in flamed brandy – when the air raid siren began to wail. Although Hillsbridge House was a good two miles outside the town the sound carried clearly across the valley and Barbara paused, spoon halfway to her mouth, waiting to follow the lead of the others.

275

They did nothing, but noticing her alertness, Lady Spindler smiled.

'We ignore it, Barbara,' she said serenely. 'It's probably a false alarm, but in any case there is nothing I deplore so much as a spoiled meal.'

'Waste of good food – nothing short of criminal in these days of shortages,' Sir Richard agreed.

'Oh yes!' Barbara said and popped the spoonful of crêpe into her mouth. But it no longer tasted quite so good. The bomb which had demolished the Chapel and killed poor Ron Hodges had made her nervous – since then she had never been able to summon up the same nonchalance about a raid – and looking across the table she realised Marcus was feeling much as she did. His handsome face was drawn suddenly, his eyes wary and she knew that like her he was listening for the drone of the bombers. That was experience for you, she supposed. A little went a very long way.

On this occasion, however, Lady Spindler's optimism was justified. After a few minutes they heard the siren again, this time the reassuring 'all clear' and Barbara heaved a sigh of relief. There would be no raid tonight – at least not on Hillsbridge.

The ladies retired while the port was passed – how old fashioned! thought Barbara. Then there were more drinks in the splendidly furnished drawing-room with portraits of Marcus's ancestors glowering balefully down from the walls.

'I'm very proud of my sons, you know!' Sir Richard said, as if addressing the portraits. 'One the best Estates Manager I have ever had, the other a hero. And now they are going to swap roles and show they can do just as well in each other's spheres, too.' He raised his glass, obviously well in his cups and enjoying it. 'Let's drink to them. Henry and Marcus.'

'Henry and Marcus,' they all echoed dutifully, but Barbara could not help thinking it was unlikely Henry would be as good a soldier as Marcus had proved to be. Of course he was cut out for it, she thought with a touch of pride. His sporting achievements, his whole personality fitted him for it. And it never crossed her mind to wonder if he could also be as good an Estates Manager as his brother.

Marcus was after all the perfect English gentleman. Success would surely follow in everything he attempted.

Glowing, Barbara finished her drink.

'Well, did you like them?' Marcus asked.

He had parked the Bentley in the usual place under the trees at Valley View and slipped an arm around her shoulders.

'Oh, I did!' she said happily. 'Your mother is so serene! And your father is not a bit frightening.'

'Did you expect him to be?'

'Just a little, maybe. Do you think they liked me?' she asked.

'I'm sure they did. All of which makes what I want to say to you a good deal easier.'

'What's that?'

'Can't you guess?'

'No.'

He turned her slowly towards him. In the moonlight he looked more than ever like a young Greek god. 'I want to ask you to marry me.'

'Oh!' she said.

He laughed, a small forced laugh. 'Is that all you can say – oh!'

'Oh!' she said again.

He had taken her totally by surprise. Though they had been seeing one another for several months now it had simply never entered her head that he might be this serious.

'Look – you don't have to say anything now,' he said.

'I can see I've given you a bit of a shock. I've shocked myself as well if it comes to that. But I'm in love with you. I think I have been ever since I first saw you that night in the George and I've known for weeks that I wanted to marry you.'

'Why have you shocked yourself then?' she asked, playing for time to get her breath back.

'Well, coming out with it just like that of course!' He smiled. 'I should have done it properly on bended knee with a bouquet of red roses and a family heirloom ready to pop on your finger. But I've had enough to drink to give me Dutch courage and all of a sudden I didn't want to wait a moment longer. Please, darling Barbara – you honestly don't have to say yes now – as long as you do say yes!'

Her head was spinning. But suddenly she was thinking of Huw. Why couldn't it have been *Huw* proposing to her? Oh why . . . ?

'I'm very honoured,' she said and her voice sounded strange and stiff to her own ears. 'But you'll have to give me time to think.'

'Of course. It's your birthday next week, isn't it?'

'That's right. You are taking me to the Sadlers Wells Ballet at the Theatre Royal to celebrate – remember?'

'It would be rather nice if we had something else to celebrate as well wouldn't it? Like an engagement?'

'Marcus, you are rushing me.'

'Sorry. But – oh Barbara, I do love you.'

She felt serene suddenly, as serene as Lady Erica, but floating on a little cloud somewhere between heaven and earth. She leaned across and kissed him lightly.

'Goodnight, Marcus. And thank you for everything,' she said.

The serenity lasted only until she was inside the front door. Then her head was spinning again.

Marcus had asked her to marry him. Marcus Spindler, Hillsbridge's golden boy, the most eligible bachelor in the district. She should be over the moon. She should be, but . . .

I don't love him, do I? thought Barbara in confusion and a small voice inside her, the voice of reason began to argue with her.

Don't you? What is love anyway? You like his company. You go funny inside when he kisses you.

Huw! What I felt for Huw was love!

But Huw doesn't want you. If you can't have Huw you might as well settle for Marcus. At least that way you would forget Huw and all your silly dreams.

Oh – I don't know. I don't know!

Write to Huw. Tell him you are thinking of marrying someone else. Give him one last chance. If he still doesn't want you . . .

That's what I'll do. I'll write to Huw.

But first she told Maureen. She simply could not keep the news to herself, much as she intended to. Maureen was ecstatic.

'Oh Barbara, you must marry him! You'd be a fool not to!'

'Yes, I know, but . . .'

'But nothing! You can't turn down a chance like that! Can I be bridesmaid? I could have a pink dress! I've always wanted to be a bridesmaid!'

'Oh, I don't know . . .'

'What does Mum say?'

'Mum doesn't know yet. And you are not to tell her.'

'Why not? Oh, it's so exciting! He's so super! Really gorgeously super! I wish somebody like him would ask *me* to marry them. I wouldn't need asking twice. But I don't suppose anyone ever will.'

'Don't be so silly.'

'Marry him, *please* Barbara!'

'Don't keep on. And don't tell Mum.'

'All right.'

But of course she did.

To Barbara's surprise Amy was cautious.

'Don't rush into anything, darling,' she warned. 'You're not eighteen until next week. You've got all your life ahead of you. I'd hoped it would be a long while before you thought of getting married.'

'People do get married quite young, especially when there is a war on,' Barbara said. Amy's opposition was turning her into devil's advocate. 'You weren't much older than me when you married Dad.'

'I was twenty,' Amy said severely. 'There's quite a difference. And I *seemed* much older than you.'

'That's probably because you insist on treating me like a little girl. And I'm not.' She was warming to the idea. It made her feel good to have someone like Marcus wanting to marry her and it restored some of the self-confidence she had lost since Huw's rebuttal. Love on the rebound was not a term Barbara would have used but it was what was happening to her all the same.

When Huw's reply to her letter came in the same envelope as her birthday card its contents were exactly as she had feared.

'I am very glad to hear that you have found someone else,' Huw had written. 'All I have ever wanted was what is best for you. Dear Barbara, I hope you will be very happy.'

She had thought she would cry when she knew for certain there was no more hope but she did not. Perhaps she had already shed all the tears from that particular well. But she did sit for a very long time staring at the letter and feeling the dark hollow inside her grow and spread. So that was it. There could be no more doubts, no more foolish secret hopes. A part of her

280

still cried out that she could not understand it, couldn't believe that what had meant so much to her had meant nothing to him. But the facts were indisputable. Huw had turned his back upon that wonderful stolen day as if it had never been.

Had it really been only one day? To Barbara it had seemed like a lifetime and perhaps that was the trouble. It had been no more than a diversion to Huw in the midst of months of hell and she had set too much store by it because that was the way she so desperately wanted it to be. Well, no more. Marcus wanted her. He could salve her wounded pride and heal her broken heart. She could stand up and say to the world – Look! Marcus Spindler wants me for his wife! And in the quiet of the night when the doubts crept in she could remind herself that she could not be so unlovable if someone like Marcus loved her.

I'll do it, thought Barbara. I'll marry him and I'll be the best wife ever. He'll never know it was because of someone else that I hesitated and I'll never give him cause to regret asking me. We'll be happy. Happy even if it kills me. Oh, I'll show that Huw James! I'll show him! Just see if I don't!

Marcus arrived to take her to the ballet bringing with him an enormous bouquet of red roses.

'Happy Birthday, darling.'

'Oh, they're beautiful! Thank you! No one ever gave me red roses before!'

'You shall have them every year from now on if that's what you want. And on other special occasions too.' His eyes held hers and she read the message there – 'I love you'. Her heart seemed to lift and she felt a little as if she had already drunk several glasses of champagne. Oh perfidy! Bought for a look of love and two dozen red roses . . .

But it was wonderful to be made such a fuss of. To be treated like a piece of precious porcelain. To be handed in and out of the car, installed in one of the private boxes at the rear of the dress circle, presented with a beribboned box of handmade chocolates. The music, rising from the orchestra pit to fill every corner of the prettily ornate theatre, throbbed within her and the whiff of greasepaint as the curtain rose heightened her elation and excitement.

The ballet was wonderful, too – Swan Lake with Margot Fonteyn and Robert Helpmann – and Barbara was entranced. This was not something Huw would have dreamed of taking her to – she could just imagine the rude remarks he would make about men in tights – and had she dragged him along he would now doubtless be fidgeting and looking at his watch, not enjoying the performance as Marcus was doing.

During the interval champagne was brought to them.

'Birthdays should be special,' Marcus said, raising his glass.

She drank, the bubbles tickling her nose.

'This one certainly is.'

He leaned towards her. 'How special?'

'Very.'

'Very, *very* special?' He paused. 'You know what I'm asking you, don't you? I know I promised not to press you, but . . .'

'Yes,' she said. It was just the right moment. She felt elated, loved, bubbly as the champagne.

'Yes, you'll marry me?'

'Yes.' And then, as an afterthought: 'If Mum will let me.'

'Don't worry about that. We'll talk her round. Oh Barbara, I am so happy I feel like standing up and announcing it to the whole theatre! Are you happy too?'

'Yes,' she said, and suddenly she was. One door had closed but another had opened and the world she

282

glimpsed through it was wide and beautiful, a new adventure laid out before her.

The orchestra was striking up again. He leaned over and kissed her, his lips touching her neck beneath the cap of shining golden curls.

'You'll never regret it, Barbara, I promise you,' he said.

She slipped her hand into his. It felt good and safe. And it never occurred to her that some promises are impossible to keep.

'Marcus! What sort of a name is that to go to bed on?' Charlotte asked.

'A very nice name, Grandma. And you need not pretend you have never heard it before because everyone in Hillsbridge has heard of Marcus,' Barbara said. She spoke with asperity but warmth; Barbara and Charlotte had always shared a special relationship since the long ago days when Charlotte had cared for her whilst Amy was working to build up the business and Barbara knew that Charlotte was only being scathing in an effort to conceal her pride. That had shown clearly in her face when Barbara called to tell her that she and Marcus was getting engaged.

Her grandfather's reaction, however, had been less enthusiastic.

'Spindler, eh? The boss you mean?'

'His son, yes.'

'Well, well, I don't know about that.'

'Aren't you pleased, Grandpa?'

'No, I don't know as I am,' James said, wheezing a little, and Barbara looked at him in surprise.

Grandpa usually took everything as it came, with a gentle smile that creased his faded blue eyes and some platitude or other. She had no way of knowing that James was totally bemused by the way his descendants had of marrying out of their class or how uncomfortable it made him feel.

It didn't seem right, he thought to himself. He and Charlotte had had a good life – hard work, yes, but they had never owed anybody a penny and there was nothing better than being nice and quiet in your own home. Why the young generation couldn't be content with the same pattern he could not understand.

'What does Mum say about it?' Charlotte asked.

Barbara pulled a face. 'She says I'm too young.'

Charlotte sniffed. 'I thought she might. She's a bossy one, your Mum, but I expect you know that.'

Barbara smiled.

'You're eighteen now, anyway,' Charlotte went on. 'I was younger than you when I married your Gramp and we've done all right. Your Mum agreed in the end, I suppose.'

'She couldn't do anything else,' Barbara said. 'Marcus asked her so nicely. She keeps going on about not getting married yet, though. She seems to think being engaged is just a game, not serious at all. It's as if she is saying to me – Well, play at it for a bit and then when you get tired of it you can forget all about it and go back to being the way you were. I can't understand her really.'

'I wouldn't take a bit of notice of her,' Charlotte advised. 'Long engagements never did anyone any good. Once you've made up your mind you might as well get on with it.'

'That's just what I say, Grandma,' Barbara replied. Her grandmother had summed up her sentiments exactly. It had taken her a little while to decide to marry Marcus but now that she had she was fired with impatience. It always had been that way with her – planning longterm was for others, Barbara preferred action.

'Let's have another look at your ring, Babs,' Charlotte

284

said and Barbara displayed it proudly – an enormous
ruby set around with diamonds. Marcus had taken her
to the grandest shop in Bath to choose it and she had
not dared to tell anyone how much it had cost in case
they should think she was boasting.

'When are we going to meet this Marcus?' Charlotte
asked, admiring the ring.

'I'll bring him to see you,' Barbara promised.

'Here?' James asked in alarm.

'Why not?'

'Well, it bain't what he's used to . . .'

'Grandpa anyone would think I was ashamed of
you!' Barbara laughed and hugged him.

'Just as long as you're happy, Babs,' Charlotte said.
'That's all that matters.'

'Oh I am,' Barbara said and she was. With Marcus's
ring on her finger and the promise of a future life in
which she would want for nothing she thought she had
almost, if not completely, exorcised Huw from her
heart.

15

In July Huw was sent to RAF St Athan for a short course on Harvards and Hurricanes. He had spent the months since his promotion on offensive sweeps over enemy-occupied territories in France and the Low Countries and as bomber escort, his accredited combat victory tally steadily rising, and had been awarded a DFC for his efforts. Now he suspected the change in direction would mean a new posting and the possibility of further promotion, perhaps to Squadron Leader, and he was very glad.

Flying was his whole life now and had been from the moment Amy had broken the devastating news to him which had ended for ever his association with Barbara. It was, after all, a way of finding oblivion from the torment of discovering he had fallen in love with the one person with whom he could never have anything more than a platonic relationship. Sharply alert, eyes scanning the skies for the first sign of danger, every sense strained to breaking point, there was no time for brooding, no emotion left over for yearning after what might have been. He devoted himself to nursing along the new pilots in the Flight, fresh-faced lads many of them, only just out of school, whose keenness to get in on the fight was soon tempered by the strain of flying night after night and whose eyes soon grew to reflect the horror of seeing friends shot down in flames. He wrote letters to the loved ones of those who were lost, packing up more photographs and personal belongings than he would ever care to remember in the years to come. And somehow, through dogged determination, skill and, he admitted, a slice of luck, he managed to remain alive himself, though more than once he had to nurse a crippled aircraft back over the dark waters of the Channel.

Lying exhausted in his bunk he still thought of Barbara, her lovely face taking its place in the parade of other faces which he would see no more and the weight in his heart was almost more than he could bear. And occasionally he broke out in a sweat when he thought of how close he had come to committing that unforgiveable sin whose name invoked such feelings of utter revulsion – incest. Christ, it didn't bear thinking about! Why had Amy not told him before? He'd had a right to know, surely, and if he had known then this terrible situation would never have arisen.

Or would it? He knew now – but he still loved her. Knowing it was wrong, knowing it could not be, did not stop him loving her.

The day he received her letter telling him that Marcus Spindler had asked her to marry him he shot down an Me109, tailing it until the wings overlapped the outer ring of his gunsight circle, then destroying it with burst after burst from his canon and Browning. As it fell in an explosion of canon shells and ruptured fuel tanks Huw felt a swell of elation as if the burning German plane could also burn Barbara out of his heart. But the respite was shortlived. Back at the aerodrome with the trampled grass beneath his feet again, he discovered she was still there, an ache which could explode at any moment into an agony of pure jealousy when he thought of her with Marcus Spindler. He walked back across the airfield, unzipping his flying jacket, ignoring the banter of the men who had returned with him.

'You gave him what for didn't you, Huw? Christ, you made sure of that poor bastard!'

He made no reply for he was feeling ashamed that he had taken it out on some unknown German, given him no chance at all, when really it was Marcus Spindler he had been gunning for.

Amy's letter had arrived the following week with the news that Barbara and Marcus were engaged and he had sunk further into depression. Only one sentence had given him consolation – 'I shall not agree to them marrying for quite a while, of course. The whole thing has been much too sudden for my liking and she needs a year at least to get to know him and be certain she is doing the right thing. Thank heavens she is under twenty-one and still needs my permission.'

So there was a respite, at least. Then he remembered that a year or ten years even would make no difference to the situation as far as he was concerned. Whether or not Barbara decided in the end that Marcus was 'the right thing', he would never again be able to give her any inkling of the way he felt about her and the depression descended once more.

When he first learned he was going to St Athan it crossed his mind that it was odd that he should be returning to within a few miles of the place where he had been born and he wondered briefly if perhaps it was an omen. He had been lucky to escape unscathed so far, perhaps his luck was about to run out. There would be some sort of poetic justice if he should die, as he had been born, in Wales.

But Huw had little time for brooding and it was only when he crossed the Severn for the first time in fifteen years that he realised how deeply he had missed his native land. It was odd the way it affected him, as if the Welsh air was somehow different to English. Breathing it in started a strange poignant nostalgia and half forgotten memories came flooding back. The grass was so green, the sky so blue above the rolling hills, more green, more blue than he had ever noticed it to be elsewhere. In his mind's eye he saw Pontypridd again, the steeply rising terraces of cottages with the black slag heaps which in Somerset were known as 'batches', the market place, the deep slow-running river. Thinking about it he seemed to hear the lilting Welsh accents, too, and the soaring voices raised in hymns of praise which floated out of every chapel in the valley on a Sunday morning so that they could have been mistaken for a thousand male voice choirs.

He had been happy here in those far off days, roaming the streets and the woods, sliding down the waste tips on an old tin tray, playing at war beneath the kitchen table with a bicycle pump for a gun with the man he had called Dad, stealing handfuls of sweets from the counter in 'Jones the Sweets'' shop when the old man was not looking, fighting – rolling, gouging and kicking – sometimes alone, sometimes as one of a gang, getting up to all kinds of mischief. It was years now since he had thought about it for the carefree pleasures of those days had been replaced, after a period of utter misery, by a new happiness with Amy's family. The changed circumstances had become his life so that Pontypridd seemed like a distant dream which had happened to someone else, not to him at all.

Now, however, it all came back to him as clearly as if it had been yesterday and Huw knew that while he was here, so close to where it had all happened, he had to go back.

He went on an afternoon when the sun was hot and bright in a cloudless sky, getting a train to Pontypridd station, and at first he was disappointed. The streets were much as he remembered them yet subtly different, altered not only by time but by his misted recollection of them. 'Jones the Sweets'' shop was gone now, replaced by a small café; Huw went in and bought himself a cup of tea and a slab of bread pudding, sitting at an oilcloth-covered table near the window to eat it and watching the faces of the passers-by in the hope that he might recognise one of them as a face from long ago. He did not and he felt oddly let down.

Was there anyone here in Ponty who still remembered him? Anyone who just once in a while when they were reminiscing asked: 'I wonder whatever happened to Huw James – Idris's boy? Remember Idris? He got killed underground – a stone fell on him and crushed him.' Probably not. Memories can be short and it was all so long ago.

He had been wrong to come, he thought. Better to have left his memories intact. But now that he was here he felt oddly driven to press on with his odyssey.

He left the café and went for another walk through the streets. And then, almost without meaning to, he found himself heading towards the pit where Idris had used to work, past it, and up the steep slope towards the cottage where he had spent the early years of his life. The cobbles felt comfortably familiar beneath his feet and he saw that here, at least, nothing much had changed. The stone with which the cottages had been built was blacker, if anything, than he remembered, for another fifteen years' coal dust and smoke had spewed onto them, the paintwork a little more faded from neglect that the war years had spawned. But the doors still stood ajar; in some of them a woman or an old man sat enjoying the summer sunshine, and the voices calling to one another had that wonderful lilt that he only now realised he had missed so much.

Two children were sitting outside the house where he had been born, squabbling over a bowl of soapy water and a clay pipe they were using to blow bubbles. He smiled to himself and stopped to speak to them.

'Live here, do you?'

They looked up in surprise at this tall stranger in uniform and the smaller of the two, a girl, gave up her struggle for the bubble pipe and ran indoors. The other, a boy, gazed at him with a shrewd and oddly worldly-wise expression on his grubby face.

'Who are you?'

'Oh, I used to live here a long time ago,' Huw said.

The door of the neighbouring house, which was ajar, swung fully open and a woman came out.

'All right, you two? What's the matter? Where's our Mary?'

'Gone in,' said the boy.

'Oh, all right is she?' She fixed Huw with a suspicious eye. 'I'm watching out for them while their Mam's gone down to shop. You're wanting her, are you?'

'No,' Huw said. 'I was just looking around. I don't suppose you remember me, do you?'

'Should I?' Her eyes were small and bright in her round face.

Huw smiled. He had recognised her the moment he saw her, though her hair, crimped across her head in neat corrugated waves, was now iron-grey and she had an extra chin and a few deep creases to mark the passage of the years. Win Williams. She had lived next door then and she still lived next door now.

'It's been a long time, Mrs Williams,' he said. 'I'm Huw – Huw James.'

Her eyes went round and waves of surprise chased one another across her face.

'Huw! I don't believe it! Little Huw James – Sibyl's boy!'

'Yes.'

'Oh duw, duw! Yes, it is! I can see it now! But – you've grown!'

'I suppose I have,' he said, smiling. 'It's fifteen years since I was playing along this rank.'

'Oh Huw – come in, come in do! Come in and have a cup of tea!' The Welsh hospitality was taking over now. 'You behave yourself now!' she said severely to the child with the bubble pipe. 'Your Mam will be back in a tick and if you two keep quarrelling I shall have to tell her all about it.' She winked at Huw. 'That's my grandchildren, you know. Our Olwyn's children. You remember our Olwyn. She'd be older than you by a bit. Been married now five years and her hubby is off somewhere in the Atlantic on the convoys. Went down to Barry, he did, soon as war broke out, and signed on with the Merchant Navy. I ask you! And a good job here in the pit and two little ones . . . I don't know . . .' She shook her head sadly. 'Still, never mind our troubles now, Huw. Come in, bach. Sit down now. Make yourself at home.'

Huw followed her into the kitchen and she fussed around making tea from the kettle that was boiling on the open fire.

'Now, Huw, tell me all about yourself,' she instructed him. 'You're in the air force, I see. Where are you stationed?'

'I'm at St Athan at the moment.'

'St Athan, is it? Well, well! The last I heard you were in Somerset.'

'Yes, that's right.' Huw filled in the details of his life and Mrs Williams kept his cup topped up with thick sweet tea made the way only the Welsh knew how, Huw thought. Drinking it he had a sudden longing for chunks of bread and jam or that special treat, drop scones made on the griddle.

'Well, Huw, I just can't get over what a fine lad you've grown into!' Mrs Williams said at last. 'I can hardly believe it! It seems like only yesterday you were no bigger than Olwyn's two. And a proper little scamp you were, too. Led your mother a proper dance. And your poor father – oh, that was a sad thing to be killed like that and after all he'd been through, too.'

Huw looked at her sharply, wondering suddenly just how much she knew. Quite a bit, no doubt. There were few secrets in the closely packed ranks in the Welsh valleys.

'Of course, things weren't quite what they seemed, were they?' he said.

He saw the wary look come into her eyes – and knew she knew.

'Oh – weren't they?'

'You know very well they weren't,' he said lightly, though suddenly he felt much the same way as when he sighted enemy fighters. 'It's all right Mrs Williams, you don't have to keep any secrets from me. I know all about it.'

She relaxed visibly. 'Well, that's all right then, isn't it? You see, I always promised your Mam that I wouldn't breathe a word to a living soul. And I never have – no, not even when there's been talk. I buttoned my lip up and said I wasn't interested in gossip. And I wasn't. Never have been – it's not my way. We're none of us as white as the lilies of the field, are we? That's why your Mam talked to me, I expect. She had to have someone to confide in, poor soul, and she knew she could trust Win Williams to keep it to herself.'

'That's very good of you,' Huw said awkardly. 'I'm sure she would be very grateful.'

'Well, who was I to lay blame? She was so lonely, see, your Mam, when your Da was away. And she wasn't the only one to make a mistake, not by a long chalk. She was just unlucky enough to get caught out. Not that I should call it unlucky when I look at what a fine young man you've grown up to be! Oh, she'd be proud of you, she would. I only wish she could see you now . . .'

'Did you know him too – my real father?' Huw asked. The tea was beginning to taste bitter in his mouth now, but he felt driven to continue the conversation.

'Oh, I did that. Did well for himself, so I've heard.'

'Yes, he had a transport business. Llew Roberts Haulage. He's dead now too, though.'

She stopped in the act of pouring more tea. '*Llew* Roberts?'

293

'Yes. He was killed by one of his own lorries.'

'No – no, I didn't mean that. Did you say *Llew* was your father?'

The cup rattled in the saucer as he set it down too quickly. 'What?'

'Oh no, she did have a bit of a fling with Llew, it's true. But he was only a boy really. His mother soon put a stop to that. But then his brother picked up where he left off. Eddie, his name was. Bit of a sly one. Sharper than Llew and not so soft-hearted. When there was trouble he didn't want to know. Would have left her high and dry and never thought twice about it.'

'But I thought *Llew*. . .'

'Llew helped out. She told me all about it. I suppose he felt guilty himself after the way that he had – well, been like friendly with her. And sorry that his brother could just wash his hands of his responsibility. After Idris was killed she wrote to him and he used to send her money. Then – well, the money stopped coming. She went off to Somerset to see him, and try and sort things out. Desperate, she was. But she never came back. She died there, poor soul. And I suppose you know the rest.'

'Yes.' He could hardly think straight, yet it was as if a great weight had lifted off his heart. 'Are you sure about all this?'

'Oh yes, how could I be mistaken? Nights I've had your poor Mam in this very kitchen beside herself with not knowing what to do. Oh, Eddie was your father all right, not Llew. Make no mistake about that.'

'Thank you,' he said. 'Thank you very much, Mrs Williams.'

'Nothing to thank me for now is there? Anyway, it's all so long ago now I don't suppose it makes much difference to anything.'

'Don't you believe it, Mrs Williams,' Huw said. 'It makes all the difference in the world.'

He bid her goodbye and went back along the rank without a backward glance. It was all part of his past now, these houses, the pit, the towering slag heaps. And the past no longer mattered. Everything about it had changed. Nothing was quite the way it had seemed.

Now it was the future and only the future that was important. A future in which there was no barrier to his love for Barbara.

There was no way he could get a pass immediately. He was being posted to a new base in Essex as he had suspected, the posting to take effect immediately he left St Athan, the station commander told him. He would have to sort things out when he got there. Huw argued but it was useless. Unless there were very pressing personal reasons the station commander was not prepared to countermand the instruction.

Huw was forced to retire defeated. He did not feel that making things up with a girlfriend would be counted as 'very pressing' by the station commander, important though it was to him. He could only hope that his new chief in Essex would be more understanding and he told himself a few days could hardly make any difference.

He could scarcely have been more wrong.

'We don't want a long engagement, Mum,' Barbara said. 'There's no point. It's not as if we have to save up to get married. Marcus is well able to keep me and we can live at Hillsbridge House.'

'That is hardly the point, Barbara. I want you to be sure you're doing the right thing,' Amy replied.

'I am sure.'

They were in the garden of Valley View, Amy deadheading the first flush of roses on the bushes which rioted around the lawn, Barbara following her to talk as she worked, but the argument was the same one which had raged constantly since the end of April when Marcus had formally asked Amy for Barbara's hand. Because she really had no concrete reason for refusal and because she hoped that it might help Barbara to get over Huw, Amy agreed to their engagement. She was still torn by guilt at the misery her daughter had been caused because she had kept silent about Huw's parentage and she was glad that Barbara had found someone as acceptable as Marcus to help heal the wounds. But marriage . . . Amy's heart seemed to fold up at the thought of it. Marriage was such an enormous step and she was still not convinced that Barbara's feelings for Marcus were anything other than love on the rebound. She had only to remember Barbara's ravaged face in the weeks following Huw's rejection to know how deeply she had cared for him. The child had gone about in a daze of misery, hardly speaking when she was spoken to. It was wrong, of course. It could never be. And Amy had fervently hoped that one day someone else would come along to make Barbara forget her infatuation. But was Marcus the right one? Amy was not sure that he was, though apart from the feeling that it had all happened much too suddenly, she could not put her finger on the reason for her reluctance to believe that he was. He seemed perfect – charming, well-educated, apparently devoted to Barbara – what more could a mother want for her daughter? Yet still Amy could not rid herself of her intuitive sense of misgiving.

'Mum – please!' Barbara said. 'Will you stop fiddling with those roses and *talk* to me? It's very important, Mum. Marcus and I want to get married now – before the end of the summer.'

'It's too soon,' Amy said. 'We could never arrange a wedding at such short notice.'

'Rubbish. Of course we could. Sir Richard has already said we can have the reception at Hillsbridge House. That only leaves the church to be booked.'

'Honestly, Barbara, you talk as if it were as easy to organise a wedding as a daytrip out in the car!' Amy said snappily. 'There's a great deal more to it than that if you want to do it properly. In any case I thought I'd made it clear I'm not agreeable to you marrying for quite a while yet. You won't be twenty-one for another three years and until then you need my permission.'

'No I don't.'

'You certainly do.'

'If you keep on refusing we can always apply to the courts,' Barbara said. As always her mother's opposition was only serving to make her more determined. 'You had your way about keeping me out of the WAAF but this time my mind is made up.'

'Sometimes I think it's a pity you aren't joining the WAAF,' Amy said with feeling. 'Apply to the courts indeed! I never heard of such a thing!'

'The trouble with you, Mum, is that you think you can run everyone's lives for them,' Barbara retorted. 'Just because you are the boss at work you think everybody will do what you tell them at home as well. But if you keep saying no that's what we shall do, and with a war on, Marcus who he is and me eighteen and old enough to be serving my country you can bet they'll give us permission if you won't.' She paused, not wanting to be hurtful, yet determined not to be talked around. 'I'm sorry, Mum, but you must realise I'm grown up now. You have to let me make my own decisions.'

And your own mistakes, Amy thought. But perhaps Barbara was right – she shouldn't try to impose her will on a child who was ready to fly the nest. With two happy marriages of her own she wanted to be certain her daughter would be equally happy. But that did not give her the right to dictate or judge too harshly, nor to pretend she knew all the answers.

Perhaps the war was to blame, she thought, for making the younger generation grow up too quickly. Boys became men overnight and girls became their wives. And no one knew what tomorrow would bring, or even if there would be a tomorrow.

'All right, Barbara,' she said. 'What date were you and Marcus thinking of?'

'August 16th,' Barbara replied promptly. 'And we will arrange everything. You won't have to worry about a thing.'

'I'd better write it in my diary then, hadn't I?' Amy said drily.

'Oh Mum!' Barbara's face was wreathed in smiles. 'Does that mean you'll give your permission?'

'Yes, Barbara, I suppose it does.'

'Oh Mum, thank you! I must phone Marcus and tell him!'

She hugged Amy and ran off towards the house. Amy shook her head, hoping fervently that her intuition was wrong and that she would not live to regret her change of heart. Then, with an air of resignation, she went back to deadheading her roses.

Two days after he arrived at his new station Huw's flight was detailed to act as target-withdrawal wing for the 'beehive' – the formation of bombers and their fighter escort which had been instructed to destroy an engineering factory in France that was producing valuable aircraft parts for the Germans.

'Immediately he had installed his belongings in his billet Huw had spoken to the Station Commander about the chances of a short leave pass and had been promised one at the earliest possible opportunity. That night, as he led his men out to the airfield, he was feeling reasonably happy and he whistled as he knotted the silk scarf which Barbara had sent him last Christmas at the neck of his flying jacket and adjusted his Mae West.

'It's a nice night for flying,' a voice beside him said and he turned to see 'Topsy' Brown hurrying to catch him up.

Topsy was one of the newest pilots on the squadron – a fresh-faced boy who had joined the RAF straight from school – and already Huw had marked him down as one he needed to keep an eye on. Though he handled his Hurricane well his keenness to make his first kill was a little worrying. When he had flown a few more sorties he would learn to temper his enthusiasm with caution, Huw thought, but for the moment he would need watching if he was to survive to fly another day.

'Should be a good chance for a bag tonight shouldn't there?' he said now, reinforcing Huw's opinion.

Huw nodded. Flying as target-withdrawal wing meant that they would arrive in the target area as the 'beehive' turned for home and their job would be to assist in any scraps that might still be going on and mop up any stragglers.

'We should have some fun, yes,' Huw said. 'But don't take any risks, Topsy. Do as you're told and fly yourself in first – right?'

'Yes sir!'

They took off into the gathering dusk, climbing and heading out over the Channel. In spite of his vigilance towards other members of his flight, Huw felt relaxed. He liked the Hurricane, liked the compact feel of the aeroplane and its marvellous manoeuvrability, though on the ground it looked clumsier than the elegant little Spitfire, and liked the stories he had heard of the amount of punishment it could take and still keep flying.

The coast of France loomed up ahead and they headed south. Flak was heavy from the harbour defences splintering the darkness of the fine clear night but they managed to avoid it and flew on keeping a sharp lookout for German fighters and aware of the need to arrive at the target area at precisely the right time – the success of these sorties depended on perfect timing.

Then, just as they expected them to, the fields beneath gave way to the build up of heavy industrial buildings starkly illuminated by a huge fire that was burning out of control and the sky was streaked with the bright criss cross of gunfire.

The bombers had done their job. They had hit their target and turned for the safety of home. But the Germans were after them like furious terriers snapping at their heels. There was work for the target-withdrawal wing as they had guessed there would be. Huw issued an instruction and they went in, drawing the German fire. An Me109 dived steeply away from Huw and he followed it, though at first his slower plane was left standing. Then the Me109 began to pull out much sooner than Huw expected and as he overhauled it he shattered its tail unit with a burst from his guns. It fell like a stone and mentally he added it to his tally of 'enemy destroyed'.

The remaining Germans had scattered and Huw and his flight were about to turn for home when the reinforcements arrived – a flock of fresh and determined Bf109s. Huw shouted a warning; it was every man for himself now. He got one with a full deflection burst at point blank range and saw his shells striking the 109's fuselage. It nose dived away, hitting the ground and exploding in a burst of bright flame.

He looked around, every nerve alert and singing, and saw another 109 on Topsy Brown's tail. Topsy seemed unaware of it. Huw went in drawing the fire and at that precise moment realised that he himself was trapped. Another 109 was heading straight for him, all cannon

300

firing. In a moment suspended in time he saw the crackling lines like deadly sparkler trails and knew the 109 had made no mistake. He was hit.

Many times, returning after seeing his friends spiral from the sky in flames, Huw had wondered how it would feel to know with deadly certainty that you were going to be shot down. He had had plenty of close shaves but always there had been something he could do. He had dived and climbed, flipped close circle, coaxed dead engines back to life in the nick of time. He had known fear, excitement, the heady crazy mix of emotions which come from surging adrenalin. But never had he faced the inevitable. He did so now and was surprised by the strange calm he found himself in. Life and death had fused, it seemed; eternity stretched before him and there was nothing whatever he could do to escape it. It was euphoric, almost, that moment of inevitability. And then the gunfire hit the Hurricane. An enormous explosion at his feet knocked him almost senseless and then his cockpit was filled with flames and he was sharply conscious once more and the momentary crazy euphoria was gone.

His plane was lost. He had known that from the moment he saw the deadly accuracy of the cannon fire. But he was alive – if he could get out of the Hurricane which would otherwise be his coffin. With fingers still numb from the force of the explosion he clutched at the release, dragged the hood open and fumbled to free himself from his harness. It gave and he raised himself up so that he was standing in the slip stream. A strange sickening stench assailed his nostrils; he realised it was his own burning flesh. His body was wholly out of the cockpit now but still he was falling with the crippled plane and he realised the toe of his boot was caught. He experienced a moment's wild panic and kicked out with all his strength. The thrust cleared him and he was hurtling down through the cold night air, tumbling head over heels. The fine honed instincts born of a hundred mental rehearsals for his moment took over where his thought processes had been arrested. He found the ripcord of his chute and jerked hard, the chute opened and he was no longer falling but floating, with the French countryside laid out beneath him ghostly pale in the moonlight and fiery orange away to his left where the factory burned fiercely.

When he saw the 109 closing in he thought that it was all over for him, for up here, suspended beneath his billowing parachute, he was a sitting duck. But the German seemed satisfied with knowing he had got the Hurricane. The wings slanted and he curled away.

The ground rushed up to meet Huw. He tried to position himself for landing but his body would no longer obey him. He hit the ground with a jolt, rolled over and tried to rise. But the blackness of the night was inside him now. A wave of pain enveloped him, the field cartwheeled around him again and as the blackness numbed and blinded him, Huw knew no more.

Amy put down the telephone and went back into the kitchen where the family were having breakfast. It was a peaceful scene repeated every morning five days a week – Ralph opening the mail as he drank tea from his extra large cup, Maureen and Barbara sharing the last piece of toast and faithfully dividing between them what was left of the butter ration. The normality of it struck at Amy as the telephone conversation had not, finding a crack in the strange calm unreality which had enveloped her as she listened to what the caller had to say. Her knees went weak suddenly and she clutched at the door to support herself.

Barbara looked up, saw her standing there and knew at once something was very wrong.

'Mum?' Her tone was sharp and anxious.

Amy tried to speak and could not.

'Amy!' Ralph rose, jerking his chair back. 'Are you all right?'

'It's Huw,' she said. 'He's missing.'

For a moment her words seemed to hang in the air. Maureen uttered a small strangled cry; Ralph asked sharply: 'When? How?' Only Barbara remained motionless, holding the piece of toast suspended halfway to her mouth.

'He was shot down last night,' Amy said. 'That was his commanding officer on the phone. He said he wanted to tell us himself.'

'You mean he didn't come back from a sortie?' Ralph asked.

'No, he was definitely shot down. His Number Two saw his plane crash in flames.'

'Oh Christ! You mean . . .'

'They don't know. They think they saw a parachute. He may have got out. If he did he is somewhere in France. But they don't know for sure. And even if he's alive he may be badly burned. He may be . . .' Her voice tailed away.

Ralph crossed the kitchen, put his arms around her and supported her to a chair. 'Sit down, my love.'

'I'm all right,' she said, almost crossly. 'Don't fuss, Ralph.'

'You're not all right. You have had a shock.'

'So have we all!'

'He'll come home safely,' Barbara said. They all turned to look at her. The glazed expression was still there in her eyes but there was an eagerness too about her face as if by the force of her own will she could make it so. 'He'll come home safely – I know he will!'

'Oh please God, I hope you're right!' Amy whispered.

'He will,' she said fervently. 'He has to!'

16

Huw came slowly through the mists of semi-consciousness to the pain which had bounded his world for the past days. Waves of burning pain seemed to envelop the whole of his body as if he were still on fire, trapped in his blazing Hurricane. For a moment he imagined that he was and a scream rose in his dusty-dry throat. Then his senses registered the dimness and the overpowering smell of hay and he checked the scream.

Quiet, you idiot, you bloody fool! Keep quiet can't you!

He lay stock still for every movement only increased the agony. He was lying on a makeshift bed, an old mattress covered with a clean sheet. On one side of the bed was a sheet of rusty corrugated iron, on the other three bales of hay formed the walls of a narrow 'room'. Beside him on the straw-strewn floor stood a carafe of water and a glass, at his feet an aluminium bucket provided primitive toilet facilities. The dryness in Huw's throat increased, aggravated by tiny particles of hay which he had breathed in and he decided that painful or not he must have a drink.

Slowly, with great difficulty, for both hands were heavily bandaged, he managed to pour some water from the carafe into the glass. As it touched his lips he winced. The burned skin had peeled from them like an overripe peach and now they were raw and tender in spite of the medication which had been spread on them and was now making the water taste bitter.

How many days had he been here – four? five? He was not sure. He had tried to keep count but time had lost its meaning. Here in the barn what little light there was was shut out by the wall of hay, so night and day were almost inseparable and the bouts of semi-consciousness had made a mockery of his own sense of the passage of time. Sometimes it seemed like only moments ago that he had come floating down with his parachute billowing above him, sometimes years, for it was difficult to remember a time before this pain which bounded his universe on all sides like the walls of hay. He was lucky to be alive, he knew, and luckier still to be free in this occupied country. On both counts he owed a debt of gratitude which he could never hope to repay to the farmer who had found him and brought him here, who was still caring for him regardless of the risk to himself and his family, and to the doctor, a general practitioner from the nearby village, who had treated his burns and given him medication to ease the pain.

His memory of what had happened that night after he had been shot down was hazy, a kaleidoscope of blurred fragments like small sharp clips from a movie. He remembered hearing voices as he lay there in the meadow-grass, tangled still in the harness of his chute, and looking up to see dark shapes silhouetted against the purple sky. The voices were rough, speaking French in a thick country dialect that made them almost impossible to understand, though stunned as he was he caught the odd word.

'Anglais?'

'Oui. Anglais . . .' he had muttered but the effort had been almost too much for him. When they lifted him he had passed out again. The next thing he remembered was being here in the barn lying on the straw-covered floor. Two men were bending over him – the two men who had carried him here, he assumed – but as his eyes came into focus he saw a girl standing in the doorway, a tall slim figure with long loose hair. The older of the two men said something to her in rapid, incomprehensible French and she came over, dropping to her knees beside him.

'Restez-vous ici,' she said. 'We you hide with straw. We bring M. le Docteur to help your wounds. M. le Docteur est notre ami – our friend. You stay – we hide you now.'

He only half understood until they began building the bales of hay up around him. It was not so much that her English was imperfect as that he was still incapable of coherent thought. Then, when they had gone and he was alone, he realised the danger. The German pilot would have reported seeing his parachute. Before long they would be combing the countryside for him. When they found nothing they would know someone had hidden him. And if he was discovered here the French farmer and his family would be shot.

I can't put them at risk! he thought. But there was nothing he could do. The wall of hay formed a prison and Huw was in no fit state to find the strength to demolish it. He lay sweating and listening, tensing at every sound and gritting his teeth against the waves of pain.

Before dawn they were back, unpacking enough of the straw bales to make a gateway to reach him. The girl stood at the barn door keeping watch while the doctor tended to him, soothing and bandaging. His English was quite good and he kept up a running commentary on Huw's burns.

'Hands – face – legs – ah, not so bad. We will have you well soon I think. You will not die this time. So long as the German bastards do not find you. Now I give you something to make you sleep. You sleep a few days. Henri will look after you. I will come back and see you again when it is safe. As soon as I can.'

Huw tried to argue but he was unable to form the words properly. Then the injection began to take effect and he became drowsy, drifting into the semi-consciousness that was to make a nonsense of the next days for him.

In his periods of awareness he knew they came to him, sometimes the man, sometimes the girl, who spoke reasonable English. He had no recollection of them making up the bed for him. He only eased out of his stupor one day to realise he was no longer lying on the floor but on a mattress, old and lumpy, but at least offering some comfort to his aching joints. As time passed he realised he was in less danger of discovery but he still worried about it, more for the sake of those who were hiding him than for his own. He had no way of knowing that the German who had seen his parachute had himself been shot down minutes later in another skirmish without ever having time to report that the pilot of the Hurricane he had claimed had survived, or that the farmer had eased his body out of the remains of his flying jacket, charred it still further in his own fire, and deposited it along with his watch and signet ring in the burned out wreck of the Hurricane so that German patrols would believe that he had died with his plane.

Now, closer to reason than he had been since disaster had overtaken him, he lay in the semi-dark and tried to think beyond his pain. He could not stay here forever; he could not continue to expose the farmer and his family to the danger of having an English flier hidden on their property. He had to get back to England. There was a very good reason why he should get back – and quickly. Only just for the moment he could not remember for the life of him what it was . . .

A small sound from the other side of the wall of hay attracted his attention and he froze, listening. Then he saw that one of the bales was moving and as it was removed the light came rushing in, hurting his eyes.

'Hello. You are awake then.' It was the girl. She removed another bale and crawled through. 'I have

307

some coffee for you and something to eat. Would you like something to eat today?'

She set down a milk churn on the floor beside his bed, removed the lid and dived inside, bringing out a jug of steaming coffee and a box containing bread and butter, cheese and a bunch of grapes.

'Thank you,' he said. He was hungry though he was not certain he would be able to eat. She emptied the remaining water from his glass and filled it with coffee. The aroma rose temptingly but he knew the hot liquid would sear his lips.

'We wait until it is cool,' she said, as if reading his thoughts.

Gritting his teeth against the pain he struggled to sit up. She smiled.

'You are better today, I think. Tell me, what is your name?'

'Huw,' he said. 'Huw James.'

She spread a hand across her chest. 'And I am Yvette. My father found you when you came down boom! from the sky. Do you remember?'

'Not very well.'

He was looking at her now with eyes clear at last from the fever. A pretty oval face framed by the long swinging hair, huge dark eyes fringed by thick lashes, well defined dark brows, a wide generous mouth. She was wearing a dress of floral cotton and though she had been strong enough to move the bales her figure was trim.

'I must go,' he said. 'It's not safe for you while I am here.'

She shrugged. 'Paw! Nothing is safe these days. Too many of our countrymen give in to the Germans. Not us! We are proud. We still fight for France. We keep you here until you are well then we will find a way for you to go home.'

'How?'

'There are some in the village who are also proud. The doctor, Father Leclerk, the priest, and some others. They will find a way. It will be dangereuse, but . . .'

'It's you I'm worried about. If they find me here you could be shot. I must go.'

'You are not well enough. Not yet. You would not last for any time.'

And then he remembered in a blinding flash just why it was so urgent for him to get back to England. Never mind these people who were hiding him, never mind the war. He had unfinished business in England. And it concerned Barbara.

'I must.' He tried to rise, was unable to and fell back on the mattress.

'You are not well enough,' she said. 'Later. For now you must stay here. Now,' she tested the coffee with her little finger, 'this is cool. Drink some.'

She lifted the glass, guiding it to his mouth and slowly, painfully, he drank.

She was right of course. He would not make it out of the barn, never mind out of France. For the moment he was as much a prisoner as if he was in German hands. There was nothing he could do but wait while they nursed him back to health. Never in his life had Huw felt so helpless.

'Thank you,' he said. And felt the drowsiness creeping up on him once more.

Preparations for the wedding were speeding ahead now. There was so much to be done and in such a short time! But Amy was glad that she had something to take her mind off her anxieties about Huw.

There had been no word of him since that telephone call which had devastated them all, not the smallest snippet of information as to whether he was alive or dead. Amy kept her hopes pinned on the fact that someone had thought they saw a parachute after his plane was hit and she half expected to hear that he was a prisoner of war, but as the silence stretched on she began to wonder if perhaps that parachute had been just a piece of wishful thinking on the part of Huw's Number Two. It could take much longer of course before there was any official notification that he was in enemy hands. Or there was always the possibility that he was being sheltered by some French family. But occupied France was overrun by German patrols and in the Vichy sector those who would be willing to risk their well-being for the sake of a British pilot were few and far between. Collaborators would be only too willing to turn him in in return for being left alone to get on with their lives. The alternatives did not bear thinking about – that Huw had gone down with his crippled plane, or that he had been so badly wounded that he had died anyway – and Amy tried not to allow herself even to consider them. But they were there all the same, dark shadows which took shape in the long hours of the night and rose to haunt her.

She was glad now that she had given in to Barbara over the wedding for she dreaded to think how Barbara would be taking this interminable wait, the awful uncertainty, without the constant round of activity which the coming wedding created. All very well for her to state confidently that she was sure Huw would be all right. Amy had seen the dark circles beneath her eyes when she got up in the mornings and knew that Barbara's thoughts were running on much the same lines as her own.

It was a nightmare, this whole thing, a nightmare from which she was unable to wake, yet they scarcely mentioned it even among themselves. The official family line was: 'Huw will be all right. Huw will be back.' To discuss it, even with hope in their hearts, might somehow weaken the defences. If one of them admitted to even a moment's despair the first crack might appear; the fragile dam would be breached.

So life – and preparations for the wedding, which was to be the biggest seen in Hillsbridge for many years – went on as if everything was the same as usual and that terrible phone call had never happened.

For Barbara the crack in the dam appeared the week before the wedding.

It was a warm evening with the threat of thunder turning the skies into a deep purplish haze above the fields and thick high hedges and she and Marcus had decided to go for a walk. They could not go too far for Marcus's leg would not allow that and in any case Barbara was tired. It had been a long day with last fittings for her dress and those of her bridesmaids – all family heirlooms which had required alteration by the dressmaker – and when that was over Amy had insisted that she should accompany her to the Denbury Court Hotel where the reception was to be held.

In spite of the Spindler's offer of a marquee in the grounds of Hillsbridge House, Amy and Ralph had decided that they should be undisputed hosts for the reception and Denbury Court, a grand country hotel in its own grounds, some six miles out of Hillsbridge, was the only place suitable for accommodating the society guests who had been invited. This had caused a slight panic for there was talk that Denbury Court was to be taken over as a POW camp, but this had not been confirmed and it seemed that the reception suite would be available for the wedding breakfast, although the waitresses and staff were more likely to be women from the nearby village instead of the usual highly trained staff of which Denbury Court boasted. Amy had driven out with Barbara to inspect the suite and make sure there would be a room where Barbara could change into her 'going away outfit' – a plain but very chic navy blue dress and jacket which they had bought by pooling every clothing coupon they could lay hands on.

Barbara was not certain when the depression had begun to descend upon her. Maybe it was as she stood balanced on a chair while the dressmaker, her mouth full of pins, trotted around her making final adjustments to the hem of her dress. It was a beautiful dress, a designer creation in silk and lace which had been worn by Marcus's mother and Barbara knew that even in times of peace she could never have afforded to buy anything half as good for herself. Irrationally, the thought had annoyed her for she hated to feel inferior, and she had transferred her annoyance to the fussy little dressmaker.

The feeling had intensified as she drove with Amy to Denbury Court. The setting was perfect, the long drive winding through parkland where, in peacetime, small deer grazed, the trees, weighed down by summer foliage, provided shade from the strong but fitful sun, the house itself gracious and impressive beyond a broad gravelled turnaround where once carriages had lined up and waited, the horses standing tall and proud in their harness. Barbara had tried to imagine herself and Marcus arriving here next week in their ribbon bedecked bridal car; in her mind's eye she saw herself sweeping up the steps on his arm, the beautiful gown spreading out behind her in a sweep of handmade lace, and felt the depression descend a little more.

Why? She gave herself a little shake. This was what she wanted, was it not? A lovely wedding day that would shine out like a bright star in the dark days of the war? Then why was she suddenly entertaining these treacherous thoughts – that if it was Huw she was marrying, she would have been content to slip away somewhere with only the family as witnesses; to wear

312

her 'going away' dress for the ceremony; to celebrate quietly at home with perhaps the luxury of a bottle of champagne; to slip away somewhere for a stolen twenty-four hours in the heart of the country instead of the week's honeymoon Marcus had promised her? Months ago, when Huw had told her to forget him, she had vowed to do just that and with Marcus sweeping her off her feet she had thought she was succeeding. But since receiving the news that Huw was missing she was not so sure.

In spite of all the excitement of the wedding, in spite of having one hundred and one things to do, there was hardly a moment when she had not thought of him, wondering where he was, whether he was dead or alive, wounded or well. Now, overseeing the last minute preparations, it seemed to her that to be thinking about wedding celebrations when Huw was missing was somehow obscene and she could not bear the thought of going through it without him. Yet could she have gone through it if he had been there? Could she have promised to love, honour and obey Marcus with Huw looking on?

Yes, she thought, her stubborn pride coming to the rescue, yes, I could. I'd have been showing him that even if he did not want me someone else did, someone handsome and brave, someone any girl would be proud to call her husband. And in truth the fact that Huw was missing altered nothing. He did not want her, that was the basic fact she must not lose sight of. He had never thought of her as anything other than the little girl he had grown up with. Anything else had been in her imagination. And that wonderful stolen day they had shared? It was the one thing she could not explain.

'Babs, are you coming?' Amy had asked over her shoulder and Barbara had pushed her tumbling thoughts to one side. But still the depression remained within her as the thunderclouds built up to blot out the sun and for

313

once the excitement of the wedding preparations could do nothing to lift it.

Now, as she and Marcus walked along the lane between the high hedges from which the sultry air was wringing a sweet heavy scent, it was still there – an unbearable weight on her heart.

Their progress was slow and after a while they stopped in a gateway for Marcus to rest. He leaned heavily against it and Barbara rested her elbows on the top bar looking across the field towards the river. The grass that would soon be winter's hay was waist deep yet motionless for not even the faintest breeze stirred in the heavy evening air and along the perimeter beneath the hedge a few clumps of poppies grew, scarlet silk with a dusting of soft deep black.

'You're very quiet, tonight,' Marcus said. 'What's wrong?'

She hesitated, raising a hand to brush a dozey fly away from her face.

'Oh, nothing. Just pre-wedding nerves, I expect.'

He reached out and caught her arm, pulling her across so that she was leaning against him face to face.

'You aren't about to change your mind, are you?' His face was brooding yet very handsome and resentment stirred in her. Marcus had everything, expected everything and automatically it was his. She felt a sudden urge to hurt him as she was feeling hurt.

'I don't know. I'm scared, Marcus. It's all happened so fast and we've scarcely had time to get to know one another. I mean – you don't know what goes on inside my head and I don't know what goes on in yours. You have to be very close to someone for years and years before you know that and even then you can be wrong . . .' Her throat ached as she said it. A moment more and I'm going to cry, she thought. 'I'm just afraid we're making a mistake,' she added quickly.

'That's a stupid thing to say.'

314

'I'm just trying to be realistic,' she said desperately. 'Marriage is for a very long time – a lifetime! I'm not sure I've been thinking of it like that. I've been seeing wine and roses and me in a lovely white dress and you in uniform and . . .'

'Runs in the family, doesn't it?' His tone was bitterly sarcastic. 'Didn't your cousin jilt his fiancée at the altar?'

She flushed. 'Perhaps he was right,' she retorted, stung. 'Better a jilted fiancée than a wretched marriage.'

She saw his face change, whiten.

'Oh God, Barbara, no! Don't say that, please! For God's sake don't leave me! I couldn't take it – not on top of everything else.'

With a shock she realised he was suddenly as close to tears as she had been a few moments ago. 'Marcus . . .' she began helplessly.

His hands gripped her arms convulsively. 'You've been my salvation. You don't know what it was like – the war I mean. You don't know what hell it was, losing all my men and knowing that I'd failed them.'

'You didn't fail them!' she said, frightened now without really knowing why. 'Everyone knows that what happened was not your fault. You're a hero.'

'I don't feel like a hero, especially in the middle of the night when I wake up and think about them. I feel . . . there must have been something I could have done. If I'd been sharper, braver . . . it's hell on earth thinking that, Barbara. I believe I'd have gone mad if it wasn't for you. You have been like a ray of sunshine coming back into my life. For the first time since it happened I have had something to plan for, someone to care about. When I was a little boy I used to have a nanny. Funny old stick. Very strict, very old fashioned. But when I had nightmares she'd come and sit with me. She made the nightmares go away. You've done the same for me.'

'Oh Marcus . . .'

315

'I love you, Barbara,' he said. 'If you left me – well, I don't think I'd want to go on living.'

'Oh Marcus,' she said again and suddenly she was melting inside, the weight falling away. 'I won't leave you.'

She put her arms around him, holding him tight, and he buried his face in her shoulder. His hair was soft against her chin, his back lean and muscled beneath her hands and she felt a spark of excitement stirring within her, urgent and sweet. She moved against him and as he raised his head she kissed him with all the desire that was suddenly singing in her body. For a moment his lips clung to hers and she pressed even closer, wanting to feel him with every inch of her body. But she felt him stiffen suddenly, pulling away from her as if she were burning him with red hot coals.

'Marcus . . . ?' She looked at him with surprised hurt and rejection, not understanding the sudden withdrawal when only a moment before they had been so close.

'Don't,' he said. His voice was odd; she could not recognise the emotion in it. 'Carry on like that and I shall do something I shall regret.'

'But Marcus – we're going to be married. Surely . . . ?'

'So isn't it best that we wait until we are?' Still that odd, unrecognisable note in his voice.

'Yes, but . . . I thought you wanted to be sure of me . . .'

'Not like that,' he said. 'Not like that, Barbara.' He moved suddenly, reaching for his stick. 'I think we'd better be going. I don't like the look of the sky. I should think we are in for a storm.'

She followed him and in spite of his limp she had to almost run to keep up with him. The depression and the doubts about her own feelings had gone now, but they had been replaced by another shadow, darker and more inexplicable. A shadow she had touched upon herself when she had remarked how little they knew about one another. But Barbara did not stop now to wonder or analyse. One way or another it would all come clear, given time.

Somewhere over the mountainous black batches the first thunder rumbled.

The sun shone for their wedding day and it seemed that half Hillsbridge was there to see them come out of church, Marcus, his fair good looks accentuated by the dark morning suit, Barbara a fairytale bride in the white silk and lace, with a veil so long it reached the hem of her skirt and beyond and a trailing bouquet of red roses and lillies of the valley.

'You look lovely, darling. I'm very proud of you,' Amy whispered, reaching up to adjust the small coronet of orange blossom and pearls that held her veil in place so that the photographer could take a perfect picture, and it was a sentiment that was echoed many times among the groups of people who had gathered beneath the trees that ringed the churchyard to watch.

But there were those who were less enthusiastic about the grandeur of the ceremony. Eddie Roberts was one of them.

'I suppose our prospective Labour candidate will be there, drinking champagne with the class he's supposed to be fighting against,' he said bitterly to Walter Martin, another of the Labour Six on the council, when he called on him to collect his insurance money the day before the wedding. 'How can he justify himself, I'd like to know? All that waste at a time when we're supposed to be tightening our belts. Not much belt tightening for the Spindlers, I dare say.'

'People like that will always see themselves right,' Walter agreed.

'Of course they will. It's them and us – always has been and always will be until the working class can get themselves organised to do something about it. But that's what gets my goat. There's Harry Hall, supposed to be the Miners' Agent and a Labour candidate pledged to get a fair deal for the ordinary working man, hobnobbing with very ones who try to keep our noses ground down in the dirt. It's not right.'

'No, I s'pose not. But when it's his niece that's getting married he's bound to be invited,' Walter said reasonably.

Eddie snorted. 'She's my niece, too, remember but you won't catch me going anywhere near those Spindlers,' he said righteously, omitting to mention the fact that he had not been asked. 'He ought to turn the invitation down if he's genuine and make a stand for what he says he believes in. You can't run with the hare and chase with the hounds, Walter. It doesn't work. But will he turn it down? I wouldn't mind betting my week's wages he won't. He's too much of a one for looking out for his own good. And that's the way it will be if ever he gets to Parliament, you mark my words. It won't be our interests Harry Hall will be looking after. It will be his own.'

'Perhaps you'm right, Eddie,' Walter said. For all that he was a good solid councillor with his heart in the right place he was a simple man and easily swayed by a well-reasoned argument. 'Perhaps you'm right.'

'I know I am,' Eddie said, pleased.

He repeated his allegations as he went on his rounds to anyone who would listen – and there were plenty who would. Eddie had always made it part of his business to be known as a friendly fellow, ready to stop for a cup of tea and a chat and he injected his poison insidiously, embellishing it, where he dared, with the story of how he had found Harry's evacuees running away because they were so unhappy with him.

'The trouble is that some people like to be seen to be doing good,' he said darkly. 'When their own front doors are closed it's a different story.'

Heads nodded and tongues flapped. There was a

318

certain amount of jealousy of the Hall family among certain members of the community and Eddie was quick to fasten on and nurture it.

On the day of the wedding he managed to arrange things so that he was in Hillsbridge when the procession of ribbon bedecked cars passed by, though he would never had admitted that his being there was anything but an accident. Sure enough Harry Hall was in one of the cars with Margaret sitting beside him. Eddie smiled with satisfaction. So he had been right. Harry *was* hobnobbing. And his wife was just as bad. War or no war she had managed to get herself a new hat for the occasion by the look of it. And she was George Young's daughter, too. It was enough to make her father turn in his grave.

The Hillsbridge *Mercury*, starved of anything but war news for many months now, made the most of the society wedding with no less than three pictures, two of them on the front page. But it was the one inside which pleased Eddie. A group of guests, all dressed up in their best with champagne glasses in their hands – and right in the middle of them was Harry Hall! Eddie fetched his mother's sewing scissors and though he knew she would 'kick up hell's delight' as he called it if she saw him cutting paper with them, he chopped out the picture and then neatly trimmed it round. Another piece of ammunition in his war to put Harry Hall right back where he belonged – nowhere! He tucked the picture into the back of his rounds book. He intended to show it to anyone who had missed it in the paper – and that included the Executive Committee who had made such a rash choice in selecting Harry for their prospective candidate.

Oh yes, I'll get him, Eddie promised himself. He's a sight too big for his boots, is Harry. One of these days he'll find he's put them down in just the wrong place. And when he does, I shall be right behind him, making sure that everybody knows about it.

17

On their return from honeymoon Barbara and Marcus moved into a suite of rooms in Hillsbridge House and Barbara soon discovered that marriage was not quite what she had expected it would be.

During the day Marcus was busy with his new job of managing the estates and she was left with time on her hands for the house was still run by a skeleton staff of servants who somehow managed to cook, clean and do the work which had once been done by a small army. At first, Barbara relished the freedom to do exactly as she wished but soon she became bored with this enforced inactivity and begged Marcus to allow her to use her year's training in business studies to help him with the estates. He refused. Spindler wives did not work, he told her firmly. They were supported by their husbands. None of Barbara's arguments or pleas could persuade him to change his mind and she flitted about the house and garden feeling a little like a guest in a grand hotel.

The evenings were almost as bad. It was the Spindler family custom to have dinner at seven and afterwards they would sit for a while in the drawing-room listening to the radio or some of their large collection of classical gramophone records. Lady Erica would bring out her embroidery, working fine delicate stitches in shaded pastel silks, and Barbara wished that she could sew – it would at least give her something to occupy her hands. But sewing had never been one of her talents – Amy and Maureen had often teased her about her 'long stitch and a lie flat' – and watching Lady Erica's nimble fingers at work she blushed to remember the only thing she had ever made – a canvas bag worked in wool, so clumsy and garish that it had been relegated to use as Mrs Milsom's peg bag. She quite liked knitting but knitting did not seem quite the thing amidst the grandeur of the Spindler's drawing-room as it had in the cosy kitchen at Valley View, and in any case clothing coupons were required to buy wool and after buying her trousseau Barbara had none left. To make things worse Marcus and his father often retired to the study to talk business – very necessary, he assured her, since he was still so inexperienced in running the estates – and Barbara was left to make small talk with Lady Erica. Since the two women had little in common the conversation was less than stimulating and Barbara found the hours stretching away interminably towards the time when she could excuse herself and go upstairs to prepare for bed.

At least on this score the fact that she was newly married worked to her advantage for Lady Spindler never made any effort to detain her. She merely smiled understandingly – for a new bride to want to take time to make herself attractive for her husband was only natural.

If only she knew the truth, Barbara thought wryly as she said goodnight one evening in early September. She wouldn't sit there smiling so sweetly if she knew just how unlike newly weds we are when the bedroom door closes behind us!

She climbed the sweeping staircase to their private suite. Spacious though it was Barbara had been surprised to find it also verged on the old fashioned, papered with a good heavy paper which had obviously been intended to last and which had darkened slightly over the years and furniture which looked as if it had been in the family for generations. The bathroom was basic white and would have been almost clinical were it not for the basket of luxury soaps and apothecary's jar of bath salts which Lady Erica had placed on a shelf above the bath and the small touches Barbara had added – a hanging basket of her favourite maidenhair fern and a large gilt-edged mirror, a wedding present from Auntie Dolly.

Barbara turned on the taps revelling in the fact that at least here there was hot running water – no need to heat a boiler and dip it out as she had used to have to do at home – and tipped a handful of bright pink crystals into the mainstream. Then she went into the bedroom to undress.

Her nightdress was in its matching case on the pillow; she took it out and spread it across the bed. It lay there, frothy pink against the heavy dark candlewick and she found herself remembering the first time she had worn it – on the first night of their honeymoon in a small but exclusive private hotel halfway between Somerset and the Lake District. Marcus had booked it because the whole distance was too great to travel so late in the day and she had been glad. Honeymoons were not about places but about being together and after the excitement of the wedding she had been tired – and ready to be alone with him.

They had eaten a cold supper in the deserted restaurant and as she tucked into the ham and salad, accompanied by a bottle of wine, she had realised how hungry she was. There had been a wonderful spread at the reception, of course, but Barbara had been too excited to swallow more than a mouthful or two. Now, she ate hungrily and by the time cold apple pie had been followed by coffee and liqueurs she was beginning to revive, the tiredness dropping away as she contemplated her wedding night.

The dining-room was dim, lit only by candles, and in their soft light Marcus looked more handsome than ever, a fairytale prince who had ridden up on his white charger to take her away from the strictures of wartime existence. Under the table his hand found hers and as their fingers touched she felt the glow of anticipation suffuse her whole body. She smiled at him, her lips becoming mysteriously fuller as they curved upwards, and she saw the answering smile in his eyes.

Let's go to bed! she wanted to say but it seemed an immodest thing for a bride to suggest and Marcus seemed in no hurry. He seemed quite content to sit there in the candlelit dining-room holding her hand.

Barbara was aware of the first small barb of puzzlement. Then he said: 'You looked lovely today, darling. You *are* lovely. You've made me a very happy man,' and she reasoned that he was simply taking things slowly because he was a gentleman.

'I'm happy, too,' she said and she was. With half the world plunged into darkness and uncertainty her own world seemed assured. Never had the war and all it meant seemed more distant. Even her fears for Huw had, for today, become part of the background of thoughts not to be entertained, though there had been a moment when she had been making her vows when she had seemed to see not Marcus's face, but Huw's. But only for a moment. She was Marcus's wife now; nothing must be allowed to interfere with that.

At last he rose and as she saw him sway slightly she wondered if he might perhaps have had too much to drink – he had certainly demolished a great deal of whisky, diluted only with the merest drop of water from the carafe on the table, while she had been sipping her wine. But Marcus always drank a lot and she had never once seen him in anything but complete control. Most likely it was his leg letting him down after the strain of a long day.

The bathroom was along the corridor; while Marcus used it she undressed quickly, glad that she did not have to take her clothes off with him watching for she felt suddenly shy. She slipped on the rose-pink nightdress, caught sight of herself in the mirror and felt her confidence returning. She looked nice – provocative yet at the same time the virgin that she was. She sat down at the dressing table and removed what make-up was still left on her face with puffs of cotton wool and brushed her hair until it shone like a bubbly golden cap. About to unfasten her necklace she hesitated. The gold locket had been Marcus's wedding present to her; it was as much a symbol of their love as the narrow gold wedding band. She looked down at it remembering the moment he had placed it on her finger: 'With this ring, I thee wed. With my body I thee worship . . .'

Where *was* Marcus? she wondered. He had been a very long time. She crossed to the bed and slipped between the cool cotton sheets to wait for him. Five minutes passed, another five, then . . . She was just beginning to be anxious when the door opened and he came into the room. He was still fully dressed except that he had undone his tie and top button of his shirt.

'Oh, you're in bed already,' he said. There was a strained note in his voice.

'Yes,' she said, suddenly embarrassed.

He stood for a moment as if uncertain what to do, then he crossed to the bed and sat down beside her taking her very gently in his arms. She responded eagerly, wanting him to sweep away the awkwardness that was suddenly there between them. Beneath her hands his jacket felt smooth, stretched taut across the rippling muscles of his back, but it rasped a little against the bare flesh of her throat and something stirred deep within her, sending small quivering darts of desire through her veins. She turned her face against his cheek, drawing back slightly so that she could see him, just a little out of focus, see the strong clean lines of his nose and mouth, though his eyes were shadowed. Their lips hovered and touched and the very lightness of the kiss started a new response in her so that she felt that a tight cord had been drawn from her very core to the place where her lips met his. He kissed her deeply then, his hand sliding around to caress the curve of her breast and as his fingers touched the nipple, teasing it erect, it seemed to her that the silken cord was joined to that too. She unbuttoned his jacket, slipping her hands beneath it, almost sobbing with the longing that throbbed through her.

Then, abruptly, he moved away, sitting up.

Puzzled, aching with a sense of loss, she opened her eyes. His head was bent, his face in deep shadow, but she saw the expression on his face and could not understand it.

'Marcus,' she said, wondering what she had done wrong.

He raised his head slowly. His eyes were hooded. For a long moment he looked at her then he leaned towards her again, kissing her forehead and smoothing the curls away from her face.

'It's been a long day. You're tired. And tomorrow we have to be on our way early. You had better get some sleep.'

'I'm all right. Really.'

He ignored her, crossed the room and undressed with his back towards her. She lay mutely watching him. The lines of his back were clean and strong, his hips narrow, his legs long and straight, but she was too bewildered by his attitude to appreciate them. He couldn't mean 'goodnight' . . . really 'goodnight' . . . could he? This was their wedding night. He had always treated her with tenderness and respect like the perfect gentleman he was, but it was different now. They were man and wife.

Marcus put on a pair of pyjamas, took time to hang his suit in the huge old wardrobe, turned out the light and came back to the bed. Neither of them spoke. As he climbed in beside her she lay waiting. Now surely he would take her in his arms again. She turned towards him expectantly, every nerve in her body once more aware of his nearness, even more so now in the soft unfamiliar darkness. But he only leaned over and kissed her on the forehead.

'Goodnight, darling. See you in the morning.'

Then his back was presenting her with a hard line and she realised she had not misunderstood him. He was not going to make love to her.

The bewilderment ached in her and she longed to curl her body around his, make him want her as she wanted him so that there was no room for caution and consideration. But she did not. She was too afraid of rejection by this strange unknown Marcus.

For what seemed like hours she lay awake staring into the darkness. Why? Why didn't he want her? Oh he must, surely! He said he loved her. The only explanation was that he was being generous, taking things slowly. It *had* been a long and tiring day. Tomorrow it would be different.

But it was not different. On the second night she was once again first in bed and when he climbed in beside her she put her arms around him and pressed her body close to his to show that tonight at least she was ready for him. He kissed her, caressed her and rolled on top of her and in the rush of desire she forgot her earlier anxieties. But after a few minutes, just as her need was almost at screaming pitch, he rolled away again.

'Marcus – what's wrong?' she asked in desperation.

'What do you mean – what's wrong?' His tone was bad tempered, unlike his usual smoothness.

'Don't you want me?' she asked. She was close to tears.

'Of course I want you.'

'Then why . . .?' There were no words to express her frustration.

'We're both tired.'

326

'I'm not tired. And neither should you be now. Surely if you wanted me . . .' The tears welled up. 'What's wrong with me? Have I disappointed you?'

'No, of course not.' He got up, sitting on the edge of the bed in the moonlight. 'You don't understand, Barbara.'

'No, I don't,' she said.

'Every time I try to make love to you all I can hear are those damned guns! They're there – in the dark. And the faces of the men I let down. I keep seeing them, Barbara. I can't think of anything else.'

'Oh Marcus!' She got up too, kneeling behind him and putting her arms around him. 'You didn't let them down.'

'What do you know about it?' he asked roughly.

'But you didn't. You were decorated for gallantry. No one could have done more. It was something that happens in war. You have to forget it.'

'I can't. I just bloody can't.'

'Marcus, please. Let me help you forget.'

He turned to her then, burying his face in her shoulder, and she stroked his hair gently. After a moment she felt the tension going out of him and she held him like a baby, hoping that now they could slip through the natural stages into the closeness that should be between them. But although she managed to ease him back into bed and lie with her body close to his, pressing gently until the hollows between them were squeezed away to intimate contact he made no move to reinstate their lovemaking. Her lips found his but now that she knew what was in his mind she could almost feel what he was feeling, see the same destruction and horror, and knew with a sinking heart that it was useless. They did not make love that night nor mention the conversation again. It was as if a barrier had been erected between them and with each day that passed it became that little bit harder to breach it.

327

Ten days they had spent in the glorious peace of the Lake District and still she was a virgin. During the day they walked in the green spreading countryside, swam when it was warm enough, and ate in the hotel dining-room, trying as best they could to ignore the awkward-ness that was there between them now, spilling over from their sterile nights. Marcus drank a good deal and only then it seemed did he become the easy charmer who had courted her. But when the bedroom door closed behind them there was no escape from the knowledge that nothing was the way she had expected it to be.

I've failed him, Barbara thought, and the knowledge was a knife thrust into her heart. He thought I could make him forget death because I am warm and alive but somehow I only remind him of it. The horror is still too real for him; he suffered too much.

Would he ever forget? With warmth and understand-ing would he one day be able to put it behind him? She did not know. She could only try to be the strength and refuge he needed, try to understand and not be affected by her own sense of failure. That way perhaps they could overcome his personal demons and begin a normal loving relationship. But sometimes, in the quiet of the night as she lay beside him listening to the murmurs of his disturbed dreams, she wondered – and doubted her own ability. A more experienced woman would know what to do, how best to make him forget. But she had no experience, nothing to fall back on but instinct.

And so they had come back to Hillsbridge, to the pressing realities of everyday life. And no one, not even those closest to them, knew that relations between them were not quite what they seemed.

Tonight, as always as she bathed and prepared for bed, Barbara nursed the hope that perhaps tonight it would be different.

Marcus had not come up yet. For the last hour he had been closeted with his father in the study, consuming, no doubt, still more of the whisky which seemed to be his lifeline. She sighed, slipped into her nightgown and crossed to the window, pulling aside the blackout and looking out.

There was no view of Hillsbridge from here, nothing but the trees standing dark sentinel against the cloudy sky. A feeling of loneliness crept into her and she thought of home. It was two miles only across the valley yet it might have been half a world away. She imagined the family gathered there – Amy sharing a cup of cocoa with Ralph, Maureen already in bed with the alarm set to wake her so that she could catch up with unfinished homework. Maureen missed her – she had told her so. 'It's not the same without you here, Babs. Remember how we used to creep into one another's rooms when we were supposed to be asleep for a chat? Remember the times we started giggling and couldn't stop and Mum would come in and catch us and tell us it was time we were alseep?' Barbara remembered and the remembering stirred a sad chord within her. Giving up the things of one's youth would not be so bad if there was something to take their place. She had never dreamed that when she was a wife she would look back with longing to those foolish happy days. But then she was not a proper wife – just a girl who had moved into a different world, sleeping in a strange bed with a strange man by her side. A man who could not be the husband she needed and who had no need of what she had to offer him. The moon came from behind a cloud, throwing the scene outside the window into sharp relief and the bleakness inside her grew.

Oh Huw, Huw, where are you now? No! Don't think of Huw! The last thing you must do is think about Huw . . .

The door opened and Marcus came into the room,

putting the light on. Quickly, she drew the blackout, fastening it tight across the window. He looked tired, she thought.

'Busy session?' she asked.

'Yes.' He had a glass, half-full, in one hand and a bottle in the other. He set both down on the dressing table. 'I just wish I'd had longer with Henry to get into the swing of things. Father seems to expect me to be able to take on exactly where he left off and it's not that easy.'

'Let me help,' she said eagerly. 'I've done business studies. I'm sure there must be something I could do to help you.'

'For God's sake, Barbara, I know I'm not much of a man. At least let me prove myself in one sphere.' He upended his glass, draining the last drop of whisky and refilled it from the bottle.

'Marcus . . .' she pleaded.

'No!' he said irritably. 'What's the matter with you, Barbara? All I want from my wife is that you should be here and . . .'

'I know that's all you want,' she retorted, stung. 'I know you don't want me for any other reason.'

'So why can't you at least make a decent job of that?'

The unfairness of it hurt; tears blinded her.

'I don't know why you married me,' she cried. 'I really don't!'

'Because I love you. Haven't I told you so?'

'Yes – but if you loved me you'd want to . . . you'd want to make love to me.'

He swigged his whisky. His face was hard.

'We've been through all that.'

'I know. And I've tried to understand and be patient. . .'

'*You've* been patient?' he snarled and she took a step backwards away from this aggressive stranger. 'What do you mean, *you've* been patient? Good God, you've got

330

everything you want – everything a woman could wish for. Can't you be satisfied with that?'

She wrapped her arms around herself.

'I want to be a proper wife to you. I want . . .'

'Oh yes, I know what you want,' he said. He was loosening his tie with one hand, still holding the whisky tumbler in the other. 'I thought you were different, Barbara, but you're not. You're the same as all the rest.'

'What do you mean?' she whispered. She was beginning to be frightened. She had never seen him like this before. Perhaps it was the whisky talking, transforming him into this embittered, aggressive stranger. 'What are you talking about?'

'You are a whore,' he snapped.

She took a step backwards, shock and horror freezing her every sense.

'A whore!' he repeated. His face was almost unrecognisable, twisted into a mask of hatred. He banged the whisky tumbler down on the dressing table so that everything on it rattled. 'All right, then. If you want it so much, by Christ you shall have it!'

She tried to move away again but she could not. She stood frozen to the spot. He grabbed her, throwing her across the room. Her legs hit the iron frame of the bed, she lost her balance and fell backwards onto it. He followed, grabbing a handful of her frothy nightdress and hoisting it up to her waist. The hem was caught between her legs and the iron rim of the bedstead; she heard the fabric tear.

'Marcus!' she sobbed.

He towered over her, holding her pressed into the mattress with one hand while unbuttoning his trousers with the other. Then he was on top of her, roughly forcing her legs apart. The weight of him squeezed all the breath out of her; as he entered her pain shot through her like a knife. A scream gurgled in her throat and she pushed at him with all her strength, fighting for breath and to free herself from his angry rasping thrusts. But he was like a madman and he had the strength of the demented.

To Barbara it seemed it would go on forever; in reality it was all over within a few minutes. A few last frenzied thrusts that seemed to tear her in two and he lay on top of her panting and sweating. She freed her face and chest, sobbed air into her bursting lungs and he rolled off her.

'I hope you're satisfied.' His voice was still ugly with hate. He got up, crossing to the window, wiping himself with his hands, and she lay trembling while the pain inside her subsided to a fierce burning throb. He went out of the room and still she lay motionless, unable to believe what had happened, too shocked to move or even, for the moment, to cry. The overhead light still shone down on the bed, glaring into her wide staring eyes and illuminating her half naked body and the moisture running in sticky rivulets down her splayed thighs. She raised her arm to shut out the light and tears began to gather in her throat.

She did not see him come back into the room, did not know he was there until he spoke.

'For God's sake cover yourself up! You look disgusting!'

She lowered her arm a fraction; he was at the dressing table, pouring still more whisky into his tumbler. She tried to move and could not. Her muscles seemed to have gone into cramp.

He tossed back the whisky.

'You only got what you asked for.' He sounded more sullen than angry now, as if the usual considerate Marcus was beginning to re-emerge and the animal he had become was attempting to make excuses for itself. 'You wanted it, didn't you? Well, you got it.'

'But not like that!' she whispered and the effort of

speaking dislodged the tears in her throat. They began to run out of the corners of her eyes and down her nose. 'It didn't have to be like that!'

He did not answer and she lay sobbing soundlessly.

'For God's sake, stop snivelling!' He crossed the floor towards her and she cringed back into the mattress but he only took her by the shoulders, pulling her up. The torn nightdress fell back over her legs. 'Go and wash yourself,' he said impatiently.

Dazed, she went into the bathroom. The bath was still full of scented water. She took off the ruined nightdress, let it fall to the floor, and got into the bath. The water was cool now against her burning flesh. She took the soap and began scrubbing herself, tears still running silently down her cheeks. She stood up, automatically drying herself with one of the large soft towels.

He appeared in the doorway and she wrapped the towel around herself protectively. Yet one glance at him and she could see his mood had changed again. He leaned against the jamb running his hand through his hair with a jerky repetitive movement. His shirt was unbuttoned, half in and half out of his trousers and his face was no longer angry but ravaged.

'Barbara – I'm sorry . . .' His voice broke. 'I'm sorry. But you went on and on and I . . .'

She shook her head. There was nothing she could say.

'Forgive me,' he said.

She wrapped the towel more tightly around her and went past him into the bedroom, pulling open one of the drawers of the chest and taking out a fresh nightdress. It was one of her old ones, cool cotton, long and voluminous with big puffed sleeves. When she had put it on she felt a little better. Still sore, still used, still shocked, but a little safer.

Marcus had followed her into the bedroom. He stood between her and the bed.

'Barbara, please. I don't know what came over me. Say you forgive me – please!'

She pushed past him and climbed into the bed.

'There's nothing to forgive,' she said and her voice seemed to come from a cold hard place deep inside her. 'I'm your wife, aren't I? At least I'm no longer your wife in name only!'

'Barbara . . .' He was following her now like a puppy dog or a naughty child seeking forgiveness.

'I don't want to talk about it,' she said.

'Well, you did keep on about it so!' he persisted. 'But I'll never hurt you again, I promise. If only you'll say you forgive me!'

He was on his knees beside the bed, reaching for her, burying his face in her breasts, and she realised he was crying now.

'It's all right, Marcus,' she said. Her voice flat, as if all emotion had drained away. 'Come to bed. But for heaven's sake, let's try to lead a normal life from now on. And forget what happened tonight.'

'Oh Barbara!' he whispered. He undressed quickly, put out the light and climbed into bed beside her. But as she lay cradling him in her arms Barbara found herself wondering. Would they be able to forget? Would they ever be able to lead a normal life? She would like to think so but somehow, remembering the crazed animal he had become before he had raped her, she doubted it.

In the darkness fresh tears gathered in Barbara's eyes and rolled silently down her cheeks.

During the long weeks that he was being nursed back to health Huw remained at the farm near where his Hurricane had crashed. At first, he was left holed up in his small 'prison' of corrugated iron and straw, then when Jacques, the doctor, felt it was safe to move him, he was supported across the muddy farmyard one dark wet night to the house, Jacques on one side of him, René, the farmer, on the other and Yvette and Raoul, her brother, keeping watch at opposite ends of the yard. Weak and dizzy from the long period of being cooped up with little light and air and no possibility of moving about, Huw gained only a fleeting impression of the farmhouse kitchen as they helped him through it – low roofed, sparsely furnished and lit by only a single oil lamp – then he was almost fainting with the pain as they manhandled him up the stairs to a tiny attic room where another makeshift bed was made up and ready for him. He collapsed onto it able to think of nothing beyond his own extremity and it was only when he awoke next morning and fought his way through the thick fog induced by René's painkilling drugs that he took notice of his surroundings.

But for the bed and a heavy old chest the attic was empty, rough bare boards beneath a sloping roof which met the floor a foot or so to the left of his bed. Almost immediately above his head a tiny window allowed a certain amount of light to filter into the attic and in the pervading peace Huw could hear pigeons cooing nearby – on the roof above, perhaps, or in an adjoining pigeon loft.

He lay for a moment taking it all in and wondering

why they had moved him. He was glad they had, of course; much more of that stuffy, stinking barn and he would have gone stark raving mad. But surely here in the house he must pose a greater risk to the family who had befriended him?

The thought worried him. He did not want to put them in danger. René presumably knew the risk he was taking as did Jacques. But René's daughter, Yvette, was only a girl, no older than Barbara, Huw judged. What the Germans might do to her if she was found to be hiding him did not bear thinking about.

He mentioned this to Jacques next time he came to see him. His English was good enough to make conversation relatively easy and after he had dressed Huw's burns he sat down on the chest, lighting a pungent French cigarette and resting his shoulder against the sloping attic roof.

'You are more comfortable here, no?'

'Yes,' Huw said. 'But what if the Germans come searching? Aren't they more likely to find me here?'

The doctor shrugged. He was a thin man; the angular bones of his shoulders and elbows jutted out through his checked cotton shirt.

'That is a risk we take, my friend.'

'I'm not thinking about myself,' Huw said quickly. 'I suppose I'd just be taken off to a POW camp. It's you I'm worried about, and the family.'

'They wish to help,' Jacques said simply. 'They are not proud of the way some of their compatriots behave. Besides we think you are safer here for the time being than in the village. This place is out of the way. There is no reason for the Boche to suspect you are here. There have been no English shot down here except for you and we made them believe you died with your plane, I think.'

'I see.' Huw felt too weak still for much argument. 'What will happen to me then?'

'When you are well we will try to arrange for you to leave France. We know people who work to that end. You will be given papers in case you are caught, identity card and the like. Do you speak French?'

'Very little,' Huw admitted.

'Then we will help you. Yvette will come and coach you, enough to fool the Boche at least. But we hope you will not be caught. English planes fly in sometimes to take out pilots like you and agents who work in the Resistance. We will arrange for you to go out with one. But that is not yet. You must be first fit or you will put us all in danger. I shall make you fit. That is my job.'

'I see. How long . . .?'

The Frenchman got up, stubbing out his cigarette in a small tin he carried in his pocket.

'Patience, my friend. We shall see. The war will go on without you.'

Huw tried to smile. The effort hurt his face and a new and disturbing thought occurred to him. Was he going to be scarred? He wished he could ask the doctor but somehow it seemed trivial and ungrateful. And his heavily bandaged hands made it impossible for him to try to discover for himself, by touch, just how badly burned was his face.

He thought of it again, however, in the long and lonely hours after the doctor had gone and he was alone. He had seen friends who had been badly burned. One, Buster Ford, had lost half his face after being shot down in flames during the Battle of Britain. Once he had been a handsome fellow, able to pull every girl who came his way; now in spite of the efforts of the plastic surgeons he resembled Frankenstein's monster. The thought that he might be similarly disfigured was not a pleasant one yet there was an irony about it which might have made him smile had it not been so painful, both mentally and physically. To have discovered there was no reason why he should not love Barbara – marry

337

her even! – and then find himself a repulsive freak was so unlucky as to be ridiculous and Huw cursed himself for his bad timing.

If only he had not flown that last sortie he would have been able to settle things with Barbara by now. As it was she was still ignorant of his true feelings – and probably even thought by now that he was dead. The knowledge frustrated him. If only he had been able to see her for just a few minutes, tell her he loved her and ask her to ditch that damned Marcus Spindler! Or that he had written while he was still free to do so. Even that would have been better than nothing.

Or would it? Supposing they had got together again, she had promised herself to him and then this had happened? If he was as badly burned as he feared Barbara might find him quite repulsive and yet feel honour bound to stick by him. Tied by loyalty to a freak. Much as he loved her, much as he wanted her, Huw could not bear the thought of her feeling nothing but pity for him. If she could not love him as a man he would rather not have her at all.

Through the long weeks that followed such thoughts continued to torment him and as he grew stronger and his periods of lucidity lengthened there was plenty of time for thinking. He was alone for so much of the time with nothing to do but nurse his increasing frustration.

Jacques still came as often as he was able and the two men would share a packet of the pungent cigarettes and talk about the war and regularly each evening Yvette came to the attic. She would give him supper – bread, cheese and wine, and sometimes a plate of thick stew made from potatoes and meat, and while he was eating it she would lift a loose floor board and take out the radio set that was hidden there. It was a tiny instrument, yet clumsy and old fashioned, but when she had fiddled with it for a while she could usually pick up the BBC news and they would sit in silence listening to it.

From the broadcasts Huw learned that the bombing raids were continuing over England and Germany, and Germany was getting the worst of it – though in his more depressed moments Huw wondered if this was a piece of propaganda designed to bolster the morale of the English under siege. He heard of the continuing fighting in North Africa where the Desert Rats were holed up and of the worsening situation in the Far East where the Japs were now on the rampage. Hong Kong it seemed was in particular danger, though that was nothing new – the women and children had been evacuated from the colony months ago, long before he had been shot down. But the danger was more imminent now, whilst it was said that Singapore, with her battery of guns facing out to sea, was impregnable.

Yvette sometimes visited him at other times during the day when her duties about the farm permitted, to coach him in the French language as Jacques had promised. As he grew stronger he began to look forward to her visits. She was a handsome girl, her long dark hair counterbalancing her strong countrywoman's features, and the fresh open air she lived in lent a healthy colour to what might otherwise have been a sallow skin. She was good natured too with a laugh which came easily – and Huw's broken schoolboy French certainly gave her plenty to laugh about.

'You pass as a Frenchman? Never!' she teased him. 'Only per'aps you could fool the Boche. They are – 'ow you say? – theeck!' And her laugh rang out filling the attic so that he was afraid someone might hear.

He shushed her and she laughed again.

'There is no one there – only the cows! Now – try again. Je m'appelle Maurice Valla. J'habite près de Paris.'

He repeated it, trying to concentrate on his pronunciation rather than on her dark eyes and thick sweeping lashes.

If it wasn't for Barbara I believe I might fancy her, he thought, and then chided himself for a fool. It was simply that he had been here too long. Under the circumstances any woman would look attractive. But he wondered about her all the same in the long hours when he was alone. For a simple French country girl her English was good, much better than his halting French would ever be, and it did not seem feasible that she should have learned it in a village school.

He asked her about it one evening when the BBC news was over and the tiny radio set had been returned to its hiding place beneath the floorboards.

'You make me ashamed that I speak your language so badly. Where did you learn such good English?'

She perched herself on the edge of the trunk.

'It is a story that takes a long time to tell.'

'What's time? It's the one thing I have plenty of.'

'You are lucky. Me – I rise each day before daylight and I do not go to bed until late. There is much to do on a farm. But then that is why I am here – to help my father. That is why I come home.'

'Where were you then?'

'Paris. I worked as a waitress. I met an Englishman there. We are friends. More than friends. I became his lover. He teach me English as I now teach you French. But I was more good pupil than you,' she teased.

'What was an Englishman doing in Paris?' Huw asked.

'He is an artist. He come to Paris to paint. But then the war come and he go home to England. I do not know where he is now. Maybe he is fighting. Maybe he is dead. I do not know.'

'I see.' Huw was surprised. If Yvette had been living in Paris two years ago she must be older than she looked. As if reading his thoughts she laughed.

'I go to Paris when I am only sixteen years old. I was – how you say? – wild. I wished to see la vie more than just on this leetle farm. Per'aps I see more la vie than I expect. Then ma mère die. Papa wish me to come home. At first I say – Non, I stay here! Then the war come and David go back to England and Paris – Paris is not so nice any more. So I return home to the farm as Papa wish. Now I am glad I am not in Paris any more. Paris is full of Boche. Here at least they leave us in peace.'

'Thank the Lord!' Huw said with feeling.

'Et tu? Have you a lover at home?'

Huw hesitated. 'I had a girl,' he said at last.

'She wait for you?'

'I don't know,' he admitted and suddenly the hopelessness of it was claustrophobic. Would Barbara wait? She did not know if he was alive or dead, did not know he loved her even. 'I think she may have found someone else.'

'Then she is crazy!' Yvette said.

He looked at her. Her button-through dress had fallen open at the hem, displaying her legs. They were nice legs, a little sturdy perhaps, but long and brown. He dragged his eyes away from them.

'She's not crazy,' he said. 'It's just circumstances.' Then the other thought occurred to him, the one that had been haunting him, try as he might not to think about it. 'In any case she wouldn't want me now, would she?' he asked. 'Who would want a man with a scarred face?'

'Oh!' Yvette threw up her hands. 'Now I think it is *you* who are crazy! If you love someone, what is a little scar?'

His stomach fell away. So he was scarred. He had known he must be by the tight feel of the skin. But how badly?

'Am I – a sight?' he asked.

'A little bit. But you are getting better. You have been lucky I think.'

Lucky. Lucky to have been shot down. Lucky to be holed up here for weeks on end, alone and in pain. Lucky to be scarred for life. He could think of another word for it which had nothing to do with luck. But at the same time, perversely, he wanted to know the worst.

'Could you bring me a mirror?' he asked.

'Mirror?'

'Looking glass. So that I can see myself.' He raised his bandaged hand in a mime of holding a mirror to his face.

'Dr Jacques say no looking glasses.'

His stomach dropped again. It must be as bad as he had feared. Worse. She saw the look in his eyes and stood up suddenly.

'But that was weeks ago,' she said simply. 'Now it is better I think for you to look. I will get you a glass and you can see for yourself.'

She slipped out through the door and he heard her climb down the steep stairs. Whilst she was gone he lay sweating for it suddenly seemed hot and airless in the attic. After some minutes he heard her coming back and tensed. Did he really want to see what he had become? But it was too late now to change his mind.

Her head and shoulders appeared through the attic door. She lay the mirror down on the bare boards while she climbed up, then brought it to him, a large old fashioned glass in a wood frame. He took it, turned towards what little light there was, and looked. Although he was prepared for the worst the sight still shocked him. One side of his face was dark red, crinkled like old parchment, lips blurred into the mass, eyebrows gone.

'Christ!' he said.

'You see it is not so bad.' Her voice was determinedly cheerful. 'And it will get better. Dr Jacques say that. It is still soon.'

342

'Yes, but . . .'

'You are still very handsome, I think.' She reached out and touched the scorched skin. Her fingers felt cool. 'What is a little bump here and there, huh? It shows you are brave. And you are still alive. Many would be glad of that.'

He jerked his face away from her touch. He did not want her sympathy. She was right – he should be grateful to be alive – but just now it seemed scant comfort.

She took the mirror from him. 'You are alone too much, I think. Soon you will be well enough to come down and eat with us. Dr Jacques says you can do that as soon as you are well enough to come quickly back up the stairs if the Boche come. It will not seem so bad then. You want to try to walk?'

He turned away from her. No, he did not want to try to walk. He had had enough this evening without the ignominy of being supported back and forth across the attic by this girl who felt nothing for him but sympathy.

She shrugged. 'Very well. But you cannot stay up here hiding forever. I go now. I have work to do. More important work than talking to a man who feels so sorry for himself. I will bring a drink when it is time for you to sleep.'

When she had gone he lay for a while sunk in depression. Then the resilient side of his nature began to reassert itself. He couldn't stay here pitying himself forever. That would do no good at all. The sooner he got himself mobile, the sooner they would send him back to England. Once there he would be able to see a plastic surgeon, someone who would be able to tell him whether a skin graft was necessary. They were magicians, those boys – and it could have been worse. At least the structure of his face was still there, unlike poor old Buster. They'd work wonders as long as it wasn't too late.

The thought spurred Huw to action. He pushed back

343

the rug that covered him, rolled onto the floor and slowly levered himself to his feet. His legs felt shaky and he balanced himself against the sloping ceiling. So far he had only made it to the toilet bucket and back. If he was going to go downstairs he would have to make it much further than that. Teeth gritted with the effort he went back and forth, back and forth, holding onto the roof until he fell on the bed exhausted with the effort, then, when he had recovered his breath, he got up to try again.

He was still at it when Yvette brought him his cup of chocolate. She paused, pushing her head and shoulders through the attic door.

'I don't believe it! I must be dreaming!'

'You're the one who told me to pull myself together and get my legs working again,' he said grimly, hanging onto an overhead beam.

'Yes, but I do not say go on until you kill yourself!' she exclaimed. 'You look terrible!'

'Thanks very much.' He didn't say that driving himself to exhaustion had given him something else to think about but she knew it instinctively all the same.

'That is enough for one night.' She climbed through the attic door, crossed to him and put her arm around him, supporting him. 'Come on, come back to bed. I will help you.'

He let go the beam, put his arm around her shoulders and she supported him back to the bed. As he half fell onto it she went down with him. She was very close. Her hair smelled nice, like the fresh air, sweet with the scent of wild flowers and new mown hay, in which she spent so much of her time. Her face turned to his. And suddenly, without meaning to, he was kissing her. The pressure hurt his still-sore lips but only added a new dimension to the pleasure of it. After a moment he drew away.

'I'm sorry.'

'Don't be sorry.' She was smiling, her hair falling rumpled around her face. 'I thought you would never do that. I thought, oh it is true what they say about Englishmen – so cold. David, he was different. He was an artist. But you – just a cold Englishman.'

'I'm not English,' he said. 'I'm Welsh.'

'Ah! So there is Gallic in you. When you are well you will show me, yes? There is not much fun here on the farm with only my father and the old men. We will enjoy it. You will see. But for now you must rest. Drink your chocolate while it is hot.' She put the cup in his hands and her teasing, patronising tone stirred something within him, something halfway between anger and the desire for her strong healthy body. The need to prove himself was suddenly much greater than the need to rest. It lent him new strength and he set the cup down untouched on the floor.

'Who says I have to wait?' he asked. 'It takes more than a bit of practice walking to wear a Welshman down! Come here – I'll show you now!'

He pulled her down beside him and the touch of her body against his seemed to infuse him with new life. She was eager, yielding, a woman who had left her lover two years before and found no one to take his place. When his strength flagged she helped him and for a little while the world outside the attic ceased to exist. But afterwards lying with her head resting against his shoulder, one brown leg thrown carelessly across his, it began to intrude once more. He glanced at her face in the fading light, at the strong bone structure and the sweep of eyelashes lying on her cheek, and saw only Barbara's rounded fairness. As he thought of her desire began again and with it impatience. He had to get back to her – had to see her again. Yvette had not found him repulsive, burns or no burns. Perhaps Barbara would not find him repulsive either. Beside him Yvette stirred.

345

'That was nice, no? But your chocolate – it will be quite cold!'

'Never mind the damn chocolate!' he said, and there was a new and cheerful note in his voice.

Although next morning Huw was weak and tired from his exertions it was as if a watershed had been reached. He grew stronger by the day. Soon he was joining the family in the farmhouse downstairs and each time he looked in the mirror he saw that the burns to his face were a little less noticeable. He and Yvette listened regularly to the broadcasts on the little radio and afterwards they would make love. He harboured feelings of guilt about this for when he was alone he thought of no one but Barbara, but Yvette asked for nothing beyond his company, never demanded more than he was prepared to give, and the union of their bodies in the small bed in the attic room had become as necessary to him now as the food and wine she had brought him when he was too weak to go downstairs and the medication Jacques had provided. It was all a part of the healing process, something as mechanical as it was pleasurable which fulfilled a need in her just as she fulfilled one in him.

But with returning strength his impatience grew. How much longer would it be before he could get home? He couldn't languish here for the duration of the war. In Yvette's company he tried to hide his impatience but when Jacques visited he asked what plans they had for him.

'It will not be long now,' the doctor told him. 'Things are in hand.'

But a few days later Jacques brought devastating news. The Resistance cell which would have arranged for Huw's exit from France had been penetrated and the leaders arrested. They sat around the table in the farm kitchen, talking of it in low voices.

'They were betrayed,' Jacques said. 'The SS called at

the house of M. Sambussi in the night. They found his
radio set. He was arrested and taken away – his wife
too. It will be a matter of days only, hours maybe,
before the rest are arrested.' His tone was matter-of-fact
yet the words reminded them all of the constant danger
they faced.

'Thank God we had not yet told them of Huw,'
Raoul said in French.

Huw was by now used enough to the language to
understand him.

'Did none of them know?' he asked.

'Only Father Leclerc,' Jacques assured him. 'We can
only pray he is not taken – as no doubt he is doing
himself! If he talks, then . . .' He shrugged expressively.

Huw stood up. 'I must go – I'll make my own way
across country. I don't want to put you into any more
danger.'

'No, my friend.' Jacques laid a hand on his arm. 'I
have my ear close to the ground. If the good curé is
arrested we must think again. For now it is safer for all
of us if you remain hidden.'

Reluctantly, Huw was forced to accept the logic of
this argument. If he were caught without identity
papers and if the Red Cross agreement was violated
and he was interrogated he might very well be the one
to betray these people who had saved his life.

'What do we do then?' he asked.

'For the moment, nothing. As soon as things quieten
down I will try to find a new contact,' Jacques
promised.

For a few days they lived in fear and the sound of a
motor vehicle in the lane would bring them out in a
cold sweat. But the days passed and no black uniformed
Germans came. Another week. Two. Blue summer was
now turning to red and gold autumn. There was a nip
in the air and Huw dreaded to think how cold it would
be in his attic if he was still there when winter came. He

347

was considering making a run for it by himself again when Jacques came with the news.

'It is arranged, my friend. If all goes well you leave for England tomorrow night.'

The blood began to pound at Huw's temples. 'How?'

'Tomorrow night, a Lysander will come for you at a field not far from here. We will take you there. Be ready by ten o'clock. We must be there waiting for them. Any delay would be dangerous.'

'I understand,' Huw said.

That night, Yvette came to the attic and he knew she expected him to make love to her one last time. He went through the motions automatically but it was an effort. He was too excited at the prospect of going home.

'I shall miss you,' Yvette said afterwards as they lay on the narrow bed.

'You will be a lot safer with me out of the way.'

She laughed softly. 'Safer, per'aps, but also much more dull. Will you think of me sometimes?'

'Of course.'

She laughed again. 'You are a liar, Huw. You will think only of your English girl. I know how it is with you.'

He felt a flush of guilt. 'Is it so obvious?'

'Oui,' she said. 'Yes, it is. I hope she has waited for you. I hope you will be happy with her.'

'Yes,' he said. 'So do I.'

It was pointless to deny that now suddenly the hours until he could see Barbara again seemed to stretch ahead of him as long as the months that had already passed. Just the thought of her was making him close up inside with anticipation though it was no longer so easy to conjure up the image of her face. 'Thank you for all you have done for me, Yvette,' he said.

She shrugged and he sensed her resignation, a girl in an occupied country, chained for the duration of the war to an isolated farm.

'I wish it could have been more,' she said.

'Why don't you fly out with me?' he said suddenly. 'I'm sure they could find room for you in the Lysander.'

'And leave Papa to go on here with only Raoul to help him? I do not think so. And what would I do in England?'

'I'm sure my family would look after you as you have looked after me.'

'And your girl – she would look after me too? Oh no, Huw. That would not be good. Per'aps when the war is over if things do not work out for you with her you will come back. I would like that. But I do not expect it.'

'I shall certainly come back if only to make sure you are all right,' Huw told her.

The next day he awoke to the sound of rain on the tiny attic window and his heart sank. If the cloud base was too heavy the Lysander would not come. But if they missed this moon it could be another month before another pick-up could be attempted. All day he watched the lowering sky, edgy now as a kitten. He had waited so long, another delay now would be unbearable. The rain continued, driving down in thick persistent rods, dripping from the poorly maintained guttering of the old farmhouse and turning the yard outside into a quagmire. Nerves tormented him – he could never remember feeling so nervous, even when he had been flying nightly sorties. He could not eat, but chain smoked the pungent dark cigarettes which the doctor obtained for him. At around seven in the evening the rain eventually stopped and Huw's practised eye noted that the cloud base was higher. Perhaps it would be all right after all. They had supper sitting around the big old scrubbed table and Huw managed to force himself to swallow the pork stew and chunks of bread so as not to be affected by the wine. He couldn't afford to have that going to his head tonight! Across the table he felt Yvette's eyes watching him and he smiled at her. She

349

was to drive him to the pick-up field in the farm truck. There they would be met by the agent in charge of the operation.

As the kitchen clock slowly ticked away the minutes Huw felt the knot of nerves tightening in his stomach. At a quarter to midnight Yvette stood up.

'We go now.'

It would take about an hour to reach the field, she had told him, and it was imperative he was there ready and waiting for the Lysander would be able to stay for only a few minutes.

Yvette fetched her raincoat and tied a scarf over her long hair; Huw put on an old jacket which René had found for him.

'I'll try to send it back to you on the next drop,' he joked.

René nodded, not fully understanding. Huw thanked him and Raoul for all they had done for him and bid them farewell. Then they squelched across the farmyard to the truck. Raoul cranked the engine to life and Yvette shot it into gear. As they turned out into the lane Huw looked back and saw the two men watching them go. He had one last glimpse of the farm before the darkness swallowed it.

Considering the condition of the roads and the truck's unreliable state of repair Yvette drove fast and well but the effort required all her concentration and they talked little. In the narrow beam of the truck lights Huw tried to see something of the surrounding country-side. All these weeks he had been in France yet he knew nothing of it outside the confines of his attic room. But there was little enough to see. The fitful moon showed hedges and fields, all too bumpy or sloping to allow an aeroplane to land, and the occasional barn or cottage.

At last Yvette swung the truck off the road and into a deeply rutted track. Some yards further on and it petered out altogether. She coaxed the truck into bottom gear and crept slowly over the rough ground and into the shelter of a thick copse of bushes.

'Is this it?' Huw asked.

'Oui. I think so. If I am wrong there will be no plane for you tonight!'

'I certainly hope you're not wrong!'

'Per'aps I 'ope I am!' she said drily.

She killed the engine and the lights and Huw turned to her. By the light of the moon he could see she was half-smiling but it was a sad smile. A strand of hair had escaped from the headscarf, lying across her forehead and brushing the corner of her eye. He reached out and tucked it back beneath her scarf, then kissed her. He felt the warm generous response of her mouth then she pulled away with a sharp determined movement.

'It is time for us to go.'

He nodded, regretful suddenly. Another time, another place, who knew what might have been between them? Except of course that wherever he went, whatever he did, there would always be Barbara . . .

'Thank you, Yvette, for everything,' he said and kissed her once more. Then he opened the door of the truck and jumped down.

Twigs and brambles tore at his coat and trousers as they made a way for themselves out of the bushes which effectively concealed the truck. Yvette led the way along the hedge to a corner of a field. She had obviously been here before to reconnoitre, Huw thought, yet she had not mentioned it to him.

A dark figure emerged from the shadow of the hedge, a torch snapped on, its light going right into his eyes and momentarily blinding him. Someone spoke in French and Yvette answered; the words, hurried and heavily accented, meant nothing to Huw. He stood and waited. The torch snapped off and as his eyes adjusted he saw that the agent was slightly built and bespectacled, looking oddly more like an insurance clerk than a Resistance fighter.

The agent spoke again, rapid French in a low voice, and half a dozen more men materialised from the bushes. Two were armed with Sten guns – guards to watch the approaches to the field and prevent interference, Huw guessed – whilst the others would be the flarepath team. Watches were checked. There was still half an hour to go before the Lysander was due. Yvette left them to return to the truck; soon she was back with two flasks of coffee which they shared by passing the plastic beakers from hand to hand.

The minutes ticked slowly by. The tension now was unbearable. Two of the flarepath team began a noisy argument and the agent intervened to silence them.

'Do you want to let every Boche within a hundred kilometres know we're here?' he snarled and though his French was rapid Huw had no difficulty in catching his meaning.

In spite of her raincoat Yvette was shivering, maybe from cold, maybe from the nerves she was controlling so well. Huw put an arm around her, drawing her into the shelter of his own coat and sharing with her the last of his cigarettes. The flarepath team occupied themselves by tying three of their torches to stout sticks. After what seemed an eternity the agent looked at his watch and signalled that it was time to move. The two men with Sten guns left silently to take up their posts, the flarepath team made their way into the open field. Huw watched from the shelter of the hedge as they staked out the makeshift runway under the eagle eye of the agent, setting the sticks with the torches attached to form an inverted 'L' shape. The agent came back to speak to Huw in English.

'We may have trouble. The rain today was bad. There is much mud.'

Huw's heart sank. Landing and take off on a

miniature flarepath in a bumpy field would be difficult enough; if it was muddy, too, the agent was not exaggerating to say he anticipated difficulties.

They stood huddled together watching the sky for the approaching Lysander and periodically checking their watches. It was late. Could it have run into trouble? Huw reckoned that with the weather as bad as it had been it was unlikely many aircraft would be flying that night for any planned bombing raids would certainly have been cancelled. It was always possible his pick-up had been cancelled, too, and the message had not got through. Or perhaps it had set out only to encounter heavy cloud or fog further north and had lost itself somewhere over the French countryside. His heart was beating a tattoo and the palms of his hands were sticky with sweat. How long would they wait before abandoning the exercise? He did not know.

Then, just when he had almost given up hope, he heard the faint drone in the quiet of the night and looking up managed to pick out a dark shape against the fitful banks of cloud with only its dark blue wing tips occasionally showing in the moonlight.

At the first faint sound of the plane the agent had left them to hurry back to his position by the first of the lamps. As the Lysander circled overhead his torch flashed a quick pre-arranged signal, dash-dot-dash. Immediately the circling plane responded the three lamps flared to life on their sticks and the flarepath team retreated.

Once, twice more, the Lysander circled, each time going through a complete approach and overshoot procedure, raising and lowering wheels and flaps, then it came in. From his position under the hedge Huw could only admire the expertise of the pilot as he landed neatly at almost exactly the right spot on the flarepath and taxied along. Just beyond the end of the flarepath the Lysander stopped, seeming to dip slightly, began to turn and stopped again. The roof slid back and as they started across the field towards it two passengers emerged and packages were unloaded and swiftly passed to one of the flarepath team.

As he reached the Lysander, however, Huw realised something was wrong. No pilot would stop at that crazy angle. The cockpit opened and the pilot shouted to him: 'I'm bloody well stuck! Can't move! What is this, a bloody quagmire?'

Huw went to the front of the Lysander and his feet sank into mire. As the pilot had suspected the wheels of the aircraft had dug deep into soft mud. Huw swore. Surely the flarepath team could have set the runway further back? They were buzzing around now like angry hornets, shouting at one another, blaming one another. The pilot jumped down and he and Huw began digging away the mud from the wheels with their hands.

'Here – try this.' Huw had not heard Yvette approach, now she stood beside them holding out a spade.

'Good girl,' he said softly, took the spade and began to dig. The pilot re-entered the cockpit, the Frenchmen and the two passengers who had disembarked from the Lysander went to the rear and pushed with all their might as he revved the engine. But for all their efforts the Lysander refused to budge by so much as an inch. For long minutes they sweated and fretted to no avail and again Huw began to despair of ever getting away. If they could not move the Lysander there would be nothing for it but to set it on fire. Then he and the pilot would have to go on the run together. It was not an inviting prospect.

The agent turned to Yvette, who was standing helplessly by.

'Fetch your truck. Give him a tow,' he said in French.

'Oui.' Yvette ran back across the field, her boots squelching in the soft ground.

A few minutes more and she was back bumping towards them. A tow rope was produced from the rear of the truck and with hands now numbed from cold and caked with mud the men began attaching it.

'Hurry it up, can't you?' the pilot shouted. He had already been on the ground for longer than he cared to be.

At last the rope was attached. Yvette had left the engine running and as she put her foot hard down on the accelerator the men once more put their weight behind the plane. And it was moving. Slowly, very slowly, but moving – back towards firmer ground.

Absorbed as they were none of them noticed the approach of the German patrol. The hard-pressed engines of the Lysander and the truck drowned the sound of engines out on the lane. Their first warning was the sharp crack of shots and they turned, horrified, to see the lights rounding the wood at the entrance to the field. More shots followed; the quick fire rat-tat-tat of the guard's Sten and the answering fire from the German patrol, and the field was suddenly illuminated by a fierce blue searchlight.

Huw swore. 'Allez – vite!' the agent shouted at him.

He half turned, then remembered Yvette. This was going to turn into a massacre. He couldn't leave her. He raced to the cab of the truck and dragged the door open. 'Come with me – come on!'

'Don't be a fool!' she yelled above the noise of the engine. 'Get out while you can!'

Her foot was hard on the accelerator, truck and plane were moving faster now on the firm ground. She reached out with her left hand and pushed him away. At the same moment the agent grabbed his arm. Caught off balance he stumbled.

'She has to move the truck,' the agent shouted, 'or you cannot take off.'

One man was slashing at the towrope with a knife while another covered him with fire from a Sten. It gave and the truck shot forward across the field. The agent was pushing him towards the moving plane. The German guns blazed again, hitting the truck. As he scrambled up the little ladder to the rear cockpit Huw saw it race forward, then career wildly. In that instant he knew he could do no more for Yvette. Someone inside the Lysander had hold of him, pulling him inside. He felt it gathering speed. For a moment he hung on crazily, sucked backwards by the slipstream. Then he fell into the plane. Shots were cannoning into the fuselage but they were just a part of the general mêlée and he hardly heard them. Then the bumping of wheels on uneven ground ceased and he realised they were airborn.

'Christ, that was a close one!' an English voice said and he turned to see a man hanging onto the luggage shelf where the machine gun mounting had been removed. He was wearing a dark rollneck sweater and jacket; Huw recognised him as one of the flarepath team – one who had kept silent while the others had argued volubly.

'Who the hell are you?' he asked.

'Never you mind,' came the reply.

With half his mind Huw registered that he must be an agent who had used the flarepath team as cover to get to the pick-up. But for the moment it was the least of his concerns. All he could think of was the close brush he had had with death – and of Yvette who had undoubtedly given her own life to ensure the safe take-off of the Lysander.

The other man calmly slid back the rear cockpit roof and Huw sank into the little seat facing aft. Below them in the muddy field the guns still made bright patterns in the dark beyond the glare of the searchlights. They would be dead soon, all of the men who had helped him

– if they were not already. Yvette probably lay dead in the bullet-riddled cab of the truck. And what of her father and Raoul? The Germans would undoubtedly trace the truck to the farm and they too would be taken.

He sat in silence, feeling sick, as the Lysander turned for England. He was going home. God alone knew what would happen to them. How the hell could he ever justify to himself the knowledge that he had regained his freedom at their expense? He should have left months ago and taken his chances on being captured. If he had Yvette would be sleeping safely in her bed now.

Or would she? Would she have found some other way to fight back at the hated Boche? He did not know. And now it was much too late to make any difference.

Wearily, Huw sank back onto the seat as the Lysander made its way home over the French coast.

19

'Appeal for Nurses. Extra Staff Urgently Needed.'

The advertisement took up almost a quarter of one of the reduced size sheets on which the *Mercury* had been printed since a shortage of paper had been declared back in the summer. Barbara read and re-read it. Then she took out her diary, noted down a name and telephone number and carefully refolded the paper. If there was one thing Sir Richard Spindler hated it was having his newspaper left in a mess. Barbara was not at all sure he ever read it – she had never seen him with his nose in anything but *The Times*. But that was beside the point. Newspapers must not be left turned inside out or with pages in the wrong order, the way they had always seemed to be at Valley View, or Sir Richard would express his annoyance in no uncertain terms.

In spite of having lived under the same roof with him for almost three months now, Barbara was still more than a little afraid of her father-in-law. His bluff manner could so easily change to bluster and he would roar his displeasure in tones that could be heard from one end of the house to the other. One could never be quite sure of him from one minute to the next. And since he did not suffer fools gladly it was very easy to feel a little like a naughty schoolchild in the presence of a strict headmaster – not an emotion which did anything to help her perpetual feeling of being simply a visitor in the house which was now her home.

If things had been right between her and Marcus she might have been better able to accept it, she thought, but they were not. Little had changed since the night when he had taken her by force and she was beginning to wonder if it ever would. Marcus was a stranger, not at all the man she thought she had married. Sometimes, it was true, he was his old charming self and she wondered if the other dark side of his nature existed only in her imagination, no more than an extension of the depressions which were understandable in a man who had suffered so much. But there was no way she could imagine the absence of intimacy. Mostly he came to bed very late after long sessions closeted with his father in the study and she knew from the way he climbed stealthily into bed that he thought she was asleep and had no intention of waking her. Once or twice she had tried to rouse him but he put her away with the same excuses – she was tired, he was tired, it was late – so that she withdrew, hurt and bewildered, to lie stiffly on her own side of the bed, isolated from him by six inches of cold sheet and the terrible barrier his unwillingness had erected.

Only when he was angry did he seem able to make love to her. Sometimes it seemed he picked a quarrel purposely, goading, needling, until she reacted, then turning on her and blaming her. Then and only then would he take her, but in no way could the act be described as making love, and far from satisfying her it left her more bewildered than ever, her body sore from the violence of his assault, her whole being crying out for tenderness.

He was drinking more than ever, too, but when she mentioned it to him he lost his temper.

'I can have a drink if I want to, surely?'

'Of course you can. But it's not just one drink is it? It's not good for you to have so much.'

'How do you know what's good for me? At least when I've had a drink I can forget for a little while.'

That, of course, was the crux of the matter. He was still suffering from the trauma of his experiences in France, she realised, and she tried to be patient with him because of it. But time was passing and he seemed to be getting worse instead of better – or was it just that he was less able to hide his feelings? He had certainly hidden them well enough when he was courting her; now she saw his black moods, his depressions, his periods of silence and his torments, and try as she might she was powerless to do anything to help. He suffered nightmares, she knew. Sometimes, he would cry out and thresh about in his sleep and when she put her arms around him he would sob against her breast like a child. But she guessed those same nightmares also haunted him when he was awake.

At times she longed to talk to someone about the problem but there was no one to turn to. She was too proud to take it to Amy, who might have had some sensible advice to offer, since she was reluctant to admit that her mother had been right in her reservations about the early marriage.

Once she did try to raise the subject with Lady Erica. Marcus had been drinking heavily and when he and Sir Richard had left them to go into the study she closed the door and turned to her mother-in-law.

'I'm very worried about Marcus.'

Erica surveyed her serenely over her coffee cup. 'Oh? Why, dear?'

'He has such terrible moods. He drinks too much. And I just can't seem to get through to him.'

'I know what you mean.' But Erica did not look in the least worried. 'I expect he'll get over it. He's still suffering over what happened to him, poor darling.'

'But surely we ought to try to help him,' Barbara persisted. 'I'm sure it's getting worse. He didn't seem at all like this before we were married.'

'That's because he was on his best behaviour, I expect. He doesn't seem very different to me. Don't worry about it. Time is a great healer they say and I'm sure it will prove to be just that in Marcus's case. After

360

all, he has his work to think about and he has you. I'm sure that's all he needs to come to terms with what happened.'

Barbara turned away helplessly. How could she tell his mother that she thought he hated his work and that she could be no comfort at all. She could not bring herself to tell the truth about their sterile relationship. It was too private. And even if she did she thought Lady Erica would remain unmoved. Nothing seemed to touch or disturb her, no emotion ever rippled the surface of her serenity. Barbara had a vision of her countering any confidence with her unruffled smile: 'Oh yes, dear, Richard is just the same. It's nothing to worry about. You mustn't let it upset you . . .'

I don't believe she's all there, Barbara thought in irritation, as Erica reached for her embroidery and began stitching a delicate butterfly as if nothing else was of any importance.

Barbara continued to suffer in silence, wondering sometimes why Marcus had asked her to marry him at all. Then he had seemed to want her. Now he did not. On more than one occasion she cried herself to sleep waiting for him to come to their loveless marriage bed and wondered what she could do to improve matters.

One evening Marcus's bad temper had caused a major upset with his father. Throughout dinner he had been quiet and withdrawn eating little and drinking a good deal. When the meal was finished Sir Richard lit a cigar and stood up.

'I want to talk to you, my boy, about the lease of the swimming bath to the council.'

For once, Marcus made no attempt to follow him.

'Not tonight, Pater. I don't feel like it.'

'That's beside the point. I saw Harry Hall today on a colliery matter and he spoke to me about it.'

Barbara pricked up her ears at the mention of her uncle's name.

'He had no business speaking to you about it,' Marcus said pettishly. 'I thought the estates were my responsibility now.'

'They are. Which is why I want to pass on his comments to you.'

'Won't it wait?'

'From what Harry Hall says it has been waiting long enough already. He tells me the Clerk to the Council has written to you on three separate occasions and has not received a reply.'

'I'll get around to it. I can't do everything at once.'

'Sometimes I think you do bugger all!' Sir Richard exploded.

Lady Erica averted her eyes and Barbara's anxiety grew, along with a desire to defend Marcus. It really was not fair that Sir Richard expected him to be able to take on all the administration work and do it as well after a few months as his brother had done after years of experience.

'He does his best,' she protested.

Lady Erica reached over, touched her sleeve and cautioned Barbara to silence with a small shake of her head. Sir Richard did not appear to notice the interruption.

'We have to remain firm on this one,' he asserted. 'The agreement on the council lease for the swimming bath does not expire for another three years. Now they want to pull out and have it revert to us – just because they allege it is it being polluted from the graves in the churchyard or some such nonsense. We can't allow that. We have their agreement in writing that they will pay us rent for it until 1944. We have to make it clear that we shall hold them to that or before we know it we shall be losing three years' rent. A letter must be sent to them tomorrow stating our clear intention.'

'All right, Pater, you've made your point,' Marcus said sullenly.

'I hope so. You can't run an estate without keeping on top of things. If you ran your unit like that it's no wonder you lost the lot of 'em.'

Barbara saw Marcus whiten. She leaped up and ran to his side.

'That's a terrible thing to say!'

'True, though,' Sir Richard blustered.

Marcus's hands were clenching and unclenching, his face working.

'I'd like to have seen you do better.'

'Give me half a chance and I would have. The trouble with you, my lad, is that you think you can swan through life like you swanned through school. But it isn't one damn great cricket match. It's serious business.'

'You think I don't know that?' Marcus yelled. 'You think seeing my men killed was no worse than having my team all sent back to the pavilion? Maybe everything did come to me too easily. But I've found out about life the hard way. And death too. I've learned more than you'll ever know!'

He turned and stormed out of the room. With an anguished look at Sir Richard, almost apopletic with fury, and Erica, still serenely sewing, Barbara ran after him. When she reached their room he was sitting on the bed, head in hands. She dropped to her knees beside him.

'Marcus – don't! He didn't mean it.'

'Oh yes he did.' His voice was muffled. 'I've disappointed my father – you know that?'

'Don't be silly. Het gets impatient, that's all.'

'I've disappointed him all my life.'

'What nonsense! Everyone in Hillsbridge knows you are a hero. You were very brave.' Her voice was soft, eager. 'You were decorated, Marcus, for what you did.'

'Decorated! For losing all my men!'

'For valour in an impossible situation.'

363

'Tell that to my father! You know something, Barbara? All my life I've tried to live up to what he expected of me and I don't believe I've ever managed it. I wasn't clever like Henry. He was always held up to me as a shining example. Make sure you do as well as Henry, my boy. Don't let the side down. I knew I couldn't keep up with him academically, no matter how hard I worked and I wasn't that keen on work. So I tried to shine in my own way.'

'And you did!' she said loyally, taking his hand. 'You did!'

'It wasn't enough for Pater. Oh no. He was still making comparisons.'

'You're wrong, I'm sure. And he is very proud of you now. He must be.'

'No. I know what he's thinking – that Henry wouldn't have lost his men.'

'Henry wasn't even there. He was here doing nothing more demanding than running the estates.'

'A damn sight better than I am! You see – I can't even manage that.'

'Oh Marcus!'

'I'm not even a proper husband to you.'

'You will be when you're well again. And I can wait.' She felt strong suddenly. She dropped to her knees beside him, loosening his tie and collar button. 'Come to bed. You're all in.'

He raised his head. His handsome face was ravaged. Then he reached for her pulling her in between his knees.

'I love you, Barbara.' His voice was little more than an anguished whisper. 'I know I have a funny way of showing it but I do. You're the best thing that ever happened to me.'

She wound her arms round him, resting her head against his chest so that she could feel the beat of his heart against her cheek. For long moments they remained that way, then slowly she was aware of the bridge of power that was building between them. Her chest was tight with tension and she was afraid to move or breathe deeply in case it was shattered. Then she felt his hands moving over her back into the curve of her waist and down to the curve of her bottom. Still she remained motionless. It had to come from him. Any move on her part and he would draw back. But beneath his touch every nerve seemed to be coming to life.

His hands moved up to the swell of her breast, slid round, unbuttoned her dress and slipped inside. Her nipple hardened as he stroked it. Then and only then did she lift her face so that she could see the clean cut profile of his cheek and chin. He eased her dress off her shoulders, she dropped her arms, a quick wriggle and it fell to her waist. He buried his face in her breasts, kissing the hollow between, then exploring with growing urgency. His lips moved to her throat and then they were on her mouth. With a small moan she parted her lips, kissing him back as she had not kissed him for weeks – months. Her fingers found the buttons of his shirt and unfastened them and she ran her hands over the muscular lines of his chest.

'Oh Barbara!' It was a sob, almost inaudible. They moved as one; somehow they were lying on the bed. As she felt his weight on her she was afraid for one wild moment that even now he would draw back. He did not. He took her quickly, desperately, and too soon it was over. As he rolled away she wanted to cry out to him 'No – don't stop – please don't stop!' but she did not dare. It was too fragile, this moment of communication between them; she had experienced so many rebuffs. And though her own need ached in her still, she was aware of a feeling of satisfaction. She reached out her hand and he took it, pressed it to his lips, then held it between them against his chest. Within moments it seemed his breathing had become deep and even and she knew he was asleep.

As her own sensitised body relaxed Barbara felt the warmth within her grow to a sense of anticipation. Tonight, for the first time, Marcus had made love to her – really made love. Tonight he had forgotten the horrors of war and his sense of inadequacy in her arms. Surely now they had overcome the barrier and from now on things would be different.

She sang next morning as she dressed and her face looked back at her from the mirror with its old healthy glow. Lately she had been looking more and more pale and peaky. Not today. Today she was buoyed up with the residue of pleasure from the previous night and the anticipation of all the nights to come. For the first time she felt like a bride. It was a good feeling. But it was not to last.

To Barbara's frustration and disappointment she soon discovered nothing had changed. After another day in his office Marcus came home as silent and morose as ever. And he made no attempt to repeat the experience of the previous night.

However, he did talk to her about his confrontation that day with the Clerk to the Council over the lease of the swimming bath.

'I couldn't get anywhere with him at all. It seems the council are determined to close the bath and not pay us another penny in rent. Father is going to be mad as a hatter – I'll bet he thinks if Henry was dealing with it he would be able to sort something out. And I expect he could. But I can't.'

Barbara said nothing. Her mind was working over-time for an idea had occurred to her. Perhaps if she was to have a quiet word in Uncle Harry's ear he could do something. If Marcus could emerge the victor in this one small thing maybe it would bring him some praise from his father and bolster his self-esteem. But he must not know what she was thinking of doing. He must believe that anything he achieved had come about from his own efforts.

The following afternoon Barbara decided to pay a visit to Uncle Harry and Aunt Margaret. It was a Saturday so she knew it was likely they would be at home. Marcus and his father had gone to watch a rugby match at Marcus's old school and Lady Erica was resting; Barbara left a note saying she had gone out without any further explanation. Then she set out to walk the mile and a half to Uncle Harry's house.

It was a bleak afternoon, a gusty wind driving the newly fallen leaves into swirls and huddles at the sides of the road and a thick drizzle which would probably become fog at nightfall dripping down from the almost bare branches of the trees. Barbara turned up the collar of her coat and shivered. She was glad she was not spending the afternoon watching a rugby match.

She reached Uncle Harry's house, went around to the back door and knocked. After a moment it was opened by Margaret. She was wearing an apron and her hands were floury.

'Barbara! What a surprise!' She opened the door with her elbow. 'Come in, dear.'

Barbara went into the kitchen. It was warm from the heat of the oven, comfortably untidy with the pastry Margaret had been rolling out on the table and a clothes horse airing laundry in front of the fire. Thinking of the elegant rooms in her new home Barbara felt a twinge of nostalgia for the life she had left behind when she had married Marcus.

'I'm just making a pie for tomorrow's dinner,' Margaret said, explaining the pastry. 'I thought I'd get it done while I have five minutes to myself.'

'Don't let me stop you!' Barbara took off her coat and hung it on the hook behind the door. 'Are you alone?' She was glancing around for some sign that Uncle

Harry was in; if he was not her plan would have to be rethought.

'Elaine and Marie have gone to the Saturday afternoon pictures at the Palace. Thank heavens for the pictures, I say! I don't know what I'd do with them otherwise. It's really hard work to interest them in anything. And your Uncle is in the front room working on some council business,' Margaret said, unknowingly answering Barbara's question.

'He's busy then,' Barbara said.

'I'm sure he'll be pleased to see you. Pop in and say hello in a minute. But first *I* want to hear how you're getting on. We hardly see you these days. How do you like married life?'

She had returned to her pastry, neatly rolling and cutting as she spoke and suddenly Barbara wished she could tell her all her troubles. Margaret was so sensible, yet so caring – the warmest person I have ever met, she thought. And she was not involved as Amy was. Any advice she offered would be wise and impartial – there would be no 'I told you so' from her. But how to begin? She could hardly blurt out that her marriage was a disaster, even to Margaret.

'It's all right,' she said.

Margaret glanced up at her sharply then her face softened. She was very fond of Barbara and she knew instinctively something was wrong.

'Adjusting is never easy,' she said. 'You think because you love someone you can live with them anywhere, anyhow, but of course it's not that simple. And you've moved into a totally different world. It must seem very strange to you.'

'It does,' Barbara agreed. 'It's all so leisurely! I'm not used to having nothing to do.'

'Oh dear – bad as that?'

'Yes. The days really drag. Most new wives have a house to look after, but I haven't got that. The

Spindlers have managed to keep some of their staff in spite of the war – the ones too old to do anything else – and they get really offended if I so much as lift a finger. It's really deathly.'

Margaret lifted the pastry lid and fitted it onto the pie dish, covering a mound of blackberry and apple slices. She led such a busy life herself she found it almost impossible to imagine the arid days Barbara described, but there was no mistaking her niece's distress.

'It would be much better if you had something to do,' she said.

'I know. I want to work – after all I'm fully trained in business studies. I can do book-keeping. I know all about commerce and economics. I'm sure I could be a help to Marcus but he won't hear of it.'

'What about war work? There must be something you could do to help the war effort. Surely no one could object to that?'

'I had to give up my fire watching because for one thing we're too far out for me to be of any earthly use and for another it would interfere with the Spindlers' dinner.' Barbara's voice held a note of bitterness. 'I *have* knitted some socks for the sailors, though. Six pairs, all in waxed wool. See – my fingers are quite sore!'

'Good for you.'

'I'm not sure. They'll probably need two left feet to wear them.' She grew serious again. 'Honestly, I don't know what to do. I could join the WVS, I suppose, but they are all so much older than me. I just long for company of my own age. But going to school in Bath I never really made any friends out here in Hillsbridge – and the ones I do still hear from have all joined the forces now.'

'Poor old Barbara!' Margaret said. 'We'll have to think. There must be something you could do.'

A thought occurred to Barbara. 'You won't tell Mum, will you, that I'm feeling a bit blue?'

'Of course not, if you don't want me to. Now, I'm going to get this in the oven. Are you going in to see your Uncle?'

'Yes, all right,' Barbara said.

She went through into the front room where Harry was sitting at the table surrounded by papers. He looked up as she tapped at the door and opened it.

'Hello, Babs! I thought I heard voices.'

'Yes, I thought I'd call in and say hello.' She went into the room and closed the door after her. 'Actually, since you're so busy I'll come straight to the point. It was you I came to see.'

'Me?' He sat back, smiling at her. 'I am honoured!'

'I don't know if you'll think so when you hear what it's about,' Barbara admitted. 'Boring old council business.'

'Since when have you been interested in the council?'

'I'm not really, but Marcus is. He's terribly worried about this swimming bath thing. You know what I'm talking about? The council lease it from Spindler estates and now they want to give it up.'

'There's no point wasting ratepayers money to keep it on,' Harry said. 'We have had a report done and the pollution from the churchyard means it's not safe for people to bathe in it.'

'Yes.' Barbara bit her lip. 'I know that's what they say. But Marcus's father is very angry about it.'

'He would be,' Harry said drily. 'If there's one saying your father-in-law believes in it's the one about looking after the pennies and the pounds will look after themselves. The rent we pay is just a flea bite to him, but I don't suppose he sees it that way.'

'He doesn't. He's blaming Marcus for not tying things up. That's why I wondered if you could help.'

'Me? How?'

'Well . . .' Suddenly it seemed a tremendous imposition but she stumbled on anyway. 'I thought maybe you could persuade the council to keep on the lease for another year at least . . .'

'Oh, Barbara!' Harry pushed the sleeves of his pullover up above the cuffs and his shirt. 'I can't do that.'

'But they take a great deal of notice of you. After all . . .'

'I was elected to represent the interests of the ratepayers of Hillsbridge, not Sir Richard Spindler,' Harry said firmly.

'Couldn't you just . . .?'

He shook his head. 'Not even for you, my love. With the pollution as it is that bit of river is no earthly use as a swimming bath. It should have been closed down years ago. It's only a mercy no one has got septicaemia yet from swimming in it. I'm afraid if Sir Richard wants his money for the next two years he is going to have to take us to court to get it.'

Barbara nodded. She knew when she was beaten.

'I'm sorry. I suppose I shouldn't have asked.'

'Forget it. Just as long as you understand there is nothing I can do.'

'Of course.' She leaned across and dropped a kiss on his forehead. 'Sorry, Uncle.'

Her feelings were mixed as she walked home. She had failed to help Marcus but talking to her aunt and uncle had made her feel better all the same. In their house she had been her old self for a little while, remembered how she had used to be before the events of the last year had altered her – before Marcus, before Huw. She hadn't sat back and let things happen to her then. She had been a rebel, ready to take risks and battle for what she wanted. She remembered the scrapes she had been in, the way she had managed to get her own way even against the Sisters at school and how she had altered her birth certificate in an effort to join the WAAF. Could that Barbara really have disappeared? Surely not. If she wanted her life to change then she was the only one who could change it. She simply was not prepared to be a victim of circumstance any longer.

Hillsbridge House was as quiet as she had left it, her note unread on the table. Marcus and his father were not home yet, she assumed. Perhaps they had stayed to have tea with one of the masters in his room. And of Lady Erica there was no sign either. Barbara crossed to the big open fireplace, warming her hands. No shortage of coal at Hillsbridge House. The thought amused her. There wouldn't be, would there, since Sir Richard owned most of the pits in the valley which produced it!

The *Mercury*, published the previous day, lay on the table. Idly, Barbara picked it up, turning the pages. A few weddings, mostly with the brides wearing sensible coats and hats, a small spray of flowers their only concession to tradition. Poor things, I wonder if they know what they are letting themselves in for? Barbara thought. An account of an inquest into yet another death in the blackout. Some war news and a photograph of a local lad, missing in a merchant ship. Barbara thought of Huw and quickly pushed the thought away. She had enough on her mind without adding to the load.

She turned the page and saw the story: 'Appeal for Nurses'. She stopped to read it and felt a quiver of excitement.

She had been wondering what she could do – now right here in front of her eyes was the answer! It was something that had never occurred to her before, now she wondered why ever not. She had no experience, of course, but the advert said that all that was needed was a pair of hands and a willing disposition. It would be menial work, no doubt, emptying bedpans and sweeping wards, but it would be work and she would be doing her bit for the war effort. After the frustration of the past weeks it was an exhilarating thought.

Marcus and his father came home while she was dressing for dinner.

'Good match?' she asked. The new positive mood spilled over into her voice but Marcus seemed not to notice.

'I suppose so.' He stripped off his shirt, shivering a little. It was not very warm in the bedroom. 'Pater is still going on about this damned swimming bath business.'

'You might just as well tell him there's nothing you can do,' she said. 'Your only recourse would be to take the council to court and it's simply not worth it. Besides it's immoral to try and squeeze money out of the ratepayers for a swimming bath that no one can swim in.'

He looked at her in surprise. 'What do you know about it?'

'I went to see Uncle Harry this afternoon. I mentioned it to him.'

She knew at once she had said the wrong thing for his face darkened.

'You haven't been interfering, have you?'

'Of course not. I just thought I'd ask him about it.'

'You have been interfering!' He swung around from the wardrobe, a clean shirt on its hanger swinging in his hand. 'Why can't you mind your own business?'

'I'm sorry,' she said shortly. 'I'm getting a bit fed up with playing the dutiful little wife. There's something else I might as well tell you while I'm about it. I want to volunteer as a nurse.'

'You *what?*'

'They're desperate for extra nurses – auxiliaries as well as trained people. It's something I could do instead of sitting around here all day. I'm going to see them on Monday and volunteer.'

'Where would you go?'

'Bath. I don't know which hospital. Part of the Royal United Hospital has been turned over to the military and there are a lot of new buildings at St Martins to deal with air raid casualties and so on. I presume I'd be sent where I'm most needed.'

'No,' he said flatly. 'No wife of mine is going to look after other men. There are plenty of girls who can do that without you . . .'

'But it's up to everyone to do their bit. I don't want to quarrel but I don't want to be kept here like a bird in a gilded cage. I'm bored out of my mind and I want to do something useful.'

'Mother and Father would never stand for it.'

'They can't stop me and neither can you. My mind is made up.' If it hadn't been before it was now, she thought.

His face contorted. 'You will do as you are told.'

She turned away. There was no point in arguing. He was simply working himself up to one of his rages. But she was determined that on Monday morning she would get on a bus and go to Bath.

She was at the wardrobe selecting a dress when he grabbed her from behind. 'I know what you want. You want a man.' He spun her round. His face had the dark shut-in look she had learned to fear. He caught at her blouse, ripping it off her shoulders.

Suddenly Barbara was more angry than afraid. She lashed out with her hand. Her fingers caught his cheek a stinging blow. He recoiled, then grabbed her, and hauled her struggling and fighting to the bed.

'Stop it!' she screamed, but his hand was over her mouth, stifling her cry. He was too strong for her. Despite her struggles he took her with the same manic strength she had come to know. Afterwards, as he rolled away, she struggled to her feet. Her mouth was bleeding and his finger marks had made angry weals on her breasts.

'That's it!' she said. Her voice was low and trembling, yet surprisingly firm. 'I won't be treated this way. I'm leaving you, Marcus.'

In a second he was on his feet. The monster had gone. In his place was the frightened, war-shocked young man. It was as if Marcus was three separate people, she thought. No doubt this afternoon he had been his third self – the charming sports-mad hero – to everyone he had met at his old school.

'No!' he begged her. 'Barbara – I'm sorry. I'm really sorry. I don't know what comes over me. But it won't happen again I promise.'

'I've heard that before.'

'I mean it. I couldn't bear it if you left me. I don't know what I'd do.'

'You'd survive.'

'I wouldn't. I'd kill myself, Barbara. God knows, I've thought about it. Before I met you I almost did. I've got a gun. I've still got my service revolver. I made up my mind to use it. But I couldn't even do that. And then I met you and you made everything seem different. I thought I was going to be all right. And I will be. I will be. Only don't leave me, Barbara – please don't leave me!'

She was amazed at the emotions flooding through her then. Her anger had died at the sight of his face. Now she felt only pity, fear that he might actually mean what he threatened, and, strangely, love. Never before had she felt that she actually held someone's life in her hands. Never before had the feeling of responsibility and of being needed been so strong. It frightened yet exhilarated her. Maybe she could still help him. Maybe she could help to restore his shattered nerves, help him rebuild his confidence in himself so that he could once more become what he had been. It was a challenge and God alone knew it would not be easy. But if she could do it the rewards would be well worth the effort.

Marcus the golden boy living up to his image once more. And only she would know the truth about the toll his heroism had taken on him.

Once again she remembered the horror of what he had been through and reminded herself that these traumas and inadequacies were as much a legacy of the war as his damaged leg. That was a wound for all the world to see – and an acceptable one. His mental state was something to be hidden, something only she knew about. Heroes were not supposed to be mentally or emotionally deranged. They should be above that. If she left him it might prove the final straw. Her departure would signal the final failure and it might push him over the brink. Whereas if she stayed, perhaps she could help him to become whole once more and in so doing become a more complete person herself.

The words of the marriage service came back to her. 'For better, for worse . . . in sickness and in health.' That was what she had promised. Usually, one would expect the better to come before the worse, the health before the sickness, building strength for what might follow. Not in her case. She had been plunged straight into a nether-world she had scarcely dreamed existed. But she would fight out of it and she would take him with her. In that moment Barbara silently renewed her marriage vows and the words had fresh meaning for her.

But she had to have an outlet or go under herself. If she was to help him, she had to establish a sound base from which to work. Now was the time to do it.

'All right, Marcus, I'll stay on one condition. I am serious about doing war work. If you try to stop me, I *shall* leave you.'

'Anything, Barbara. Only please – don't go!'

'All right, we'll try again.'

She did not add a second condition. She did not tell him as she might have done a few minutes ago that she would also leave him if he continued to take her by force instead of in love. With an instinctive wisdom beyond her years Barbara knew that was a promise he would be unable to keep.

She went to Bath on Monday morning to the Headquarters of the Civil Nursing Division where she was interviewed by the Honorary Organizer herself.

Facing her questions across the table Barbara felt hopelessly inadequate. No, she had no formal training and no nursing experience either, just a few classes in first aid which she had attended when she was fire watching, to her credit. Yes, she was willing to learn. As credentials she gave details of her education and the business training she had received.

The Organizer sat for a moment reading the form which Barbara had completed. Then she looked up at Barbara directly.

'I'm not sure that enrolling you as an Auxiliary would be the best way to aid the war effort, Mrs Spindler.'

Barbara's heart sank. 'But it said in the advertisement that experience was not necessary,' she argued. 'I'm young and fit and I'm ready to do whatever is required of me. The Minister of Health himself has launched a campaign for more nurses, it said so in the paper. If you turn me down I shall just have to go elsewhere to offer my services.'

The Organizer smiled. She admired spirit, particularly in the young.

'I didn't say I was turning you down. I simply said I think there may be better ways for you to help the war effort than by nursing.'

'Such as?'

The Organizer straightened the papers in front of her. 'I need help here at my HQ. Administering the

377

Civil Nursing Reserve involves a lot of clerical work. With your education and business training background I am sure you could be of great assistance to me. It doesn't sound as glamorous as nursing, I agree – not that nursing is as glamorous as people seem to think it, in any case. But it is very necessary and I must have staff I can depend on. Would you consider working here with me, Mrs Spindler?'

'Oh!' Barbara said, the wind taken out of her sails.

The Organizer continued to look at her with that disconcertingly direct gaze. It was not what she had expected, but yes, now that she came to think of it, working here at HQ did have a certain appeal. No awkward shifts. No bedpans. No brooms. And the chance at last to put her training to good use.

Barbara nodded. 'Yes. Yes. I think I would consider it. And yes, I think I would like it very much.'

Whilst she was in Bath she took the opportunity to look around the shops, though she did not buy anything. She was amused by the queues which had formed outside some shops and joined one for the fun of it.

'What are you queuing for?' she asked the woman in front of her.

The woman shrugged. 'Don't know. But as soon as I saw the queue I knew it must be for something. We'll find out when we get there.'

Briefly, Barbara shared her excitement, but after ten minutes with no appreciable movement she began to be bored, left the queue and followed it to its head to see where it was leading.

A chemists' shop!

Curious, thought Barbara. Why should anyone queue outside a chemists' shop? Oh well, perhaps they knew what they were doing. But then again, perhaps they did not.

Barbara wandered on.

By killing the rest of the afternoon she managed to be at the bus station at exactly the same time as Maureen. Her sister, who now travelled to school alone, was delighted to see her and it seemed just like old times as they sat side by side on one of the hard wooden seats rattling along and chattering all the way.

'Why don't you come home for an hour?' Maureen suggested when the bus reached Hillsbridge. Barbara glanced at the town clock. She still had more than three hours before she needed to begin getting ready for dinner and the thought of spending at least a couple of them at her old home was an inviting one. Besides, if she was going to begin working for the Civil Nursing Reserve it might be the last opportunity she would have for quite a while.

The girls walked along the lane.

'Shall we call in at the office and see Mum?' Barbara suggested as they approached the yard.

'She isn't there today,' Maureen told her. 'She's gone to a meeting of the Haulage Association or whatever they call themselves.'

'Does that mean she'll be late home?' Barbara asked, dismayed.

'I shouldn't think so. I know the men tend to rabbit on a bit but Mum is very good at getting a meeting closed when she wants to go home. And she and Ralph are supposed to be going out tonight to some function in connection with the Comforts Fund.'

In the months since she had left to be married little had changed at Valley View. Mrs Milsom was at the sink peeling potatoes for the evening meal and she dried her hands to greet Barbara warmly.

'Well, well, Miss Babs, fancy seeing you! I thought you'd gone and deserted us.'

'Now would I do a thing like that?' Barbara asked, helping herself to a few crumbs of a cake which was cooling on the table. 'This looks good – what is it?'

'Carrot cake,' Mrs Milsom told her. 'It's not the same as a nice slice of Dundee, but there you are.'

'Can I have some?' Barbara asked. 'I'm starving.'

'It shouldn't be cut yet. It's still warm,' Mrs Milsom said severely, then smiled, setting her multiple chins wobbling. 'Well, go on then. But don't blame me if you get indigestion.'

'I won't.' Barbara cut herself a thick slice and bit into it. 'Hey, not bad! Do you want some, Maureen?'

'She does not. You'll have your mother after you if you spoil your appetite, Miss Maureen.'

'When have I ever done that, Milsy?' Maureen laughed and the girls munched carrot cake together. Then Maureen went upstairs to change out of her school uniform and Mrs Milsom departed to lay the table – something she liked to get out of the way before the cooking reached what she referred to as 'the crucial stage'.

Barbara sat by the fire glancing through the *News Chronicle* which had been discarded in Mrs Milsom's rocking chair and toasting her toes. She felt good and comfortable, happier than she had done for weeks.

Perhaps everything was going to come out right after all, she thought. Her new job would give her a different perspective on things and she was determined to make a success at last of her marriage to Marcus. Patience and understanding were what was required and in the end she would see his mind mend as his body had, so that he would once again truly be Hillsbridge's 'golden boy'.

Lost in her thoughts she did not hear the footsteps approaching the back door, but when the handle creaked and began to turn Barbara looked up in surprise. Too early for her mother, surely, and Ralph never used the back door. She half rose as it swung open, then gasped and froze.

It couldn't be. She must have fallen asleep and be dreaming.

The apparition smiled.

'Hello, Barbara.'

And then she moved, running across the kitchen and throwing herself into his arms. And her voice, though only a whisper, was so full of joy it seemed to come from every bit of her being.

'Huw – oh Huw! I don't believe it! Huw!'

20

He held her. Her hair was silky soft against his face, her body felt firm and sweet and whole. A thousand dreams and now she was in his arms. Unexpectedly, tears filled his eyes. He buried his face in her hair and hugged her close.

After long moments she pulled back, still holding him, but tilting her head so she could see him.

'Huw! You're all right! You're here! Oh Huw!'

She was crying, too, and laughing at the same time. He pulled her close again, not wanting her to see his tears.

'Oh Barbara!' Her name was like a liturgy. He heard himself saying it over and over. Time had stopped, the world stood still. The cosy kitchen around them ceased to exist. He kissed her, felt the eager response of her lips, held her close again. Time for questions and explanations later. For now all that mattered was being here. With her.

They did not hear Maureen coming back downstairs. The first warning was her excited squeal and then there were not two bodies embracing but three. After the first ecstatic moment it brought him back to reality.

'What are you doing here?' Maureen asked. 'We thought you were dead! Oh, Mrs Milsom, come quickly! It's Huw! He's home!'

'Whatever is going on? Whatever . . .?' Mrs Milsom stopped in the doorway, her hands full of cutlery. Then she added her voice to the clamour.

'Oh Master Huw! Oh my goodness!'

He put his kitbag down on one of the chairs.

'Why didn't you let us know, you naughty boy?' Mrs

Milsom asked. And then: 'Oh my Lord, whatever happened to your face?'

He touched the still-bubbled skin defensively. 'I got burned when my kite came down. It's not so bad now.' He looked around. 'Where is Amy? I called in at the yard and she wasn't there. They thought she'd be at home.'

'She'll be here soon. Oh Huw, tell us, where have you been?' Maureen bubbled.

'In France. It's a very long story. I got back this morning. They flew me out.' He glanced towards the stove. 'Is the kettle on Mrs Milsom? If there's one thing I could do with it's a nice cup of English tea!'

'Yes, of course, Master Huw. Oh my goodness. I'm all of a dither!'

'Sit down, Milsy, and I'll see to it,' Barbara said.

Huw watched as she set out cups and saucers and though he was now trying to answer their hundred and one questions he could think of nothing but Barbara and how lovely she was. Christ, he could eat her. Devour her. The way she moved started a fire within him, her smile touched his heart. Barbara – I love you! I've always loved you and I was too stupid to realise it. But I'm here now and everything is going to be all right. There's nothing to stand between us now. Nothing . . .

She made the tea, poured it, and brought a cup over to him.

'I was lucky,' he was saying. 'Lucky not to be captured and even more lucky not to be killed. My kite went down in a mass of flames.'

'Oh Huw!' she said. 'Oh your poor face!'

As she stretched out her hand to touch the scorched skin of his cheek he saw it. A wedding ring, a plain circle of gold on the third finger of her left hand. He caught her hand, held it, looking at the ring.

'What's this?'

She turned pale as she remembered what the excitement had made her forget.

'I'm married,' she said.

'Married?'

'Last August. Marcus and I were married.'

'Oh,' he said. The joy was dying in him. Was dead already.

'You missed it, Huw!' Maureen bubbled. 'It was a lovely wedding. She's practically the Lady of the Manor now, aren't you, Babs?'

Married. She was married. He was too late.

'I wrote to tell you I was engaged,' she said defensively.

'But I didn't think . . . Amy wrote that it would be at least a year . . .'

The others had fallen silent, aware suddenly of a drama in which they had no part being played out.

'There didn't seem any point in waiting.' Her voice was brittle.

No point. He had discovered there was no reason why he should not love her, been unable to tell her, and now it was too late. The injustice of fate was staggering. Somehow he managed to compose himself.

'Congratulations. I wish I hadn't missed it. I hope you're very happy.'

She did not answer. She had felt him go away from her and the agony of it was almost too much to bear.

They heard the sound of a car outside.

'It's Mum!' Maureen cried, excited again. 'Wait till she sees you, Huw! Mum!' She ran to the door, wrenching it open.

For a moment Huw and Barbara remained motionless, looking at one another. There was so much to say and none of it would make any difference. She was married. It was as final as if she had been dead.

Amy came in, her face alight, and it all began again.

'Huw! I knew you'd come back! I knew you would!'

384

He hugged her, trying to ignore the empty leaden place inside him.

'You knew you wouldn't get rid of me so easily, you mean? It takes more than the Boche to kill me.'

'The Boche!' Maureen giggled. 'Oh Huw, how French you sound! What was it like? Tell us all about it!'

'Give Huw a chance! He'll tell us about it over dinner,' Amy said and turned to her elder daughter. 'You'll stay, won't you, Babs? Ring Marcus and tell him you must stay for dinner. I'm sure they'll understand this is a very special occasion.'

Barbara bit her lip. In the midst of all the excitement she was suddenly thinking of Marcus and his threats of suicide. If she stayed away tonight he might think she had left him and heaven only knew what he might do.

'I'm sorry, but I don't think I can,' she said.

'Oh surely . . .' Amy began.

Another notch tightened in Huw. 'Don't worry, Barbara, if you have to go I understand.'

'I'm really sorry . . .'

'Well, I think that you married into a very peculiar family,' Amy said briskly. 'How long are you here for, Huw?'

He hesitated. He had been given a week's leave but he knew now he was not going to take it. At least, not here. A week around Barbara, looking at her and knowing she could not be his? Seeing her perhaps with that damned Marcus Spindler? Knowing, even when they were together, that she would be going home to bed with him? It was more than flesh and blood could stand.

'Twenty-four hours,' he said, trying to smile. 'And I assure you, I intend to make the most of it!'

When Maureen had at last been persuaded to go to bed Amy and Huw sat talking in the fading light of the fire.

Any thought of attending the function in aid of the Comforts Fund had been abandoned for Amy had no intention of going out with Huw home safely after so long. There was so much to talk about and Amy assumed that Huw's slightly withdrawn air had something to do with the experiences he had been through. Ralph, however, was more perceptive and although he had no inkling of the reason behind it he knew instinctively that Huw wanted to talk to Amy alone. He made some excuse about wanting to check on his ARP post and went out.

'I can't understand them not giving you more leave, Huw,' Amy said, getting out her cigarettes and offering him one. 'I know we're fighting a war, but all the same I think it's a bit much expecting you to start operational flying again without a break. How do they know you're fit?'

'I was given a thorough medical as soon as I got back. They came to the conclusion that the French doctor who looked after me did a pretty good job.' Huw flicked his lighter, igniting both Amy's cigarette and his own.

'Well, I still can't understand it,' Amy said. 'I should have thought at least a week at home would have done you the world of good.'

Huw was silent for a moment wondering whether it would make things better or worse to tell Amy the truth. In some ways it seemed pointless. When she had warned him not to become involved with Barbara she had only been doing what she had thought she must and he knew it was unfair to blame her for what had happened. But this was something she had a right to know.

'I feel like taking it up with the Air Ministry,' Amy was going on. 'It's not right, Huw, and . . .'

'Never mind my leave, Amy,' Huw said. 'There's something else I want to talk to you about.'

She tilted her head to one side, a tiny frown puckering between her eyebrows. 'You sound very serious.'

He drew on his cigarette. After the French ones he had become used to it tasted unsatisfyingly mild.

'I've been living here all these years under false pretences,' he said.

She tucked her feet up into the chair, sitting on them like a child.

'What on earth are you talking about?'

'You took me in because you believed Llew was my father. That's right, isn't it? That's what you told me?'

She nodded. 'That was the reason in the beginning, yes. But . . .'

'Suppose I told you he wasn't?'

She stared at him uncomprehendingly. 'Huw – what is this? He was your father. Your mother told me so.'

'I don't think she was telling the truth.'

She passed a hand over her eyes. 'Huw – I know it's hard for you to accept that you and Barbara are brother and sister, but . . .'

'We aren't. Just before I was shot down I was in South Wales. I took a trip to Ponty to have a look at my old home. I talked to the woman we used to live next door to. I mentioned my father – Llew. And she told me I was mistaken. Llew wasn't my father.'

'But your mother said . . .'

'I know. I think she did it because she was desperate. Llew had been good to her, helped support me. But he wasn't my father.'

'Then who . . .?'

'Eddie,' he said. 'Eddie Roberts was my father.'

'Oh my God!' she said. The cigarette was burning down unheeded in her fingers. 'You mean he knew all the time and he let me . . .'

'Yes. It's not very nice, is it, knowing that bastard is my father.'

387

'Oh Huw!' She could hardly take it in yet already all the implications were there, flapping at her like a flight of disturbed bats. 'Dear God, I never knew. I never for one moment suspected . . .'

'I know. Don't think I blame you, Amy. You only did what you thought was right. But it's a mess, isn't it?'

'Oh Huw, I'm so sorry . . .'

'I was coming back,' he said. 'I was coming back to tell you and put things right with Barbara only I never got the chance.' He paused. 'Is she happy, Amy?'

She ground out her cigarette and wrapped her arms around herself.

'I think so. She's never given me the slightest indication that she's not. But I didn't want her to marry him, Huw. It was all much too soon. I know he's the type to sweep any girl off her feet but . . . I couldn't help feeling it was on the rebound. She worshipped you, Huw. Something died in her after you left. I can't describe it. It was as if a light had gone off. Oh, if only I'd known! If only I'd persuaded her to wait . . .'

'Well, it's too late now,' he said bleakly. 'As long as she's happy, that's all that matters.'

It wasn't and they both knew it. But as he said, it was much too late.

'The pig,' Amy said, thinking of Eddie. 'The bloody sanctimonious pig! Do you know they wanted you to be sent to the Reform School, he and his mother, because they were worried about what people would say about the Roberts family? He had the gall to tell me the scandal would ruin his business – men wouldn't want him calling on their wives to collect insurance if they knew that his brother . . . And all the time it was him!'

'Do you think he knew?' Huw asked.

'He must have. Oh, I wish he was here now! I'd like to wipe the grin off his face! I'd like to . . .' She looked up at him. 'What do you want to do about it, Huw? Do you want to confront him with it?'

He was silent for a moment. 'I don't think so. I don't see the point in bringing it all up again now. If Barbara was still free and single and you didn't believe me it would be different. I'd drag the truth out of him somehow. But Barbara is married to someone else – and you believe me anyway. Don't you?'

'Yes,' she said. 'Yes, I do. I'd believe anything of that slimy object. How someone like him managed to father a son like you is what I can't understand.'

He pulled out his own cigarette case and offered her one. She shook her head. He lit his own cigarette. There was something else he had to say.

'It won't make any difference will it Amy – to us?'

She caught his hand, holding it between her own. She could feel the ridged skin where it had been burned, and twisted inside with love for a boy she had taken in who had grown into a young man to be proud of – a young man who had inherited none of his father's unpleasant characteristics.

'Of course it won't, Huw,' she said. 'Not on my part. But will it make any difference to you?'

'Not to the way I feel about you, Amy. I just thought that maybe now you know the truth you might wish you'd let me go into that home.'

'Never!' she said. 'I'd never wish that.'

The telephone shrilled. For a moment neither of them moved.

'Who can that be at this time of night?' Amy asked.

Inexplicably she felt frightened. This was a night when anything could happen. Ralph . . . she thought. But there had been no air raid warning.

'I'll get it,' Huw said.

He got up. A moment later he was back.

'It's for you. Peggy Yelling.'

'Peggy? On the telephone?' She hurried into the hall. 'Hello – Peggy?' Her voice was anxious.

'I'm sorry to worry you, Amy, but I'm ringing for

your Mam. It's your Dad. He's been taken bad again and I don't like the look of him at all. We've sent for the doctor. But I think you ought to come, Amy, soon as you can.'

Amy felt the pit of her stomach fall away. For years she had been expecting a call like this. Now it had come and she could only feel sick with dread.

'All right, Peggy, I'll be there right away.'

She replaced the receiver and turned to Huw, who was standing in the doorway.

'It's my father. I'll have to go.'

'Do you want me to come with you?' he asked.

'No. You stay here. Ralph will be home soon. Tell him I don't know when I'll be back.' Already she was reaching for her coat from the stand, slipping into it. 'Oh Huw – what a home-coming!'

'Don't worry about me, Amy,' he said. 'And don't worry about Maureen either. I'll take care of her.'

She squeezed his hand. 'Thank you, Huw,' she said.

Her heart was thudding as she drove along the Rank. All was darkness, even now. No lights showing at the windows to tell her which households were still up. Not so much as a glimmer even from her mother's windows. But there was a car parked outside and she knew it must belong to Dr Hobbs.

She parked, hurried to the door and lifted the latch. The murmur of voices reached her from the kitchen. She went in. The tiny room seemed overcrowded. Mam, sitting at the kitchen table, feet planted wide apart, skirt falling between splayed legs, hair rumpled behind the kirby grip as if she had been running her fingers through it. She looked old suddenly, old and white and heavy lidded. Harry, stood beside her, pullover buttoned incorrectly beneath his overcoat as if he like Amy had answered a summons in haste. Peggy

390

Yelling hovered as she always did in moments of crisis, her smooth placid face looking worried. And Dr Hobbs was kneeling beside the sofa where James lay.

The uneven rasp of his breathing filled the room. As Amy entered the doctor rose, shaking his head slightly. Amy ignored the others and looked at her father. He had been propped up so as to assist his breathing but every bit of his being was concentrated on it all the same. His eyes were closed with the effort of trying to take air into lungs turned concrete-hard with the accumulation of dust. Amy had seen his 'turns' before but knew that this was worse than any. He was dying.

She ran to the sofa, knelt down beside him in the space vacated by Dr Hobbs and took his hand in hers. Already it felt cold.

'Dad!' she said. There was no response but that awful rasping breathing. 'Dad, it's me! It's Amy!'

His eyes opened. Tired eyes, faded blue and rheumy, looking at her as if he was already a great way off. Then his chest heaved again with the effort of drawing breath.

'Amy,' he said, his voice surprisingly clear. 'Our Amy!'

'Don't try to talk, Dad,' Harry said, coming to stand beside Amy.

James looked at her for a moment longer and only he knew that he was seeing not a grown woman with children of her own but a little girl in petticoats with ribbons in her hair, a little girl who had brought sunshine into his life. Then his eyes closed again, his fingers clasped hers convulsively and he drew one last shuddering breath.

'Dad!' Amy sobbed.

Her hand still clasped his as she moved to make room for Dr Hobbs. He bent over James, then straightened.

'He's gone.'

Now that the rasp of his breathing was stilled there was silence in the room, broken only by Charlotte's gasp. 'Oh no! No!'

'He's gone, Mam,' Harry said. 'It's all over.'

Amy did not move. She sat on the floor looking at her father's pinched face already taking on the peace that only death could bring and she seemed to hear his voice saying as he always had in moments of crisis: 'Worse things happen at sea, m'dear.' But it was only in her head. He would never speak those words again. Tears blurred her eyes and she felt Peggy's hand on her shoulder.

'Come on, Amy, love. Leave it to me.'

She glanced up uncomprehending. Then as Peggy's meaning came clear she almost cried out. Peggy was going to lay her father out as she had laid out corpses up and down the Rank for years. The thought had always turned Amy cold inside and now suddenly the final impersonality of it offended her.

She looked down at her father's hand, still in hers, at the raised veins, black with coal dust, and saw the hands that had comforted her as a child. Dad had always been the one she had turned to in distress. Mam might have been the strong one, but Dad had been the comforter. It seemed a long time since she had been this close to him.

Gently she loosened her fingers and looked up at Peggy, in her element now for all her genuine concern for a family who had always been her friends.

'Can I help you please, Peggy?' she asked. And saw the imperceptible softening of her features.

'Of course you can, Amy. If that's what you want.'

'I do,' she said. 'Oh yes, I do.'

James was buried in Hillsbridge churchyard the

following week and though their hearts were heavy there were few tears.

He had lived a good life and his time had come, years perhaps after they had expected it. Many miners of his generation had failed to live to see their half-century; against all the odds James had survived beyond his seventieth birthday. And so many young men were dying now, men who should have had their whole lives before them. Every week it seemed they were reported in the *Mercury*, sailors lost with their ships, airmen shot down or crashed, soldiers dying in battle or torpedoed on their way to fight. There were still the blackout deaths, a steady stream of pedestrians killed on the road and older folks who had fallen in their homes in the panic of a raid or because they had been trying to keep the lights low.

James's children were all here with the exception of Ted, far away in Australia, and though saddened by their father's death they had come to terms over the years with its inevitability. They stood, sombre-faced, side by side in the two front pews of the chapel, looking at the flower-decked coffin which contained his earthly remains and cherishing their own memories of him. Charlotte was in the front pew, flanked by Jack and Harry. Her best black straw hat sat squarely on her hair, once as gloriously honey coloured as Amy's and Barbara's, now iron-grey, her black gabardine pulled slightly at its buttons for the relative inactivity of the last few years had caused her to put on weight. Nor were her legs as good as they had been. She had difficulty in standing for the singing of 'Abide With Me' and Harry glanced anxiously at her as he helped her to her feet.

They had tried to persuade her not to come today.

'You aren't well, Mam, and it will only upset you,' Amy had said. 'Peg will stay with you until we get back.'

393

But Charlotte had been adamant.

'I wouldn't think of not going! All these years James and I have been together and you think I'd stay away from his funeral! A fine thing that would be!'

And Margaret had taken her part.

'Of course it wouldn't be right. It would be awful for you to stay at home. Don't worry, we'll look after you, Mam.'

And they had, though none of them, except perhaps Amy, knew the bleakness inside her. And even Amy could not help feeling her own experience had been different. She had been young, Llew had been young, and it had all been such a terrible shock, while Charlotte . . . well Charlotte was old and must have been expecting James's death just as they all had. Unlike herself and Llew, Mam and Dad had had all their lives together, unlike them it was a long, long time since they had stood before the altar where the coffin now rested to make their vows.

Only to Charlotte it did not seem a long time. Strangely enough it seemed like only yesterday. Though her body felt stiff and bloated, though her legs ached and her ankles when she looked down at them were swollen over the tops of her sensible black shoes, still Charlotte found herself looking at her family unable to believe the passage of years which had turned her babies into adults – almost middle-aged adults, some of them – Jim, in particular, with his shoulders bowed by the weight of his years underground and Sarah, quite matronly. They had had a lot of worry of course over Alec, who was now in Burma, they said. But all the same it was almost inconceivable that Jim should ever have been her little boy – even now she could see him sitting on the edge of the kitchen table while she bathed his grazed knees after he had taken a tumble playing along the Rank. And Jack, so smart in his dark suit and black tie, every inch the schoolmaster – was he really

394

the result of an afternoon's folly with a young man who had eased her suffering when she had been out of her mind with grief over the death of little Florrie? Florrie. Now Florrie seemed real to her – Florrie who would be forever a golden haired toddler unlike the sombre-faced strangers who purported to be her children.

Charlotte's eyes were drawn back to the coffin which had stood on trestles in the front room for the last five days and to which she had returned again and again, seeking comfort and consolation in the unbearable loneliness which had descended on her even before Dr Hobbs had pronounced James dead.

Sometimes in the busy years when the children had been growing up she had felt she had little time for him. In the winter he had been at work from before dawn until after dark had come again, in the summer evenings he had spent long hours cultivating his garden. And when he had been there she had been too tired out by her own exertions to be able to enjoy his quiet company. But afterwards, when the children had grown up and left home, they had found a companionship which the years of their youth had been denied. James had never scintillated or sparkled, never been a source of wit or amusement. But he had been a rock on which she had come to depend. Even when he was weak and sick, needing constant attention, his uncomplaining nature and the gems of good sound sense he dispensed from time to time had kept her sane and his infirmity had made her feel needed.

No one needed her now. Not James. Not her children. She was old. And yet within the confines of her now cumbersome body she felt somehow she was still the young bride who had left her home in Bath for what had seemed to her the romance of a pit village, carried off by her very own knight on a white charger. Where had the years gone? They had flown by in the twinkling of an eye. And now it was over, all over, and soon to be buried with that narrow oak coffin. Charlotte felt stunned by the finality of it, part of her unable to believe even now that when she went home James would not be there. The house that had once overflowed with her growing family would be empty and silent with no one to make meals for, no one to share bits of gossip with. But she had no intention of being persuaded to leave it.

'You must come back to Minehead with us,' Jack had said when he and Stella had arrived that morning. 'We have got a room all ready for you. You can stay as long as you like.'

But as she declined. 'I have to get used to it, Jack, and the sooner the better. Perhaps later on, in the spring, I'll come down for a week or a fortnight. But not yet. I'd rather be in my own home.'

They had looked at one another, shaking their heads and knowing further argument was useless. Once she had made up her mind to something Charlotte was immovable. Already, Jim and Sarah had suggested she should make her home with them, as had Amy, and she had turned them both down. She did not want to share a kitchen with another woman and she did not want to leave the house which had been her home all her married life. Especially, she thought, she could never live with Amy. They were too alike in temperament; sparks always flew when they were together for too long. And she could never have been comfortable leading the kind of life they led, the days turned upside down so that they had their dinner in the evenings instead of half-past-midday and so much talk of business it made her head spin. They had plenty of room for her, of course, as Amy had pointed out, with Huw away and Barbara married. But Charlotte had found herself wondering just how long that would last. Marrying out of her class was something Charlotte had never agreed with and the child did not look as happy as she should. She was so pale now where once she had had lovely rosy cheeks and there was an expression in her eyes that Charlotte did not like at all.

The simple service ended and the family filed behind the coffin to where the hearse waited to convey the coffin to the churchyard.

It was over. All over. That was all she knew. All over almost as soon as it had begun. It would be her turn next. And when it came she would be ready.

21

It often happens in families that a death and a birth follow close together and the Hall family was no exception. Two weeks after James was buried Barbara began to suspect that she might be pregnant and by the beginning of December she was almost certain. The thought of it set her mind in a turmoil and she did not know whether to be glad or sorry.

To all practical intents and purposes it could not have come at a worse time. She had begun working for the Civil Nursing Reserve for four days a week, surprisingly encountering no resistance from the Spindlers who seemed to look upon her choice of war work as not only acceptable but also laudable, as if she was making some great sacrifice instead of enjoying herself hugely, which was much closer to the truth. But Barbara had the uncomfortable feeling that their attitude would change when they knew she was pregnant with their grandchild and her heart sank at the thought of being confined once more by the stout old walls of Hillsbridge House. It was such a pleasure to be travelling to Bath on weekdays once more, even if the trains were sometimes delayed so that she was left waiting on the platform for anything up to three quarters of an hour. Although it was cold enough to chill her in spite of her good thick coat and fleecy lined boots, it was still quite fun for Barbara had soon become popular with the regular travellers and she could bank on having someone to talk to to pass the time.

As for her job she adored it. To some office routine might seem deadly dull but the challenge of orderliness had always appealed to Barbara. Even as a child she had longed to get to grips with the piles of papers and files on her mother's desk and her year's business training had done nothing to diminish her enthusiasm while at the same time teaching her office skills. Under the guidance of the Organizer she had set to work with a will and soon it had become apparent that she had inherited some of her mother's organizational capabilities as well as her enthusiasm. After a very short time she was acting not only as clerk and secretary, but interviewing too, taking details of the volunteers who flocked into the office and making preliminary assessments of their capabilities. Since she knew nothing of nursing herself she was able to see the amusing side of this, but the Organizer was delighted with the work she was doing and delegated more and more responsibility to her as time went by.

I should be very sorry to have to give it up, thought Barbara, and she could see no reason why she should – at least not until her pregnancy was a good deal more advanced. It was not as if it was onerous work. If she had been a nursing orderly as she had originally intended it would have been different. Yet she suspected Erica would feel an expectant mother should be at home, preparing for the birth, and Marcus, as always, would be quite unpredictable.

His state of mind continued to concern Barbara. A baby needed a stable background and two loving parents; Marcus just now was hardly likely to be able to provide that. Sometimes she felt that humouring his moods was almost like having a baby already, though no one outside the walls of Hillsbridge House would ever have guessed it. Would telling him that he was to be a father make him even more unstable? Would it spark off another violent attack on her? And if so would that cause harm to the baby?

She was distressed, too, to think that one of these unloving occasions had been the cause of her pregnancy.

399

A baby should be conceived in love, surely, if it was to be a happy child. And supposing Marcus's instability was passed on to his child? This thought she tried to dismiss. Marcus was like he was now because of his terrible wartime experiences. He had been perfectly normal before and he would be normal again, when he finally managed to overcome his shock and the quite unfounded guilt he felt at having seen his men slaughtered. But it haunted her all the same.

Lastly, Barbara worried that she was not the type to have a baby at all. In all her life she could never remember having had a single maternal thought; not for her the cosy dreams of a small sweet-smelling bundle suckling contentedly at her breast. Even now she was a little frightened by the thought of having responsibility for a tiny human being and the prospect of broken nights and lines full of nappies, even if she did not have to wash them, left her cold. And she was still so young! It was no time at all since she had been a schoolgirl. Now, with practically no warning, she was going to become a mother.

For all this, there was inside her a small bubble of excitement. Barbara had always been thrilled by the unknown, attracted by fresh adventures. And having a baby was perhaps the greatest adventure of all.

At the beginning of December she visited Dr Hobbs. The Spindlers were private patients and Dr Hobbs would have called to see her at Hillsbridge House if she had asked him to, but she did not want that. Better to retain a little privacy as long as she was able. But there was no question of her going to his surgery and waiting in his corridor-like waiting-room with all and sundry speculating on the reason for her being there. When she telephoned him Dr Hobbs suggested she should come to his home where a former lounge had been converted to a consulting room. And there, when he had examined her, Dr Hobbs confirmed what she already knew.

Yes, she was pregnant, he was almost certain of it. He asked her questions, did quick calculations on the edge of his blotter and told her the baby would probably be born towards the end of June.

'Let's say the 28th, shall we?' he suggested. 'I'll book it into my diary. You will want me to attend you, I expect? If I'm still here, that is. I'm expecting to be called up for military service at any time. If that happens I shall be patching up wounded soldiers, not delivering babies.'

She nodded. June seemed so far off she was not going to concern herself yet about that. It was now that mattered.

'It will be all right for me to go on working, won't it?' she asked. She had already told him about her work with the Civil Nursing Reserve and found it was not news to him – the Organizer had already complimented him on 'that excellent girl of yours' as if coming from Hillsbridge had somehow made him responsible for Barbara.

'Good gracious, yes. Carry on just as long as you feel fit to do so,' Dr Hobbs told her. 'It's fashionable, I know, to give up work as soon as you hear you are pregnant but I should think they will be very sorry to lose you a minute before they have to. And certainly it won't do you any harm.'

'Thank you,' Barbara said. 'I shall quote you to my mother-in-law. I can imagine her insisting I put my feet up and rest the minute she hears about it.'

'Nonsense! How do you think working class women with families manage? No, you'll be fine, Barbara. You are a strong and healthy young woman. You will sail through this pregnancy, I'll bet my socks on it.' He paused, looking at her over his half-moon spectacles. 'I should think Marcus will be delighted, too. Something like this is just what he needs to help him get over what happened.'

She glanced up sharply. Did he know then the state that Marcus was in? Had she at last found someone in whom she could confide?

'Do you really think so?' she asked eagerly.

'I'm sure of it. An experience like that is bound to leave its mark on a man. We must be grateful Marcus is such a strong character. A lesser man could have his nerves shot to pieces by such a thing. But at least your husband has the satisfaction of knowing he came out of it a hero. That has helped him, I think. And becoming a father will be just the fillip he needs to heal the wounds completely. Life in place of death. Trite but true.'

She nodded, but she was thinking: he doesn't know. He doesn't know how bad Marcus is. And if he did not know then she could not tell him. It was not her place to do so, even if her pride would allow her to admit it. But it had given her an idea, all the same. When the opportunity arose she would suggest to Marcus that he ought to seek help. It seemed as if Dr Hobbs would be understanding and 'nerves shot to pieces' as he had described it sounded almost as treatable as a broken leg. The load on her heart lightened a little and as she walked home she felt brighter and more hopeful than she had done for weeks.

The elation lasted until she reached home. Marcus was already there and she could tell from his expression that he was in a surly mood.

'Where have you been?' he greeted her brusquely.

'To see Dr Hobbs.'

'What for? There's nothing wrong with you is there?'

Her heart sank. She did not want to tell him like this. She wanted to choose her moment.

'I'm not ill, no.'

'So what did you go to see him for?'

There was no avoiding it.

'I wanted him to confirm something I already

suspected,' she said. 'I'm going to have a baby, Marcus. *We're* going to have a baby.'

For a moment he stared at her in disbelief. Then his eyes narrowed with the dark look she had come to fear.

'All right. Whose is it?' he barked at her.

It was her turn to stare blankly.

'What do you mean? Yours, of course.'

'Don't give me that!' He crossed the room, taking her by the arms. 'I'm not capable, Barbara. We both know that. So whose is it? Who have you been with? Tell me or I'll beat it out of you!'

'Marcus, for heaven's sake, you're mad!' she cried, frightened by the violence in his face. 'Of course I haven't been with anybody else. When would I have the chance, anyway?'

'You're out often enough. Off to Bath. How should I know what you get up to? But I'll find out. And when I do I'll break his bloody neck . . .'

His fingers were biting into her arms. She jerked angrily.

'Let go of me! You're hurting me!'

'I'll hurt you a lot more if you don't tell me the truth!'

'It is the truth! It's your baby!' she sobbed. 'Though I wish to God it wasn't!'

His face contorted and she thought he was going to hit her. But he did not. Instead, he hurled her away from him, across the room. She cannoned into the edge of the bed and sank onto it, trembling with shock and fear. He followed, towering over her and she shrank back.

'Don't touch me! Don't dare touch me! If you harm my baby I'll never forgive you!'

For a long moment neither moved. Then suddenly he was on the bed beside her, his arms around her. His mood had swung once more with the terrifying abruptness she had come to expect and now there was tenderness in his touch and contrition in his voice.

403

'I'm sorry, darling, forgive me! Are you really going to have a baby?'

'Yes. And it is yours.'

'Oh, I didn't know . . . I didn't know . . . I'm so useless, so bloody useless. How could I manage to . . . ? Am I really going to be a father?'

Her heart melted. It was almost as if he only remembered his failures, she thought, the times when he had tried to make love to her and been unable to and those other times, the times when he took her by force, had been wiped clean from his memory. Perhaps he was more of a Jekyll and Hyde than she had realised and he not only acted differently but became someone else, someone who ceased to exist and all his deeds with him, when he reverted to the other, normal Marcus.

'Yes, you are going to be a father,' she said. 'In June.' She paused. 'Do you think – please, do you think we could make a fresh start?'

He held her. 'A baby. My baby. I can't believe it! Oh Barbara, it's wonderful news. Wonderful!'

She smiled, smoothing the hair back from his face.

'I'm glad you're pleased,' she said. And thought: maybe, maybe at last everything is going to change. Maybe at last it is going to be all right.

They told Sir Richard and Lady Erica that evening after dinner and because they were talking about the baby they did not listen to the news as they usually did. When Milly, the old and faithful maid, came to serve coffee, she commented on the fact.

'You haven't got the wireless on tonight then, sir.'

They looked at her in surprise. It was unlike Milly to venture such comments.

'No, we haven't, Milly,' Sir Richard said. 'Why do you ask?'

'You'll have missed it then, won't you?' She sounded excited.

'Missed it? Missed what?'

The coffee pot was shaking in her hand. 'They gave it out just now. We were listening in the kitchen.'

'Gave *what* out?'

'The Japs have bombed Pearl Harbor.'

Sir Richard banged his napkin down on the table so hard that all the crockery and glasses rattled.

'Have they indeed? The American fleet! You realise what this means? The Yanks can't sit on the sidelines any longer. They'll be in the war now.'

Suddenly, they were all as wildly excited as Milly had been. If the Yanks were in the war, Britain was no longer alone. For the moment they spared no thought for the ships which had been destroyed and the men who must have been killed. The Yanks would be in and their help would shorten the war by years, perhaps make victory all the more certain.

'That's wonderful! Wonderful!' Marcus exclaimed.

'Oh, I'm so glad!' Barbara added.

'The Axis powers have made a bad mistake this time!' Sir Richard pronounced.

Only Lady Erica remained as unmoved as ever.

'Darlings, this is all very well, but don't you think we should have our coffee before it gets cold?' she cooed.

One Wednesday afternoon in late February Joan Tiley walked down the sloping road that led to Combers End and the cottage that should have been her home. She plodded along solidly, head down against the biting wind, but her legs, clad in her calf-length zip-up boots felt heavy as lead and the hand which held the knot of her headscarf inside the neck of her coat was trembling a little.

It was the first time that Joan had been to the cottage

since Alec had jilted her. From the day he had marched into the recruiting office and signed on for the army the door had remained locked and the house untouched – a monument to the marriage that had not been. It was folly, Joan knew. She should have done something about it long ago. Alec had left it to her to sell the place, trusting her to give his share to his mother once she had deducted enough to compensate her father for the expense over the cancelled wedding. But she had not been able to bring herself to do it. She could not face going coldly through the rooms which had once been the cradle of all her dreams taking down the curtains she had sewed with such love and hope, packing away the bits and pieces she had installed to make the place homely, and she did not want to let her mother do it either, though she had offered. For one thing it seemed cowardly to delegate the task; for another Joan had clung to the superstitious hope that so long as they still had the cottage Alec might one day come home, marry her, and live with her there as they had planned. In spite of what he had done to her, in spite of the fact that almost two years had gone by, there was nothing she wanted more. And strangely enough with the passage of time it had begun to seem to her that it was nothing but the war that was keeping them apart. The cruel hard fact that Alec had jilted her first and joined the army afterwards had been blurred by her own wishful thinking and she had clung to the hope that when the war was over and Alec came home everything would be as it had once been – just so long as she kept the cottage.

But still she had kept away from the place without really knowing why. It was not a conscious decision, but something which had begun when she had been so heartbroken she had felt she never wanted to see it again and which had become habit. Sometimes her mother would raise the subject, telling her she must make up her mind one way or the other – it was stupid to just leave the place there getting damp and cold.

'Much longer and it won't be fit for anyone to live in!' she would say. 'Much longer and you won't be able to *give* it away.'

'I'd rather Alec saw to getting rid of it,' Joan said stubbornly. 'He paid for it mostly and I don't feel it's my place, whatever you say.'

'You don't owe that little bugger a thing,' Arthur Tiley, her father said. 'Not after what he did to you. And anyway he's not here, is he? He's off in India or somewhere. Meanwhile, as your mother says, that house is going to rack and ruin.' He managed to make it sound as if Alec was on a holiday rather than fighting for his country.

'The war won't go on for ever, Dad,' Joan argued. 'He'll be back.'

Arthur had snorted angrily but Joan remained firm. She could be as stubborn as a mule when she wanted to be. A few more months wouldn't make any difference. The Yanks were in the war now – it couldn't go on much longer.

But throughout December and the first weeks of the New Year the news from the Pacific grew worse and worse. With a sinking heart Joan followed what seemed to be the unstoppable advance of the Japanese. After the fall of Hong Kong they were swarming all over the islands and the Malay Peninsula. She lay awake at nights worrying about Alec for it was so long since they had heard from him and consoling herself that if anything had happened they would have been notified. But the news became blacker still and when Singapore followed the fate of Hong Kong in the middle of February. Joan was shocked into facing facts. Singapore was impregnable, they had said. Now she had fallen and those Allies who had not been killed in the fierce fighting were now prisoners and would be for

407

the duration of the war. It would be a very long time before Alec came back – if he came back at all.

And so Joan came to the conclusion she had spent so long trying to avoid. She would have to do something about the house. And the first step was to go there and see what sort of shape it was in.

Wednesday afternoon was half-day closing in Hillsbridge and when she had drawn the blind down over the door of the newspaper shop where she worked, Joan put on her coat and zip-up boots and started out in the direction of Combers End. Though she had spent most of the morning nerving herself up, she still had to fight the almost irresistible urge to turn and go home to the bacon-and-potatoes that was the regular Wednesday fare before she and her mother went upstairs to 'do the bedrooms', sharing a mop and a dustpan and brush and calling cheerfully to one another as they worked.

As she approached the cottage Joan felt in her bag and found the key, but when she attempted to fit it into the lock her hand was shaking so much she had to make more than one attempt. Then she turned the handle of the door and pushed it open for the first time in almost two years.

The stale mustiness came out to meet her just as she had known it would and with it a cold that chilled her to the bone. Two winters had permeated the very stones of which the cottage was built. Joan shivered and closed the door behind her.

Apart from the mustiness and the cold there was an air of unreality about the kitchen – like the *Marie Celeste* it had been abandoned suddenly and the evidence of occupation remained – a mug, the dregs of tea long since turned to murk in the bottom, on the draining board, a newspaper on the table, Alec's paintbrushes still in their jar on the window ledge. But there were the dead flies, too, scattered about the cobwebs festooning the corners and hanging in long unbroken streamers from the centre light.

Joan brushed through the cobwebs and went up the stairs, numb with the cold and the feeling of desolation. But when she entered the bedroom a lump began to choke in her throat as she remembered how she and Alec had made love here on this bed in the days when the future had seemed to stretch ahead like a rosy summer day. She stood for a moment biting her lip and looking around and the echoes of the past sounded ghostly murmurs in her ears – Alec's voice as he humped the heavy old wardrobe into position – 'Well, what do you think of that?' and her own reply: 'Looks quite good. Unless the light might be better on the mirror over there . . .' Oh happy days, when the biggest problem in life had been the best position for a wardrobe! The lump grew, tears pricked Joan's eyes and she sank down onto the bed, unaware of the damp cold of the blanket through her thick coat.

How long she sat there she did not know, weeping for the past and what might have been, and for Alec who might be a prisoner or who might be dead and past making plans with anyone ever again. Suddenly, through the thick walls she heard the sound of what she took at first to be someone crying. She sat listening, head bowed, hands pressed over her mouth. Things were no better next door then, no better than when Alec had taken pity on that . . . that woman. Then it occurred to her that what she had thought sounded like sobs was actually closer to laughter. The back door slammed but the squealing continued and in spite of herself Joan got up and crossed to the window.

In the yard below were Bryda Deacon and a young soldier – one of those whose regiment was billeted in the Scouts' Hall, Joan guessed, and she was indeed squealing with laughter as he chased her. As Joan watched he caught her in the coalhouse doorway, grabbed and kissed her, pushing her back into the darkness. Joan stood riveted, hardly able to believe her eyes. Was this the poor downtrodden wife for love of whom Alec had jilted her and fought a man? Why, she was no more than a trollop, getting off with any man who came her way behind her husband's back.

Angrily she moved away from the window. The spell had been broken, her nostalgia was all gone. Just as well to put the house on the market and everything in it. Even if Alec did come back, even if they did make things up – and the way she felt just now that seemed fairly unlikely – she couldn't live here with him next door to that . . . that cheap little cow. She looked around, swept a few knick-knacks into the leather patchwork bag she had brought with her and clattered down the bare stairs. Let the rest of the stuff stay here. She didn't want it. It could be sold with the house and good riddance.

As she went out slamming the door behind her she heard movement across the yard and saw Bryda and the soldier peeping curiously out of the coalhouse. She lifted her chin, turned abruptly with the intention of ignoring them. But as she passed the coalhouse Bryda giggled. The sound infuriated Joan and she swung round on her.

'What do you think you're laughing at?'

Bryda's thin face sobered though she looked as if it would not take a great deal to make her laugh again.

'Excuse me!'

'Standing there sniggering!' Joan exploded.

'Hey, wait a bit!' the soldier said. He had a ruddy round face and he was wearing the uniform of the Devons. 'Lay off, missus. What's she done to upset you?'

Joan was battling mad now. 'You really want to know? My bloke is out in Singapore now because of her. She led him on, just like she's doing with you, no doubt, made him feel sorry for her and came between us. He even came to blows with her husband over her. Have you met her husband yet? He's a big man, bigger than you, I should think. So watch out. Just blooming well watch out!'

The soldier was staring in amazement but at least Bryda was no longer laughing.

'You want to watch what you say!' she flared at Joan. 'Just because you can't keep a man don't go blaming me.'

'You little cow!' Joan flew at her, grabbing a handful of hair. Bryda retaliated, lashing out at Joan's face with her fingernails.

'Hey ladies, ladies!' Careless of his own safety the soldier managed to get between them. 'You're worse than bloody Hitler!'

Joan took one last swing at Bryda with her shopping bag. As it connected she heard one of the ornaments inside smash but she did not care. It was worth it. She started down the lane, shouting over her shoulder. 'That's one man you won't deceive, Bryda Deacon. At least that's one that's seen you in your true colours!'

She was still shaking as she walked back up Combers End, but now her mind was made up. She would have to sell the cottage now whether she liked it or not. She never wanted to see that Bryda Deacon again.

The next day she visited the estate agents where Eddie Roberts used to work and put the cottage on the market. They would be able to sell it easily, they reckoned, for the bombing had put the housing market in short supply. As for Bryda Deacon, Joan never gave her a second thought. Sometimes, in the months that followed, she saw her in the town with her little girl but never close enough to speak to and with some satisfaction Joan guessed that the soldier was unlikely to be paying her any more visits. It was a small enough triumph, and not really enough to make up for the misery and heartache Bryda had caused her but it was some consolation all the same. Enough to sustain her while she waited for news of Alec at any rate. Joan hid her heavy heart behind her inexpressive features and carried on with her life as before.

Throughout the spring months Barbara bloomed. Incipient motherhood suited her and for the first time since her marriage she was truly happy. And Marcus it seemed was a new man. From the moment he had accepted that the baby was his he began to revert to his old charming self. He was gentle with her; he was considerate. It was as if the achievement of fatherhood which most men take for granted had somehow miraculously restored all the confidence that had seeped away when he had lost his men.

One person had heard of Barbara's pregnancy with mixed feelings, however. Margaret was genuinely delighted on Barbara's behalf and congratulated her niece warmly, for there was not a jealous bone in her body. But the news had also touched the deep pool of sadness within her and reawakened her longing for a baby of her own.

For the most part she had put her grief at her miscarriage behind her; her days were busy and there was no time for brooding. But nevertheless, odd little things could touch it off and sometimes she would lie awake thinking that if things had not gone tragically wrong her baby would have been a toddler by now, into all kinds of mischief, and she wondered what he would have looked like and whether he would have taken after her or Harry. She wished, too, with all her heart, that she could conceive again. But it had not happened and sometimes she wondered if it ever would.

To some extent little Marie had filled the gap. In the

two-and-a-half years they had been with her, Margaret had watched Marie grow from a skinny frightened urchin to quite a plump little girl who would sit on her knee to enjoy a bedtime story and could be as affectionate as a puppy dog. Elaine she had never been able to get close to and for all her efforts the girl still regarded her with suspicion and resentment, greedily accepting whatever benefits came her way yet remaining a stranger whom Margaret found it difficult to trust.

The suspicion she felt went against the grain for Margaret. She liked to believe that no child was really bad, only mischievous or misguided, and she made excuses for Elaine both to Harry and to herself – the girl had never been taught right from wrong; she was lonely and afraid in an alien world; and her hard-boiled calculation and moments of dishonesty were symptoms of her deep-seated insecurity. But as time passed she began to doubt her own conviction. Elaine didn't seem cowed or frightened. There was never a chink to suggest anything soft and childlike beneath the surface. Margaret did not like the sly way she caught her looking at her sometimes; she did not like the ease with which lies rolled off Elaine's tongue; and she did not like the children Elaine had chosen as her friends. There was a gang of them now, made up of the hardest roughest cases from Batch Row and a handful of other vackies. They stayed out long after dark in the evenings supposedly playing but Margaret suspected they were roaming the streets and getting up to mischief. The company the girls were keeping worried her. The *Mercury* often carried stories of vackies breaking into lock-up shops and even houses, causing wanton damage and generally making nuisances of themselves, and she felt that Elaine, though not necessarily an instigator in a gang situation, would certainly be easily led. But she could not prevent Elaine from going out to play nor choose her friends for her, and could only keep an eye on what was going on and remonstrate with the child if she became too disobedient.

Fortunately, Marie no longer followed her sister as blindly as she had done when they first came. Sometimes she would go out with Elaine and the others, but more often than not she would soon be back, popping her forlorn little face around the kitchen door and creeping inside as if she half-expected to be yelled at to 'Get back out!'

'Home already?' Margaret would say and Marie would nod, sucking on her thumb and regarding Margaret with huge solemn eyes.

'What are they up to, Elaine and the others?' Margaret would ask, but she could never ascertain the reason why Marie had come home. Though she now followed Margaret with the same puppy-like devotion she had once shown towards her sister, she still maintained her sense of loyalty. Sister did not 'split' on sister. Whatever it was that Elaine was up to, Marie had no intention of telling.

During the spring of 1942 several more of the Hillsbridge evacuees went home. Since the previous summer there had been little aerial activity over London and parents who missed their children were only too ready to convince themselves that the worst danger had passed. Against the advice of the authorities they arrived to take them home. But Elaine and Marie were not amongst those claimed and though for herself Margaret was glad, she was also hurt and angry on behalf of the children that their mother took so little interest in them.

'I think I'm going to write to her,' she said to Harry one day. 'It's not right that she should abandon them like this. Surely she could at least come down and visit them once in a while.'

'It seems to me she's glad of the war as an excuse to be rid of them for a while,' Harry said. 'I doubt if

414

anything you can say will make the slightest bit of difference.'

'But I have to try,' Margaret insisted. 'You don't give up on hopeless cases – why should I?'

Harry had not argued. He was too busy with council work and meetings he had to attend as prospective Labour candidate to be able to give much thought to his evacuees. His work, too, was all-consuming for in addition to the daily cases he had to fight for the union he was involved with pressure groups which were struggling for the early nationalisation of the coal industry.

That evening, when the girls were in bed, Margaret sat down and composed a letter to their mother, inviting her to stay and pointing out how much it would mean to the girls. Then, after a great deal of thought, she folded three one-pound notes into the envelope and wrote a postscript.

'I hope you will not be offended if I offer to help with your train fare. Since the authorities pay me for having the girls to live with me, I feel in a sense that it belongs to them.'

It was not true, of course, that she was making anything out of them. On the contrary, she was so generous in buying their food, clothes and books that she was often out of pocket. But she felt that the three pounds would be well spent if it persuaded the girls' mother to make the trip she might otherwise be unable to afford.

With the letter in the post Margaret sat back to await a reply. It did not come. Margaret began to worry that the letter had not reached her. She had not heard that the girls' old home had been bombed but it was always possible. Or perhaps the woman had been killed and never identified. There were such tragedies in the cities, she knew, cases where bodies had been recovered but their papers lost so that they became no more than countless pieces of flotsam and jetsam to be buried in unmarked graves. Then one morning just as she had given up hope, a letter arrived. It was addressed to Elaine and Marie in the childish almost unintelligible hand and there was a note enclosed for her: 'I got your letter. Sorry but I can't come just now.'

No more. No promise for the future. No mention of the three pounds.

'I can't understand it, Harry,' she said as they washed the dishes after the evening meal. 'How can any mother treat her children that way? Sometimes I think the world has gone mad. There's me, who'd do anything to have a child of my own, while she . . . well she just doesn't seem to want to have anything to do with them.'

Harry muttered something. He was deep in his newspaper. Since newsprint had been restricted by government order he was not able to get one everyday and when he did he made sure he read it from cover to cover.

'She must be a terrible woman,' Margaret said, clattering dishes. 'I even offered to help pay her train fare and still she hasn't made the effort.' She dared not tell Harry she had actually sent money – she knew he would be angry with her. 'You can say what you like, Harry, she just doesn't want them. People like that shouldn't be allowed to have children.'

She turned to wipe the kitchen table and froze. Elaine was standing in the doorway and from the expression on her face Margaret knew she had heard every word.

'Elaine!' she said helplessly. 'What are you doing here?'

The child had been out up the road, playing off-ground touch and 'ghosties' and Margaret had thought she was safely out of the way.

'I came in to go to the lav,' Elaine said. 'And I heard

416

what you said. I heard what you said about my Mum.' Her voice was tight and she looked close to tears. Margaret crossed to her.

'Elaine, I didn't mean it. It's not true that your Mum doesn't want you. You had a letter from her this very morning . . .' She reached out and the child spun away, her weaselly face a mask of hate.

'Don't touch me! You said things about my Mum! You're wicked! I hate you! And I hate it here!'

'Elaine!'

'Leave me alone! You're horrible – you poxy bitch!'

Margaret gasped. She had thought at least Elaine's language had improved. The child spun around, eyes blazing, and ran out of the door. Margaret tried to follow but she had gone, disappearing down the path into the gathering dusk.

'Oh dear – I didn't know she was there!' Margaret said, distressed. 'I wouldn't have said what I did for the world if I'd known. Oh Harry . . .'

'It' no good worrying about it,' Harry said, sounding a little like a reincarnation of his father.

'But she heard what I said – that her mother doesn't want her . . .'

'It's no more than the truth. But I doubt she believed it anyway.' Harry turned over a page of his newspaper. 'She's as hard as nails, that one.'

His refusal to be ruffled did nothing to ease Margaret's anxiety. As she finished clearing up she continually went to the door, looking out to see if she could see the girls. But there was no sign of them. They were further up the road with Elaine's gang, she supposed, but it was now almost dark and she thought it was time they came in. Added to her distress was a fear that Elaine might relay her remarks to Marie. Elaine was, as Harry had said, pretty resilient, but she hated to think how Marie would react if told of what she had said. Eventually, she could stand the waiting no longer.

417

'I'm going to look for them,' she told Harry.

'Leave them be. They're all right.'

'They should be in. Goodness only knows what they're up to.'

She got her coat and set out up the road in the direction of Batch Row. Part way along was a small square of recreation ground where a metal slide had stood until it was requisitioned in the drive for scrap metal for armaments and she saw some shadowy figures running about. Relieved she approached them and recognised one of her pupils from the Church School, a ragamuffin boy, last of a long family from Batch Row. She called to him.

'Colin! I'm looking for Elaine and Marie. Do you know where they are?'

Colin approached warily. 'No, Miss.'

'What do you mean? I thought they were playing with you.'

'They were, Miss, but they've gone. Ages ago.'

'Gone? Gone where?'

'Don't know, Miss. They went that way.' He pointed in the direction from which she had come. 'I thought they were going home.' He was sidling away from her and she knew she would get no more from him.

She stood for a moment looking around as if she expected them to materialise from the darkness, then started back down the road. Perhaps she had missed them somewhere or they were hiding. But she was aware of a qualm of misgiving and the sudden panicky thought that she might never see them again.

She reached the corner and stood looking up and down the hill but the road was deserted apart from a man walking his dog. A car came up the hill and suddenly its shaded lights picked up someone coming up on the pavement. A small figure. One, not two. But somebody. Too soon the hill was in darkness again but

Margaret started down towards the figure. It could have been . . .

It was. Marie. Dragging her feet and coming slowly up the hill.

'Where have you been?' Margaret demanded. 'Where is Elaine?'

'She's gone home.'

'Home?' Margaret looked back up the hill, puzzled, then realisation dawned. 'What do you mean – *home*?'

'Home – to London.' Marie was shivering. She had no coat and now her teeth were chattering so much she could hardly speak. 'She's gone to find Mum. She wanted me to go with her but I didn't want to.'

'Oh my goodness! But where is she now?' Margaret was on the point of dragging Marie back to Hillsbridge but the child stopped her.

'She's gone on a train. To Bath.'

'How can she? She hasn't got any money.'

Marie shrugged and Margaret groaned. She should have known Elaine would not let a little thing like lack of money stop her.

'How long ago?' she asked.

Marie shrugged again. Margaret checked her watch, holding it close to her eyes to see the dial by the fitful light of the moon. Eight o'clock. There was a train at twenty minutes to eight. If it had been on time it would almost have reached Bath by now. She grabbed Marie's hand and began dragging her up the hill.

'Come on – hurry! I shall have to get the police to meet the train at Bath.'

She was out of breath by the time they reached home so an astonished and annoyed Harry had to do the telephoning for her.

'They'll do what they can,' he said, replacing the receiver, 'though a child like Elaine might very well slip past a dozen special constables.' He faced Marie

419

sternly. 'Have you any idea of the trouble you are causing us?'

Marie hung her head, her eyes filling with tears, and Margaret put a protective arm around her.

'Not Marie,' she said. 'Not our little Marie.'

Harry snorted. His patience was very nearly exhausted.

'All I can say is, it's time they learned a little gratitude and a lot about how to behave themselves!' he said snappily.

Marie had been bathed in the recommended six inches of water and was tucked up in bed when the telephone rang.

'They've got her,' Harry said replacing the receiver. 'But not before she had raided the chocolate machine on the platform. Now she's on her way back to us – more's the pity!'

'Shh!' Margaret admonished, looking towards the stairs. Bad enough that Elaine should have overheard her earlier this evening, if Marie heard Harry saying such things she would be disappearing next!

'Something has to be done about those children,' he returned. 'They are out of control.'

She was too relieved that Elaine had been found to argue. She went upstairs and looked in on Marie. 'Are you asleep?'

'No.' The voice was muffled, coming from beneath the bedclothes.

Margaret sat down on the edge of the bed.

'Elaine has been found,' she told Marie. 'They are bringing her home.'

Marie did not answer. Margaret smoothed her hair where it lay on the pillow.

'You wouldn't do anything like that, would you, Marie?'

'No,' the child said. 'I told you she wanted me to go but I wouldn't. I don't want to go back to London. I like it here.'

Margaret felt a wave of tenderness. 'Really?'

'Yes, it's nice. Much nicer than London. And I like you too. You're always here.'

Perhaps I haven't failed totally, thought Margaret. If I've made Marie happy, I haven't failed totally. Suddenly, in the silence, she heard Marie begin to cry softly.

'What is it, darling?' she asked, thinking that perhaps Elaine had after all repeated what she had overheard.

It was a long time before Marie would answer. Then she whispered between sobs: 'You won't send us away, will you, because of what Lainey's done? You won't send us back to London?'

A lump rose in Margaret's throat and she took Marie's hand in hers beneath the covers.

'No, darling, of course I'm not going to send you away. You can stay here as long as you like.'

The child's sobs subsided. Margaret went on holding her hand until she fell asleep.

The idea came to her that night and it was enough to keep her awake as it flowed through her veins like adrenalin. But it was the next evening before she had the chance to mention it to Harry.

'I don't suppose we could adopt them, could we?'

Harry had been lucky enough to get a newspaper two days running. He looked up from it reluctantly.

'Adopt who?'

'Elaine and Marie.'

He gazed at her in astonishment. 'But they have a mother – and a father somewhere I presume.'

'They're glad to be rid of them, you said so yourself.

And we could give them a good home. We don't seem to be having much luck starting a family of our own.'

'But Elaine and Marie!' Harry exclaimed. 'They've given us nothing but trouble since they came.'

'I know, but that's because they're so unsettled. If they knew they were really wanted, not just dumped on us, things would be different.'

'I can't say I agree with you there,' Harry said. 'Marie isn't a bad kid but Elaine . . . she's a real handful. Personally, I think she's a lost cause.'

'No child is a lost cause! That's a dreadful thing to say!'

'You are too idealistic, Margaret. You think that all the ills of the world can be cured by love and understanding. You don't believe some people are just plain bad. I believe you'd try to reason with Hitler if you met him.'

'How can you compare Elaine with Hitler!' Margaret blazed. 'She is just a child who has never had a chance.'

'She has had every chance since she's been here. You have fallen over backwards to make her feel at home, you have bought her decent clothes, tried to find her interests, tucked her up in bed warm and dry and probably better off than she has ever been in her life. Not for two weeks, not for two months, but for two years and more. And nothing has changed. She is still resentful and untrustworthy. I still don't care to leave my wallet lying about or my cupboard doors unlocked. And now you tell me you would like to have this liability strung around our necks for the rest of our lives!'

'Amy did it!' Margaret said defensively. 'She adopted Huw.'

'Amy had her reasons and yes, I grant you, that turned out very well. But it might not have done. It could have been disastrous. In any case the circumstances were quite different. Huw was an orphan. He

422

was going to be sent to an Industrial School. Elaine and Marie, as I keep pointing out, have a mother, however inadequate she may be. It is nonsense for you to even think of adopting them, Margaret.'

'It isn't nonsense!' Margaret suddenly felt close to tears as yet another dream came crashing down. 'I could make them happy, I know I could. Oh, Elaine is difficult, I grant you, but Marie . . .'

Harry folded his paper and put it down, looking at her squarely.

'That is the crux of the matter, isn't it? Marie. If it was just Elaine I'm sure you'd never have suggested such a thing. It's Marie you want to adopt and you feel you can't do that without including Elaine. Your sense of fair play is in action again.'

She could not deny it.

He shook his head, reaching out for her and putting an arm around her waist.

'Oh Marg, Marg, what am I going to do with you?'

She did not answer, simply drew a pattern on his newspaper with her fingernail.

'Just as long as you don't become too fond of Marie,' he said. 'I don't want to see you hurt again.'

She nodded. For the moment there was nothing more to say.

22

Eddie Roberts was not a happy man. He was in fact a very worried one.

Saturday was usually a day of rest for him, a day when he would shut his briefcase on the pile of insurance books, turn his back on any outstanding council business and relax, pottering in the garden, listening to the wireless or indexing his collection of cigarette cards – an activity he was slightly ashamed of, since he regarded it as a little juvenile, but which he enjoyed far too much to give up. He had collected the cards from the time he began smoking – filling gaps in his sets had provided him with the excuse to buy one packet and then another, for his mother heartily disapproved of the habit and refused to allow him to indulge inside her pristine house. The stringencies of war meant the cards had been stopped, of course, but Eddie still enjoyed arranging his albums.

But on that last Saturday in April Eddie was quite unable to concentrate on any of his usual leisure activities. Instead, he had made at least three trips to the shed at the end of the garden where his bicycle was kept to reassure himself a certain two cardboard boxes were still there behind the pile of waste paper which was waiting to be taken to the collection point, prodding them and anxiously rearranging the old sacks which covered them. After each visit he stood in the doorway nervously fingering his chin and telling himself that no one visiting the shed would notice anything amiss, before trekking back up the path, kicking off his shoes in the back porch (shoes, like cigarettes, were taboo in Mrs Roberts's home) and attempting once more to get back to Saturday normality.

Impossible. After only half an hour or so with his mind running in frantic circles, Eddie once more felt the need to assure himself that the boxes had not done some magical disappearing trick or his camouflage had not been interfered with.

'Why do you keep going in and out, Eddie?' his mother asked him as he padded across the kitchen in his stockinged feet for the fourth time in two hours. 'You're letting the cold in opening and shutting that door.'

'Sorry, Mam.' Eddie might be a local councillor who would never see forty again, but he had learned long ago not to argue with his mother. It simply did not pay. She always emerged the victor and even if she did not she was quite capable of making life unpleasant in a hundred ways in order to gain her revenge.

'If you're going out I wish you'd stay out. Dinner won't be for another hour. I'll call you when it's ready.'

'OK, Mam.' Worried as he was he managed to make his voice sound quite normal, as if he did not have a care in the world.

As Mrs Roberts had said it was chilly for the time of year, a cold breeze whipping along the backs of the houses, but several of Eddie's neighbours were out in their gardens 'digging for victory'.

'Got your beans in yet, Eddie?' Fred Brock from next door called to him. 'T'was South Compton Fair Day last week, you know.'

'Yes, I know,' Eddie called back. He was not the world's keenest gardener – his own patch was usually still overgrown with last year's cabbages and strewn dead potato haulms long after the others were neatly planted and he was used to being gently upbraided about it by Fred Brock.

'I'm going to build myself some rabbit hutches when my garden is ship-shape,' Fred said, leaning on his spade. 'Get myself a breeding doe and we shall soon be well away for rabbit meat. All you have to do is join the rabbit club and you can get all the bran and food stuff you need – I've been finding out about it. You could do worse than do the same. Plenty of room in that shed o' yourn for a couple of hutches.'

Eddie, on the point of trying to escape, went cold inside. What did Fred Brock know about his shed and what was in it? But there was no hint of leering suspicion on Fred's weatherbeaten face.

'I haven't got time to look after rabbits,' Eddie said rather pompously. 'I've got enough on my plate as it is.'

'Oh ah. Got you in the Home Guard now, haven't they?' Fred remarked.

Eddie snorted. He had not been pleased at being conscripted into the Home Guard. He hated having to turn out when he had finished a day's work to do their silly drills and work on plans for combatting an invasion. Waste of time that was, in his opinion. If the Germans came the Home Guard, however good their intentions, would be no match for them and as a new and insignificant member he felt it was undignified to be ordered about by men he considered his inferiors. It was just another of the petty inconveniences which seemed to dog him these days and had done ever since he had crossed swords with Harry Hall. Why, if Harry himself had been responsible for Eddie's conscription he wouldn't have been surprised. Harry was always hobnobbing with the powers-that-be. And why wasn't *he* wearing a scratchy uniform and crawling round hedges and ditches practising manoeuvres to outwit an enemy, Eddie would like to know!

He escaped from Fred Brock and went down the garden path to the shed. The door was latched – he'd made sure of that for he did not want anyone poking inside. He went in, pulling the door behind him, and the sunlight streaming in through the spiders' webs on the small window showed him that the boxes were, of course, still there where he had left them.

Still there – but even covered by the sacks, so blooming obvious! If the police should come looking that pile would be the first thing they would investigate. A fine sweat broke out on Eddie's forehead and he dashed it away.

Why *should* they come here, for goodness sake? Unless Jiggles Johnson talked. And he wouldn't. He'd have more sense – wouldn't he?

Eddie crossed the shed, moved some of the waste paper and rags and turned back the corner of the sack. Inside the box he could see the corner of a packet of Players – just one packet, but there were plenty more. Four hundred packets of ten, Jiggles had said. Four thousand cigarettes in all. And a hundred bars of chocolate, razor blades, shoelaces and shaving soap. Stolen goods obviously. And here they were in his shed. The knowledge made Eddie feel sick all over again and he stood rubbing the sore place on his chin where his razor had slipped while he was shaving this morning and wondering what the hell he was going to do about it.

He knew now what he should have done, of course. When Jiggles had telephoned him two nights ago and said he had some nice 'stuff' which might interest Eddie, he should have hung up and had nothing more to do with it. But he had not. He had been curious and unable to resist the chance of what he knew must be black market goods. The result was he was now in a fine mess.

Why the hell did I ever get mixed up with Jiggles in the first place? Eddie asked himself. Jiggles was a rogue and he'd always known it. But Eddie was not above doing business with rogues if they had something to offer and what Jiggles had offered him was something Eddie wanted very badly – petrol.

427

The subject had first arisen one afternoon when Eddie had called to collect Jiggles's mother's insurance money. Unlike her son, Mrs Johnson was an honest and upright soul who had spoiled the weaselly-faced lad in every conceivable way from the moment she had brought him into the world rather late in life. Throughout his childhood, Jiggles (so nicknamed because of his rather jerky manner, though his mother always referred to him as Raymond) had wanted for nothing and the unexpected departure of his father with a lady from Tiledown had only left his mother even freer to indulge his every whim. He was not strong, she was fond of telling people – he had a weak chest and a heart murmur, the legacy of a bout of scarlet fever as a child – and if he was not taken care of goodness only knew what would happen to him. That Jiggles did indeed have some weakness was apparent from the fact that he failed to pass a medical when conscripted for the army, but this weakness did not seem to stop him from involving himself in various dubious activities. In his youth he was brought before the Juvenile Courts several times for petty larcenies, on one occasion he was caught defacing the War Memorial and on another, after indulging himself with a great deal of cider, swinging from a bus stop. Whenever trouble threatened Mrs Johnson defended him fiercely with a string of excuses and she kept up small but regular payments on a succession of endowment policies on his life because, as she said, you never knew what might happen with a boy as delicate as Jiggles.

On the afternoon in question Eddie had made his regular twice-monthly visit to the Johnson home in 'Twelve Houses', a rank on the main South Compton road. Mrs Johnson had paid him with the exact money as she always did from a cup on the dresser where she kept it in readiness for him, but when he bade her 'Good afternoon' Jiggles, who had been sitting in a

428

corner of the kitchen reading the 'Beano', got up and followed him outside.

'Must be hard going for you these days,' he said to Eddie, indicating the pedal cycle Eddie had propped against the garden wall.

'It is a bit,' Eddie admitted. 'Still, I suppose it keeps me healthy.'

'If you had a bit of extra petrol you'd be able to drive your car,' Jiggles said meaningfully.

Eddie looked at him sharply.

'And where would I be able to get that?' he asked.

'I might be able to do something for you. If you're interested.'

'Oh, I'm interested,' Eddie said. He was thinking not so much of his insurance round, hard though it might be to make it on a pedal cycle with winter approaching, as the fact that the shortage of petrol had meant he had been able to make far fewer trips to Bath than he wanted to. Eddie had a friend, a 'young lady' as he called her, who lived in Oldfield Park and whose husband was in the Merchant Navy. She was a very accommodating young lady and lately it had seemed a terrible waste that on so many evenings she should be lonely in Bath while he was lonely in Hillsbridge and unable to do anything about it because he had no petrol for his car.

'What's it worth, then?' Jiggles asked slyly.

Eddie did a quick calculation, estimating the black market price for petrol and subtracting as much as he thought he could get away with. Jiggles wasn't clever enough to be greedy, he reckoned.

As he had expected Jiggles accepted his offer. The arrangements were made and two nights later Jiggles delivered the petrol to Eddie in an old oil can. Eddie paid him in cash and asked no questions as to where the petrol had come from. What he didn't know couldn't hurt him. As he drove into Bath that evening to pay a visit to Doris, his 'young lady', he felt ridiculously elated. Doing himself a bit of good in small underhand ways had always pleased Eddie. Like the 'backhanders' he had managed to elicit from local firms for putting contracts their way – a nice little earner until Harry Hall had put a stop to it. In the weeks that followed Jiggles kept Eddie supplied with petrol and before long there were other things too. Packets of cigarettes and chocolates and on one occasion several bottles of Scotch. Eddie had his doubts about those, but Jiggles was prepared to accept such a ridiculously small amount in payment it seemed a crime to let the opportunity pass and in any case Eddie had had an idea for making himself a little money on the side.

Whilst doing his rounds people frequently complained to him about shortages and Eddie, with his infallible instinct, knew who would be prepared to do a deal with him and ask no questions and who would be outraged enough to go straight to the police. Soon he had established a profitable little sideline in black market goods, buying from Jiggles and reselling at a profit. At first he was nervous about it but he could not resist the chance to make something for nothing, especially as his ladyfriend was proving a great deal more expensive than he had expected, and as time went by he gained in confidence. It was easy! And he got a kick out of knowing he was flouting the authorities and taking risks.

When Jiggles had phoned him on that Thursday morning, however, warning bells had rung in his head. To begin with it was unusual for Jiggles to telephone at all. To do so he had to walk up the road to a call box and he had a deep dislike of speaking into an inanimate instrument to a person he could not see.

Then again, his request was peculiar to say the least – that Eddie should meet him with his car after dark underneath the railway arch on the New Road that could be reached by driving across a piece of waste ground. Lastly, Eddie was alerted by the fact that Jiggles was obviously not alone in the telephone box. He could hear another voice prompting him.

'Who have you got with you?' Eddie asked.

'Just a mate,' Jiggles replied. 'Nobody you'd know. Are you going to come? It'll be worth your while.'

Eddie's curiosity was aroused but still he hesitated.

'I don't know that I can make it tonight.'

He heard the whispered prompting, then Jiggles said: 'I hope you will. I wouldn't like to have to tell anybody how I've been letting you have stuff when I shouldn't have.'

Eddie had begun to sweat. His mind raced furiously over his association with Jiggles. Surely nobody would take the word of a little no-good against his own? But he could not afford to take any chances.

'All right, I'll be there,' he said.

That night he took his car and drove to the railway arch, taking care that there was no one to see him turn in across the waste ground. Once off the road he switched his lights off and bumped softly forward over the thistles and stones. There was little chance now of being seen. As he came to a halt he saw two figures emerge from the deep shadow of the bridge. One was Jiggles, the other a lad wearing the uniform of a soldier.

'What's all this about then?' Eddie asked, speaking in a hushed tone although there was no one else about. Everyone knew that the railway arches set up an echo which carried around the valley.

'We've got some stuff for you,' Jiggles said.

'What sort of stuff? Why did you get me down here about it?'

Jiggles had a pocket torch. He snapped it on and the thin beam picked up the boxes stacked beneath the arch and half hidden by broken branches.

'Crikey!' Eddie said.

'It's fags,' Jiggles informed him. 'Oh – and a bit of chocolate too. But mostly fags.'

'How many?'

'Four thousand we reckon, and six dozen bars of chocolate.'

'Where did they come from?'

'Never you mind.' The soldier spoke for the first time. 'Do you want 'em?'

Eddie's mind was boggling. The odd gallon of petrol and hundred cigarettes here and there, no questions asked, was one thing. Goods on this scale which must have been stolen were quite another. Good God, if he got caught with this little lot it would be the end of him in politics, the end of his career. He'd probably go down for a spell.

'Not bloody likely!' he said.

'I'll let you have 'em cheap,' Jiggles offered.

'No. I've got nowhere to put a lot like that anyway.'

'That's your problem,' the soldier said. He had what sounded like a London accent. It added an edge of insolence to his voice. 'Twenty-five quid the lot – or like Ray said, he'll start talking about his little business deals with you.'

Eddie went cold. He had been surprised when Jiggles had made his attempt at blackmail on the telephone. It didn't seem his style. Now he understood. This soldier lad, whoever he was, was putting him up to it.

'Now wait a minute . . .' he blustered.

'No, you wait,' the soldier said. 'Twenty-five quid is nothing for this lot. You've got yourself a good deal. Better take it or we might decide to ask more.'

'We could get double and treble elsewhere,' Jiggles put in.

'Then why don't you?'

''Cos we want to get rid of it quick.'

'And 'cos you're in it with us.'

432

'Oh no I'm not!' Eddie protested. 'This is stolen. Got to be.'

'And where do you think I've been getting the stuff I've been letting you have?' Jiggles jeered. 'Hillsbridge Market? Come on, twenty-five quid, Eddie. It's dirt cheap at the price.'

Eddie hesitated. He did not like being blackmailed but it seemed he did not have a lot of choice. And besides . . . He did a quick calculation. Twenty-five pounds for this lot was a bargain. He could get rid of the cigarettes and chocolate to the customers he'd built up over the months at a good profit that would keep him in clover. Perhaps it wasn't such a bad deal after all . . .

In that moment Eddie was possessed of a mad greed. He forgot the blackmail threat, forgot even that the cigarettes were stolen, and saw himself as a business entrepreneur presented with a deal he could not refuse.

'All right. Twenty-five pounds. But that's it. I don't want anymore. This is a one-off, understand?'

Jiggles grinned. 'I knew you'd see it our way. Got the dough?'

Eddie nodded. The wallet he carried his insurance collections in was in his inside pocket. He pulled it out and counted out the notes.

'Couldn't you make it thirty?' the soldier asked, seeing the wad of money.

'No, I couldn't,' Eddie snapped.

He gave the money to Jiggles and the two lads helped him load the boxes into the boot of his car. As he cranked the engine he saw them dividing up the money. There was a bicycle coming along the road as he reached the edge of the waste ground. Sweat broke out on his neck again. Should he wait until it had gone by and hope it didn't see him? Better not take the chance. The driver would be less likely to recognise the car if it was moving. For the first time Eddie realised what a criminal feels like. For all his dubious dealings he had never felt like that before. He drove home, overawed by the enormity of what he had done, terrified there might be something wrong with his lights which would mean he would be stopped by a special constable, or that he might be involved in some kind of accident. Such a thing had never occurred to him before. Now, with his boot full of stolen cigarettes, it seemed a very real danger.

He drove around to the rear of his house and humped the boxes into the shed where he kept his bicycle, hiding them beneath the waste paper and rags they had been saving for the war effort. Then he went indoors, glad his mother was out at a whist drive. He felt flushed and nervous but also exhilarated. Oh, he was going to do all right out of this and no mistake! He poured himself a glass of whisky from a bottle Jiggles had obtained for him a few weeks ago and sat down to do a few sums and work out how quickly he could dispose of the first lot of his loot to enable him to make up the £25 he had borrowed from his insurance collections. He was still feeling pleased with himself when his mother returned from the whist drive with the news that she had won five shillings for the 'travelling prize' and he almost laughed at her. Five shillings indeed! His evening had been a great deal more profitable than that!

His elation lasted until next morning when on his rounds someone told him that the Catholic Hut, which served as a NAAFI canteen, had been broken into two nights ago and over four thousand cigarettes stolen. The theft had not been discovered for twenty-four hours but when it was someone had remembered seeing two men pushing a pair of trucks up the New Road in the small hours and they thought it had looked like that little rogue, Jiggles Johnson. When he went back to his bicycle Eddie was shaking so much he did not dare attempt to ride it. He pushed it along the road, his mind working furiously.

The Catholic Hut! He had never dreamed the stuff had come from so close to home! And what atrocious luck someone recognising Jiggles with a pair of trucks! He must have known he'd been seen and that was why he had been so keen to dispose of the loot. The police would search any likely places in the vicinity of the New Road and the evidence would have been discovered. Now it was safely out of the way as far as Jiggles and his pal were concerned – in Eddie's garden shed! In his agitation Eddie walked into the pedal of his cycle and almost fell. If the police picked up Jiggles, would they worm the truth out of him? They might. Jiggles was not the world's brightest. But surely even he would have the sense to know that if he indicated where the goods were now he would also be incriminating himself?

Eddie hardly knew how he got through his rounds that day. He did so quite mechanically and when one woman asked if he was feeling unwell he made the excuse that he thought he might be coming down with the 'flu. It was hardly a lie. His head ached and his knees felt shaky. Added to the knowledge of guilty possession was the realisation that with talk of the theft rife in Hillsbridge it would be some time before he could dispose of his assets through his usual channels and from somewhere he had to find the twenty-five pounds to make up his insurance collections. What the hell was he going to do? Eddie Roberts, blustering fast talker and sly bully that he was, had gone completely to pieces now that he was faced with the possible consequences of his dishonesty and greed.

Saturday morning and he still felt as if he was living in a nightmare. He was half afraid of a knock on the door that would herald his downfall, alert enough to realise his frequent trips to the shed were drawing attention to it, panic-stricken enough to be quite unable

435

to stop checking on the hastily arranged camouflage.

By the time he made the fourth visit to the shed in two hours he had come to a decision. He had to get rid of the stuff, dump it if necessary, and cut his losses. The thought of throwing it away and losing the chance of retrieving his twenty-five pounds made him feel sick but anything was preferable to the risk of being caught with it in his possession.

Staring at the boxes Eddie decided on his best course of action. He had arranged to see Doris that evening so he had every excuse to take his car out again. When it was dark he would load the stuff into the boot and take it with him to Bath. He would spend the evening with Doris and then on the way home he would make a detour around Wearley Pond. It was only a few miles out of his way, a deep natural pool surrounded by plenty of bushes. He would put the stuff in a sack with a few good-sized stones to weigh in down and throw it in. It would sink without trace. Just as long as he left it late enough to be sure there weren't any courting couples or potential suicides about. Wearley Pond was a favourite spot for both.

His decision made Eddie feel a little better, but as the day wore on his nerves began to get the better of him again. How the hell was he going to load the car without being seen?

Luck was on his side. When he left the house after dark the Rank was deserted and all the blinds drawn for blackout. He reached Doris's house without incident and parked the car outside, making certain the boot was locked.

Doris, Eddie's ladyfriend, was what he might have described as a 'good type'. By this he did not mean virtuous – quite the opposite. But she was that rare thing – a woman who was easily pleased. She enjoyed Eddie's company, enjoyed the little presents he brought her, enjoyed frolicking with him in the bed which had become very large, cold and lonely since her husband had sailed away on the convoys. And she certainly knew how to please him in return. Since he had been visiting her Eddie had dropped every one of his other ladyfriends; he simply could not be bothered with them and their demanding ways any more. Doris, with her well-endowed bosom and generous hips, gave him everything he could wish for and more. If she had not already had a husband Eddie thought he might have considered marrying her. But the fact that she did have a husband and he had no decision to make in the matter he considered could only be an advantage. In the cold light of day Eddie did not see himself as the marrying kind.

Tonight, however, with his mind full of his troubles Eddie was unable to relax and take advantage of Doris's hospitality.

'Whatever is the matter, dear? You do seem ever so edgy,' she chided him gently. She was sitting on the sofa, legs crossed, leaning forward so that her ample décolletage was displayed at the sweetheart neckline of her dress, scarlet lips parted invitingly. This was usually the first step in an inevitable routine which ended up in Doris's cheerfully untidy bedroom, but tonight Eddie knew his performance as a lover was likely to be woeful.

'I fancy a drink,' he said. 'How about you?'

Doris gazed at him in frank amazement.

'You've got to be joking! Everyone down the local knows my Alf.'

Eddie did not bring to her attention that with his car parked outside her door regularly his being here was hardly a state secret.

'We could go into town,' he suggested.

She considered. 'Well, I suppose we could . . .'

'There must be plenty of pubs where you aren't known,' he said. 'We'll make it a quick one, eh?'

'Oh, all right.' Doris's good nature made her amenable to any suggestion.

Once outside, Eddie began to wonder about the wisdom of his idea and he wished he could leave the car with its incriminating cargo here in the suburbs rather than driving it into town where some keen and conscientious young copper might take more than a passing interest in it. But Doris would think it most odd if he suggested taking a bus. There was nothing for it, he would have to drive the car and hope he didn't do anything to attract attention to himself – or the car boot!

They went to a public house in the centre of Bath and after a few drinks Eddie began to feel better. In the public bar someone was hammering out popular songs on a honky-tonk style piano and voices raised in chorus floated through to the lounge bar where Eddie and Doris sat squeezed into a leather-covered settle. Doris hummed along with the music – 'You made me love you, I didn't wanna do it, I didn't wanna do it . . .' and looked at him coquettishly from beneath half-lowered eyelids, and each time she leaned forward to get her gin and orange her breast brushed against Eddie's arm. He felt a sweat begin to break out on his forehead that had nothing to do with the stolen goods hidden in the boot of his car. Perhaps after all he would be able to forget his worries for a little while if he and Doris went back to her place . . .

'Drink up,' he said.

'Oh my!' Her eyes teased him across the rim of her glass. 'I don't know what's the matter with you tonight, Eddie. First you want to come out, then you can't wait to get home again. Talk about messing a girl about!'

'Do you want another drink then?' Eddie asked. 'I'll get you another if you like.'

'No, no,' she giggled. 'It's all right. There's some things more intoxicating than liquor, wouldn't you say?' She leaned over and touched his knee and he stood up, lifting the glass-topped table aside so that they could both get out.

'You're right there, my girl, and I shall be showing you what one of them is right here unless you watch your step!'

She skipped in front of him very nimbly in view of the size of her ample behind.

'Promises, promises!'

They drove back. To Eddie's annoyance the space outside Doris's gate had been occupied by a motor cycle and sidecar and he had to park some way down the road.

Once inside the house Doris wasted no time in leading Eddie upstairs and soon his worries about the stolen goods were forgotten in the delights of Doris's voluptuous body.

They were still in bed when the air raid siren sounded. Eddie swore but Doris merely nestled closer.

'I 'spect it's just a false alarm. Let's ignore it, shall we?'

Eddie was not so sure. He did not care for air raid sirens. But Doris's big comfortable breasts felt good against his bare chest and her arm lay across him, pinning him down. He ran his hand down her back, gripping the plump rounded bottom.

'Sounds like a good idea to me.'

The mournfull wail of the siren was still echoing in their ears when they heard the heavy bomber engines. The house began to vibrate to them and Eddie's natural caution made him stiffen.

'It's not a bloody false alarm.'

The words were scarcely out when they heard the first bomb fall, screaming down through the air, and the dull thud as it hit the ground made all the windows in the house rattle.

'Jesus!' He sat bolt upright, thrusting Doris aside

and reaching for his shirt, discarded on the floor beside the bed. 'Where's the nearest shelter?'

'Down the road. But we're too late to go there.' She still sounded calm and lazy, unruffled by the German planes overhead. Eddie controlled an urge to shake her.

'For God's sake, we can't stay here! Not with a raid on!' He was pulling on his trousers now, his shirt still unbuttoned, flapping around him. Another bomb fell. He heard it whistling down, followed swiftly by another and another.

'They're bombing Bath! The bastards are bombing Bath!' He was beside himself now with fear and Doris's seeming indifference only served to heighten his panic. 'Have you got a cupboard under the stairs?'

'Yes . . .' She was out of bed now too, standing naked in the patch of moonlight that filtered through the half-open curtains, but the sight of her plump white body did not excite him now. He threw her a robe that was hanging over the door.

'Get some clothes on, you silly bitch! Come on!'

He grabbed her arm, bundling her along the landing. Another bomb whistled down and the explosion this time was so close that the ground shook beneath their feet.

'Christ almighty!' Eddie yelled. He started down the stairs at a run, holding onto the bannister with one hand and his trousers with the other for his braces were dangling uselessly down over his backside. Doris was on his heels, stirred at last out of her lazy calm.

They had reached the bottom of the stairs when the next bomb fell. Eddie made one last hopeless rush for the cupboard, Doris froze on the bottom step, an expression of utter surprise on her normally immobile features.

'Oh Eddie!' she said in a pained voice, as if he personally was to blame for the sudden disaster.

And then the world caved in around them.

*

Hillsbridge was buzzing with it. The fact that Bath was in ruins would have been news enough for three heavy raids had left a trail of death and destruction across the beautiful city with churches gutted, schools in ruins and stately Georgian buildings reduced to a pile of rubble. But for the people of Hillsbridge there was one particular aspect which added spice to the otherwise bare facts. Eddie Roberts was among the dead – and the circumstances in which his body had been discovered were discussed with a mixture of ribaldry and relish but very little sympathy. In spite of his hail-fellow-well-met manner Eddie was not the most popular man in Hillsbridge.

'What's think of Eddie Roberts then?' Ewart Brixey asked the gathering of regulars in the Miners Arms. 'Bit of a turn up for the books, ain't it?'

'What be on about?' Stanley Bristow enquired, slurping his beer with relish – it was not always possible to get his brand of bitter nowadays.

'Eddie Roberts. He was killed when they bombed Bath Saturday night.'

'Oh dear, oh dear!' Stanley shook his head and wiped the foam from his lip with an unsteady hand. 'You never know what you'm going to hear these days and that's a fact.'

'And you haven't heard the best of it,' Ewart chortled. 'You'll never guess where they found 'un. In some woman's house. Both pinned down by rubble as they was coming down the stairs to look for shelter, I suppose. And neither of them had a stitch on, or so I heard.'

'You want to mind what you'm saying,' Walter Clements warned him. 'You can get your clothes torn off with the blast, you know.'

'Maybe, but I'll bet it weren't *bomb* blast that tore off Eddie's!' Ewart laughed.

'You mind his mother don't get to hear what you're

saying. She'll be having you up for defamation of character,' Walter warned.

Ewart laughed again. 'That's a long word, Walter! Your missus give you the dictionary for yer tea, did she? Anyway, that's not all. His car was parked up the road a bit and were hardly touched by the bomb, 'cept all the windows were broke. And what do you think they found in the boot? All that stuff that was nicked from the Catholic Hut!'

'That's never right!' Stanley Bristow said in disbelief.

'Oh ah 'tis. Tich Carey told me and he's a Special Constable so he ought to know. So what d'you think of that? Our councillor not only having a bit on the side but a thief as well!'

'I don't know, I'm sure!' Stanley muttered. 'Well, I never did!'

'You never know with folk, do you?' Walter added.

They shook their heads and sipped their beer. It was true – you never knew. Eddie Roberts had been a dark horse and no mistake.

The subject was a nine-days wonder in Hillsbridge. But with the war providing new topics of conversation almost daily it was soon forgotten.

23

Barbara's baby was born a week later than Dr Hobbs had predicted, on Friday, 3rd July.

'Friday's child is loving and giving,' smiled the midwife, a trained and uniformed professional employed by Lady Erica to stay at Hillsbridge House as long as she was needed, as she placed the small, tightly wrapped bundle in Barbara's arms.

Barbara looked down at the child with a feeling of wonder. She had never thought of herself as a maternal type and was totally unprepared for the rush of love she felt as she looked at the small round face beneath a cap of silky hair, the button nose, the little rosebud mouth. Tired as she was she found the energy to loosen the wrappings sufficiently to examine one tiny hand, marvelling at the little fingers each tipped with a pearly nail and wonder that this new little person could actually be the lump which had been weighing her down over the past months.

She was still engrossed in the baby when Marcus came in to see her. He had an armful of roses which he deposited on the bed to the annoyance of the midwife.

'Goodness me, whatever next!' she fussed, grabbing them up.

'But they're beautiful!' Barbara objected. She was always thrilled when Marcus brought her flowers.

'Beautiful they may be. They could also be crawling with insects. They must go in a vase on the dressing table well away from baby!' the midwife said sternly and disappeared to find someone to carry out her orders.

'Bossyboots!' Barbara whispered and she and Marcus

exchanged smiles. Things had been much better between them lately – and it showed. Once Marcus had accepted that the baby was his it had done wonders for him and he had become every inch the proud father-to-be. His temper had improved and he had indulged Barbara's every whim, including agreeing to her continuing to work for the Civil Nursing Reserve as long as Dr Hobbs had allowed it. His newfound confidence spilled over into his work, too, and Sir Richard found less cause to criticise his handling of the estates. All in all life had been a good deal more pleasant and Barbara hoped that their shared joy in the baby would help this happy state of affairs to continue.

'Isn't she beautiful?' she said, still feasting her eyes on the little miracle which she had produced.

'You both are,' Marcus said – and it was true. Propped against the pillows, wearing a new silk bedjacket and with a touch of lipstick to lend colour to her pale face, it was difficult to believe Barbara had so recently been through eighteen hours of labour. 'What are we going to call her?'

'I've been thinking about that,' Barbara said. 'I'd like to call her Hope.'

'Hope, eh?' He had been thinking more on the lines of a family name – Elizabeth perhaps, or Frances, after his grandmothers. But still . . . 'I suppose it's a pretty enough name,' he said.

'I think so,' Barbara said without explaining her reasoning.

That Hope might be an omen for the future.

Throughout the months while summer became autumn and autumn winter it seemed that Barbara's optimism might be justified. She was engrossed in her baby in a way she had never believed possible and life took on a new meaning. Now that she had Hope to care for the days were no longer endless but full and satisfying. She was a good child who rarely cried and soon she was sleeping through the night and giving her mother a long unbroken rest. Barbara delighted in pushing her out every day while the fine weather lasted, talking to her constantly though she was too young to understand and often calling in to see Charlotte who was now all alone and taking a great delight in her newest great grandchild.

Marcus's good humour, too, appeared to be lasting. It was as if becoming a father had gone a good way to restoring his confidence in himself just as Dr Hobbs had predicted and he even discussed the estates with Barbara in the evenings when they sat with Hope during her wakeful period, instead of sharing the company of his parents as they had done in the days before Hope's arrival.

Only two things marred the halcyon days. The first was that Alec had been reported missing after the fall of Singapore and there was still no word of him.

Charlotte talked a great deal to Barbara about Alec on the occasions when she visited her, recalling the agony she had been through when Ted had been missing in the Great War, and expressing her sympathy for Sarah, her daughter-in-law, who was now experiencing the same torment.

'It's not knowing that's the worst,' she said, jiggling Hope on her knee. 'You don't know whether to go on hoping or prepare yourself for the worst. I was lucky. Our Ted came back. I only hope it's the same with Alec.'

Barbara nodded. She did not repeat what Marcus had said to her – that if Alec was in the hands of the Japs he would probably be better off dead. The Japs were even more inhumane than the Germans, he had said, the conditions in the Far East were intolerable, with disease rife and wounds turning septic in the

445

steamy tropical heat. There was no point in worrying her grandmother any more than she was already.

'The sad part is, if it hadn't been for all that other business I don't suppose this would ever have happened,' Charlotte went on and Barbara knew she was referring to his affair with Bryda Deacon. 'I saw Joan the other day, you know, and she was asking after Alec. She's still carrying a candle for him if you ask me. You'd think she'd have found somebody else by now, a fine girl like her. But no, she hasn't, and somehow I don't think she will.'

'It must have been awful to be jilted at the altar like that,' Barbara said. 'I shouldn't think you'd ever get over something like that.'

'I don't know what Alec was thinking of,' Charlotte said sadly. 'Still, there you are, that's life, I suppose. At least you've done well for yourself, Barbara, though I might as well say I had my doubts about whether it was the right thing in the beginning.'

Barbara smiled, but her grandmother's words served to remind her of Huw and the recent worrying news of what he was doing – no longer flying Spitfires and Hurricanes but taking Ansons and Lysanders into France on secret missions.

'I don't like it one bit,' Amy had said when she told Barbara about it. 'It sounds terribly dangerous to me. But Huw was so grateful to have been brought out himself and so impressed by the work the Resistance are doing that he wanted to help. And I suppose with a war on all flying is risky. All we can do is pray it's all over soon and Huw will be all right.'

Barbara now silently repeated the prayer she said every night when there was a moon and a sky clear enough to make her think Huw might be flying.

'I don't think it will go on too much longer now,' she said, trying to be her old optimistic self. 'Things are bound to be better now the Americans are in.'

Charlotte snorted. She had less faith than most people in the 'Yanks'. Too flashy for her liking, they were, with their chewing gum and their parcels of butter, chocolate and nylons, and their belief that they could put the world to rights the minute they wagged their little fingers. But at least it was true that Hitler now had most of the civilised world to contend with.

'Let's hope you're right, Babs,' she said, shifting Hope to reveal a wet patch on her skirt. 'Now, I reckon you'd better change this baby's napkin if you don't want World War III starting right here in my kitchen!'

As winter set in Barbara continued to push Hope out whenever it was fine enough, covering her thick fair hair with a woolly bonnet and muffling her in blankets up to her chin. She was amused at the way the baby's button nose turned into a little cherry and she refused to pay any heed to Lady Erica's warning that Hope should not be out in the cold.

'Fresh air is good for her,' she argued. 'She's never had so much as a sniffle yet and I don't believe she will.'

By the middle of November Hope was settling down to a pattern of three feeds a day with a late top-up at about eleven at night and Marcus sprung a surprise on Barbara. *The Desert Song* was playing at the Theatre Royal in Bath the following week and he had got tickets.

Barbara was ridiculously excited at the prospect. It was so long since she had been anywhere and though she had been too engrossed in Hope to care, now that an outing had been arranged she could hardly wait. When the day arrived she laid her clothes out in good time and washed her hair. She was giving Hope her feed when Marcus arrived home earlier than usual and she sat on the nursing stool in the bedroom with Hope at her breast, chattering with him about his day as he changed from the tweed jacket he wore for work to a dark suit and pristine white shirt.

Once Hope had been settled – something which took a little longer than usual as she seemed to sense something different in the air – they were able to leave for Bath. Driving through the city Barbara was shocked by the devastation the air raids had caused – beautiful churches reduced to piles of rubble and houses with only one wall left standing, chimney breasts exposed, torn wallpaper flapping forlornly. She remembered that Uncle Eddie Roberts had died in one of the houses and shivered. She hadn't liked Uncle Eddie – she had been brought up to regard him with mistrust – but it was still unpleasant to imagine him lying dead beneath a hail of masonry, his clothes torn off him by the blast.

Her morbid thoughts were soon forgotten in the theatre, however, when the orchestra struck up, the smell of greasepaint wafted out into the auditorium and the curtain rose. *The Desert Song* was such a romantic show, the tunes were hauntingly beautiful and Barbara fell instantly and deeply in love with The Red Shadow. Marcus had bought her that rare treat, a box of chocolates, but they lay untouched on her lap as she was carried away, along with the heroine, into the desert.

When it was over, they ate in a small but exclusive restaurant close to the theatre and with the aura of romance still surrounding her Barbara was transported back to the days of their courtship when Marcus had seemed as glamorous to her as the Red Shadow himself. It was as if the traumas of their married life had never been and as she looked at his face, golden and handsome in the candlelight, something melted inside her.

'Happy?' he asked, leaning across to take her hand, and she nodded.

'Very happy. It was a wonderful evening. I don't want it to end.'

'It's not over yet,' he said and the promise in his eyes

448

made her heart lurch. Perhaps tonight was going to be one of those rare occasions when he made love to her without aggression to motivate him. Small tingles ran through her veins and she curled her fingers round his. Suddenly she could not wait to be alone with him.

The dreamy sensation lasted whilst he paid the bill and as they walked back to the car, hand in hand, she felt she might be floating on air. Driving back through the city she hardly noticed the bomb scars and she relaxed against the soft leather seat humming the words of one of the songs from the show:

> Blue heaven and you and I
> And sand kissing a starlit sky,
> The desert breeze whispers a lullaby
> With only stars above you
> To see I love you . . .

She hardly noticed a car overtaking them at high speed until Marcus swore.

'Crazy idiot! What does he think he's playing at?'

She opened her eyes to see tail lights disappearing around a bend in the road and smiled. Marcus liked to think of himself as a fast driver and hated to be overtaken. Then suddenly there was a screech of tyres followed almost immediately by a crash and a terrible tearing sound of metal on tarmac.

Her dreamy mood shattered. At once she was stone cold sober and trembling. Marcus was braking but they were now into the bend themselves and as the car shot to a stop so abruptly that she had to steady herself against the dashboard, the muted lights picked up the dark shape slewed across the road.

'He lost it! Bloody fool – he lost it!' Marcus's voice was high-pitched. His foot was on the accelerator again and he was pulling the wheel to the right, passing the crashed car which lay on its roof. She thought he was going to pull in in front of it, then suddenly realised he was not going to stop.

'Stop!' she screamed at him. 'Marcus – stop!'

He did not reply. He was past the crashed car, accelerating away.

'Stop!' she screamed again and reached over for the handbrake. The car lurched a little as it bit and as if her intervention had brought him to his senses he slowed, pulling into the side of the road.

'We can't just drive off!' she cried. 'That man must be hurt!'

Marcus sat silent and tense, holding onto the steering wheel.

'Back up!' she ordered.

He made no move, simply stared straight ahead like a man in a trance. She reached over to shake him and felt his arm rigid beneath her touch.

He was not going to do anything. She realised it with a mixture of horror and disbelief. Marcus the hero was going to leave a man in a crashed car, injured, maybe dying. And she could not be a party to it.

'Wait here then,' she said.

She got out of the car. Her legs were like jelly as she ran back up the road. It seemed she lived a hundred years in those few moments for she, too, was terrified at what she might find. But she knew she had to do whatever was necessary. She could not live with herself if she did not.

The car, a boxy Morris, was on its roof. Glass was scattered all over the road; it crunched beneath her feet. She could see the driver half in, half out of the windscreen. Her breath caught painfully.

The engine had cut out but the wheels were still spinning and steam gushed from the shattered radiator in a thick hissing cloud. She wrenched at one of the doors. It was jammed. Panic stricken she ran around to the front of the car.

'Are you all right?'

It was obviously a foolish question. The driver lay, blood streaming from his face and head, and he made no reply.

Her mind was chasing in frantic circles now. She had to get help, but how? They were miles out in the country. And she could expect no help from Marcus – he may have driven off without her for all she knew. She ran around to the other door, trying it, and to her immense relief it gave a little. She wrenched at it harder and it jarred open a fraction. She felt about inside. There was no way she could free the driver by her own efforts and she was not even sure she should try. She knew it was possible to cause worse injury by moving someone without medical knowledge. But if she could find something to make him more comfortable and perhaps stem the bleeding . . .

She found a cushion and a car rug, got them out and placed them under the driver's head where it lay on the road, after knocking out some more of the sharp shards of shattered glass. What now? She was just trying to remember where the nearest telephone box was when she saw more lights coming along the road from Bath. She leaped up and ran into the road, waving her arms wildly. For a moment she thought that it, too, was going to pass by, then to her relief it slowed to a stop. She ran around to the driver's side.

'There's been an accident,' she said breathlessly. 'I think the driver is badly hurt. Please – oh please – can you help?'

There were two servicemen in the car and they immediately took control. The driver executed a neat three-point turn to drive back to Bath in search of assistance, the passenger got out and approached the crashed vehicle with Barbara.

'Cor – bit of a mess, ain't it?' he commented. 'Were you in it?'

451

'No, I – we – came upon it.' She was unwilling to draw attention to the fact that her husband had done nothing to help.

They stayed with the injured driver until help arrived, some ten minutes later, in the shape of an auxiliary ambulance. He had begun to come around a little, making moaning sounds, and Barbara was glad of the soldier's company. Then, as the injured man was being loaded into the ambulance, a police car arrived, bell clanging.

Barbara gave her name and address to the policeman and told him all she knew of what had happened.

'Where's your husband now then?' the policeman asked, looking puzzled.

'Further up the road, in the car – or he was,' Barbara said, feeling ashamed, and added quickly: 'His nerves were shot to pieces after something that happened to him in France.'

'Oh, I see. You can get home then can you?' the policeman asked.

'Yes – so long as he's still there . . .'

He was, still sitting exactly as she had left him. She got into the passenger seat. Her knees were trembling and she was glad to sit down.

'That's it then. He's been taken away by ambulance,' she said matter-of-factly.

Marcus did not reply and made no attempt to start the car.

'Marcus!' she said sharply. 'We can go home now.'

He remained immobile.

'For heaven's sake do something!' she snapped. 'Don't just sit there!'

His breath came out on a shuddering sob.

'Well, there you are then,' he said. 'Now you know.'

Barbara was too shocked herself to play guessing games.

'What do you mean? What do I know?'

'What I'm like. What I'm made of. The man you married.'

'Oh, for heaven's sake! What are you talking about?'

'A hero. You thought you married a bloody hero. Now you know the truth.'

'Oh Marcus!' She leaned across and touched his hand. It felt cold. The magic of the evening was shattered now and she knew it had been a vain hope that he had put his guilt and inadequacy behind him. It was rooted too deep. Well, she would just have to go on trying to help him as she had promised she would. In some ways he was as much her baby as Hope. 'You *are* a hero. Everyone knows that,' she said gently.

'No!' He was crying, tears running down his face.

'Don't be silly. You were decorated for heroism.'

'I wouldn't have been if they'd known the truth. I'm not only a coward. I'm a bloody liar as well.'

She froze. There was something in his tone which made it impossible for her to utter further platitudes.

'It wasn't the way I said it was,' he went on, speaking slowly now and deliberately, as if the words came from deep inside him. 'You really want to know what happened that day when we were ambushed? I ran away. That's why I survived. I ran away and left my men to die. I left them. That's why I'm alive and they're dead. I deserted them, Barbara.'

'Oh my God,' she said. 'Marcus, you don't know what you're saying.'

'Oh yes I do. Why do you think it haunts me like it does? I'm no hero, Barbara. You've seen what happens to me when the crunch comes. Look at me!'

His hand, stretched on the steering wheel, was taut and shaking. She looked at his face, drawn and white in the light of the moon, and knew without a shadow of doubt that he was telling the truth.

Afterwards, Barbara knew that it was in that moment that any feeling she had left for him died. Not

453

in the bedroom when he had beaten and abused her. Not when he had failed to take her in love and instead had taken her by force. She had still felt sympathy for him then and been able to make excuses for him. But now the last shreds of the charade had been stripped away and there was nothing left between her and the naked truth. Marcus the golden boy did not exist. He never existed, perhaps.

For a moment she sat with her hand on his. The full implications of his revelation had not yet had time to be absorbed but the shock of them had made her suddenly very calm.

'Well, we can't stay here all night,' she said and her tone was still matter-of-fact. 'Are you going to drive or do you want me to?'

'Yes – will you . . .?'

'Move over then,' she said.

The world seemed to have collapsed around her. She went on automatically with the everyday tasks of caring for Hope exactly as before but she could think of nothing but Marcus's anguished confession. Over and over again it played itself over in her mind and she kept seeing his face, white and strained, and his shaking hands. Fragments of past conversations came to her, too, and she slotted them into place in the overall picture. So many things made sense now that she knew his terrible secret. She could understand the ghosts that haunted him, knew why his self-disgust ran so deep, even pity him in a way. But any respect that had remained for him had died along with the remnants of love and Barbara felt more alone and frightened than she had ever felt in her life.

How could she live like this? How could she continue to share her bed and her life with a man for whom she could feel nothing but scorn and a little pity? So long as

454

he had been a hero to her there had at least been something to hang onto – the hope that in time he would be able to put tragedy behind him and become once again a man to be admired. But his revelations had put an end to that once and for all. To outsiders it might appear that he had the world at his feet; Barbara now knew those feet were made of clay. There was nothing, nothing at all for her to cling to, no single peg for a dream and nothing but her own stubbornness and dogged determination to keep her going.

If only I could talk to someone about it, it wouldn't seem so bad, she thought. But there was no one. Sir Ralph and Lady Erica were remote from her, they had never shared confidences and in any case Barbara knew that if they learned the truth it would be disastrous. The knowledge that their son was a coward and a liar, responsible for the death of his men, might not actually destroy them but it would certainly destroy the somewhat tenuous relationship which existed between them. No, she could not confide in the Spindlers. If Marcus chose to tell them at some time that was between him and his parents. It was not for her to do it.

Sometimes when the knowledge weighed on her so heavily that she did not think she could bear it alone, Barbara wondered if she could talk to Amy or even Charlotte. But she could not bring herself to do it. It was as if Marcus's failings had diminished her in some way, she felt. She was ashamed of him, yet even now reluctant to admit that her marriage was a disaster.

I was so determined to show Huw I could forget him that I fooled myself over Marcus, she thought, and the longing for Huw overwhelmed her. He had always been the one to whom she could turn, the one to whom she had confided her hopes and dreams and fears. But Huw was far away. And even if he were here now she did not think she could bring herself to tell him. So Barbara

455

kept her own counsel, determined that no one should know of the darkness inside her heart.

But Amy knew. She looked at her daughter, missed the sparkle in her eyes, and knew that something was very much amiss in her life.

'She's not happy, I know she's not,' she said to Ralph.

Ralph, engrossed in sorting out the details of a timber deal with the government for the building of prefabricated houses, barely glanced up.

'She seems the same as always to me.'

'I suppose to you she would,' Amy said stiffly. 'She has always been very good at putting up a front. But I'm her mother and I *know*.'

Ralph put down his pen and reached for the cup of coffee at his elbow.

'Don't start interfering, Amy. You'll get no thanks for it. She's married now and if there are any problems between her and her husband it's for them to sort out.'

'I know that,' Amy said irritably. She felt helpless and it was not a feeling she liked. 'But I can't bear to think of her being unhappy, Ralph. She's so isolated, living with those Spindlers. They're queer people. Him all bluster and her – well, she's strange. She has peculiar eyes, Ralph.'

'Only you, Amy, could think your daughter is unhappy because you don't like her mother-in-law's eyes.'

'Don't be so silly!' she snapped. She and Ralph rarely quarrelled but there were times when she felt like hitting him.

The subject was dropped but Amy continued to worry about Barbara and when she came to visit on Sunday afternoon and they were alone together Amy decided to take the bull by the horns.

'Is everything all right, Babs?' she asked.

They were in the kitchen, warming their toes by the fire. Hope was asleep in her pram in the hall, Maureen had been invited to a friend's house for tea, and Ralph had retired to his study with the Sunday papers.

The moment the question was asked she saw the wary look creep into Barbara's face.

'Of course it is, Mum. What makes you ask?'

Amy hesitated. 'I'm not sure, Babs. Except that I probably know you better than anyone else and I know when you're hiding something. Everything is all right between you and Marcus, is it?'

'Fine.' But there was no mistaking the brittleness of her tone.

'Babs, I don't want to pry,' Amy persisted. 'But if you ever do feel you want to talk – well, you know where I am.'

'Yes. Thanks Mum.' She was silent for a moment, staring into the fire, and Amy saw her swallow hard. There was something. She knew it. She waited, watching Barbara try to control herself. At first she thought she would manage it – there was so much of herself in Barbara, so much stubborn pride. But the suppressed emotion was too strong. The muscles of Barbara's face tightened, her eyes squeezed shut and still the tears came rolling down her cheeks in silent rivers.

Amy went to her going down on her knees in front of her and taking her hands.

'Babs, darling, tell me – please.'

Barbara's head was bowed, the firelight made the tears shine on her cheeks. 'There's nothing you can do. Nothing anyone can do.'

'But tell me, at least *tell* me. Is there something wrong with Hope?'

'Oh no, nothing like that.'

'Then what?'

457

'Oh Mum . . .' And suddenly it was pouring out, stumbled words becoming a steady flow. Amy listened in shocked silence. Whatever she had expected it was not this.

'Oh darling, I don't know what to say!' she said when at last Barbara faltered into silence.

'You see?' Barbara raised her chin, looking at her mother through her tears with a hint of her old defiance. 'I told you there was nothing you could do. All that has happened is that now you're worried too.'

'But I'm so glad I know! Oh Babs, why did I ever agree to you marrying him? I knew it was a mistake. I knew it!'

'Oh, don't start that now please!' Barbara was on the verge of tears again. 'The last thing I want is you saying I told you so.'

'I know but . . . Babs, you can't go on like this! You made a mistake. You can't go on paying for it all your life.'

'What else am I to do?'

'Leave him! Oh, I know it won't be easy. But you've always got your home to come back to.'

'No, I couldn't,' Barbara said. 'I promised him, Mum, that I'd stay with him. If I left him I don't know what he'd do. He's threatened to kill himself and I wouldn't put it past him.'

'Then he needs help. There are doctors who understand these things.'

'He'd never seek help,' Barbara said. 'That would mean admitting the truth. He'd never do it.'

Amy sat back on her heels, shaking her head. She did not have much faith in doctors who claimed to be able to heal broken minds. She was remembering Grace, Oliver Scott's wife, who had suffered with her nerves. She had attempted suicide and all the treatment in the world had failed to make her well. She had been better for a while perhaps, but the weakness was always there, the first stress of some seemingly normal occurrence and she would be ill again, depressed and thoroughly unpredictable. Amy knew the worry and unhappiness Oliver had had to live with because of it and she felt sick with wretchedness at the thought of Barbara enduring a similar experience.

'You have Hope to think of too,' she said. 'If he's like that, heaven knows what it will do to her. He might . . .' She broke off, shocked by her own thoughts.

'I am thinking of her, Mum,' Barbara said. She was no longer crying. Her expression was set, her hands squeezing Amy's very hard. 'If I did leave him he'd never let me take her. The Spindlers would never allow it.'

'But you're her mother!'

'And she's a Spindler. Can't you imagine the way it would be? They are very influential people. They could afford the best lawyers.'

'So could we. I'd fight for her if it cost every penny I have.'

'And we still might lose. The Spindlers *own* Hillsbridge, don't forget. They have the county in their pockets.'

Amy was silent, thinking.

Barbara moved suddenly, taking her hands away from Amy's and fumbling in her bag for a handkerchief. 'Mum, I'm going to have to go.'

'Oh Babs, no!'

'I have to. It will be time to feed Hope. And Marcus will be wondering where I am.'

Damn Marcus, Amy wanted to say. But she knew it would do no good.

'Well, promise me you'll come again soon, darling. And think about what I've said. We'll both think.'

'All right, Mum.' Barbara was composed again now. Only her pale face and haunted eyes showed the depth of her despair.

After she had gone Amy paced the kitchen. Dear God, she had known something was wrong but she had never suspected it was as bad as this.

And it's all my fault, thought Amy. My fault for interfering between her and Huw. She always wanted him and he wanted her and I . . . But I only did it for the best. I truly believed they were the same flesh and blood. Damn Eddie Roberts. Damn him! But it was a little late for that now . . .

She poured herself a stiff whisky and lit a cigarette. Then she carried her glass into the study. Ralph had nodded off over his Sunday paper. Unusual for him, but he had been working very hard lately. When she opened the door it disturbed him and he sat up, rubbing his eyes.

'I must have been asleep! Has Barbara gone?'

'Yes.'

He noticed the glass in her hand and raised his eyebrows.

'What are you doing drinking at this time of day?'

'I needed it. And I have to talk to you, Ralph. I'm out of my mind with worry.'

'Whatever is wrong? I haven't ever seen you like this before, Amy.'

She laughed, a small mirthless sound.

'I don't think I've ever been like this before! Or not for years and years. Are you properly awake, Ralph?'

'Now I am.'

'Good. Because it's going to take quite a time.'

'Well?' she said when she had finished. 'What do you think?'

Darkness had fallen while they were talking. Amy got up, fixed the blackout and put on the light. Ralph still sat chin resting on his hand.

'What do I think? I think you shouldn't interfere.'

'But Ralph, she's so unhappy! She can't go on that way.'

'It's for her to sort out, Amy. If you start poking your nose in you'll only make things worse.'

'But she's my daughter! I can't just . . .'

'Support her. Listen to her if she wants to talk. But don't try to manage her affairs. Look what happened when you interfered between her and Huw.'

'That was different. I had to, Ralph!'

'Yes, I suppose you did. I'm sorry, Amy. But it just shows the mess that the very best of intentions can lead you into. I really think you must leave it to Barbara.'

All very well to say. Not so easy to do. Being a mother meant bleeding with your children, wanting to make things better for them, if not perfect. Amy found herself remembering Charlotte's maxim: 'When they're little they are a weight on your arm, when they're grown they're a weight on your heart.' Now, despite Ralph's warning, she felt she simply could not sit back and do nothing.

The idea came to her in the middle of the night, astounding her with its simplicity.

She would write to Huw. If Huw knew that Barbara was unhappy he would be here 'like a shot' and there was no reason now why they should not be together if that was what they both wanted. She wouldn't suggest it, of course. She would take Ralph's advice that far. But she couldn't see Huw standing for Barbara being treated this way and he had always had more influence with her than anyone else. And at the same time she would be going some way to putting right the wrong that she had instigated.

Quietly, she slipped out of bed without disturbing Ralph and went down to the study to find pen and paper. In the small hours she wrote, pouring out the story to her adopted son. Then she slipped the letter into her bag. It could be posted tomorrow with the office mail. Amy went back to bed feeling a good deal happier and at last she slept.

Her relief lasted a few hours only. When she rose next morning the day's post was already stacked on the small table in the hall waiting for her and amongst it she saw an envelope bearing Huw's distinctive handwriting. Eagerly she tore it open, then felt her heart sinking as she read what he had to say:

I expect this will come as quite a shock to you, but in wartime things move at a different pace for you never know from one day to the next what is going to happen.

The fact is, Amy, I am married. To a wonderful girl. Claire is a WAAF and we met when she was posted to my station. We were going to wait a while until I had had the opportunity to meet her people and bring her home to meet you. But service life being what it is it looked as if we were going to be separated and we did not want that. So we applied for a special licence and tied the knot.

I know you'll love her, Amy, as I do, and I hope you will understand and forgive me for not being able to include you in one of the most important events of my life. And I pray the war will soon be over and we will all be able to be together again.

I remain, as always, your loving son – Huw.

Amy stared at the letter and felt the hope drain out of her, leaving only disappointment and despair. She was too late. He had found someone else – 'a wonderful girl'. There was nothing else she could do for him or for Barbara.

Never had the war seemed more endless or the night blacker. Amy folded the letter, wondering how on earth she would break the news to Barbara. Then, she tore up her own letter to Huw and alone in her office she laid her head down on her folded arms and wept.

24

In the spring of 1944 Margaret Hall had an unexpected
visitor – or, to be precise, two unexpected visitors. She
opened the door one Friday afternoon to a flashily
dressed woman with crimped hair and too much paint
on her face and a man in GI's uniform. Her eyes
widened with surprise and she looked from one to the
other of them enquiringly.

It was the woman who spoke, fussing with the fur
tippet at her throat and touching a scarlet tipped nail to
her equally bright scarlet lips.

'You'll be Mrs Hall, I dare say.' The broad Cockney
accent was unmistakeable. 'Well, I'm Mrs Cooper.
We've come to see Elaine and Marie.'

Margaret was so astonished she was rendered almost
speechless. 'Oh!' was all she could manage.

The woman tittered shrilly. 'Well, that's a nice
welcome, I must say! After we've come all the way from
London, too. Aren't you going to ask us in?'

'Yes, yes of course!' Margaret opened the door wide
and stepped aside. The woman took the GI's arm and
pulled him into the hall. An overpowering smell of
cheap perfume came with her. Margaret led the way
into the front room and the woman looked around
appraisingly.

'Well, this is nice, isn't it, Joe? This is Joe, by the
way. My fiancé.' She pronounced it 'feeanc-ey'.

The American grinned and thrust out a big hand to
take Margaret's in a bear-like grip.

'Joseph Z. King, honey. That's me. Pleased t' meet
you, I'm sure.'

'Yes,' Margaret said faintly.

463

'Joe had some leave so I thought I'd bring him down to meet the girls. Seeing we're going to be married as soon as we can get through all the red tape, it seemed only right.' The woman squeezed the GI's arm, simpering at him coquettishly then looking around again. 'Where are they then?'

'I'm terribly sorry but I'm afraid they're not here,' Margaret said. 'They're in Minehead, staying with my brother for a few days. It's half term at school and we thought a change and the sea air would do them good.'

'Well!' The woman looked more affronted than disappointed. 'That's a nice thing! I thought *you* were supposed to be looking after them.'

'I am,' Margaret said patiently. 'I have been looking after them for the last four years and in all that time you haven't been to see them once. How was I to know you were going to choose this week to visit? If you had let me know you were coming I'd have made sure they were here, of course, but under the circumstances . . .'

'It hasn't been easy,' the woman said defensively. 'We've had a rare old time of it in London, I can tell you. And I haven't had the money to fling about on train fares. But I've wrote to them. You can't say I haven't wrote.'

'Oh yes, you have occasionally,' Margaret conceded. 'But I wouldn't have thought it would have been beyond you to make the effort to get down to see them at least once in a while. And I really don't see that I should take the blame for them not being here now. They needed a holiday, Mrs Cooper, and I'm sure my husband's brother will give them a good one. He's a schoolmaster and well used to dealing with children.'

'I see,' the woman sniffed, slightly mollified.

Margaret indicated the sofa. 'Well, now that you are here, perhaps you'd like to sit down. I'll put the kettle on and make you a cup of tea.'

She left them and went into the kitchen bristling slightly. The nerve of the woman, turning up out of the blue after more than four years and expecting the children to be here and waiting for her! Margaret thought of the first Christmas they had been with her when they had eagerly awaited her arrival with the other evacuees' parents and been disappointed, thought of the mornings when she had seen them waiting in vain for the arrival of the postman and the problems which she had been forced to sort out for them unaided, and her blood boiled. After all this time, the woman had virtually given up her rights to them – abandoned them to be looked after by somebody else – then she had the gall to criticise Margaret for arranging for them to have a holiday!

She made the tea and took it into the front room. The woman was cuddling up to the GI and there was now more lipstick on his face than there was on her mouth. Margaret pulled up a table and set down the tray.

'Actually, I am very glad of the chance to meet you at last, Mrs Cooper,' she said, attempting to make a fresh start. 'I've grown very close to the girls in the time they've been with me. In fact there are times when it seems they have always been here and I can't imagine life without them.'

'Oh!' Mrs Cooper looked surprised. 'They can be a couple of little beggars at times, though. I hope you've kept them in order. A good hiding and off to bed wiv'out any supper and they soon see sense.'

'You're too hard on them, sugar,' Joe said affectionately and Mrs Cooper patted his knee.

'You'll spoil them, given the chance, Joe, I know! Joe an' me'll be taking 'em over to the States with us after the war's over you see,' she added for Margaret's benefit. 'I shall be a GI bride!' she giggled.

Margaret poured the tea, trying to hide the shock waves that were running through her.

'The children don't know anything about this yet, of course.'

'No, but they'll be thrilled.' Joe put an arm around Mrs Cooper and hugged her. 'It's a great life for kids in the States. A great life for everyone!'

Margaret said nothing. She was thinking of Elaine, who thought of London as her home, and Marie, whom she had grown to love as her own child, going to the States, to a strange country, to live with a woman who cared so much for them that she had not visited them once in more than four years and a man who was a total stranger. It was dreadful; unthinkable! A great empty space yawned open within her and she remembered her own idea, planted so long ago now and nourished and watered over the years, to adopt them herself. She had not mentioned it to Harry again since his first unfavourable reaction, but that did not mean she had forgotten it. Far from it. It was just that she had almost seemed to have become the children's mother unofficially. And now they were to be snatched away from her. Her mouth felt dry. This was the moment to speak or it would be too late.

'Of course, if you like they could always stay here with me,' she ventured. There was a slight tremble in her voice and it was echoed in her hand as she set down a tea cup. She looked up quickly and caught the gleam in the woman's small mean eyes.

'Stay here wiv' you? What d'you mean by that?'

Margaret heard the eager note in the question and was heartened.

'As I said, I like having them. I should miss them terribly. As far as I'm concerned they can stay.'

'You mean when I go to the States? You'd keep them here?'

Margaret nodded, holding her breath. The woman straightened in her seat with a jaunty little movement.

'Well, that's very civil of you, I'm sure . . .'

'Hey wait a minute!' the GI interposed. 'This is all going a mite too fast for me. You know what you're saying, sugar?'

'Yes, 'course I do! They've got a nice home here, Joe. They're settled like. You an' me – well, we could have a good time on our own. They could always come over for their 'ollerdays,' she added as an afterthought.

Margaret's heart was beating so fast it was making her feel a little sick.

'I should want to do things properly, Mrs Cooper,' she said. 'Be legally responsible for them, you understand.'

The woman's eyes narrowed. 'How d'you mean?'

Margaret's hands were clasped so tightly in her lap that the nails bit deep semi-circles into her palms.

'I'd like to adopt them.'

She saw the woman's face change. The thin scarlet lips tightened, high spots of colour showed on her cheeks through the dark smudging of rouge.

'Adopt my kids?' Her tone was incredulous. 'You want to adopt my kids?'

Margaret swallowed hard. 'Yes. They're happy here and I'm very fond of them. You seemed quite willing for them to stay with me a moment ago.'

'Yes – but adopt them! Oh, I don't know about that!' She got a packet of cigarettes out of her bag and lit one, drawing on it fiercely. 'That's going a bit far, isn't it?'

'I don't think so,' Margaret said levelly. 'There would be things that would arise – I'd have to be in control, Mrs Cooper. And to be honest I don't really think *you* want them . . .'

'Now wait a minute! Who says she doesn't want them?' Joe interrupted and the woman quickly followed his lead.

'That's right! Who says I don't want them? You've got a nerve, I must say, just because you're . . .'

'You don't seem to. You never come to see them.'

467

Margaret was on the defensive suddenly, her dream slipping away from her.

'I told you about that!' Mrs Cooper snapped. 'We aren't all living in clover like you, you know. Some of us finds it hard to make ends meet, never mind chasing round on trains.'

Margaret was on the point of mentioning the three pounds she had once sent to enable Mrs Cooper to visit, but before she could do so Joe spoke.

'That'll all change, sugar,' he said, putting an arm around Mrs Cooper. 'When we get back to the States you'll want for nothing and I'll make sure your kids don't either.'

The woman simpered at him and drew on her cigarette, picking bits of tobacco from her scarlet lips. She seemed to be torn between the tempting thought of a new life alone with Joe and outrage that a stranger should suggest adopting her children, unable to decide which part Joe wanted her to play – the fun-loving lover or the devoted mother. Margaret felt a wave of contempt. Little wonder the children had been so insecure, little wonder Elaine lied and stole, and Marie clung to her, the first person she had ever been able to depend on in her young life in all probability.

'Will you at least think about it?' she begged.

Mrs Cooper rose, enjoying her new found power.

'All right, I'll think,' she agreed. 'But I'm promising nothing. Me and Joe have got to talk, haven't we, sugar?'

'We sure have, honey. When will the kids be back, ma'am? Seems to me they ought to be included in this. And I'm kinda keen to meet them.'

'Jack is bringing them back on Saturday,' Margaret said. 'Do you know when you will be able to come down again?'

'Not offhand, no. All depends on my duties. But we'll make it soon as we can.'

'It would be best if you telephoned first,' Margaret said. 'That way I can be certain you won't be disappointed again.' And be prepared myself, she added silently.

'Well, there you go!' Joe held out a big hand, squeezing hers, but though Mrs Cooper smiled tightly she did not offer her hand and Margaret was aware of the thinly veiled animosity. More because she had dared to criticise her treatment of the children in front of the man she wanted to impress than because of any jealousy, Margaret thought – and yet perhaps that was part of it too. Unwilling to put herself out in any way for them, she resented Margaret for doing just that.

When they had gone, walking down the hill arm in arm, Margaret found herself seeing again that hard calculating over-made-up face and hating the woman with a depth of dislike she had not realised she was capable of feeling. It wasn't her nature to take so violently against another human being. She was more likely to make excuses for them and their behaviour whatever they did. But she was quite certain that Mrs Cooper was the shallowest, most selfish person she had ever come across.

She did not want her children but she would be prepared to use them as pawns in her game to be whatever Joe wanted her to be. If it suited her she would happily abandon them for years on end and if it had not been for Joe, Margaret felt sure she would have agreed to the adoption. But Joe was a typical Yank, big-hearted and enthusiastic about family life. He plainly did not care for the idea of his wife leaving her children in England and if he said as much Margaret had the uncomfortable feeling that Mrs Cooper would go along with him rather than risk his disapproval.

Margaret climbed the stairs and went into the room that had been the girls' domain for the last four years. It was tidy now, tidier than it ever was when they were there, for she had taken the opportunity to give it 'a good going over' while they were away but their things were still very much in evidence – the rag dolls she had given them last Christmas propped up on their pillows, a heavy book in which Marie was pressing wild flowers weighted down by the leg of the dressing table, colouring books and crayons neatly stacked to await their return.

A terrible weight of emptiness flooded through Margaret. Dear God, how she would miss them – particularly Marie. She knew what had happened, of course. They had come into her life just when she had been at her most vulnerable after the loss of her baby and she had let them take his place in her heart. Stupid of her really. They were not hers and she should never have allowed herself to care so much. But she had so much love to give and they seemed to have had so little. How could she have cared for them day after day, sorted out their problems and looked after them, and *not* come to feel this way? If their mother had come to see them it might have been different. Margaret would have seen them together and known she was a temporary replacement only. But she had not come and without any formal recognition of it, without really realising it herself, she had come to think of them as her own. Now, she saw all too clearly that they were not and the knowledge ached in her painfully.

'Oh Marie – oh Elaine!' she whispered.

She reached out and picked up one of the rag dolls. Then, cradling it to her, she sank down onto the bed and wept.

Harry was in a temper. Margaret had seldom seen him so angry.

'What do you mean, you told their mother you'd adopt them? Have you taken leave of your senses?' he

470

demanded. Margaret twisted the tea towel between her hands, saying nothing. 'It's madness!' he went on. 'Two scruffs from the East End who don't even know the meaning of the word honesty!'

'That's not fair,' she objected. 'Marie has never done anything dishonest and Elaine has been much better lately. She's changing for the better, Harry, living here with us. But if she goes back to her mother she'll be back to square one again. And Marie won't want to go. I know she won't. She thinks of this as her home.'

'And what about me?' Harry asked. 'This is my home too. You've gone ahead and suggested this without even consulting me.'

'We talked about it ages ago,' Margaret said. She was close to tears.

'Exactly. Ages ago. And I thought I made it clear then what I thought about it. But you've never mentioned it since. Not once. I imagined you'd seen sense.'

'I haven't talked about it but I've thought about it often enough. I love them, Harry. I've come to love them as my own. If they go now I don't think I can bear it.' The tears were streaming down her face. She could not stop them. She seemed to have been crying all day. 'Oh Harry, I'm sorry. I don't know what's the matter with me. I'm sorry! If we had a child of our own I expect I'd feel differently. But we haven't. And I'm beginning to think we never will have.'

Harry shifted impatiently. 'That's stupid talk.'

'Is it? It's not for the want of trying, is it? I'm beginning to think something happened to me when I had the accident. Something they didn't tell me about.'

He did not answer. In truth the same thought had occurred to him.

'Look, Margaret, when this war is over and we have a General Election, there's always a chance I might be a Member of Parliament,' he said after a moment. 'No,

471

don't look so incredulous. It could happen. The whole country is ripe for change and this constituency is there for the picking. If that happens you'll have far too much on your plate to worry about those girls.'

'Oh!' she flared. 'And I suppose that means you don't want a child of your own either!'

'Of course it doesn't,' he said. 'There's nothing I'd like better. But Elaine and Marie aren't ours. And what if Elaine starts stealing again? Or running away and telling cock-and-bull stories about us? Can't you see what an embarrassment it would be to me?'

'I see. Now we're getting down to it. It's your reputation you're thinking of. How can you be so selfish, Harry?'

'Selfish? Well, I like that! You want to bring two children, one of whom I don't even like, into my home, make me responsible for them – and you have the nerve to call *me* selfish? And what about them? You haven't ever asked them what they want, have you? Oh no, you just go steaming ahead with your plans to disrupt four – no six – lives because it happens to be what *you* want. If you ask me, it's you who are the selfish one!'

'Oh!' The shock of his words cut through her haze of self-pity. Her hands flew to her mouth, staring at him with tearful eyes over the tips of her fingers. 'Oh Harry, I'm sorry. It's just that . . . you're right, I am being selfish. But Elaine and Marie – well, it's as if they took the place of my baby . . .' Her voice wobbled, she wrapped her arms around herself and suddenly she was sobbing as if her heart would break. 'My baby! Oh, I want my baby! I want my baby so much . . .'

His anger died. He reached for her, pulling her roughly into his arms and she wept on his shoulder.

'My baby . . .' The pain was sharp in her, as sharp as it had been the night she had lost it, a steel band tightening around her, squeezing out breath.

The depth of her grief frightened Harry. He had not

472

realised how painful it still was for her; for him the baby had never been real. He had been upset, of course, when she had lost it, but his main concern had been Margaret, that she would come through, and his regret over the loss of his son and heir had been tempered by thankfulness that she was going to be all right. As time had passed he had accepted the loss and he had imagined that she had too. Now he saw how wrong he had been. Margaret had accepted nothing. She had simply bandaged the wound and concealed it and the analgesic she had used for the pain had been concern and love for two little London girls whom she had accepted into her heart and her home as her own.

'Oh Marg!' he said, feeling utterly helpless. Oppressed miners who brought their grievances to him he could deal with; bullying blustering bosses he could deal with; sharp political opponents he could deal with – or at least, have a damn good go at it. But his wife, his dearly loved wife, in such a state as this . . . this was something Harry did not know how to deal with.

After a while her sobs subsided, a few moments longer and she raised her face, ravaged by tears but calm now.

'I'm really sorry. I'm being stupid, I know.'

'No, you're not,' he said awkwardly. 'I didn't know, Marg, you felt this way. I thought you'd got over it. I should have realised.'

She wiped her cheeks with her fingers.

'Perhaps I should have told you. But I didn't want to sound self-pitying. And besides, it's not always this bad. Since we've had the girls . . .' Her voice faltered again.

'I know,' he said. 'Well, I suppose that's it then. If it means so much to you, I suppose we'll just have to keep them. If they want to stay that is – and if their mother agrees.'

'Really?' Her eyes were starry bright again, shining

473

with tears still but happy tears now. 'We really can keep them – you don't mind?'

'I suppose I'll get used to the idea. But Marg, please don't go building up your hopes again. Their mother may decide to take them.'

'Oh, I'm sure I can persuade her. She really doesn't want them. They're just an encumbrance to her.'

'They might not want to stay.'

'Marie will want to. I know she will.'

'Well, first I think you should ask them how they feel. And after that there are still a lot of bridges to be crossed.'

'Yes, yes – I know . . .'

But hope was springing again. She couldn't help it. She had to have something to cling to. And that something was Marie.

She told them on their return from Minehead. They had arrived with Jack and Stella during the afternoon brimming over with excitement over the week they had just spent, the walks along the beach, the trips onto Exmoor, the new and different flowers Marie had pressed for her collection. Looking at them Margaret found herself thinking how little resemblance they bore to the two thin pale children she had taken in. The pinched look had gone now, their faces tanned to a healthy glow by the fresh sea air and the good food they had grown used to over the last four years had filled out their skinny frames. But if they went back to their mother how long would it be before they were deprived urchins once more? Perhaps if they went to America with her and Joe it would be all right, Joe seemed well-meaning enough, but that might be something which would never happen. Plenty of English girls were picking up with the American GIs and believed they were heading for the promised land, but Margaret thought some of them might yet be disappointed. A pretty girl to ease the loneliness of a foreign country was one thing, especially with the aura of war to enhance the romance of it. But there would be those who would see things differently when the time came to go home. Not all, she was sure, had the affluent backgrounds they boasted of, and there were those with a little more responsibility than they would admit to, in the shape of girlfriends and wives. Joe might not be one of them but how long would it be before he saw through the surface charms of Mrs Cooper was anyone's guess. It could be that she and the girls would find themselves left alone in London for a very long time.

When Jack and Stella had left to visit Charlotte and Margaret was alone with the girls, she decided to have a talk with them.

'You had a visitor while you were away,' she began, setting plates of bread and butter and their favourite seed cake on the table in front of them. 'Your mother.'

Two pairs of eyes widened. 'Mum – here?'

Margaret nodded. 'She was very sorry to have missed you. She had something to tell you and someone she wanted you to meet.'

She had expected them to bounce up and down with excitement, instead she encountered suspicion. 'Who?'

'A friend of hers. A man.'

'Oh, she has lots of those,' Elaine said off-handedly.

'This one was rather special,' Margaret said carefully. 'It seems he is going to be your stepfather.'

That aroused their interest. They gazed at her wide-eyed.

'His name is Joe and he's in the American army. Your mother and he are planning to get married and after the war is over they want to take you to America to live with them,' Margaret said.

The girls looked at one another.

'America? *Us?*'

'Yes. It's rather a surprise, isn't it? What do you think of it?'

'America!' Elaine repeated. Her eyes were huge. Marie said nothing.

'What is it like in America?' Elaine asked.

'Well, I don't really know since I've never been there. But they certainly have a lot of things we don't have here at the moment, like chocolate and candy. And everything is much bigger, so they say – the houses, the towns, the open spaces . . .'

'Oh!' Elaine said. 'I'd like that!'

'Would you?' Margaret hesitated. 'Better than being here?'

'Oh yes. If there's chocolate . . .'

'I wouldn't,' Marie said. She looked as if she might be about to cry. 'I don't want to go to America with Mum. I don't care how much chocolate there is. I don't want to go!' She reached out suddenly and caught at Margaret's skirt. 'I want to stay here with you, Auntie Marg! Can't I stay with you?'

Margaret felt a lump rise in her throat. 'I'd love you to stay, Marie, but it's not really up to me. It's whether your mum would let you.'

'Oh, please let me stay!' The look on Marie's face was one of sheer desperation. 'Don't send me to America!'

Margaret laid her hand on the child's head. Her hair had grown now from the ugly shorn look she had had when she came to a flattering bob. It felt silky to the touch. Margaret turned Marie's face into her skirt and the little spark of warmth within her fanned to a flame.

'Is that what you really want?' she asked.

'Oh yes. Oh please let me stay!' Marie whispered.

It was all Margaret needed to hear. If Marie wanted to stay she would fight for her all the way.

'I'll do what I can, Marie,' she promised.

*

It was three weeks before they heard from Mrs Cooper again, three weeks when Margaret had to endure the girls' eager faces every day on their return from school and try to alleviate their disappointment whilst coping with her own turbulent emotions. She was as much on edge as they were, watching for the postman and jumping each time the telephone rang, and she did not know whether to be glad or sorry when the letters that plopped onto the mat turned out to be only bills and circulars and the telephone calls were almost always for Harry. Each passing day gave her cause for hope and strengthened her conviction that Mrs Cooper did not care two figs for the girls beyond their usefulness as 'the family' which lent her credibility in Joe's eyes, but she could not rid herself of the constant nagging fear that her bubble was about to burst. The more she built up her hopes, the more possible – and devastating – was the prospect of the girls leaving. An hour of optimism seemed to be followed inevitably by a depression of exactly inverse proportion. All the wretched woman had to do was turn up and announce that she was taking the children away with her and there was nothing that Margaret or anyone could do to stop her.

The uncertainty ate into Margaret, making her snap where normally she would have been good tempered, ruining her appetite and keeping her awake at night. She was usually able to fall asleep from sheer exhaustion the moment her head touched the pillow but by three or four o'clock she was awake once more, her head spinning with a crazy whirl of thoughts.

Was it this way for Sarah, her sister-in-law, she wondered? Did she lie awake at night wondering about Alec? A year after the fall of Singapore they had received a postcard from him, saying he was well and in the hands of the Japs but it had brought little comfort. The wording had obviously been dictated and since the card had taken so long to get through Alec could have

477

been dead of malaria or beri-beri even before Sarah received it and there had been no news since. And Dolly, too, had to live with the worry of having both Fred and Bob in the fighting forces, for both had joined up as soon as they were old enough.

But at least for her there was some prospect of the end in sight. Little by little the stranglehold of the Axis had been whittled away and now the talk was that the Allies were going to land in France and hound the Germans back over the Rhine.

'It can't last much longer – we've got Hitler on the run now!' people said optimistically. 'Churchill will make his move soon now – and then woe betide them!'

Listening, Margaret felt a small teacherous dart of despair. To them it meant the end of the killing and fighting, the end of shortages and nights of waiting for the wail of air raid sirens. To them it meant the boys would be coming home. But to her it could mean the loss of her beloved evacuees. So Margaret lived from day to day unable to do anything but wait. And one evening when the telephone rang it was not the union or the constituency party for Harry. It was Mrs Cooper.

'We thought we'd come down at the weekend,' she said. Her voice was loud, false and nervous, as if she was not used to speaking on the telephone, 'Is that all right with you?'

'Of course,' Margaret said, making a great effort to sound normal, though she was clutching the receiver so hard that her palm felt sticky against the solid black instrument. 'What time do you expect to get here?'

'Trains allowing, about dinner time. Course, me and Joe *could* have something to eat at the Station buffet before we leave Bath, but . . .'

'Oh, don't do that. I'll get you a meal,' Margaret said.

'That's very civil of you, I'm sure.' She paused. 'The

girls will be there won't they? We shan't be coming on another fool's errand?'

'They'll be here,' Margaret promised.

She replaced the receiver and turned to see both girls in the hall behind her, Elaine with her *Radio Fun* comic, Marie clutching a coloured pencil she had been using to do some colouring.

'Was that our Mum?' Elaine asked eagerly.

'Yes. She's coming down to see you at the weekend.'

'There you are!' Elaine said triumphantly to Marie. 'I told you, didn't I? She wouldn't go off to America without us!'

But there was no look of answering delight on Marie's face and her thumb went into her mouth in the childish gesture she still reverted to when she was upset. Elaine nudged her impatiently.

'Don't be stupid, you!'

'Don't want to go to America!' Marie mumbled over her thumb.

Margaret put an arm around her. 'Come along, both of you. Tea will soon be ready,' she said brightly, though it occurred to her that whatever the outcome of Mrs Cooper's visit it would be impossible to please both girls.

On Saturday the girls were ready for the visit by mid morning, dressed in their best fair isle jumpers and pleated kilts. Elaine was excited, Marie solemn, though Margaret did manage to enlist her help in making a 'treacle tommy' tart for dinner and as she rolled a piece of pastry into strips to criss-cross the pie, her small face pale and set above the apron Margaret had put around her to protect her best clothes, Margaret's heart went out to her.

She had been so pathetic when she had first come but this was her home now. At her age, four years must seem like a lifetime and her mother a virtual stranger. I'll fight for her – I will! Margaret promised herself.

By noon Mrs Cooper had still not arrived. Elaine had spent the last hour watching for her out of the front bedroom window and Marie was following Margaret around like a nervous puppy dog, getting under her feet at every turn.

'Do you think they're coming?' Margaret asked Harry when he brought her in a freshly cut cabbage.

'They've just been held up, I expect. Stop worrying, love.' At times Harry's unruffled attitude, so like his father's, could be infuriating.

'I'm not worrying!' she snapped.

He grinned. 'All right, you're not worrying. So why are you putting sugar instead of salt into the potatoes?'

'Am I? Oh!' She glanced down at the jar in her hand and shook her head in disbelief. 'Oh Harry, whatever is the matter with me?'

Ten past twelve and she was beginning to hope that perhaps Mrs Cooper might not turn up after all. She was ashamed of the thought for she knew she was being selfish but she could not help it. She was not looking forward to the meeting, and to its outcome even less.

At twenty past twelve she heard Elaine's footsteps flying down the stairs.

'They're coming! They're coming!'

She ran past Margaret and Marie out of the back door to meet them. Margaret tried to untie the strings of her apron and found Marie clinging to her skirt. Her face was upturned, her eyes huge and afraid.

'Oh Auntie Marg – I'm scared!'

'It will be all right,' Margaret comforted with more confidence than she was feeling.

'Don't let them take me away! Please!'

Margaret rumpled her hair, bent down and kissed her. Her heart was full. There was nothing she could say to comfort her. She resorted to bustle.

'Come along, darling, we'd better open the front door for them.'

Marie was still hiding behind her as she opened the door. They were just crossing the road, Joe looking enormous in his GI uniform, Mrs Cooper 'done up to the nines', Elaine hanging onto her arm.

'There you are, Marie. There's your Mum,' Margaret said.

She was aware of Marie peeping from behind her as they came up the path. 'Hello. So you made it,' she said.

'We sure did.' Joe's voice was hearty.

'Marie? Where's our Marie?' Mrs Cooper asked shrilly.

'She's here. She's . . .' Margaret broke off. At the sound of her mother's voice Marie had emerged from behind her skirts and now she darted forward, running down the path and throwing herself at Mrs Cooper with all the enthusiasm of the young puppy she so often resembled.

'Oh, our Marie!' Mrs Cooper, almost bowled over by the onslaught, teetered on her high heels and made to hold the child away. 'Mind my skirt! Oh, you're all over flour!' Her welcome was less than warm but Marie seemed not to notice. All her reservations, all her fears, had flown as if they had never been and she was oblivious to everything but that her mother, whom she had not seen for four years, was here. She clung to her legs, sobbing, and Margaret felt the emptiness yawn inside her.

She had lost her. All her pleas to be allowed to stay had been merely the whimperings of an abandoned child, clinging to the one person who had offered her love and understanding in this alien world. But now her mother was here and nothing else mattered. Not the privations of life in London, not the neglect, not the days of waiting for a letter which did not come. She was here, a highly coloured figure in a two-tight skirt and a pair of American nylons, and everyone else had faded into shades of sepia. Even Margaret, who had fed her, cared for her, tucked her up in bed at night. She had been a caretaker mother only, now Marie's real mother had come to claim her and Margaret knew the child would go with her without a backward glance.

She should have been glad for her, Margaret knew, but she could not be. She felt numbed, empty, heavy as lead. Automatically, her lips formed a smile and she heard her own voice, steady and amazingly normal.

'Won't you come in? If the children will let you, that is! You've had a long journey.'

'That's it then. It's all decided. There's nothing more you can do,' Harry said.

It was late evening, Mrs Cooper and Joe had departed, the children were in bed and Harry and Margaret were drinking cocoa by the fire. Harry was tucking into the last of a pound of Osbornes but Margaret felt as if even a nibble of biscuit would choke her.

'Just a few more weeks and they'll be gone,' she said forlornly. 'Oh Harry, I shall miss them so!'

'You'll get over it,' Harry said placidly.

It had all been arranged that afternoon in the stiff formality of the front room. Mrs Cooper had decided the children should definitely accompany them to America after the war and Joe thought they should return to London as soon as possible so that they could become accustomed to living with their mother again and get to know him.

'Seems safe enough now,' he had stated in his slow drawl.

'Are you sure?' Margaret was still clinging to any straw in an attempt to keep the girls in Hillsbridge.

'We haven't had a raid now for months,' Mrs Cooper

assured her. 'They'll be as safe at home as they are here, judging by the look of Bath.'

'Oh, we don't get bombed out here,' Margaret said quickly, omitting to mention the incendiaries and the bomb which had demolished the chapel.

'That's decided then,' Joe said. 'The girls will come back to London.'

'As soon as I can get things ready for them,' Mrs Cooper added. Margaret heard the slight reservation in her voice and was heartened. Even now, she was not sure that Mrs Cooper was sincere in her desire to have them back.

'Why don't you let them finish out this year at school?' she suggested. 'They are doing so well. It's a pity to unsettle them just now.'

Mrs Cooper hesitated but Joe was clearly the force behind her new found interest in her children.

'I reckon they should come as soon as possible, sugar,' he insisted.

And so it was arranged. As soon as she was ready for them Mrs Cooper would send for Elaine and Marie.

'They can come on their own, can't they?' she said. 'I don't have to trek all the way down here again, do I? You put 'em on the train here, Mrs Hall, and I'll meet them at Paddington. That'll be all right, won't it?'

Margaret thought it would be far from all right, but did not see how she could say so.

They were, after all, not her responsibility any more.

The knowledge hurt more than she would have believed possible.

25

On 6th June 1944 Charlotte sat down to a solitary meal of a rasher of bacon and potatoes moistened with fat from the pan. The house was very quiet for she was unable to use her wireless as the batteries had run low and she was waiting for Jim to recharge them for her when he came to visit. She ate slowly, because one of her teeth had come loose and ached a little when she bit on it and also because she suffered from terrible indigestion these days if she swallowed a meal too quickly.

When she had finished she washed the dishes and went outside to hang her tea cloth on the line to dry. Perhaps she would sit out for a while on the bench in the sun, she thought. It was a nice afternoon and she had nothing to hurry back inside for. How different from the days when she had had all her family at home and there had never been a moment to spare!

As she settled herself, Peggy Yelling emerged from the outbuilding across the yard where Colwyn carried on his shoe-mending business.

'Afternoon, Peg!' Charlotte called, glad of someone to pass a few minutes with.

Peggy approached, beaming. 'Well, Lotty, and what do you think of the news then?' she asked.

'News? What news?' Charlotte asked, puzzled.

'The invasion of course! What do you think?'

'Invasion?' Charlotte repeated blankly.

'Yes! Where have you been all day?'

'Here, of course. Where else would I be?'

'And you haven't heard? On your wireless?'

'My batteries have gone,' Charlotte said. 'What's going on?'

'We've gone and invaded!' Peggy said importantly. She had spent half the morning glued to her own wireless. 'Our boys and the Americans landed in France about six o'clock this morning. They're going to show that little blighter Hitler what's what at last!'

'Oh!' Charlotte said. It was news they had waited for for so long; now she could hardly take in the fact that it had actually happened and she knew nothing about it. 'How's it going, do you know, Peg?'

'Quite well, it seems. Not a bit like last time. If you ask me, Lotty, this could mean it's all nearly over. Thank the Lord!'

'Oh Peg, that is good news!' Charlotte said.

'I'll have to go.' Peggy turned back up the Rank. 'I've got some prunes stewing on the stove. But I'll let you know straight away if I hear anything else.'

'Oh, I wish you would!' Charlotte said.

Too excited to sit in the sun now she went back into the house and suddenly she was remembering the day when Charlie Durrant had come running along the Rank, just as Peggy had today, waving his newspaper and announcing that war had been declared. Only that was the last war, Charlotte thought, puzzled that it could seem like only yesterday. That was almost thirty years ago. She shook her head wondering where the years had gone. Then she crossed to her wireless, turning it on and hoping that there might be just a little juice left in the tired batteries. It would be nice to be able to hear that the war was over for herself. Although, if it came to that, it didn't much matter how she heard it. Just as long as it ended soon.

I should like to live to see the boys come home, Charlotte thought. Our Alec and our Fred and Bob. And as the first thick, slurry crackles emitted from the wireless set she offered up a silent prayer that it would be so.

The day after the D-Day landings Margaret received a letter from Mrs Cooper saying that she had now completed her arrangements for the children's return and giving instructions as to which train they should travel to London on, but no mention of money to pay their fares.

'She's the absolute limit!' Harry said crossly. 'You'd think she'd have put in a postal order, wouldn't you? She seems to think we're made of money!'

Margaret did not reply. Her heart had dropped like a stone when she opened the letter as Mrs Cooper had taken so long to send for the girls that Margaret had begun to hope that she had had second thoughts. Now, however, there was no more room for hope.

'I think I shall go up with them,' she said now, trying to be practical. 'I don't like to think of them going all the way to London on their own. And I don't trust that woman to meet the train, either. If something else cropped up she'd leave them high and dry. At least if I go with them I shall know they're safely with her before I leave them.'

Harry shook his head sadly. He couldn't imagine Margaret ever being able to stop worrying about the girls even when they were no longer her responsibility. She had allowed herself to become too involved with them emotionally for that.

Margaret wrote to Mrs Cooper telling her of her decision to accompany Elaine and Marie and received a reply by return. This was so unusual she could scarcely believe it when she saw the envelope with the blotchy writing and the London postmark, but when she opened it the reason for Mrs Cooper's hasty reply soon became clear.

486

She was very glad Margaret would be with them as she was working at lunchtimes as a barmaid in a pub and meeting the train might prove to be difficult. Could Margaret shepherd them across London? It wasn't far on the underground, just a few stops down the Bakerloo line, and Elaine would be able to point the way from there. The pub where she was working was almost opposite her house – she would certainly be able to be there when they arrived, but if anything happened to prevent her she would leave a key out – 'Elaine will know where'.

Margaret was incensed and her misgivings about Mrs Cooper's intention to turn over a new leaf where the children were concerned redoubled. But there was nothing she could do about it and she kept the details of the letter from Harry, whom she was sure would be furious at the imposition and perhaps even forbid her to act as unpaid nursemaid beyond the confines of Paddington Station.

During their last week she helped the girls get all their things together, providing them with an old brown suitcase she got out of the attic, for they now had a great many more clothes and possessions than when they had arrived. Jumpers, skirts, raincoats, sandals as well as their walking shoes . . . what would happen when they grew out of them? Margaret wondered.

Their books, too, she packed, along with their crayons, jigsaws and Marie's collection of pressed flowers, and her feeling of utter desolation grew.

On the last Friday afternoon, Marie came home from school proudly clutching a 'pattern' she had made that afternoon in art class.

'It's called a potato cut,' she told Margaret, offering the smudge of blue, green and violent orange for approval and Margaret felt her throat thicken. Next week there would be no footsteps on the path, no noisy yells as the girls came in from school, no garishly painted artworks to adorn the kitchen walls.

'It's lovely,' she said. 'Do you think I could keep it when you go back to London tomorrow?'

Marie's face clouded. She folded the paper protectively against her chest. 'Oh, I don't know . . .'

'I'd like to put it on the wall,' Margaret said. 'And you won't miss it, will you? I'm sure you'll soon do lots more like it.'

'Yes, but . . .' Marie was still hugging the painting as if she was afraid Margaret might snatch it from her, 'this one's special. I did it for my Mum.'

'Oh, I see,' Margaret said. There was a pain inside her. 'Well, in that case you'd better go and put it away safely, hadn't you?'

The child looked at her as if suddenly aware of Margaret's hurt but she ran upstairs with the painting. When Margaret went to their room later to finish the last of the packing it was still on the dressing table and she wondered if Marie had had a change of heart. But next morning she had it with her when she came down ready to leave for her train.

'You can't carry that loose,' she told her. 'It will get spoiled. Look, we'll put it in this carrier bag along with the things you want for the journey.'

Harry drove them to Bath to the station. As usual the train was late – did they ever run on time these days? Margaret wondered. Harry waited with them until it arrived, packing them into a carriage and putting the brown case on the rack and telling Margaret to telephone him when she got back so that he could come and fetch her. Margaret agreed. She knew that when she returned alone she would be feeling totally bereft and she dreaded the thought of returning to the quiet house.

As the train pulled out Harry stood on the platform waving but the girls hardly bothered to wave back. It was as if they had already put their life in Hillsbridge behind them.

The journey seemed endless. There were repeated stops, often in the middle of open country with nothing to look at from the windows but green fields stretching away beneath a blue June sky. The girls plays 'I-Spy', joined by an American serviceman who shared their carriage and who reminded Margaret of Joe in his open friendliness, if not his physique. During the game he continually 'gave her the eye' so that she was forced to stare out of the window to avoid encouraging him.

At last, there were houses and factories instead of fields alongside the railway line, thin at first, then fast thickening into a concrete jungle, and the train was slowing as it came into the great smoke-blackened glass dome that was Paddington Station. The platforms were crowded with travellers, many of them in uniform, and Margaret was glad she had decided to accompany the children. She guided them across the platform to the Underground noticing that they seemed a little awed by the rush and noise after their years in the peace of Hillsbridge and somewhat bemused herself by the overpowering bustle.

A cold rush of air came up to meet them as they descended into the caverns beneath the streets and Margaret found herself remembering that many Londoners had practically lived in warrens like these when the Blitz had been at its height, sleeping in rows on the cold hard platforms and trying not to think of the bombs that might have reduced their homes to rubble by the time they emerged into the grey morning light.

When the tube train slid from the tunnel like a great curling rattlesnake with glowing eyes the girls became excited again, jumping aboard so eagerly that Marie almost left her precious carrier bag on the platform and Margaret had to rescue it and give it back to her.

Margaret had only been on a tube train once before,

when she and Harry had spent a week in London seeing the sights and she was a little worried about missing their station. She need not have worried. Four years or not Elaine knew exactly where she was and she was on her feet, strap hanging, when the tube whined to a stop.

'This is it. This is where we get off.'

They emerged once more into daylight. The buildings here were grey and mean and there were many gaps of rubble strewn ground, the legacy of Luftwaffe raids, to add to the air of desolation.

'Oh look – the old *Crown*'s gone!' Elaine said, skipping along the pavement and pointing to one tottering wall above a water-filled bomb crater. But she seemed more interested than dismayed.

Unerringly, she led the way past warehouses whose bleak walls stretched up towards the grey sky and pubs where the smell of beer and stale cigarette smoke hung in the doorways and spilled out onto the street. Some of the windows had been boarded up, others taped to protect them from blast. They turned a corner into a street of terraced houses which were separated from the pavement by narrow strips of garden.

'This is it,' Elaine said. 'This is our street.'

She skipped on ahead leaving Margaret to struggle along with the case and turned into a path where the gate hung, paint peeling, on one rusty hinge and the strip of what had once been lawn was overgrown with weeds and scattered with stones.

Like the gate the front door was peeling, brown paint revealing an earlier coat of dark green. She knocked on it, thumping the tarnished knocker so that Margaret thought it was in danger of falling off, and lifted the letter box to shout through: 'Mum! Mum – we're here!'

At first there was silence then the door creaked open, dragging against the floor. Mrs Cooper stood there wearing a dressing gown which had once been cheap

490

but cheerful but which now bore the stains of spilled tea and fat splashes. Her hair was in curlers beneath a brightly coloured scarf, her lipstick and rouge had been applied to a face which was devoid of any other make up and was deathly pale.

'Mum!' Elaine shrieked, hugging her briefly then rushing past her into the house. But Marie hung back, shy suddenly.

'Oh, you're here then,' Mrs Cooper said. She sounded less than welcoming. 'Do you want to come in?'

Margaret hesitated. There was a stale smell emanating from the house, a mixture of fried food and cigarette smoke and plain old fashioned dirt. She was suddenly struck by the claustrophobic thought that if she went in through the peeling door she might never come out again. But she still held the brown case containing the children's things and Marie was hiding behind it. Elaine came darting back along the hall and rushed at her mother. Mrs Cooper put her away impatiently.

'Elaine, don't! I don't feel too rosy. I haven't been to work today. I've got one of my bad heads.'

The child's face fell and Margaret wondered if the 'bad head' might be the result of having had too much gin the previous evening.

'Come in, if you're coming,' Mrs Cooper said. 'I'll make a cup of tea.'

Margaret, who was parched after the long journey, would normally have jumped at the suggestion. Now her stomach revolted. She couldn't face drinking tea or anything else in this smelly house and she hated the thought that the children she had cared for for the last four years would be living here from now on. If she did not go at once, this minute, she thought, she would never be able to leave them at all.

'It's all right, thank you,' she said. 'I think I ought to

491

be getting back. With the trains as they are I don't know how long it will take me.'

'Please yourself, I'm sure. Are you coming in, our Marie, or are you stopping out there on the doorstep all day?'

Margaret put the case inside the hall, gagging at the smell. Then she bent to kiss Marie, checking the urge to take her in her arms and run.

'Goodbye darling. Come and see us soon – if you can manage it before you go to America,' she added, looking at Mrs Cooper across the top of Marie's head. The woman snorted.

'Gawd knows when that'll be! Joe's gorn, ain't he? Gorn off to France with the Invasion Force.'

'He'll be back though when it's all over, won't he?' Margaret asked.

Mrs Cooper pulled a face, her scarlet lips making a downward turned slash in her pasty skin.

'I s'pose so. Who can tell what these Yanks'll do?'

Margaret smoothed Marie's hair, tucking a strand into her kirby grip.

'Write to me if you can, darling. And I'll write to you.'

Marie's small face creased suddenly. She nodded, her eyes brimming with tears. Margaret straightened. This was the moment she had to be strong.

'Goodbye, then.'

She kissed the girls again and walked away down the path. At the gate she turned to wave. Mrs Cooper and Elaine had already disappeared back into the house but Marie stood in the doorway watching her go. She looked very small and forlorn. Tears filled Margaret's eyes and she turned and walked quickly away down the street. She did not dare look round again; the effort of walking and holding back the tears was all she could manage. She had reached the corner when she heard footsteps running after her. She checked and turned to see Marie, out of breath and waving the potato cut pattern.

'Auntie Marg! You can have this if you like.'

Her heart melted. She took the pattern, a little crumpled now from being squashed into the carrier bag for the duration of the journey.

'Oh thank you, darling! I shall treasure it . . .'

Marie threw her arms around Margaret.

'I don't want you to go, Auntie Marg. I want to come with you . . .'

Raw anguish flooded her. If only she could take Marie with her! But she could not.

'Go home to your mum for now, Marie, and we'll see what we can do.' But the child was not listening. Her head was buried in Margaret's coat.

At first, neither of them noticed the peculiar honking sound and if they had done they might have thought it was a small-engined motor cycle down on the main road. Had they listened carefully, however, they would have realised that the sound came not from the road at all but from the sky. But even then it is doubtful whether Margaret would have realised the danger they were in.

She had heard rumours, it was true, that the Germans had a new 'secret weapon' which they hoped to unleash upon an unsuspecting British public in an effort to stem the tide of the war which was now running against them, but she had been too preoccupied with the children's future to take much notice. Secret weapons belonged in the realms of science fiction. And bombs, when they came, came at night, preceded by the wailing air raid siren.

So as the V1 came in, one of the first of the 'flying bombs' launched like so many pilotless planes from the Pas de Calais coast and pointed in the general direction of London, the thought of imminent destruction and death never so much as crossed Margaret's mind. As it came closer, a dark crossbow shape silhouetted against the sky, she hugged Marie close; when its engine cut out and it began to fall to earth she was thinking only: can I take her back with me? Will Mrs Cooper let me take her?

It was only when she heard the peculiar whine and the rush of air almost directly overhead that she looked up, startled, and saw it. There was no time to feel fear, only surprise, and she stood transfixed, holding Marie to her and watching its descent. Down, down, closer, closer, and suddenly all her senses were screaming danger. But it was too late to run, too late for anything but to stand and watch. And then the world seemed to be disintegrating around them, the air cracking and rending, the earth beneath their feet shaking. In that moment Margaret faced eternity and saw only a vision of hell. A hell of noise and exploding colours. And she was falling, falling, with Marie still clutched to her. Falling into a pit where there was only darkness . . .

The doodlebug hit the row of houses at an angle, slicing through stone like a knife through butter. The first caved in, the others followed like a pack of dominoes placed end to end. The force of the echoing blast flung Margaret and Marie ten yards along the road, away from the scene of the destruction, knocking the breath from their bodies and rendering them senseless so that in the first vital minutes they had no idea what had happened. As bricks and mortar settled in a thick cloud of choking dust, as whole strongly built walls tottered and collapsed, they lay in the road, Margaret's body shielding the child's. At last the tumbling rending noise stopped and over the whole area there was a hush of deathly quiet.

In the gutter a tattered sheet of paper covered with

494

blue green and orange potato cut, patterns fluttered like a dying bird.

The child's soft whimpers reached through the blackness, jabbing persistently at Margaret's unconscious mind like tiny sharp barbs. With returning awareness the horror came flooding in, too great to comprehend, concentrated at first merely around herself and Marie. She moved awkwardly but with some panic thinking she was suffocating the child, trying to coordinate limbs which seemed clumsy and refused to respond properly to the commands of her fogged brain. She saw the blood on the road, a bright pool, darkening as it spread, and it shocked her to full consciousness.

'Marie!' she screamed. The child sobbed, throwing herself at Margaret's half prone body and she realised the blood was her own, pouring out of a deep gash in her leg where a piece of flying debris had cut into it. She tried to rise and could not.

A man was running towards them, gibbering. 'Christ Almighty what next? What bloody next? Stay there, missus, don't try to move . . .'

As if his words had been some magic lever the unnatural stillness erupted into chaos, a new vision of hell Margaret had glimpsed. There were shouts, cries, the jangle of bells as the rescue services arrived. And in the midst of it, before the darkness began to threaten again, Margaret was aware of only two things, one filling her with relief, the other with a dawning horror so enormous it almost took her breath away.

Apart from deep shock Marie seemed to be quite unharmed. She had been protected by Margaret's body.

But the street of houses, including the one into which Elaine and Mrs Cooper had disappeared, was gone. Nothing remained of it but rubble and beams, snapped like so many matchsticks. Her leg pouring blood, her head swimming, Margaret clutched Marie to her and knew with absolute certainty that they were dead.

Then, mercifully, she and Marie were being loaded into a Civil Defence ambulance and the horrific sights of the afternoon's destruction were hidden from them by the clanging shut of its doors.

They were kept in hospital overnight and the next day Harry drove to London to fetch them.

He had been shocked when news of the doodlebug had reached him; he had no idea Margaret would be going into danger by escorting the children to London. Now he went down on his knees and thanked God that she was safe.

Fifteen people had been killed in Marie's street, the oldest a great grandmother of eighty-two, killed as she headed out with her canvas bag to buy her regular Saturday night's bottle of beer, the youngest a baby whose pram had been pushed out into the small square of garden at the rear of the house for his afternoon nap.

Mrs Cooper and Elaine were among the dead as Margaret had known they must be. It had taken the rescue workers a very long time to dig them out of the rubble but the time lapse made no difference to them. They had both been killed instantly in the evil smelling kitchen of their home.

'Thank God, you didn't go in for that cup of tea she offered you!' Harry said when Margaret related to him the sequence of events before the flying bomb had struck. 'If you had . . .'

Margaret nodded. She had slept only intermittently last night in spite of the painkilling drugs the hospital had administered to her, for her rest had been broken by nightmares when she had lived and relived it all and experienced cold sweats as she realised how close she had come to death.

But to Margaret by far the greatest miracle was that Marie had been saved because of a sheet of garishly-daubed drawing paper. If she had not expressed a wish to have it, if Marie had not decided to run after her to give it to her, if it had been in the suitcase as it should have been instead of in the carrier bag . . . Margaret's stomach turned over at the thought of what the consequences would have been, and she pulled Marie's head against her shoulder, holding the child very tight.

'We'll look after you, Marie, don't worry,' she whispered.

And she remembered another car journey home from hospital when she had been empty and bereft. At least this time she was not alone, cocooned in her misery. This time the object of her love was with her, silent, shocked and tearful perhaps, but alive and unharmed. It might so easily have been different.

Suffused with love and gratitude, Margaret vowed that she would move heaven and earth to ensure that from now on Marie's life was secure and happy. She would do everything in her power to make up for the loss of the child's mother and sister, devote herself to erasing the horror from her mind. Once again she thanked God that she and Marie had been spared.

What had she done to deserve to live when so many had died? she wondered. Humility added itself to the cocktail of other emotions as Harry drove them back to Hillsbridge.

That summer of 1944 just when it seemed to a war weary world that victory might be in sight, it seemed the news of deaths and casualties came thicker and faster than ever.

Hillsbridge was shocked by the news of the death in a V1 raid of Margaret Hall's 'vackie' girl, saddened to hear that Farmer Brunt's grandson Ron had died of his wounds in Italy and concerned for one of the Talbot boys, missing in France since the D-Day landings.

'It doesn't sound good to me,' Peggy Yelling said to Charlotte. 'You'd think they'd have heard something by now if he was a prisoner. I saw his mother when I was in the chemist's this morning getting some Beecham's Powders for my lumbago and she's in a terrible way about it.'

'You never know, there's hope yet,' Charlotte said. 'Look at our Alec. It was over a year before our Sarah heard that he was alive.'

She did not add that sometimes she wondered if Alec *was* still alive. It was so long since that one meagre postcard. But there was no point being pessimistic. With James not there to annoy her with his constant platitudes Charlotte found herself harking back more and more to his philosophy of quiet hopefulness, almost as if he was behind her shoulder soothing her as he had so often in life – and with more effect.

But the news of one death came as a great shock to the Hall family, all the more so since it was more of a side effect than a direct consequence of war. In a terrible accident involving explosives at the camp where she was stationed, Huw's wife Claire had been killed.

Claire had only been to Hillsbridge twice when she and Huw had managed to snatch a few days leave at the same time, but Amy had liked the quiet, straightforward girl in spite of the feeling she could not suppress – that it should have been Barbara by his side rather than the pretty brown-haired WAAF. When Huw's letter arrived her heart bled for him and she wished desperately that he was here so that she could offer him some comfort. She knew of old how he reacted when he was hurt, shutting himself up in a shell and hiding from the world, and she was certain the bald words spelling out what had occurred hid a depth of feeling that no one but she could guess at.

That night she could not sleep, but lay tossing and

498

turning until at last Ralph woke and asked her in disgruntled tones what was the matter.

'How can you ask that?' she snapped. 'After all he's been through, now Huw has lost his wife, and before they even had the chance of a life together, too. It's cruel, Ralph, really cruel. Oh, this war has a lot to answer for!'

'I know, love, I know.' Ralph sighed and pulled her into his arms. Amy buried her face in his pyjama jacket and thought of all the couples, less lucky than she was, who would never again be able to lie in bed in one another's arms. And then she was thinking of Llew, who had been snatched from her in just the same way, though there had been no war to blame for his death. But she had gone on to find happiness with Ralph. Please God some of those mourning tonight would be as fortunate. Please God one of them would be Huw.

The prayer was still on her lips as she finally fell asleep.

26

In August Huw came home to Hillsbridge on two weeks' leave. It was the first time he had been away from his base for more than forty-eight hours since he had joined the Lysander flight and he would not have accepted the leave now had he not been ordered to do so by his Medical Officer.

'You're a stubborn sod, James,' the MO had said, looking at him over the top of half-glasses which had kept him from doing the one thing he had wanted to do himself – pilot planes like most of his patients. 'Getting you away from this dashed camp is like prising a Yank away from his chewing gum. This time, I'm glad to say, you have no choice in the matter. You're not operational and you'll be a dashed sight more use to us when you've had a dashed good rest and recovery.'

Huw had shaken his head impatiently. They had had this argument before. When Claire had been killed the MO had done his best to send Huw home on compassionate leave and on that occasion Huw had resisted. There was work to be done and he would be far better off doing it than moping around at home with time on his hands for thinking. It was bad enough here with operations to fly and his pals around him. In quiet moments he thought he would be eaten up by grief, a grief which seemed to have a hundred different faces ranging from the sense of utter desolation and loss to anger at the unfairness of it. That was ridiculous, he knew – the war had taught him that nothing in life was fair and he had lost so many friends that he had thought he had come to accept death as inevitable and indiscriminate. But for Claire to have died so needlessly as a result of a stupid moment of carelessness – it was that which tasted so bitter in his mouth, no matter that he told himself the accident was probably as much a result of the war as anything else – a man too tired out by the constant strains and alerts to pay proper attention to the safety of a dump of ammunition. Her loss ached in him constantly like a nagging tooth and exploded to fierce agony when he was alone with time to think. Claire had been warm and loving, yet also down-to-earth with a wicked sense of fun. In some ways she had reminded him of Barbara – it was that which had attracted him to her in the first place, he thought. But he had soon come to love her for herself. Claire had been the future. In the little time they had had together they had planned what they would do when the war was over – Huw would remain in the RAF, for there was nothing he had ever wanted to do but fly – and they would set up home within striking distance of his base. 'I'd like at least six children,' Claire had said and laughed at the look of horror on his face. 'I think big families are nice. And you need not worry, you'd be away half the time so it would be *me* who'd have to look after them.'

'That's all right then,' he had said and thought yes, he could certainly picture her surrounded by children. It was one respect in which she differed totally from Barbara, who had never struck him as a maternal type, in spite of the fact that she now had a child of her own. That thought he had pushed quickly aside and concentrated instead on Claire and their plans for the future.

Well, those plans were in ruins now, blasted sky high with a load of dump ammo. And Huw was as shell-shocked as if he too had been caught in the blast. But he had been determined not to take compassionate leave no matter how hard they pressed it on him. Far better to be here, doing what he did best.

The trouble was there were not so many operations

501

to fly now. With the Allies moving victoriously through France there were fewer pick-ups to be made for the occupied area was shrinking rapidly. At the end of July they had broken out of the Normandy beachhead, in mid-August they had landed in the south, and by the end of the month Paris was liberated. In other areas the Maquis, so long hunted, and revered, as the fighting wing of the Resistance, were at last scoring successes of their own, so that it was obvious that before long there would be virtually no area left under German control and in need of undercover air transport from England.

With the end of the war in sight Huw felt nothing but resentment that just when he needed to be as fully occupied as it was humanly possible to be, there was less and less call for him to fly the dangerous secret missions which had been his life since his own escape from France. In August, the Lysanders had been moved to a forward base in Devon as the previous station was now too close to the beachhead and the part of France that had already been liberated by the Allies and Huw immediately flew two missions, one a mail pick-up and one to bring in an evading pilot and an agent of the Resistance on his way to discuss tactics with the hierarchy of the SOE. It was this mission which had almost led to disaster. The pick-up had been touch and go for the retreating German army were rumbling noisily along the main road only a few hundred yards from the designated field and on the way back he was hit by flak. With a damaged tail-wheel and elevator he had limped home only to find the whole of south-west England blanketed in thick fog. With difficulty he managed to land but he was too close to the end of the air strip. As he fought to control his crippled Lysander he had struck the corner of a small hanger and a jagged piece of metal dislodged into the cockpit by the flak had gashed his forearm. At the time he had taken little notice of it, but when he had finally delivered his passengers he had felt the throbbing pain begin and looked down to see the sleeve of his tunic was soaked with blood. Several stitches had pulled the gash together but the MO was insistent. This time Huw must take some leave and give the wound a proper chance to heal before he flew again.

Huw had no choice but to agree. He telephoned Amy to tell her to expect him. She gave herself an afternoon off from the office, drove to Bath to meet his train and took him home to Valley View.

It was a pleasant summer day, not swelteringly hot but bright enough with the sun shining through a shimmery blue haze and turning the valley a hundred shades of green. The trees were heavy with full leaf, the gardens full of roses, snapdragons and granny bonnets, though the flower beds beneath the chestnut trees in the centre of town were bare as a gesture to wartime austerity. Huw watched the familiar vista unfolding and found himself remembering the first time he had seen Hillsbridge as a small boy of eight. He had hated it then, seeing only the dust-blackened lias stone buildings and the ugly railway lines bisecting the main street and comparing them with his beloved 'Ponty'. Now, they were part of his growing up, scenario for more memories than Ponty would ever have – to see them was to know that he had come home. Yet there was no comfort in the familiarity. It merely added somehow to the yawning emptiness within him. There was nothing of Claire here, but there were other hurts, other losses, that he rarely thought of now but which were all the same, so deeply embedded they had almost become a part of his soul.

Maureen greeted him enthusiastically and he tried to respond but he knew he was being less than successful when he happened to catch Amy warning her off with a tiny quick shake of the head.

It's all right, he wanted to say, you don't have to

treat me with kid gloves. But he merely retreated into silence.

After dinner Maureen left to pay a game of tennis with the Bray girls whose father owned the iron foundry – now working overtime – at Midlington.

'Don't run about too much on top of a full stomach. It's not good for you!' Amy warned.

'I'll be all right, Mum. Don't fuss!' Huw smiled in spite of himself – some things never changed. Then Maureen turned to him: 'Are you sure you don't mind if I go out, Huw, on your first evening home?'

'Of course not.' He slapped her bottom, neat beneath her tennis skirt. 'Go on Maureen have a good time. You're only young once and it doesn't last long.'

He saw her smile falter, saw her exchange a quick glance with Amy, and thought again: oh God, they *are* going to treat me with kid gloves whether I like it or not.

When Maureen had gone, pedalling off along the lane on her bicycle, Amy touched Huw's arm. 'Shall we go into the garden for a while? It's still warm.'

'If you like.' He knew she wanted to talk. He could sense it and he was not exactly pleased at the prospect. Some things were best kept inside. It wasn't easy to control emotion with others probing your soft under belly and since nothing anyone could say could help he preferred to nurse his grief alone. But he could tell that Amy was determined and when Amy made up her mind to something it was a waste of time and effort to try to persuade her otherwise. He had learned that long ago.

The gardens of Valley View were as riotous as ever – more so perhaps since the old man who used to work there part-time had died the year before and both Amy and Ralph were too busy to do much about keeping them in order. The rose bushes still ran wild around the path, a lilac tree hung heavy branches across the jungle of shrubs and bushes and around the door the honeysuckle dripped pendulous heads to give off a sweet scent to the early evening air. Amy led the way past the fish pond where tiny orange and gold specks darted up for light between the meat-platter-sized water lily leaves and across the lawn, dotted with daisies, clover and even the occasional dandelion clock. Two deck chairs had been set in the far corner to catch the last of the dying sun; brightly striped they looked faintly incongruous as the deep golden light accentuated the garish orange and blue canvas.

Amy adjusted one to a sitting position and lowered herself gently into it. She did not totally trust the aged canvas not to rip beneath her weight. But Huw ignored the other chair, sitting instead on the grass.

'I'm so glad you've come home, Huw,' Amy said. 'I've been so worried about you.'

'Oh, I'm all right.' He said it lightly but she knew him better than that.

'You've had a terrible time.'

'No worse than thousands of others.'

'Oh Huw!' To her he was a little boy again, desperately hurt and trying to hide it. She reached out and put a hand on his arm. 'Don't bottle it up, darling, please. I want to help. It does no good to bottle it up, truly it doesn't.'

'And no good to talk about it either. Claire's dead. That's all there is to it.'

'I do understand, Huw,' she said. 'Believe me, I do. I lost my first husband, remember.'

'It was different for you though.' He picked a clover, stripping the leaves methodically. 'Claire and I never had a proper life together. Never had a home. Never really shared anything except what seemed like a "Boys Own Annual" adventure. It wasn't real. Not like it was for you and Llew.'

'I suppose not. But it would have been, Huw. When all this is over. Now . . . .'

'No point in talking about it is there?' Huw said shortly, tossing away the denuded clover stalk. He did not add the doubt that in spite of all their hopes and plans it would never have been that way for him and Claire; the unspoken fear that in spite of everything he had simply not loved her enough. She was dead now, it was irreverent to her memory to think such a thing even for a moment.

They sat in silence, Amy feeling rejected, Huw reluctant to begin another line of conversation. Then he said casually:

'How about you? How have you all been?'

'Us?' Amy said, surprised. 'Oh, we're all right.'

'And Barbara?' Amy heard the note in his voice, the deliberate throwaway masking the deeper feeling, and knew suddenly that nothing had changed.

'Oh yes, Barbara's fine too,' she said from force of habit, then stopped. Why lie to Huw? Once long ago she had written the truth to him in a letter only to rip it up when she heard of his marriage. Now there was no longer any reason to keep it from him. It might take his mind off his troubles, might even help Barbara, though how this was possible now she did not know.

He was looking at her directly now as if he knew there was something she was hiding.

'She really is happy with that Marcus character?'

Amy drew a deep breath. 'Actually no, Huw.'

He did not speak. He was sitting very still. Only the narrowing of his eyes betrayed any emotion.

'No, she's not happy,' Amy went on. 'I think there's something wrong with Marcus. Maybe because of what he went through in the war – that's what Barbara thinks. But I can't help wondering if it's some defect that has always been there.'

'Defect? What sort of defect?'

'I don't think he's quite normal. Whatever normal is.' Amy reached for her cigarettes and lit one. 'Look, what I'm going to tell you, Huw, is between ourselves. Barbara told me it in confidence. I don't think she'd have told me at all if she hadn't been terribly upset at the time and we've hardly mentioned it since. Whenever I try to raise the subject with her she simply shrugs and says she is all right. But I don't think she is. I don't think anything has changed and frankly I'm worried about her.' She hesitated. 'This isn't going to be easy. You'll have to bear with me and let me tell you in my own way.'

'That's all right. Go on.'

She told him. Haltingly and with some embarrassment though she and Huw had always been close. She did not look at him as she spoke for she could not bear to see the darkening of his eyes. When she had finished they sat for a moment in silence, then Huw drove his fist down hard onto the grass.

'The bastard!'

'I know, Huw, I know.'

'The bloody bastard! If I could get my hands on him I'd . . .'

She laid a restraining hand on his arm. The years had rolled away and she was being transported back in time, remembering how Ted, her brother, had said much the same about Rupert Thorne, the solicitor who had raped Ted's sweetheart Becky and indirectly killed her, and how it had ended with Rupert dead and Ted in Assize Court, accused of murder. Suddenly, she was terrified that history might repeat itself.

'You mustn't do anything foolish, Huw. I'd never have told you if I thought you'd do that. Please promise me . . .'

'If he was here now I wouldn't be responsible for what I'd do.'

'I know. But it would just make things worse. Please Huw . . .'

He sat in silence and Amy quaked inwardly. Then he said: 'When will I see her?'

'She usually comes to visit at least once a week. But I'm sure when she knows that you're here . . .' Her voice tailed away.

'Phone her,' Huw said. 'Tell her to come over. If she doesn't come here than I shall go out to Hillsbridge House to see her whatever anyone says.' He paused. 'And if that bastard is there when I do I'll break his bloody neck.'

Amy nodded. She was afraid, yet also strangely relieved. The problem was no longer hers alone. Huw knew and Huw cared, just as she did. It was what he might do about it that scared her. She didn't want him going out to Hillsbridge House and causing a scene. Better for Barbara to come here, where they could sort it out privately – if such a thing was possible. She stood up. The sun was going down over the lilac tree in a ball of flame.

'All right, Huw,' she said. 'I'll phone her.'

The following afternoon as soon as Hope had had her lunch Barbara washed the child's face, combed the cloud of soft gold hair and put her into a clean smocked dress. Then much to Hope's disgust she strapped her into her pushchair.

'Don't want! Don't want!' Hope protested.

At two years old Hope was very like Barbara had been at her age – and Amy before her. She was sunshine and showers, a happy child who radiated warmth and fun. But when the mood took her she could be as wilful as she was charming, and as stubborn as she was pleasing. Today, the indignity of being strapped into her pushchair brought on one of those moods.

'Hope *walk*!' she demanded, kicking her heels furiously against the foot rest. 'Hope *walk*!'

'I'm sorry but you can't,' Barbara said. 'It's too far for you and we'd never get there at your pace.'

'Hope *walk*!' All along the drive she continued drumming her heels furiously and beating the air with her arms. The commotion rasped on Barbara's already taut nerves and at last her temper snapped.

'All right, Hope, that will do! If you don't behave yourself, I shall slap your legs.'

The tone, if not the words, communicated themselves to Hope. She opened her mouth to yell again, peeped over her shoulder at Barbara, and thought better of it.

'Just look at you!' Barbara said. 'You're all red in the face and messed up just when I wanted you to look nice. Goodness only knows what Uncle Huw will think of you.'

'Uncle Huw,' Hope repeated.

'Yes, Uncle Huw. He hasn't seen you since you were a baby.' Her voice was uneven. Just saying his name could do this to her. When Amy had telephoned to say Huw was here and wanted to see her the strange dark excitement had begun in her and the longing that he always generated. She had been able to think of nothing else all day. It seemed so long since she had seen him herself – a lifetime really. There was nothing between them now, of course. She was a married woman and he was a widower. But nothing would ever change the way she felt. Nothing could touch the dreams that were still there in her heart.

Although the afternoon was warm she walked quickly for she could not wait to see him. She stopped once to pick a couple of purple flower spears from the tall grass at the side of the road for Hope. The child sat quietly now, exclaiming now and then as a bird darted in the hedges or a butterfly fluttered past and Barbara chatted to her intermittently without giving a thought to what she was saying. The lane dipped down into the valley, the sun exposing patches of tar in places beneath

509

the worn grey coating and Barbara steered the push-chair between them holding back to keep it from running away in the steepest part. Past Midlington Pit she went, where the huge wheels that raised and lowered the cage turned slowly against the blue August sky and men worked in the yard, shirts off in the warm afternoon, dust-blackened bodies riddled with pale rivers of sweat. A coal lorry passed her, the driver honking on his horn. She pulled into the side of the road, then turned into the track that would lead her along the valley floor to the house that had been her home.

It was narrow, much narrower than the lane, and the ground beneath her feet was liberally dusted with black coal dust. Fronds and branches spread out from the hedgerows to brush at the pushchair in the most narrow places and Barbara pushed them aside. Her heart was beating fast now, hammering against her ribs, and it owed nothing to the pace at which she had been walking.

Huw. Each beat of her heart repeated his name. Huw –Huw – Huw.

Don't be stupid, she told herself. But it made no difference.

The path widened and the house came into sight, square and grey, its chimneys spiking the blue of the sky. Barbara quickened her step.

'Walk!' Hope chirped again. 'Hope walk!'

Barbara ignored her.

Up the lane, through the gate. The door was ajar. Then suddenly it swung open and he was there – tall, dark, the same Huw she had loved for as long as she could remember. He must have been watching for her from the window. She ceased to think. Dropping the handles of the pushchair she ran to him.

She was in his arms, her face pressed tight against the cool cotton of his shirt. They hugged, not speaking, though her heart still clamoured his name. Oh it was so good to be here with him. So good! Emotion overwhelmed her. Tears squeezed from the corners of her eyes and warmth began in the pit of her stomach, surging up into every vein. The world around them had ceased to exist. There was nothing, nothing outside the circle of his arms.

Nothing but Hope. Her small plaintive voice found a chink in the armour. 'Mummy! Mum-mee!'

Reluctantly, Barbara pulled free.

'All right, darling, Mummy is here.'

Hope was tugging at the pushchair straps, struggling to get out.

'Sit still, you'll tip over!' Barbara warned. She glanced back at Huw. He was looking at her, just looking, his eyes deep pools as he drank her in, seeming to see into her very soul. Her stomach flipped.

'I'll have to get Hope out of her pushchair,' she said, her voice trembling slightly. 'Don't you think she's grown? Isn't she a little picture?'

'Yes.' But his eyes were still on Barbara.

She got Hope out of the pushchair and lifted her up. 'It's Uncle Huw. Look!'

Hope turned her face into her mother's shoulder. Barbara and Huw continued to smile at one another across her head. After a moment Hope began to wriggle. Barbara set her down and she toddled into the house.

'We'd better go in.' She noticed the bandage on his arm. 'What have you been doing?'

'Oh, legacy of war. It's nothing.'

The hall was dim, heavy with the scent of roses. Her fingers found his and twined. 'Oh Huw, it's so good to see you!'

'And you.'

It had been so long. There was so much to say. Yet they said none of it. Nothing was important but being together.

A voice from the kitchen: 'Hope! What are you doing here?'

It was Mrs Milsom. They looked at one another and smiled, then Barbara followed her daughter along the hall. 'Hello, Milsy.'

'Miss Barbara! Come to see Master Huw, have you?' Mrs Milsom nodded and smiled, her multiple chins wobbling. 'Go on then, the pair of you. I'll look after Hope. She'll be all right with me. Do you want a biscuit, Hope? Come on, you know where they're kept, don't you?'

'She's only just had her lunch,' Barbara said automatically.

'Never mind. This is a special occasion, isn't it? I'll keep an eye on her for you. I expect you and Master Huw want to talk.'

Master Huw. At any other time it might have amused Barbara the way Mrs Milsom still referred to a man of twenty-six as 'Master Huw'. Not today. She was aware of nothing but a wave of gratitude. Mrs Milsom knew a great deal more than she ever let on. She had been a part of the household for so long it was impossible to imagine life without her, always unobtrusive yet always there when she was needed.

'Shall we go out then?' Barbara asked. 'It's a lovely day. A pity to waste the sunshine.'

'Good idea,' said Huw.

Ordinary conversation. Just mundane words. Yet behind them so much emotion.

'Be a good girl, Hope,' Barbara said.

Hope, her mouth full of biscuit, did not reply.

Huw held the door open and they walked out together into the sunlight.

Up the steep lane, Porters Hill, where Amy had run into Ralph's Morgan with the lorry so long ago, they

512

went, through the 'V' gate and into the first of the big uneven meadows.

Here there was shadow as well as sunshine, from the oaks and chestnuts that scattered the meadows and provided shade for the herd of cows that Farmer Miles moved from one field to another throughout the summer. They followed the well-worn track across the first meadow, then climbed through a gap in the hedge so that they were in a steeper, more bumpy field, streaked by marshy patches where the underground streams ran and dotted by cowpats. The field was less pleasant than the first one but it was also more secluded, and as such had a magic of its own. The steep little banks were covered with springy grass and a carpet of tom thumbs and the occasional thistle scratched at Barbara's bare ankles.

As the path flattened and widened Barbara fell into step beside Huw and linked her arm through his.

'Huw, I was so sorry to hear about Claire.'

'Thank you.' Claire seemed to belong to another life now; he realised with a shock he had not thought about her once since Amy had spoken to him last night about Barbara's troubles.

'It must have been terrible for you.'

'Yes.'

'Don't you want to talk about it?'

'No.' He turned, looking at her directly. 'I want to talk about you.'

'Me?'

'Yes, you. You're not happy, are you, Barbara?'

'Of course I'm happy.' But her eyes were giving the lie to the words.

'Tell me about it,' he said.

She shrugged helplessly. 'I wouldn't know where to begin. Anyway you don't want to hear about my problems.'

'Barbara, I have always wanted to hear about your

problems. Do you remember when that Riddle boy was bothering you? You didn't want to tell Amy, but you told me. And I sorted it out for you, didn't I?'

'Yes, but that was just childhood problems. This is different. We're grown up now. We don't just think molehills are mountains. They really are.'

'All the more reason why you should share them. I want to know.'

'It sounds as if you already do. I suppose Mum has been talking to you. She shouldn't have. She had no right.'

'She's worried about you – and so am I. But she only told me what she knew. She said you haven't talked to her for months.'

'Talking does no good. I'm married to him, Huw. That's all there is to it. I made my bed and now I have to lie on it.' She gave a small strangled laugh. 'That might almost be funny if it were true. The thing is we don't often lie on it – not together anyway. Thank goodness.'

'Oh Barbara.'

They were at the edge of the field, near the hedge. He sat down, pulling her down beside him. She sat upright, her feet drawn up beside her, pulling blades of grass and splitting them as if her life depended on it.

'Tell me,' he said.

She shook her head. She did not want to talk about it even to Huw. She did not want to think about the coldness interspersed with childish outbursts or the anger that seemed necessary to arouse him. And she did not want to admit even to Huw that her husband was one big sham, not a hero at all but a rank coward. That was the final indignity. If he had lost his reason through the trauma of war yet been a hero she could have stood it. But he was not a hero. When danger had threatened he had failed and in doing so had failed her too, negated her dreams, demeaned her somehow. With

514

her head she had tried to understand and in part had done so. But her heart had refused to follow. To the outside world she could make excuses for him. But there was no remedy for her loss of respect for him. Nothing could erase her shame and scorn.

Tears blurred her eyes and she turned away so that Huw should not see them.

'He doesn't hurt you, does he?' Huw asked. His voice was ragged.

She could not answer.

'Barbara?' His hand gripped her arm. 'Does he hurt you?'

She swallowed, wishing she could lie, knowing she could not.

'Not very often.'

'Bastard!' He spat it out between gritted teeth.

She twisted her head quickly. Her eyes were agonised. 'He's sick. He can't help it . . .'

'He'd be sick if I got my hands on him.'

'Oh no, Huw, you mustn't . . .' She reached across, laying a restraining hand on his arm. At her touch she felt the muscle quiver and her breath caught in her throat. For long moments they sat unmoving, looking at one another as they had outside the house, only now Barbara felt as if all the life force was draining out of her limbs and she was being drawn up like a magnet into his eyes. Time was suspended. Then the magnetic pull grew stronger and they were moving almost imperceptibly closer, closer, until she could see only the blurred outline of his cheek and chin. She felt her lips tremble, drawn by that same magnetic force. They hovered, a breath away from his, then they were touching, clinging.

He raised his hand to her face, brushing the curls away and leaving his hand there cupping her ear and holding her head steady while he kissed her. After a moment they drew apart, looking at one another with

515

that same intensity, then they came together all of a rush as if they could no longer bear the wasted years.

'Barbara . . . Barbara . . .'

'Oh Huw . . .'

The excitement was now a tight spiral at the very core of her sending tiny sharp shivers to spread through her like ripples from a stone thrown into a pond. The light breeze which stirred the grass whispered over her skin and started a million pinpricks of awareness. Her whole body, it seemed, was sensitised, her soul a deep pool of longing and she was drowning in it.

Almost without being aware of moving she sank back into the grass, saw his face above her blotting out the sky, smelled his sunwarmed skin, felt the hard rippling muscles of his back beneath her hands as he leaned over her. Her heart was full. This was right. So right. They were together, isolated from the world by their love. He kissed her again, pushing back her dress from her shoulders and buried his face against her. The touch of his lips made her shiver again, a shiver of delight that linked the very core of her to the place where his mouth was pressed against her breast. The beauty of it made her weak. She shifted slightly beneath his weight and the grass scratched the back of her neck, but she was unaware of it except as a part of the overwhelming beauty of the whole. He took her gently with a restrained passion that made her ache with the need to be one with him, lifting her through the planes of delight to a pinacle of vibrant ecstacy, heights she had never dreamed existed, up, up, until she thought she would faint with the completeness of it. And then it was over and she was drifting back down the same path, warmed now, replete with love, until at last she lay contented in his arms.

He rolled away and she half turned with him, unwilling to relinquish the contact, her face still buried in the open neck of his shirt, tasting the salt of his skin.

For long moments they lay there in one another's arms, the grass scratching beneath her bare legs, the sun warming above. She wanted to sleep, sleep here in this cave of love and seclusion, with the only sounds the drone of bumble bees in the clover and the distant lowing of one of Farmer Miles's cows in the field beyond. But Huw moved, raising himself on one elbow and looking down at her.

'I love you, Barbara.'

'And I love you.'

'I've always loved you.'

'I know.' It seemed like nothing less than the truth now; she *had* always known. 'I've always loved you too.'

A moment's silence. Then he said: 'You will leave him, won't you?'

It was as if someone had doused her with a bucket of cold water, shocking her back to reality. If he had said those same words a moment ago when she had been drifting on that beautiful plane she would have had no doubts. But now the real world had come close again.

'Leave him?' she echoed.

'Yes. You can't stay with him now. I won't let you. Not now.'

'Oh Huw.' She sat up, covering her face with her hands. She did not want to face reality. Not yet. But there was no escaping it.

'Look, I know it's not easy with a war on,' he said. 'It's almost impossible to plan from one week to the next and I have to be honest, I haven't had time yet to work out how we can manage to be together. But I will. Leave Marcus, bring Hope and live with your mother for a time – she'll be only too pleased to have you, I know. And as soon as I can work something out I'll send for you.'

She swallowed. Her throat was aching. 'I couldn't do that.'

517

He tutted. 'Of course, I know it's not ideal. I suppose if you really wanted to stay with Amy it wouldn't be so bad. Now I'm to be based at Exeter it's not that far away. And to be honest I don't think the war is going to last that much longer anyway. Then things will be much more settled.'

'No,' she said in a small voice. 'You don't understand. I can't leave Marcus.'

'What do you mean, you can't leave him?' He was sitting up too now and there was an angry edge to his voice, a cover for emotion.

'I can't leave him.' She felt small and lost, yet quite sure of what she had to do. 'I married him. He needs me.'

'But you don't love him.'

'No, but what has that to do with it?'

'Everything. You don't love him. He doesn't even treat you properly. I won't let you go back to him. You can't!'

'I have to. I don't know what would happen to him if I left him. He'd fall to pieces completely. He might even commit suicide. He's threatened to. If that happened I'd never forgive myself.'

'That's his problem.'

'And mine too. I'm his wife. He's sick, Huw. I couldn't be happy with you if . . .' Her voice tailed away as imagined horrors paraded before her eyes. 'Besides,' she went on, 'there's Hope. He'd never let me take her. I told Mum that. Can't you imagine what would happen? The Spindlers would fight for her. There would be a terrible tug-of-war. Suppose I was to lose?'

'You wouldn't lose. No court would take a child away from her mother without a very good reason.'

'The Spindlers could be reason enough. I can't risk it, Huw.' She covered his hand with hers. 'Not even for you.'

Their eyes met. He saw the absolute decision in hers

and dropped his own. For a moment they sat in silence. Then he said, 'Well, what are you going to do?'

Her resolve wavered. 'I don't know.'

He curled his fingers round her wrist. 'I'm not letting you go again, Barbara. Not now.'

'No,' she said. 'Oh no. Please don't let me go, Huw. I couldn't bear it.'

'Though I don't know how I can bear to let you go back to him.' His voice had a hard edge. 'To know you're with him – to wonder what he's doing to you . . .'

She made up her mind. 'I'll tell him I want separate rooms. I'll go that far. Only I can't leave him. Not at the moment.'

'And we'll stay in touch?'

'Oh yes, yes please. You can write to me at Mum's. She'll pass the letters on to me. And we'll meet whenever we can. How long are you here for?'

'Fourteen days.'

'Can I see you? Every day?'

'Try keeping me away!'

'Oh Huw . . .'

He pushed her back into the grass and once again she forgot everything but his nearness as he kissed her, caressed her and their bodies met in a fusion of love.

'Why did you leave me?' Barbara asked. 'All that time ago, why did you write and tell me to find someone else?'

They were in the field again; over the past week it had become their special place where they could be alone together, talking, loving, cherishing the stolen moments. Every day she had walked from Hillsbridge House to Valley View with Hope in the pushchair, then left the child in Mrs Milsom's care while she and Huw were together. The housekeeper had been wonderful. She asked no questions, made no comment about their

519

preoccupation with one another, yet seemed to understand their need for privacy. Her support was unexpected for she came of a generation raised on strict propriety, but in this instance her collusion was absolute. Perhaps it was because she had never liked Marcus, Barbara thought, whereas over the years she had grown as fond of Huw as the son she herself had never had and this was her way of 'getting her own back' at the golden boy from the leisured classes she so resented. Or perhaps over the years she had secretly hoped that the undeniable bond between Barbara and Huw would deepen into love and cement together the family which had become her life. Whatever the reason, she had made things easy for them and Barbara was filled with warmth and gratitude.

The weather, too, seemed to be on their side. The skies remained high and blue and the air warm and what rain there was fell at night and was gone again by morning.

'Why did you write me that dreadful letter telling me to forget you?' Barbara asked again. 'Was it because you thought I was too young?'

It never occurred to her to ask if it had been because he had not loved her. She knew now that could not have been the reason.

Huw was silent for a moment. Obviously Amy had never told Barbara of her fears. He sought around for an answer and decided on the truth.

'Amy thought you were my sister.' He felt her stiffen. 'It's not true,' he said quickly. 'But she thought we shared the same father. Haven't you ever wondered why she took me in? Well, that was the reason. She thought Llew was my father.'

'But he wasn't?' Barbara said after a moment.

'No. I discovered the truth too late. I was going to tell you everything was all right – there was nothing to stop us being together. But then I was shot down and by the time I got back to this country you were married.'

'Oh my God,' she said. Her thoughts were churning. 'You mean . . . ?'

'You can understand how I felt, stuck in France, knowing you were carrying on with that . . . that bastard . . . and not able to do anything about it.'

'Yes.' Tears began to roll down her cheeks. 'Oh Huw, if only I'd known! I thought you didn't want me. I was trying to forget you and Marcus seemed so charming. But I'd never have rushed into marrying him if it hadn't been for thinking you didn't want me. I was just trying to forget.'

'I know.' And he did. Somehow without long explanations they were both able to read the other's thoughts. But there was still something he had to ask her. 'Have you told him yet that you want separate rooms?'

She was silent for a moment. She could not lie to him, yet did not want to tell him the truth either, that she had not yet summoned up the courage to make the final break.

'I haven't had the chance yet. But I will.'

'Oh Barbara! I can't bear to think of you with him.'

'It's all right,' she said hastily. 'He hasn't touched me. He very often doesn't – for weeks on end.'

'Well, I hope he doesn't. And I hope you soon find the opportunity to tell him. You're mine!' His voice was fierce, his hands on her shoulders demanding and proprietorial.

'Oh yes, I'm yours,' she whispered and let him push her back into the grass.

27

On Huw's last evening Barbara dined with the family at Valley View. Marcus had had to be invited too, but he had declined, pleading a prior engagement with the manager of one of the Spindler farms, and Barbara was relieved. It was bad enough sitting through the meal with only Amy, Ralph and Maureen to witness her efforts to hide her misery, if Marcus had been there as well it would have been impossible.

As always on occasions such as this Mrs Milsom had excelled herself and in spite of the shortages the meal was superb – Barbara found herself wondering how the family were going to manage with their rations for the remainder of the week. But doing justice to it was an impossibility. The food stuck in her throat and she felt faintly sick. Each time her eyes met Huw's she tried to smile, but the clock on the mantelshelf was ticking the minutes away and the despair gathered within her until it was almost akin to panic.

They were talking but the conversation seemed to spiral over her head.

'I don't know how much longer I shall be flying special ops,' Huw was saying in answer to a question Ralph had asked him. 'The more of France that is liberated the less need there will be for my brand of specialised pick-ups. I could end up doing nothing more exciting than transport services – and maybe a parachute drop or two over Germany if I'm lucky.'

His words penetrated through to her and Barbara looked at him sharply. Was this how the dangers of war had affected Huw? Would he ever be able to settle to a normal life again or would he continually seek the thrill of danger to set adrenalin pumping like a drug through his veins?

When Mrs Milsom had removed the dishes they sat for a while around the table, then moved to the drawing-room. Barbara sat beside Huw on the low comfortable settee, aching to touch him yet knowing she must not. Whatever their relationship in private, however aware the others were of it, in public propriety must be maintained.

At last Ralph moved.

'I don't want to break up this party but I'm afraid I must. It's a working day tomorrow.'

Barbara stood up. Her limbs felt like lead. At least Huw was going to drive her home in Amy's car (his own had no petrol in it though it was still in the garage under wraps) and they would have that little time together. But on the short journey she could not bring herself to speak. If she did she was quite certain she would break down altogether.

Huw turned into the drive of Hillsbridge House. Behind the blackout it looked dark and unfriendly against the deep violet of the sky. He pulled into the yard at the side of the house, well out of view of those blacked-out windows, and turned off the engine.

'Oh Barbara, I wish I could take you with me.'

'I wish you could.'

Such ordinary words, filled with so much emotion.

He reached for her and they were in each other's arms, kissing, clinging, each unwilling to let the other go.

'You will write?'

'Try to stop me! And you will tell Marcus – separate rooms?'

'I will, I promise. I couldn't bear it now if he . . .'

'Oh Barbara, I love you.'

'I love you.'

More kisses. More caresses, increasingly frantic.

'I want you!'

'We can't! Not here!'

'There's nobody about.'

'No!' But they did. It was awkward and fumbled, yet equally as loving as any of their unions.

Afterwards she said: 'I'll have to go.'

'You can't. I won't let you.'

'I have to!' Her panic had a new dimension now, a dark fear she could not explain. At last he released her.

'Go on then.'

'Huw . . .'

'Go on, quickly, before I change my mind, start this car and get the hell out of it taking you with me.'

'Huw . . .'

'For God's sake, Barbara, go!'

She went, kissing him one last time. He waited until he saw her open the door of the house then drove away. She watched his tail lights disappear down the tree-lined drive and the tears ran unchecked down her face. But they did nothing to ease the bleakness in her heart. When she could no longer see the lights or hear the engine she went in, shutting the door behind her.

There was no sound from any of the downstairs rooms. The Spindlers had all retired to bed. She crept upstairs, hoping Marcus was asleep. More darkness. But when she opened the door of their room and entered stealthily the light snapped on.

'Where the hell have you been?'

He was standing by the window and the blackout curtain was slightly awry. His hair was a little tousled and he was wearing his silk dressing gown. Barbara's eyes flicked to the bed; the covers were thrown back untidily as if he had already been in bed and jumped up hastily to look out of the window – when he heard the engine of the car, perhaps? Hot colour flooded her cheeks and automatically her hands flew to check the buttons of her dress and pat her hair into place.

It was a mistake. She saw his eyes narrow.

'We stayed talking. There was such a lot to say since it's Huw's last night.' She knew she was babbling.

'You were with him.'

'He brought me home, yes.' No point denying it. 'Someone had to. You wouldn't expect me to walk.'

'You've been out there with him close on an hour.'

'Oh surely not!'

'You think I don't know? I've been here watching and waiting. You must have had a hell of a lot to say!'

'We did – I told you . . .'

He came towards her. His eyes were bright with the fever she had grown to fear. She took a step backwards but his hand shot out, gripping her arm.

'If you let him touch you, I'll kill you!'

'Marcus – please – you're hurting me!'

'And I'll hurt you more before we're through. You are my wife and don't you forget it!' His hand was a vice on her arm; still holding her fast he ripped open her blouse. She sobbed.

'Marcus! Stop it!'

He ignored her, freeing one breast from its covering of silk and lace. She sobbed again as he pushed her back towards the bed.

'Marcus!'

He was on top of her now, one hand covering her mouth to stop her cry. Her skirt he bunched up, tearing at her panties. She struggled, knowing it was useless but desperate to stop him. She couldn't let him take her now, with the touch of Huw's body still on hers. His weight was squeezing the breath out of her, his knee forcing her legs apart. As he entered her she threw back her head, closing her eyes tightly, her lips parted in a silent scream. He moved in her roughly, his body tearing at her tender membranes, still moist thankfully from her time with Huw, and she lay submissive now, knowing there was no point in resisting further.

When it was over she lay feeling used and sore. Then her anger began, creeping slowly through her, until it built to a crescendo. She jumped up, pulling her torn dress round her and facing him with fire in her eyes.

'How dare you!' she blazed. 'How dare you do this to me?'

'I'm your husband!'

'Yes, God help me, you are! But I won't be used like this. Not ever again. I want my own room. With a lock on the door. If you won't give it to me, I'm leaving you!'

His supremacy had been expended along with his twisted lust. He looked like a frightened small boy.

'Barbara . . .'

'I mean it!' she said. 'I won't sleep with you any more, Marcus.' She turned her back on him, collecting her hairbrush from the dressing table, her nightdress in its case from the pillow. 'For tonight I'll sleep in Hope's room. After that you can work something out. This is a big house. There are plenty of rooms in this wing. Deny me one of them and I leave.'

'Please . . .' He was crying now. She looked at him scornfully.

'I don't care what you tell your mother and father, or if you tell them at all. But as far as I am concerned, Marcus, our marriage is over. Do you understand?'

She swept into Hope's room. Miraculously, the child was still sleeping peacefully, one thumb in her mouth. Barbara leaned over her protectively for a moment, half expecting Marcus to follow her. He did not. She collapsed onto the bed that had been provided for the nanny they had never employed, her anger dying once more into despair, and wept as if her heart would break.

28

If the first five years of the war had dragged by interminably the last months seemed like a lifetime. Everyone had assumed that once a successful invasion had been launched in France, the Third Reich and its allies would collapse. France had been liberated, it was true, but as Christmas approached things dragged on with the boys still in uniform, the Japanese fighting for their lives and their prisoners as far from being freed as ever.

At the beginning of December the Home Guard were stood down in a grand Final Parade, when two hundred out of the two hundred and sixty-four members presented themselves for a final march through Hills-bridge. 'We shall be forming an Old Comrades Association,' Ralph told Amy after she had watched, moist-eyed. 'It's important that we keep all the old ties intact when things get back to normal.'

One family, however, approached Christmas in a happy mood. Margaret and Harry had set the wheels in motion to formally adopt Marie and for the first time since she had grown to love the little girl, Margaret felt a glow of security and happiness as she pinned up the paper chains Marie had glued together and wrapped parcels in sheets of wrapping paper she had saved from last year and carefully ironed to remove the creases.

Thankfully, Marie seemed to have recovered from her ordeal very well. She had settled back into the bedroom she had once shared with Elaine with remarkably little fuss and though she had become a little tearful when the Christmas decorations came out and she saw the squashed trimmings she and Elaine had made the previous year, Margaret never once heard her cry for her mother.

In a way, Margaret supposed, it was as if she had lost her at the beginning of the war when they had been evacuated; the brief reappearance of Mrs Cooper had been a little like a dream to the child whose roots now seemed to be firmly entrenched in Hillsbridge.

As always the Hall clan gathered at Greenslade Terrace for tea on Christmas Day, though for the first time ever Charlotte had been persuaded not to cook her own Christmas dinner but to go instead to Margaret and Harry's. Theirs had been only one of a number of invitations, which she had turned down for various reasons.

Jack and Stella had asked her to stay with them at Minehead over the holiday but she had not wanted to go so far away from the rest of the family even though they had all thought the change would do her good; Dolly's house was too far for her to walk back in the afternoon in time to prepare the family tea she was determined to put on as usual, since Victor had no transport except for his trusty bicycle; and she could not face the thought of waiting until the evening for her main meal as she would have had to do if she had gone to Amy's. So, instead, she accepted the invitation to spend the first part of the day with Harry and Margaret, who were also entertaining Margaret's mother, Gussie. The two women had never been close, in spite of their relationship by marriage, but since they were both now widowed they formed a slightly awkward alliance, sitting together on the front room settee to chat whilst Margaret prepared lunch, sipping the sweet sherry that Harry poured for them and taking it in turns to help Marie crochet with the brightly coloured oddments of cotton which Father Christmas had left for her in her stocking.

Lunch and the ritual of listening to the King's

Speech over, it was time for Charlotte to go home and prepare for her guests. The plan had been for Gussie, Margaret and Harry to spend the remainder of the day at Margaret's house, but by this time Charlotte and Gussie were getting along so well that she and the others were readily persuaded to join the gathering at Greenslade Terrace.

There was method in Charlotte's madness. She wanted the house to be as full as was humanly possible in order to help her through this first Christmas without James. That morning, waking for the first time to find herself quite alone in the house on Christmas morning, she had felt more lonely and vulnerable than ever before, even in the early days after James's death, and the carols that were being played when she tuned in on her wireless and the shrieks of children along the Ranks as they showed off their presents to one another only served to heighten the feeling of isolation. She had wept quietly over her cup of morning tea, remembering the days when her own house had been full of love and laughter, impatient with her own self-pity, yet quite unable to stop the tears.

The loneliness had ebbed a little in the warmth and companionship at Margaret's house but once back in Greenslade Terrace it returned once more, in spite of the arrival of Dolly and Victor with Noel, whose birthday it was, and who was still as boisterous as if he were eight instead of eighteen, Jim, Sarah and May with May's two little terrors and the Porter contingent. No matter how many of them there were in the house, they could not fill the gap left by dear quiet James; though he had seldom contributed more than a word or two to the proceedings his absence was a raw wound, a void in Charlotte's heart which she knew would never be filled. And there were other gaps, too – Alec, Fred and Bob, and Huw and Barbara, besides Jack and Stella and Ted and Rosa whose absence, though customary now, was still a cause for regret.

'If they were all here we'd never get into the house!' Charlotte thought with a wry smile as she sliced Christmas cake, made from the special wartime recipe, but that did not stop her from thinking how wonderful it would be to have all her family under one roof.

Ah well, perhaps next year . . .

Perhaps, by next year the war would be over and all the wanderers returned at least, safe and well, please God . . .

Charlotte, though once a staunch chapel-goer, was not a woman who often prayed. But she prayed now, silently and fervently, that soon this terrible everlasting war would end and they would all be together again.

The end came haltingly, not with one great final moment of glory, but in a series of death-throes for Hitler's Germany and the regime which had threatened the whole of the civilised world.

For a week before the end finally came the wireless was predicting victory, but the whole country was too war-weary and worn down to jump for joy as it had at the end of the Great War. The pictures of Mussolini and his mistress hanging upside down on a Milan lampbracket after being shot by Communist partisans caused a mild stir when they appeared in the newspapers and Charlotte, amongst others, branded the display of the mistress's voluminous undergarments as disgusting. But since Italy had been out of the war now for almost two years it was not an event of any great significance.

Much more heartening was the news, two days later, that Hitler and Eva Braun, whom he had married the previous day, had killed themselves in Hitler's bunker and that their bodies had been burnt in the yard outside. But still the end did not come for there was a new name to be reckoned with – one which few people had heard before – Admiral Doenitz. Although he made an attempt to end the war on the western front whilst continuing the fight against the Russians, this proposal was rejected and so for more confusing days the news remained inconclusive.

'I don't know, they seem to be enjoying themselves!' Stanley Bristow remarked in the bar of the Miners Arms. 'Would'st think they'd be only too pleased to end it, wouldn't 'ee? But no. They've still got to hang on to their little bit of power.'

It was a sentiment echoed wholeheartedly by the other men.

'I'm going to tell 'ee some'ut,' Stanley went on. 'I blame Churchill meself. He's a warmonger, al'us was.'

There was a moment's shocked silence. To criticise Winnie out loud was to commit a heresy of the worst kind. But privately many of them agreed. All very well to have a leader of Winnie's stature to lead them into battle. Now all any of them wanted was a bit of peace.

'T'wouldn't surprise me if Atlee don't get in next time,' Walter Brixey said. 'One thing's for sure – I shall be voting for 'im.'

The others nodded. But that was no 'turn up for the books', as Walter might have phrased it. Hillsbridge miners were Labour to a man and had been from the moment the party had risen from obscurity.

On the evening of 7th May, Londoners at least decided they had waited long enough. With the announcement of Victory in England imminent, thousands converged on the West End and the sky which had once been lit up by the Blitz glowed red for victory as bonfires blazed throughout the capital, rockets streaked into the sky and a pile of straw filled with thunder-flashes salvaged from some military dump cracked and spurted darts of flame. But though London might have gone mad with uncontrollable joy, the more conservative Hillsbridge waited for the official announcement before joining in the celebrations.

It came at 3 p.m. the following day.

Charlotte heard it in Peggy Yelling's kitchen where they and Colwyn, who had abandoned work for the day and shut up the shed where he carried on his boot-mending business, were gathered around Peggy's wireless set. As the stentorian voice boomed out above the crackling air waves there was a hush in the kitchen, broken only by the fall of the coals in Peggy's fire.

'Yesterday morning at 2.41, at General Eisenhower's Headquarters, General Jodl, representative of the German High Command and of Grand Admiral Doenitz, designated head of the German State, signed an act of unconditional surrender of all German land, sea and air forces in Europe to the Allied Expeditionary Force and simultaneously to the Soviet High Command.'

'What's he say?' Colwyn, who had been slightly deafened in the trenches in the Great War, enquired, and the others shushed him to silence, straining to hear every word. Only as it came to an end with the stirring words: 'Advance Britannia! Long live the cause of freedom! God Save the King!' did they break into uninhibited cheers.

'It's over, Lotty! It's over!'

'Oh Peg, thank the Lord!'

'It's over! Colwyn, see if there's a drop of sherry left over from Christmas in the sideboard. I'm sure we didn't finish it all. This calls for a celebration if anything does!'

The sherry was found, the glasses carefully dusted out and they were drinking a toast to victory when there was a knock on the door, which was then immediately opened before Peg could reach it.

'Have you heard the news? Were you listening to the wireless?' It was Molly Clements, Walter's wife. She was invited in and another glass dusted out and filled.

'Oh, it's lovely! It's over – it's over!'

'I've still got the Jubilee bunting in the cupboard under the stairs. We ought to put it out.'

'They're selling bunting down at the Co-op too – they took it off the rations as long as it's red, white and blue!'

'Well, whatever colours would we want, I'd like to know!'

'We must have a bit of a "do". I've got a tin of salmon and some evaporated milk.'

'I've got a couple of bottles of fruit.'

'And a blancmange.'

'Oh, thank the Lord it's over! I can't believe it, really I can't!'

Warmed by the sherry they caught one another's waists and began to dance so that the Yelling cat, Fluffy, whose tail was inadvertently trodden on, ran yowling out of the house and still they laughed, too delighted to care about anything but that at last, at last, there would be no more air raids or clothing coupons, no more blackout, no more goodbyes to loved ones off to fight a war from which they might never return.

'Oh, give me land, lots of land, and a starry sky above. Don't fence me in!' Peggy sang loudly and tunelessly, and the others joined in.

After six long years it was freedom, wonderful freedom. For the moment all cares were forgotten and it seemed that nothing else mattered.

Barbara listened to the broadcast alone on the small modern wireless set in her room with Hope crawling around her feet playing with a wooden duck-on-wheels. She immediately went in search of her mother-in-law, but Lady Spindler as always refused to be excited by the news.

'We've known it was coming. Didn't they celebrate it in London last night?'

'Yes, but it's still wonderful news that it's official.'

'Yes, dear, it is,' Lady Erica said and her emotionless calm made Barbara ache for the spontaneity of her own family.

A few minutes later her unspoken wish was realised when Maureen, unable to restrain her excitement, telephoned.

'Isn't it great? Isn't it super-whizz-cracko?'

'Yes. Yes, it is! Oh Maureen, I'm so glad you rang! My mother-in-law is taking it so calmly I could hit her!'

'Oh Babs, I wish you were here! I do miss you. And you know what it means, don't you? Huw will be able to come home if he wants to!'

'Oh yes!'

Huw. Her heart leaped at the thought. It seemed so long since she had seen him now. Shortly after their last parting he had been transferred to the north of Scotland, flying Beaufighters over the North Sea and the Norwegian coastal areas. They had corresponded regularly, long loving letters, but the arrival of each letter, longed for though it was, only increased her restlessness and the deeply felt yearning. But though Maureen's words started that leap of joy, she knew that the end of the war would make no difference at least to their separation. Huw would not be among those to come home. He had always intended to make the RAF his career. And besides, with things as they were . . .

Much as she longed to see him, desperately as she ached for his touch, she knew it was better that he did not come home. If he were here she could not bear to go on living this lie with Marcus. And, for the moment, she was still determined this was what she had to do.

Later, perhaps, when Hope was older or when Marcus stabilised a little, but not now, not yet.

At least Marcus was leaving her alone now. Since

534

that terrible night when Huw had gone and she had moved into Hope's nursery, he had made no attempt to touch her and for that at least she was grateful. If he had tried she thought she would have killed him. Relations were strained between them, naturally, but it was a long while since they had been otherwise and Barbara lavished all her love and pent-up affection on Hope, who was growing into a lovely child, a little spoiled, perhaps, but a bundle of fun and laughter for all that. Barbara had begun to teach her her letters and bright as she was Hope was already learning to recognise them. Barbara was proud of her, proud of her bright gold hair and pert pretty little face, proud of her small sturdy body and lively intelligent mind.

'You're not a bit like your Daddy. You're mine, all mine!' Barbara would whisper to her as she hung over the cot when the child was sleeping.

Sometimes she regretted the fact that Hope was an only child. She would have liked her to have companionship, a little brother or sister to play with, fight with, and love. But she did not want it so much as to submit to Marcus's so-called lovemaking and besides, she did not want Marcus's baby. She wanted Huw's.

There had been a time, soon after he had left, when she had wondered if she might be pregnant. The thought had half thrilled, half frightened her. And with it had been the dread that if she were pregnant she would not know for certain who was the father – or not for nine months anyway. Then she would have known, she felt sure, for Huw's child would certainly have something of him about it. He would be dark, for one thing – for dark hair always takes precedence over fair, or so she had been told. There would be some signs of Huw's strong features. And it would be a boy. Huw's son. The thought made her go weak inside as she allowed herself the luxury of imagining the joy of it – bearing Huw's son.

But she was not pregnant and after the initial disappointment she realised it was probably the best thing. One day, God willing, she would be able to be the mother of his children. But not yet. Not yet.

And so life had gone on . . . Day after day, night after night, doing what she had to do, caring for Hope, humouring Marcus, making conversation with her parents-in-law, visiting her mother, working occasionally for some war charity, and always keeping the dream alive in her heart.

She and Huw, one day, one day when it was all over . . .

It had seemed to her that the end of the war would somehow signify the moment for change, that when the world returned to normal her life too would move into a different plane. She had not stopped to wonder why she felt this but it had comforted her all the same.

Well, now the war was over. And suddenly it came to Barbara that unless she did something about it, it would make no difference to her life. None at all. The joy died in her.

'Babs – are you still there, Babs?' Maureen asked.

'Yes, I'm here.'

'Are you all right?'

'Yes.' She glanced down at Hope. The child had tired of playing quietly with the duck on wheels and was now banging it noisily against the leg of one of the nursery chairs. 'Tell Mrs Milsom to set an extra place for dinner. I don't care what anyone says – tonight I'm coming home!'

For the POWs in the east, VE day went by unheralded and unsung. For though Germany had been vanquished, the Japanese were still deeply embroiled in their own war, battling and counter battling with the Allied forces in every part of the Pacific.

Alec Hall spent VE day just as he had spent every day for the last three years, under armed guard in his prison camp in the Malay peninsula. Once there had been a time when the Jap guns had been needed to keep the raggle of prisoners under control. No more. The steamy tropical climate, flies, disease and starvation had proved better policemen than the guards ever could. The men had been marched from place to place until they dropped and then marched again, to work day after endless day on the building of the Burma railroad. When they faltered they were urged on by rifle butts, when they fell they were trampled and left to die. Disease had taken its toll. Malaria, dysentry and beri-beri were rampant and wounds which festered in the mosquito-ridden heat killed many more.

Alec had suffered a tropical ulcer and he had seen half his leg rot away before an Australian medical officer, himself trembling with fever, had amputated it. For weeks Alec had lain close to death, then somehow, miraculously, his body had reasserted itself and he had recovered. He had thought it was the end for him – as he could no longer march with the others he thought the Japs would finish him off, but luck sent a new Commander to his camp, a man with more humanity than Alec had come across in his dealings with the sour little yellow men, and he was found jobs to do around the camp.

Whilst others died like flies, Alec somehow survived. Perhaps it was his wiry build which saved him, for always it seemed it was the biggest and strongest of the men who succumbed to the terrible conditions. Weak, thin as a skeleton, eyes sunken in their sockets, skin yellowed and covered with sores, armpits chafed by the makeshift crutches Alec had fashioned for himself, yet somehow alive, Alec waited for the end of the war which he knew, with typical Hall optimism, must one day come. And when he saw mate after mate buried in shallow graves marked only by a simple wooden cross, he held fast to his belief that he at least was not going to die in a foreign land.

England seemed like paradise in his tortured dreams, Bryda and Joan were like people he had known in another life. Time had ceased to exist beyond the cut he made daily in the wall of his hut to mark its passage; and even counting these he was unsure how many weeks, months or years had passed, for he had lost count during the time when he was feverish after the amputation of his leg and again during a bout of malaria.

To him, VE day was just another mark on the wall with nothing to make it different from all the other days. But as always when the heat began to make the steam rise in suffocating clouds from the jungle vegetation, when his wounds ached and his body felt too weak from exhaustion and starvation to carry on, he stopped to thank God that he, unlike so many of the others who had been taken prisoner with him, was alive.

That in itself was a victory.

For Harry VE Day held an extra edge of excitement.

'You know what it means, don't you?' he said to Margaret as they were getting ready for bed.

'Hmm?' Margaret enquired idly without turning round. She was standing at the window, luxuriating in the fact that there was no need now for blackout and watching the fireworks that were streaking bright paths of sparking light into the sky from the direction of the football field.

'The end of the war – you know what it will mean,' Harry said patiently.

'Yes. It will mean no more carrot cake and tins of Spam. We'll be able to get bananas again. I am looking forward to bananas! I've almost forgotten what they taste like, but I know I love them. Oh Harry – look at that rocket! What a beauty!'

'Never mind the rocket and the bananas. I'm talking about important things.'

'So am I. Bananas are very important. I could eat one right now . . .'

Harry buttoned his pyjama jacket.

'It's useless trying to talk to you in this mood.'

She turned away from the window, all contrite.

'I'm sorry, Harry. I'm just excited because it's all over. What do you want to talk to me about?'

'Nothing. It doesn't matter.'

She went across and put her arms around him, smiling up at him.

'Yes, it does. It mattered just now. So go on and tell me and don't sulk.'

'I was only going to say there could be a big change in our lives soon.'

'I know. No more Spam and plenty of bananas.' She giggled, then straightened her face. 'Sorry. I'm just finding it very difficult to be serious.'

'I know you are. But serious is just what you might have to be. The war is over, Margaret. The coalition government will come to an end. There'll be a General Election.'

'Oh!' Suddenly she was as sober as he was. 'You mean . . . ?'

'I mean that I shall be in the thick of things. I might even be elected. You could be an MP's wife before long.'

'Oh my goodness!' She dropped her arms as the full implications of it came to her, remembering that day when he had come home to discuss with her whether he should let his name go forward. It had seemed unreal then, just a very distant possibility. In the intervening years she had come to accept it as something which might one day happen without giving it much thought. Now, suddenly confronted by the imminent transformation of vague imaginings to reality, she felt swamped by the enormity of the way in which their lives could be changed forever.

'Oh Harry!' she said.

'I know. It's a bit staggering, isn't it?'

'You can say that again!' She looked up at him, anxious suddenly. 'You're not going to change your mind and back out, are you?'

He sat down on the edge of the bed. He, too, was thinking back in time, remembering a young man who had decided his mission in life was to improve the lot of working men like his father. He remembered the burning desire to see fair play for the men who gave their health and sometimes their lives to make the coal owners wealthy, the determination to fight, fight and fight again for those who were in no position to fight for themselves. He remembered the anger and impotence he had experienced watching fellow strikers make a fool out of poor old Nosey Parker when he had been forced to strike break in order to feed his family and the way his own resolve to change things had come with a far-sightedness which had been far beyond his tender years. And he remembered too the personalities who had influenced him – plucky, gritty little Mr Cook, General Secretary of the Federation, Owen Wynn-Jones with his rolling oration, even Margaret's own father, George Young, who had worked all his life with quiet passion and self-effacing dedication for the party he believed in.

Now, as he stood facing the very real possibility of his election to Parliament, it seemed to him to be a culmination of everything he had worked for. Every small effort came together to help make the whole – the nights when he and Margaret had sorted piles of used clothing donated to aid the families of impoverished miners during the General Strike of 1926, the political meetings, the circulars he had addressed, the errands he had run. All the studying that had gone into getting his Manager's ticket had played its part, too, just as he had known it would. Useless to be enthusiastic without having the necessary knowledge, qualifications and sheer weight to back it up. All his life, it seemed, he had been working towards this moment; now, daunting as it was, he felt the excitement bubbling in him like freshly poured champagne.

He looked at Margaret, at her eager face smiling up at him. She had been with him all the way. He could never have come this far without her.

He caught her hand, pulling her down so that she was kneeling between his knees. His chin rested against her hair, his eyes, staring across the top of her head into a future as uncharted as a stormy sea and as great a challenge.

'Oh no, I'm not going to change my mind now,' he said. 'Maybe I won't be elected, but if I am I promise you this. I shall go to Westminster prepared to work until I drop for the causes we both believe in. And I'll make damned sure that they sit up, all of them, and take notice of the ordinary working man.'

29

Just as Harry had predicted VE Day was closely followed by developments on the political front. In spite of Churchill's efforts to persuade the other parties that the coalition should continue until the end of the Japanese war, he finally decided that a General Election should be held in early July.

'Atlee will only guarantee the coalition until October,' Harry explained to Margaret. 'And Churchill won't go on that long with a General Election hanging over him.'

'I should think not!' Margaret retorted hotly. 'It's about time ordinary men and women had their say again – and I'm pretty sure what they will say too!'

Harry wished he had Margaret's faith; in spite of all his convictions he lacked her straightforward trust in the good sense of the British people. Churchill was riding high after leading them to victory. But Margaret remained convinced that this time, fielding more candidates than ever before, the Labour party would triumph.

'We've all had enough of this war,' she said simply. 'And besides, people won't have forgotten what happened after 1919. They were promised the earth then, too – and look what happened. The depression. Thousands of men with no work. Ordinary folk paying for a great act of folly. Oh no, they'll make sure that socialism gets a chance this time, I'm convinced of it. We've won the war, now we have to give everyone a chance to benefit from victory, not just those with power and money.'

Harry smiled. 'You put a good case. You should be on the platform, not me.'

Margaret smiled back. 'I believe in the cause and I

believe in you. That's all.' She did not add that there was a further reason for her optimistic mood. This was not the time, in her opinion, to complicate the issue by introducing personal matters.

In the run-up to the Election she worked tirelessly, making certain she was at Harry's side whenever possible. She wanted the world to know he had her complete support and besides, there were plenty of people who remembered her as George Young's daughter. If the memory of her father could swing a few extra votes Harry's way then Margaret was not above exploiting it.

Even Marie was pressed into action. Caught up in the wave of enthusiasm she soon learned to fold election addresses and stick down envelopes with the help of a pad of damp foam – though she had to be talked out of licking them, for unlike the other party helpers she actually liked the taste of the gum.

Voting day was 5th July and by the time the polls closed everyone in the Hall household was exhausted. There followed an unbearable wait for the results – three weeks until the votes of the widely scattered servicemen and women could be gathered together for counting. Those three weeks were the longest of Harry's life. Realising that his fate was already sealed in the ballot boxes, yet not knowing what it was, made for a tension which kept him on a knife edge of uncertainty. Margaret tried to persuade him to take a holiday without success. He had too much to do for that, he said, for work had taken second place to electioneering over the past weeks and no one could be appointed to take his place until the election results were known and it was certain that the union would be looking for a new agent.

The days dragged by and people followed the news of the war in the East while awaiting the results. The Japs were on the run now, the only question being how much longer they could hold out. The Philippines had been liberated, Japan itself had been attacked by air and sea, and the Allied troops were making advances in Borneo, but fierce fighting continued in New Guinea and Malaya. Still, surely it was only a matter of time . . . ?

At last, the waiting for the election results was almost over. The ballot boxes were collected, stacked and ready for the count just as if the election had taken place only yesterday instead of three weeks ago. Harry and Margaret went to the Victoria Hall where Harry's count was taking place, Harry now so tense with anxiety he could only pace and perspire in the oppressively hot room, Margaret still as serene as she had been all through the campaign.

'Stop worrying, Harry!' she said as the piles of his votes grew, dwarfing those of the Conservative candidate. 'You see – I told you. You're home and dry.'

But Harry was still afraid to be too optimistic.

'There are still a lot of boxes to be opened. Things could change yet.'

She shook her head. 'They won't. You'll be the next MP for this constituency, you'll see.'

Then it was completed. There was plainly no need for a recount – the thing Harry had most feared – but he had to be fetched from the Committee Room, the small kitchen behind the stage where he had retired exhausted to drink a half pint of beer, for the announcement of the result. As he took his place on stage with Margaret at his side she squeezed his hand and they exchanged smiles. The hall had an atmosphere of excited triumph, for here in the heartland of Labour supporters there were more than enough people delighted by the way things had gone to outweigh the long faces of the Conservatives.

As the result was announced a cheer went up to raise the roof – 'I should think they heard it over in South

Compton!' Margaret said later – and when Harry stepped forward to make his victory speech he had to wait a full minute before there was the slightest chance of being able to make himself heard.

Afterwards, he did his round of the hall shaking hands with all the party helpers, with an excited Marie, a huge red bow in her hair, hanging onto the tail of his jacket. The congratulations were endless, everyone wanted to slap Harry on the back and claim their part in making him their MP. Only Ted Phillips, the 'Union Man' from Midlington Pit, introduced a note of sadness.

'We shall miss you, Harry, darned if we shan't. You've done a good job for the lads. Still, I suppose our loss is Westminster's gain and if you can make our voice heard there it will have been worthwhile.'

Harry grasped the man's arm, all wiry muscle. 'I shall do my best, Ted, you may be sure of that,' he promised. 'This is what I've been working towards all my life. I don't intend to let the opportunity slip away now.'

Harry found Margaret in a corner of the hall talking to her mother. She looked tired now, whereas his own exhaustion had turned to adrenalin-releasing elation.

'I think it's time Margaret went home,' Gussie greeted him.

He looked at Margaret, surprised. 'What's the matter, love?'

'Nothing. I'm fine.' But she did indeed seem to be wilting.

'I'm sorry. I never thought. You seemed to be enjoying yourself.'

'I'm fine,' Margaret repeated. 'But I think I will go home all the same. I expect someone will take me if you're not ready to come yet. It's time Marie was in bed too,' she added.

'I'll have a word with Reg Morris. He's got his car,'

Harry said. 'I think I ought to stay on a bit longer.' He turned to Gussie. 'Aren't you going to congratulate me, Mum?'

She smiled, her sweet face an older version of Margaret's, and stood on tiptoe to kiss his cheek.

'Of course I am, Harry. I can hardly believe it – my son-in-law an MP! I just wish George was here to see it. He'd be so proud.'

'I know he would. And it's mainly due to him, you know. I'd never have had the courage to get started on this road if it hadn't been for George.'

'He was a great man,' Gussie said fondly. 'But I believe you'd have done it anyway, Harry. You always had the will. And now you've got a foot in the door you'll speak up for all the things you believe in. You'll do us proud at Westminster.'

'I'll certainly do my best,' Harry vowed. 'Now, if you really want to go, Margaret, I'll find Reg Morris and ask him to take you.'

'Thanks, love,' Margaret said.

She was in bed when he got home two hours later but not asleep.

'I'm so pleased for you!' she whispered as he climbed in beside her, too tired to have done anything but throw his clothes down in a heap in a corner of the bedroom, yet still strangely vibrant with excitement. 'I knew you could do it. Didn't I tell you so?'

'Yes you did. You had more faith than I did.' He suddenly remembered how tired she had looked when he had packed her into Reg Morris's car outside the Victoria Hall. 'Are you all right now?'

'Fine.'

'You suddenly went so quiet. It was all the excitement that did it, I suppose.'

She curled around him. 'Not just the excitement.'

He put an arm around her, pulling her head against his shoulder. Her body felt good, warm from the bed and soft. He thought he would like to make love to her.

'Why not just the excitement?' he asked lazily, trailing his hand across her shoulder to her breast.

For a moment she did not answer. Then she whispered: 'Are you sure you haven't had enough momentous news for one night?'

Something in her tone arrested his attention. His hand stopped moving on her breast. 'What do you mean?'

'I've got a piece of momentous news of my own. You've been so preoccupied with the campaign I've been saving it up. But I don't think I can keep it to myself any longer. I'm pregnant, Harry.'

He thought the beer he had been drinking on an empty stomach must have gone to his head; or that he was asleep already and dreaming.

'*What?*'

'I'm going to have a baby. After all this time.'

'Why didn't you tell me?'

'At first, I wanted to be sure. I didn't want to disappoint you. And then – well, as I said, you had other things on your mind. I thought I'd wait until I could claim your full attention.'

'Oh Margaret! That's wonderful! But will you be able to cope now I'm an Honourable Member? I'm going to be away a lot, bound to be. Are you . . . ?'

'Harry!' She was laughing now, a soft laugh, tired but happy. 'Of course I can cope!' She curled closer, moving his hand to cover her breast once more. 'And wasn't there something you had in mind just now – something to celebrate your becoming an MP – and a prospective father?'

He lay very still. 'But if you're pregnant we shouldn't take any chances, should we?'

'We won't be taking any chances,' she whispered.

547

'And I want to celebrate if you don't. Please make love to me, Harry.'

And tired as he was, overcome by heady joy, he acceded to her request.

On 6th August the US Air Force dropped an atomic bomb on Hiroshima and its reverberations echoed around the world.

'That's it – teach the buggers a lesson!' Ewart Brixey commented enthusiastically to the assembled regulars in the Miners Arms, but others, including Margaret and Harry, were shocked by the wanton destruction of life.

'Oh God, what is the world coming to?' Margaret asked, and Harry echoed her sentiments.

'Let's hope this is the end of it, and that this war really will be "a war to end wars", not like last time.'

But Harry couldn't see it. Sick and tired of fighting the people might be; but their leaders had tasted absolute power and he couldn't see them giving it up easily.

Two days later a second atomic bomb was dropped, this time on Nagasaki, and although less devastating than the one that had destroyed sixty per cent of Hiroshima, about forty thousand Japanese were killed. President Truman was in the ascendancy now, broadcasting threats to continue the destruction of Japan by atomic bombs unless she surrendered and the Soviet forces, too, were launching a powerful offensive. On 14th August Emperor Hirohito recorded a broadcast to the Japanese people; the following day it was played over the air to a disbelieving population, but it was another two long weeks before the official surrender was signed aboard the battleship *Missouri* in Tokyo Bay. And at long last the task began of freeing the Allied prisoners still held in Japanese hands.

Alec Hall was amongst the first to be freed. As the liberating troops marched through the Malay Peninsula finding camps that were tucked away in the jungle and prisoners who had rotted there since the surrender, shock waves echoed round the world. But Alec knew nothing of this. He was too sick to feel anything but mild relief when a convoy of trucks arrived to carry him and the others out of the camp. The previous evening they had taken a walk into the nearby village for the first time since they had been incarcerated but as they passed the weeping guards, the pits which had been dug ready for men to be machine-gunned into, and the makeshift Union Jack which the prisoners had sewn from scraps of red white and blue material and hoisted over the camp, Alec merely wondered where the hell he was going – and why. Like a caged bird suddenly afraid of freedom he wanted nothing but to go back inside the camp and stay there, unwilling to venture out again until the trucks came for him.

It was mid-September when he arrived back in Hillsbridge, bemused by all the changes that had taken place in his absence, unable to eat anything but the simplest food, and suffering from recurrent nightmares that he was about to be shot and his body tipped into the pit that he had seen dug outside the prison camp.

The family had arranged a party to welcome him home but when Sarah saw the state of him she cancelled it. 'I think all he wants is to be quiet,' she explained. So his visitors came instead in twos and threes – May and the children, Charlotte with Dolly, because they were afraid Charlotte would be too upset to see him alone, Amy and Ralph with a shocked Maureen.

'I've never seen anybody so thin!' she told Barbara afterwards. 'He's just like Farmer Miles's scarecrow, but burnt black by the sun. A sort of foreign scarecrow, if you know what I mean!'

When Alec had been home a week Alec had another visitor – Joan Tiley.

The last years of the war had been eventful for her. Her parents had moved to a small isolated cottage on the outskirts of Hillsbridge which gave Joan a long walk to the newsagent's shop where she worked and when the call had gone out for nurses Joan had answered it, choosing to work in Bristol rather than Bath. Her new life had widened her horizons and she had made many new friends including some men, but for her there would never be anyone but Alec. In spite of everything she loved him still and compared with him the others were but pale shadows.

After the family had heard that Alec had been taken prisoner she had written to him several times but had never received any reply and had no way of knowing whether her letters had reached him. When she learned that he was home it was almost a week before she could summon up the courage to go and see him. Whilst she had known he was a prisoner of war it had been possible to cling to her dream that when he returned everything would be as it had been in the past, long before Bryda Deacon had spoiled everything. Bryda had left Hillsbridge now, run off with a Polish airman, and Joan had felt that when Alec learned the news any feelings he might still have harboured for her would melt like snow in the Sahara. Surely he would not allow a moment's madness for a woman like that to spoil two lives? But now that Alec was back in Hillsbridge all Joan's doubts and fears returned and as she walked up the path to his mother's front door she was consumed with nervousness. Supposing Alec should treat her like a stranger? Worse, suppose he did not want to see her at all?

Sarah answered the door. She looked surprised to see Joan but not displeased. She had always liked the girl and had been thoroughly upset when Alec had jilted her.

550

'Joan! How nice to see you!' she greeted her.

Joan hesitated. 'I heard Alec was home. I wondered if he'd feel like a visitor.'

It was Sarah's turn to hesitate. This, perhaps, was exactly what Alec needed. But one could never be sure. He was so different now to the son who had gone to war, withdrawn, snappish if things did not please him, jumpy as a kitten.

'I don't know, dear. I'll see. Come inside and wait while I ask him.'

She disappeared into the living-room and was back after a moment.

'Come in, Joan. But I'm warning you, you may have a shock,' she added quietly.

Joan followed her into the living-room. Alec was sitting hunched in a chair by the fire wearing a woollen dressing gown over his clothes although it was a warm September day. His faced was pinched and blotchy, his eyes sunken and his hair was now thin over his sunburned scalp. A lump rose in Joan's throat. She did not know what to say.

From the depths of the chair Alec tried to move and Joan found her voice.

'Hello, Alec. Don't bother to get up. Stay where you are.'

'Hello, Joan.'

'Well, you're a fine one I must say,' she began. Then suddenly the words dried up, her inhibitions fell away and she ran across the room to where he was sitting. 'Oh Alec, thank God you're all right.'

'I'm not all right,' he said tetchily. 'I'm a bloody mess. And I've only got one leg.'

'But you're home.' She sank down onto her knees on the floor beside him. 'You don't know how I've prayed for this!'

He looked at her, mildly surprised. '*You* have?'

'Well, of course I have! Oh Alec . . .'

He moved irritably. 'Huh! So now I know who to thank for all those bloody months when I wished I was dead and out of it.'

Her head jerked up, her eyes full of horror.

It was a terrible thing to have said and he knew it. He'd been saying a lot of terrible things since he'd come home, almost as if he wanted to shock the family and friends who had lived here in comparative peace while he had been suffering untold torments at the hands of the Japs. They said they understood – but how could they? They talked blithely of their own sufferings and deprivations and it all sounded so petty that he could not resist jabbing at them time and again. Over the past week it had almost become a habit.

Now he looked at Joan, knew he had hurt her, and was sorry. She had come out of the goodness of her heart, because she cared for him in spite of what he had done to her, and he had taken the ground from under her feet.

'I'm sorry,' he said. 'Don't take any notice of me. This is what it damn well does to you, four years in a bloody Jap prison camp.'

She swallowed, trying to regain her composure.

'It's all right. I understand.'

'No, you don't,' he said. 'But don't let it worry you.'

'Alec . . .' Sarah was hovering anxiously, treading a fine line between upsetting her son and allowing him to upset Joan.

Joan looked up at her. 'It's all right, Mrs Hall,' was all she said, but her eyes spoke volumes.

'I'll go and put the kettle on,' Sarah said. Why was it that always at moments of crisis one turned to making a pot of tea?

'Well, Joan,' Alec said when she had gone. 'How's the world been treating you then?'

'Oh, all right. I've been nursing.'

'Not married then?'

552

She couldn't look at him. 'No.'

'Why not?'

'What sort of a question is that?'

'Quite a sensible one I should think. Most girls your age are married.'

'I was going to be married once, Alec, or have you forgotten?' Joan asked quietly. 'Perhaps that was enough for me.'

He nodded. His reactions were strange – slow and detached.

'What happened to the house?'

'We sold it. Your mother and father had your share to keep for you. Didn't they write to you about it?'

'Oh yes, I think they did.' It seemed so long ago now. 'Does Bryda still live down there?'

He saw the pain in her eyes again. She knew; oh yes, she knew.

'No, she's gone. Left her husband and ran off with a Pole.' She said it nonchalantly but it jolted him to the quick. Bryda had refused him because she had said she had to stay with her husband and then she had run off with a foreigner! Well, of all the . . . ! But it no longer mattered. Nothing much mattered any more.

'What are you going to do now you're home?' Joan asked.

He shrugged. 'What can I do? I'm a bloody crock. Now this show is over and all the men are coming home there won't be enough jobs to go round for those that are fit. I won't stand a chance.'

'Don't say that.'

'It's true. Who'd want me?'

She knelt up, taking his hands in hers. In spite of the warm room and the thick clothing he was wearing they felt like ice.

'I want you, Alec.' She was trembling. Dear God, she was laying it on the line, asking to be rejected for a second time.

'You can't.'

'But I do. I've always wanted you, only I was afraid to say so. I still do.'

'But I'm a crock!'

'Not to me. Let me help you, Alec. I can help you, I know it. I've been a nurse – well, not exactly, but I've got to know how to do all the messy jobs anyway, so looking after you would be dead easy and . . .'

'Thanks very much! I'm a messy job am I?'

'No! You know what I mean. Oh Alec . . .' She was scared suddenly, overcome by embarrassment at her own boldness. 'I'm sorry, I didn't mean to say any of this. I just came to see you. Perhaps I'd better go . . .' She went to get up. He reached out and took her hand, half expecting her to recoil from the almost claw-like yellowed fingers. She did not.

'I'm glad you came,' he said. 'Will you come again?'

Her eyes went moist. She bent down and touched the yellowed fingers with her lips.

'Oh Alec, of course I will – if you want me to.'

'I do,' he said.

It was a beginning.

30

Early in October Huw came home on leave – a few days only – and Barbara went over to Valley View to see him. Since Sir Richard and Lady Erica were away she had no excuses to make and she toyed with the idea of asking Huw to come to Hillsbridge House instead. It would be lovely to be able to entertain him in her own room and she liked the idea that his presence would be there even when he had gone. But the servants were still in residence and it would be all too easy to cause talk.

October had come in wet and windy and although the trees were still mainly green, the first leaves had turned colour and begun fluttering down in sad wet drifts. Beneath the lowering sky Hillsbridge looked grey and grimy and not even the bright berries in the hedgerows could do anything to dispel the depressing feel of winter just around the corner.

It was too damp now and too cold to walk through the fields as they had done in summer, so when Hope had been settled in the kitchen with Mrs Milsom, who had promised to allow her to help with the baking, Barbara and Huw went into the drawing-room. The moment the door closed behind them they were in one another's arms.

'Oh Huw, you don't know how I've been waiting for this!'

'Come here. Don't talk.' His mouth was on hers, his arms squeezing her tightly, lifting her almost on tiptoe. They kissed with the fervour of reunion and almost at once the desire began to creep in, setting fire to her nerve endings, making her weak. His hands moved the length of her back, caressing, exploring; tucked in beneath the curve of her bottom to hold her close to him; then as one they moved to the couch. He sat down, pulling her down on top of him until they could bear it no longer and he pushed her gently back onto the hearth rug. Because she had known they would be using the room Mrs Milsom had lit a fire; it crackled comfortably, bathing them in flickering light.

'She won't come in, will she?' Huw whispered and even his breath against her ear was erotic.

'No. She has more sense.' Then, as an afterthought, she said, 'Perhaps we ought to lock the door just in case.'

He got up and she lay languorously in the firelight while he crossed the room and turned the key in the lock. She watched him come back, loving every movement of his tall dark figure, stretching up her arms to him as he lowered himself beside her once more.

'Oh Huw . . .'

'I love you, Barbara.'

'And I love you.'

They were close again, closer than before, limbs entwining, bodies merging to one. Too soon it was over – it had been so long, so long! – and she pressed close against him still moving her body to the delicious contact, unwilling to give up the delight.

After a few minutes he moved to look down at her.

'We can't go on like this.'

She opened her eyes. 'What do you mean?'

'I love you, Barbara. I want you with me all the time. It's not enough, snatching a few hours like this. The war is over now. I shall be getting a permanent posting somewhere. It may be in England, it may not. There's no need for us to be separated any more. Wherever I'm sent, I want you with me.'

'But Huw, it's not just the war that's been keeping us apart. Marcus . . .'

'Damn Marcus.'

'I have to stay with him. If I left him he might flip completely. Heaven knows what he would do. And there's Hope to think of. We've been over all this before.'

'I know we have. But it's no answer. Don't you want to be with me?'

'Of course I do! You know I do! But . . .'

'Then leave him. If he'll divorce you we'll be married. If he won't . . . well, we'll just have to cross that bridge when we get to it.'

Panic was setting in, taking the place of passion.

'Huw, I can't! Maybe in a few years . . .'

'In a few years we shall be old. We may even be dead. If this war has taught me one thing it's about my own mortality. I've seen too many friends die – come too close to dying myself. We have to take what we have *now* while we're young and strong. Tomorrow may be too late.'

She was silent. He was right, of course. She felt the wasteland of her own life as a bleak emptiness deep within her. Only with Huw was she truly alive. Only with Huw could she ever be happy. But to abandon Marcus would be to take her happiness at his expense. She was not sure she could live like that. And it could mean losing Hope . . .

'Well?' he said. There was a new, hard note in his voice.

'I don't know. You're rushing me.'

'If I don't rush you it will drag on this way for ever.' He leaned over, pinioning her arms. 'I'm not letting you go until you promise.'

'I can't promise.'

'Then I shall just keep you here.'

'Don't be silly, Huw,' she said sharply. 'You're behaving like a child.'

'You're the one behaving like a child. Refusing to face up to life.'

557

'I am not! I've explained and explained. I can't make myself clearer. And will you please let go of my arm. You're hurting me.'

He released her and got up with an abrupt movement. She felt the ache of loss and with it a stab of fear. They had never quarrelled before. She hated it. But she couldn't let him push her into something she would regret.

'There's no point talking to you in this mood,' she said.

'There's no point talking to you at all. You're so bloody stubborn. Just like your mother.'

'Leave my mother out of this. After all she's done for you, too.'

They were all but shouting at one another now. A rattle at the door knob made them both start.

'Mummy – Mummy, are you in there?'

Barbara got up, straightening her clothing.

'It's Hope. Hush up, now. You'll frighten her.'

He caught her wrist. 'Barbara . . .'

'Let go! I must open the door and see what she wants.'

'All right. But think about this. I'm not prepared to go on like this for ever, Barbara. If I can't have you properly, show the world you're mine, I'd rather not have you at all.'

'Huw . . .'

'I mean it. I'm serious. You'd better think about it – and think soon.' He let go of her wrist. 'Now open the door if you want to.'

She stared at him for a moment, feeling tears gather in her throat. It was so unlike Huw, shouting at her, giving her ultimatums. It was horrible. The door knob rattled again.

'Mum-mee!'

'All right, Hope, I'm coming,' she called.

She opened the door. The child came in, wearing a

little pinafore over her dress and with flour streaks on her nose.

'What were you doing, Mummy? Why were you shouting?' She broke off, sensing the atmosphere, looking from Barbara to Huw and back again. Barbara composed herself.

'I wasn't shouting, darling. Now, what's the matter? Why do you want me?'

Hope ran to her, wrapping her arms around Barbara's legs.

'Just want you!' she piped. 'Just want you, that's all.'

The tears thickened Barbara's throat again as she looked down at the golden head, felt the small sticky hands clutching her legs. She couldn't do anything to jeopardise Hope's happiness. She simply could not. But Huw's face was as set as before. He had no intention of giving in, she knew. Once Huw had made up his mind to something no power on earth would make him change it. And his mind was made up. He was going to force her to choose. Barbara faced the knowledge and went cold at the thought.

One way or the other, it was up to her. She held the happiness of four people in her hands. And she did not know what to do.

They played with Hope a little, they had lunch – delicious homemade oxtail soup and freshly baked bread – and because the weather had cleared a little they went for a walk, taking Hope with them in her pushchair. But the lovely magical atmosphere had been spoiled and in desperation Barbara wondered if it could ever be the same again.

By the end of the afternoon it was raining again.

'I'd better take you and Hope home,' Huw said. 'I'm sure Amy won't mind me using her car.'

They folded up the pushchair and put it in the boot.

'I must get my car back on the road again,' Huw said. 'If I'm going to be stationed in this country, anyway. If not I suppose it will be laid up indefinitely.'

Like me, Barbara almost said, but did not. There was no point in making things worse than they already were.

Hope sat on her lap in the front seat, laughing at the swish of the windscreen wipers and pointing out things they passed.

'Look – man!' as she saw a man on a bicycle, riding head down into the rain. 'Dog-ee! Dog-ee!'

'Yes, dog-ee,' Barbara said patiently and felt that her voice was coming from somewhere near her boots.

They turned into the drive of Hillsbridge House. The rain had brought down more leaves here; it seemed as if winter had come in just one day. To Barbara's surprise Marcus's car was parked in front of the house. He must have come home early.

'It's Marcus,' she said, her voice bleak.

Huw stopped the car, switched off the engine and turned to her.

'Are you going to tell him?'

Barbara glanced meaningfully at Hope. 'Not now!' she said through clenched teeth.

'Well, it's your decision now.' His voice was hard. 'I've said all I'm going to say on the subject.'

He got out, opened the boot and carried the pushchair up the steps for her, depositing it just inside the front door. 'Goodbye, Barbara.'

'Will I see you tomorrow?' she asked, frightened suddenly.

He shrugged. 'That's up to you.'

'I see.'

'I hope so.' He caught her wrist, kissed her hard on the lips. She pulled away, looking round in panic.

'Huw! You shouldn't – not here!'

His lips twisted slightly. 'In that case it looks as though I've had my answer.'

'Huw . . .' But he was striding away towards the car. She checked the urge to run after him. He's only trying to frighten me, she thought. He wouldn't walk out on me. Not now . . .

Wouldn't he? came back the answer. Huw had a somewhat unpredictable streak. And in his own way he could be as stubborn as she was.

The car was pulling away. She watched it go holding onto Hope's hand. Hope was waving madly. 'Bye-bye, Uncle Huw! Bye-bye . . .'

'Come on, Hope,' Barbara said sharply. They went in and she closed the door.

For the moment, because of the gloom in the hall, she did not see him standing in the doorway. Then, as her eyes grew accustomed to the light, he seemed almost to materialise. Just standing and looking as he had stood and looked that other night beside the window.

'Marcus – I didn't see you,' she said foolishly.

'I'll bet you didn't.' His voice was silky, but the undertones were unmistakeable. 'That was Huw, I imagine.'

'Yes.'

'I thought as much. What have you been doing with him?'

'Oh, for heaven's sake!' she snapped, taking off Hope's coat and going to walk past him.

His hand shot out, grasping her arm. 'What have you been doing?'

'What do you think I've been doing? Take your hand off my arm.'

He ignored her request. 'I don't trust you with him. I don't like the way you look at him. If you've been deceiving me . . .'

Her chin shot up. 'What if I have? The way you treat me it's hardly surprising!'

'You bitch!' She felt his anger rising, that terrifying anger that turned him into a monster before her very eyes. She tried to pull away but he held her fast, dragging her in close so that his face was just a few inches from hers. 'You bitch, I'll teach you a lesson you won't forget!'

'Don't touch me!' she screamed.

He threw open the drawing-room door, dragging her in, then hit her full in the face. She staggered back beneath the force of the blow and would have fallen but for the fact that he was still holding her. She sobbed with pain and fear and he hit her again so that the whole of her face was searing with pain and her head sung.

'Bitch!' He hit her yet again. Her knees gave way beneath her, she sagged to the floor and he was on top of her. As if from a long way off she could hear Hope crying and she struggled wildly. Dear God, surely he was not going to take her here, with Hope looking on! But she was weakened by his blows and his was the strength of a madman. Though she fought him all the way, she was helpless. Only at the last did she manage to get her nails to his face, scratching savagely at his cheeks and thrusting at him with her knees, but by then the pain and the frustration of losing her at the moment of his climax only maddened him further, so that he pushed her back, kneeling astride her like some insane animal.

For a terror-struck moment she thought he was going to kill her. He grasped her by the hair, pounding her head against the floor. Hope was screaming now and her terrified wail brought Barbara back from the verge of unconsciousness. As his hands fastened round her throat she brought her knee up again and more by lucky chance than design caught him in the groin. He yelled, relaxing his hold of her, and somehow she managed to roll away. The heavy sofa connected with her singing head. She grabbed the arm of it and hauled herself up. Marcus was still rolling on the floor holding himself. Fear lent strength to her shaking legs. She ran to Hope, scooping her up with the child's face turned into her.

'That's it!' she cried. 'I'm leaving you, Marcus. I warned you. I'm going now and I'm taking Hope with me.'

She ran out of the room, Hope in her arms, and up the broad staircase. The suitcases were stored in a cupboard at the head of the stairs; she jerked one out and another fell clattering to the floor. She left it there, took the other into Hope's room and began throwing clothes into it. Hope whimpered beside her.

'It's all right, it's all right!' Barbara reassured her, but still the child cried and her anger grew to fury. What he did to her was one thing. But to do it in front of a child . . .

I'm taking her away from here, Barbara thought, and if he tries to stop me I'll tell everyone the reason. They can employ the fanciest lawyer in Bath but he won't stop me telling the truth about Marcus. Not now. Oh, not now . . .

Hope sobbed again, her small face contorted, her eyes wide. 'Da-da!'

'Hope don't!' Barbara begged. Then, a thrill of fear turned her spine to water and she swung round.

Marcus was in the doorway, holding his service revolver. The shock of it ran through her in waves yet suddenly she was icy cool.

'Put that thing down,' she said.

He took a step into the room. The gun was pointing directly at her.

'You're not leaving me, Barbara. I'll kill you first.'

'Don't be so silly,' she said.

She heard the click as the safety catch came off.

'I mean it, Barbara. He shan't have you. I won't let him. I'm going to kill you.'

563

Dear God, he means it! she thought.

She caught Hope's dress, gave her a little push towards the door.

'Go downstairs, Hope,' she said. Although she was shaking, her voice was very level. 'Go on, quickly now!'

The child hesitated, ran to the door, looked at her father in terror then darted back to Barbara, burying her face in her skirt and sobbing.

'I'm going to kill you both,' he said.

The revolver moved slightly in his hand. She stared at it mesmerised, holding tightly to Hope's small shaking body. From somewhere downstairs she heard the sound of a door slamming and a voice – Huw's voice – called: 'Barbara – are you there?'

'Huw!' she screamed.

She heard him running up the stairs, saw the expression on Marcus's face and thought it was all over. She held her breath, bracing herself for the bullet. It did not come. Instead, Marcus leaped into the room but before she could move he was behind her, one arm folded tightly around her throat, the gun muzzle pressed against her temple.

Huw was in the doorway. Though her head was strained back she could see him, see his rushed approach and the sudden stop as he took in what was happening in the room. He stood like a statue, bracing himself against the door jamb, his face momentarily frozen in an expression of shock and horror.

Marcus spoke, 'Stay there, James. Another step and I'll kill her.'

Huw eased himself upright, the tension making him move like a cat.

'Don't be a fool, Spindler.'

Marcus laughed, a high-pitched unhinged sound.

'I mean it. She's my wife. My wife, do you hear? You won't have her, I'll see to that.'

Barbara tried to speak, tried to say 'He means it,

564

Huw!' and could not. The pressure of his arm around her throat was cutting off breath and in any case she thought she was beyond words.

'Look, Spindler, this isn't doing anyone any good.' Huw's voice was deliberately level now, though the same tension that was holding his body like a tight-coiled spring was there in the air. 'Put that gun down and let's talk about this sensibly. No one wants to hurt you. No one wants to upset you. We just want to help.'

'Get out and leave my wife alone!'

'I'm not going anywhere while you've got that gun on her and you might as well realise that. Put it down, man, for God's sake!' Sweat was trickling down Huw's face but he did not dare wipe it away for fear that the movement might trigger Marcus into doing something terrible.

'Get out of here, James, and leave us alone!'

Realising he was getting nowhere Huw tried a new tack.

'What's the matter with you, man? What are you so worked up about?'

'You and her. You think I don't know? I'll kill her before you shall have her. I will!' He was sounding like a gramophone record with the needle stuck in a groove, unable to think of anything but his insane jealousy and the blackness that threatened to split his head wide open.

For seemingly endless minutes Huw went on talking. Barbara could hear his voice yet she was strangely unaware of what he was saying. Her face was throbbing badly now where Marcus had hit her, her neck ached from being stretched at an unnatural angle and her head was swimming. I'm going to faint, she thought and then: no, I mustn't. If I faint, God alone knows what will happen. Hope was still clinging terrified to her legs and she tried to concentrate on willing the child to stay still, quite still . . .

In the muzzy blackness she heard Huw say: 'Look, Spindler, I know you've had a rough time but this is no way to make things better. You're not the first one to get things all muddled up and wrong. It's what the damned war did to men. But you can get help. Just as long as you don't do anything bloody stupid. After all, you're supposed to be a hero, aren't you?'

Don't Huw! she wanted to shout. For God's sake, don't bring that up! It'll send him over the top! But she could not speak. The truth about Marcus's cowardice was the one thing she had not been able to bring herself to tell him. And now it was too late . . .

'You did your best for your men, didn't you?' Huw was going on. 'Think about that and . . .'

Marcus's arm tightened around her neck, the muzzle of the gun bit into her temple.

'Are you trying to be funny?' he barked.

'Of course not. I . . .'

Marcus laughed, that same insane laugh that chilled the blood.

'I killed them!' he screeched. 'All my men! I killed them! What difference does it make if I kill her too?'

The faintness passed over Barbara in a wave again; she fought it and saw that Huw had moved. Tensed now, both hands braced against the door jamb, head down, eyes levelled at Marcus.

'I'm the one you want to kill', he said, enunciating the words clearly. 'If you want to take it out on someone, take it out on me. But for God's sake, let her go!'

'No!'

'I'm the one you want. Look at me. I'm here. I'm alive. I'm laughing at you. Go on, Marcus. Shoot *me*. Shoot me – if you dare!'

The tension hung in the air. For a moment none of them moved, then Barbara felt the quiver run the length of Marcus's body. And miraculously the pressure on her throat reduced and his arm was no longer strangling her.

'All right, James, you've asked for it! You've bloody asked . . .' The gun was levelled at Huw, his finger tightening on the trigger.

'No!' Barbara screamed. At the very moment he squeezed she struck at his arm from underneath and the bullet cracked harmlessly through the ceiling. For a moment, Marcus stood as if frozen by the shock of having actually fired and in that second in eternity everything happened at once. Huw stepped forward, grabbed Barbara and Hope and practically threw them through the open door. Barbara scooped Hope into her arms and stumbling on legs gone weak she ran for the stairs.

'Get out of here, Barbara!' Huw shouted behind her and she needed no second bidding.

She was at the foot of the stairs, Huw behind her, when she heard the second shot. She froze.

'Go on – get out!' Huw yelled at her.

She dived for the door, down the stone steps onto the drive, then turned around to look for Huw. He was not there.

'Huw!' she sobbed. Her brain and senses were in total turmoil. Where was he? What was happening in the house? She had to know, yet she could not go back. There was Hope to think about . . .

Clutching the sobbing child to her she stared, wild-eyed at the open front door. My God, if he had killed Huw . . . she couldn't stand it. She honestly could not stand it.

Where *were* they? Why was it so quiet? In the trees around the park a rook cawed. It was the only sound now to break the silence. Wordlessly, without sense or meaning, Barbara prayed as she had never prayed before.

A movement from inside the house. She stood poised

for flight. But it was Huw who stood framed in the doorway, Huw who came down the steps towards her, took her in his arms, holding her tight with Hope squashed between them.

'All right, my love?' he whispered.

She moved convulsively. 'Marcus . . . ?'

He held her steady. 'It's all over. He's dead.'

She gasped.

'He turned the gun on himself,' Huw said.

'Oh!' She tried to break away to go to him. He was, after all, despite all he had done, her husband. Huw prevented her.

'Don't go in there. There's nothing you can do.'

She held taut, then half fell against him.

'Oh Huw – Huw!'

'It's all right, my love,' he whispered. 'It's all over now. It's all over.'

In the trees above the park the rook cawed again.

The news spread round Hillsbridge like wildfire.

'Have you heard? Marcus Spindler has gone an' shot himself!' As always Ewart Brixey liked to pass on information in the crudest possible manner – and the regulars at the bar at the Miners Arms were agog for it.

'Never!'

'Marcus Spindler? Go on!'

'He has. It's in the paper.'

'I saw the paper,' Stanley Bristow said. 'It didn't say he shot himself. It said he'd died in a shooting accident.'

'Same thing, isn't it?'

'Well, no . . .'

'It's what they would say, isn't it? They wouldn't put it in black and white, not with somebody like him. They wouldn't dare. But you can take it from me that's what happened right enough. His wife was carrying on, they reckon.'

'What – Barbara Roberts?'

'Ah.'

There was silence. The old ones hadn't forgotten how her mother, Amy Hall, had 'carried on' before her, running a business in a man's world and marrying Ralph Porter. She was respectable enough now, it was true, but all the same . . .

'I don't know what the world's coming to,' Stanley Bristow said. 'Give me the old days, before the First War. You knew where you were then.'

'Ah, them Spindlers have got it coming to 'em,' Ewart went on, quaffing his beer. 'Things will be different now we've got a Labour government, you mark my words. The pits will be nationalised soon and we'll see how the Spindlers like that. They'll have their wings clipped then, I'da know.'

'And you'll probably end up living in Hillsbridge Hall, Ewart,' Tommy Clements joked.

They all laughed. It was an amusing prospect. Things had not changed *that* much. They could not imagine that they ever would.

'Well, Babs, I'm very glad you found the time to come and see your Gran before you go off to – where is it?' Charlotte poured tea into her best china cups and set one down in front of Barbara and another before Huw as they sat at the chenille-covered table in her kitchen.

'Cyprus, Gran – and of course you know I wouldn't go without coming to see you!' Barbara said.

'Cyprus. My goodness me. I hope it will suit our Hope there. I hope it won't be too hot for her.'

'She'll love it, won't you Hope?' Barbara smiled at Hope, who was sitting in the centre of the floor, turning out her great grandmother's handbag for the hairpins which she loved and which were always to be found at the bottom. Miraculously, she seemed unscathed by her terrible experience when her father had finally gone berserk − thank God for the resilience of children, Charlotte thought.

'Anyway, after the cold weather we've been having, it will be lovely to be warm!' Barbara said, and smiled at Huw.

It was difficult for her to stop smiling at him these days. She could hardly believe that at last, at long last, they were going to be together. She would not have cared where it was just so long as she could be with him. But Cyprus sounded like heaven on earth.

'Well, I just hope I'm still here when you get back,' Charlotte said.

'Oh Gran!' Barbara reached out and took her hand. 'Whatever are you talking about? I don't like to hear you say things like that.'

'You never know,' Charlotte said seriously. 'I'm not getting any younger, Babs.'

'You have years and years yet and you know it.'

Charlotte smiled. The prospect of dying held no fears for her now.

'I don't know, Babs. But when my time comes I shall be ready. I've been lucky really. I've seen all of you settled − not just my children, but my grandchildren too. There's our Fred and Bob safely home, our Alec going to marry Joan, and you . . .' Her eyes softened. Barbara was the favourite of her grandchildren, there was no denying it. She was glad she had lived to see Barbara truly happy. 'No, since your grandpa died I feel I'm just biding my time really. I've had my life.'

'Gran!' Barbara scolded her. 'We've come to share our happiness with you, not talk about dying!'

'I know.' Charlotte patted her hand, then moved away decisively to put the cosy on the teapot. 'And I

570

am happy, really I am. Now – tell me all about Cyprus!'

They stayed with her for a pleasant half hour, but when they got up to go she was not sorry. Much as she loved to see them she did get so tired these days.

In the doorway she hugged them all and kissed Hope.

'You'll be a big girl when you get back, my love. Gran won't know you!'

'We'll send you photographs – lots of photographs,' Barbara promised.

'I shall look forward to that. Well . . .'

'Bye, Gran.'

'Bye, my love.'

They got into the car and drove off, waving until they were out of sight. Charlotte sighed and shook her head. The world was such a small place these days – Ted in Australia and now Barbara off to Cyprus. She would get out Jack's old atlas in a minute and look to see exactly where it was. But an island on a map would mean little to her. In all her life she had scarcely been outside Somerset, never mind England. It was almost impossible for her to imagine foreign climes.

She paused for a moment in the doorway of her home. Beneath her the valley spread out, grey in the afternoon, the market hall and the horseshoe of shops, the pit chimney and headgear, the church tower. A cloud of smoke rose from the railway line where a train shunted to merge with the grey sky and from one of the factories where wagons were made a hooter sounded four o'clock, proof, if any were needed, that Hillsbridge had returned to normal after the enforced silence of wartime.

On the opposite side of the valley the ranks of houses ran like long grey fingers and beyond them she could see the batches, girdled with fir trees on their lower

571

slopes, rising like the black guardian mountains she had always thought them to be.

As she stood there it seemed to her that she was transported back in time to the day when she had first seen them, standing with her arm tucked through that of James, a young bride surveying the town that was to be her home. It was so long ago now, so much had happened, and yet it seemed like only yesterday. 'I think it's wonderful!' she had said – and so it had been. With all the anxieties and heartaches, with all the hard work and worry, with all the losses and crosses, she knew she would not have changed any of it.

She half turned to look along the Rank where she had lived ever since that day and noticed her door ajar behind her.

'Good Lord, I'm letting in all this cold!' Charlotte said to herself. 'And I reckon if I'm lucky there's still a cup of tea left in that pot.'

With an impatient, if slightly rheumaticky movement, Charlotte turned her back on the valley that had seen all her triumphs and sorrows, went back inside the house and shut the door.

	DATE DUE	

9211963

Tanner, Janet
The hills and the valley